Conflicted

Michael Culp

ibooks
new york
www.ibooks.net

DISTRIBUTED BY SIMON & SCHUSTER, INC.

For Debi,
The best securities analyst
I've ever known

A Publication of ibooks, inc.

Conflicted copyright © 2003 by Michael Culp

An ibooks, inc. Book

ibooks, inc.
24 West 25th Street
New York, NY 10010

The ibooks World Wide Web Site Address is:
http://www.ibooks.net

ISBN 0-7434-9768-6
First ibooks, inc. printing October 2004
10 9 8 7 6 5 4 3 2 1

Special thanks to Neeti Madan,
whose instincts were flawless
and insights invaluable

Printed in the U.S.A.

Equitable Finance Securities
Research Department

Director of Research
David Meadows

Associate Director
Matt Speiser

Basic Materials/
Industrials

Aerospace & Defense
Doyle Linden

Business Services
Evan Moroney

Chemicals/Commodities
Arthur Litt

Chemicals/Specialty
Laura Payden

Environmental Svces.
Rebecca Sues

Ground Transportation
Timothy Laboy

Machinery
James Fullmer

Metals: Non-Precious
Frank Bueller

Metals: Precious
Nick Denisovich

Multi-Industry
Wes Persico

Paper & Forest Prods.
Alan Gildersleeve

Telecommunications
Wireless Equipment
and Services
Steven Kalagian

Wireline Services
Donald Ferber

Consumer

Airlines
James Brell

Autos
Mitch Potvan

Auto Parts
Alan Loparco

Beverages
Joe Altschuler

Homebuilders
Paul Regal

Retail: Broadlines
Robin Lomax

Retail: Food & Drug
Phillip Suprano

Retail: Specialty
Richard Geyer

Energy
Electric Utilities
Robert Magrath

Integrated Oils
Nancy Natoli o

Oil Exploration
Toni Tooke

Oil Services &
Equipment
Robert Groody

Financial Svces.

Banks
Tim Omori

Insurance:Non-Life
John Henriksen

Mortgage Finance
Brian McCrady

REITs
Alan Bellone

Technology
Computer Svces.
Toshihiko Hikima

Enterpr. Hardware
Mark Noel

Semi Equipment
James Hovanian

Semiconductors
Martin Hogue

Software/Applicat'n
George Schuler

Software/Infrastr.
Byron Shatz

Health Care

Biotechnology
Ken Lavery

Facilities
David Rosinsky

Managed Care
Matt Burlingame

Medical Supplies
Will Rivas

Pharmaceuticals
Michael Mellman

Technology (Health)
Ulla Schager

Media
Advertising
Ron Vargo

Cable/Entertainmt.
Keith Jackman

Publishing
Denise Cybulski

Radio & TV
Eileen Olivero

Macro
Economics
Bruce Soslow

Portfolio Strategy
Linda Logan

SEPTEMBER

"Is Nick there?"

The caller's accent was thick and, to Linda Chute, who had started at Equitable Finance Securities the week before, unfamiliar.

"He's not. May I ask who's calling?" Linda thought she heard traffic in the background and female voices that were too soft to understand.

"When do you expect him?"

"He's at an analysts' meeting and should be back by noon." It was 10:35. "May I take a message?"

"I'll call back."

Linda hung up, stared out Nick Denisovich's window at New York Harbor and the Statue of Liberty, and tried to place the accent. It seemed sort of eastern European, she thought, but she couldn't really tell. At the same time, a tall, dark-haired man with broad shoulders and a broader belly stepped away from a pay phone on the corner of 24th Street and Broadway, walked south a block and descended the stairs to the subway. A downtown N train pulled in behind him.

Good, he thought. He'd take it to Union Square and switch for the Q to Brighton Beach.

* * *

"You should've been a broker."

Paul Pitcher, a senior manager in the Private Client Group at Equitable Finance Securities, smiled as he stood at Ken Lavery's door. Ken, the firm's biotechnology analyst, was surprised both to see Paul and by what he'd said.

"Why?"

"Did you see how much stock we moved in the four branches you hit last week?"

Ken shook his head.

"In downtown L.A., Century City, Newport Beach and Beverly Hills we've purchased almost 1,000,000 Amgen, almost 1,000,000 Genentech and more than 500,000 Biogen for our clients since last Wednesday."

Ken had been in California the week before, visiting bank trust departments, insurance companies, mutual fund companies and other "institutional" investors. He'd also visited four EFS retail branches where he'd pitched EFS's brokers on Amgen, Genentech and Biogen. He knew they'd do some business in those names after he'd left but, if Paul's numbers were right, those brokers had channeled $90 million of their clients' liquid assets into those three stocks in less than 72 hours.

"I've gotten calls from two dozen brokers and three of the managers saying how much they appreciated seeing you and how good your work is" Paul added. "I think you've got a bigger following in the field than you might've guessed."

Ken was pleased because Paul, who carried a lot of weight inside EFS, had clearly become a friend in a high place.

"Great job," Paul repeated, pointing his right thumb toward the ceiling and smiling broadly as he walked away.

Ken sat quietly for a moment, his eyes down,

thinking hard, but not about Amgen or Genentech or Biogen, each of which had risen a point or two between Wednesday and Friday. Far more striking had been the price action in a fourth stock that Ken had pushed, Regeneron Pharmaceuticals, one that Paul hadn't even mentioned. During the same 72 hours, about 3,000,000 shares of Regeneron had traded, including 700,000 shares purchased for EFS clients in those four branches, and Regeneron had jumped more than three points. Ken had singlehandedly generated almost 25% of the total NASDAQ trading volume in Regeneron during his three days in California, far more than the fraction of trading in Amgen, Genentech or Biogen that could be attributed to his marketing skills.

Ken speed-dialed.

"The other Tom Hanks." Ken's broker had made peace with having a famous name and entertained himself by acknowledging it and having fun with it.

"Tom, it's Ken Lavery."

"Ken! It's great to hear from you. What's up?"

"I can only talk for a second. Buy me $300,000 worth of REGN, okay?"

"Put $300,000 into Regeneron at the market."

"Thanks, Tom."

Ken dialed a second number. His palms and the insides of his arms felt wet.

"McCarron."

"Bob, it's Ken Lavery."

"Ken Lavery! To what do I owe this honor?" Bob managed EFS's retail branch at 220 Park Avenue, which comprised almost 100 brokers and was the fourth-highest-grossing office in the firm. Over the years, Bob had asked Ken on several occasions to meet with his brokers and Ken had always obliged.

"Bob, I've got an ImClone meeting at the Hyatt next Tuesday. Can I stop by after the market closes and talk to your guys again for 15 or 20 minutes?"

"They'd love that, Ken. How about seeing me at 4:00 and the brokers at 4:15?"

"Perfect. See you Tuesday."

Ken dialed a third number.

"Jim Molloy." Jim headed Compliance inside EFS's Research Department.

"Jim, Ken Lavery."

"Ken, I'm on another line. Is this something we can do quickly?"

"I just want approval to buy $300,000 worth of Regeneron." Jim pulled up Ken's account on his computer. He saw Amgen and Genentech holdings valued at $900,000 and a cash balance of about $500,000 but no Regeneron. "You don't own any currently."

"No."

"Do you plan to write any reports or raise your rating on it any time soon?"

"No."

Jim checked the Restricted List, which showed companies for which EFS was currently doing investment banking work, possibly unbeknownst to the analysts. Regeneron wasn't on it. "Okay, Ken, you're clear."

Ken thanked Jim and hung up. This time he was done dialing. He tried to relax and to contain a smile but couldn't do either.

* * *

Alexander Volkov was panting as he finished climbing the stairs at the Newkirk Avenue subway station on the Q line. Brooklyn, it seemed to him, was enormous; his train had left its last stop in Manhattan almost half an hour earlier but he was still only two-thirds of the way home to Brighton Beach. Volkov knew Newkirk Avenue well. Over the years, he'd placed several important calls from the pay phone near the subway station, at which he now stared, but his belly told him it was too early and, when he checked his watch, he saw that his belly was right. It was 11:20.

One and a half blocks past the Newkirk station stood Manhattan Bagels, which Volkov had also befriended over the years. "Blueberry or chocolate chip?" he pondered. Manhattan Bagels had good bagels but better muffins. Volkov grabbed a *New York Post* at a newsstand three doors down, slipped unnoticed into the bagel shop, and spent the next 45 minutes savoring a blueberry muffin *and* a chocolate chip muffin with a large black coffee.

At 12:05, his belly full, Volkov walked back slowly to the pay phone near the Newkirk Avenue subway station and again called Nick Denisovich, EFS's precious metals analyst. On the second ring, Linda Chute picked him up.

"Is Nick there?"

"May I say who's calling?"

"Joe from the JG office." All of EFS's branch offices used two-letter codes to identify themselves inside the firm. Linda put Volkov on hold, saw that Nick, who had just returned from his all-morning analysts' meeting, was eyeing the fifty-odd e-mail messages that had arrived while he'd been out, and waved an arm to catch his eye. "Joe from the JG office?"

Nick looked up, considered whether he wanted to

take the call, and then nodded. He walked to his door, closed it, sat down at his desk, swivelled so his back was to Linda, and picked up the phone.

"Denisovich."

"Nick, this is Joe from the JG office. How yuh doing?"

"I'm great, Joe, and you?"

"Good, good. Look, I know you're busy, but I'm thinking about doing something in your group. Could you tell me quickly what you'd recommend?"

"Of course. We're estimating that gold will average $325 an ounce in 2003, up from $310 in 2002 and $271 in 2001, and that it will inch up further into the $325–$350 range in 2004 and 2005. Unless Bin Laden bombs more buildings, India and Pakistan go to war, America gets bogged down in Iraq, or there's some sort of major, negative financial 'event,' there's no reason to think gold can move up 10% or more from current levels over the near term. Obviously, we can't predict external shocks so we're using $325 and $335 for this year and next, and that makes us quite cautious on most precious metals names. These companies are very capital-intensive, have high fixed costs, and really need gold prices to rise more than 3% annually to do well. We don't think they will so we're recommending being under-weighted in the group.

"However, if you have clients who insist on owning gold stocks, I'm continuing to recommend ASA Ltd., which is an investment company that is 80% invested in gold stocks and 20% in other natural resources. The stock doubled in price between 2000 and 2002, largely because gold prices moved higher, but ASA's gold holdings are currently worth almost $35 a share so, with the stock around $30, downside risk is limited. I think ASA can sell in the $35 area a year from now so upside potential is about 15% and the stock is rated Accumulate."

"Anything else?" Volkov asked.

"That's about it. I'm getting lots of questions about Yellow Gorge Mining from bargain hunters because they remember when it was $50 and now it's $18, but I'm not recommending it. I just don't see the upside."

"Great, Nick. Thanks."

"My pleasure."

Nick and Volkov hung up. Nick opened his Palm Pilot and wrote "spend more time with your nephew" into his calendar exactly two weeks hence.

Volkov got back in the subway and took the next Ω train to Brighton Beach, briskly approached his fourth-floor walk-up on Brighton 5th Street, and huffed and puffed up the stairs. At the top, he turned keys in three locks, entered his apartment, locked himself in and then, from his big, cushy, living room Stratolounger, picked up his wireless phone and began dialing.

011–7–095–…He heard lots of static and then a pause so long that it would have made most people assume their call hadn't gone through. But not Volkov. He knew what business as usual sounded like in Moscow, and 45 seconds later he heard the first ring, then the second, then the click.

"Piotr," said a 60-year-old man with short-cropped gray hair and spectacles, whose name had never been Piotr.

"I want to speak to Yevgeny."

"No Yevgeny."

"Sorry." Volkov hung up.

Piotr looked at his calendar and put a dot on it two

weeks hence. Then he turned to a beautiful woman less than half his age with jet-black hair and large, brown eyes that had been focused intently upon him and said, "Anna dear, short Yellow Gorge."

* * *

Behind the dais inside the large conference room on the 74th floor of 3 New York Plaza stood David Meadows, EFS's Director of Research; Matt Speiser, his Associate Director; John Mansfield McLain who headed Institutional Sales; Paul Pitcher from the Private Client Group; and Lisa Palladino, David's administrative assistant. And on the dais, a name card read "Thomas C. P. (Tom) Mennymore III," who headed Investment Banking and was MIA. All around the conference room over 100 senior and associate analysts grabbed chairs and readied themselves for another of David's "Working Luncheons."

"I wish I could stay for the whole meeting" John apologized, "but I've got something at 1:00 I couldn't get out of."

"Not a problem," David said understandingly. In truth, John had asked to speak first because he simply didn't want this meeting to waste more of his lunchtime than it had to. He couldn't have cared less about what Paul and Tom had to say because he never thought much about what the "retail swine" (as he called EFS's brokers) were doing and he thought Tom was a pompous asshole.

At 12:36, David walked to the podium and welcomed his seniors and associates back from their summer vacations. "We have a lot to cover today so let's get going. First, let me introduce our two newest senior analysts. For the benefit of anyone who hasn't attended a working luncheon before, let me explain that all newly hired analysts are asked at their first Working Luncheon to publicly predict who will take EFS over and at what price."

As always, this elicited lots of laughing and buzzing in the audience. For many years EFS had been a rumored "takeover candidate" which worried many members of Research because, when brokerage firms are taken over, analysts lose their jobs. David had found that one of the best ways to minimize his department's chronic unease about a prospective takeover was to make light of it, which he did at every working luncheon.

"Robin, where are you?" A late-thirty-something-ish brunette in a blue St. John suit stood up and waved hesitantly. "Robin Lomax joined us this week from CIBC World Markets as our new department-and-discount- store analyst. Robin was a Runner-Up in last year's *Institutional Investor* All Star Poll in the Department Stores category. Robin, welcome."

"Thank you, David." Robin started to sit.

"No no, Robin, please remain standing," David instructed with a silly, sadistic grin that his analysts knew well. Robin complied.

"And where is Alan Gildersleeve?"

Alan, who was in the second row, also rose. He was in his mid-twenties, tall, very thin, an athlete no doubt, with short-cropped blonde hair and ears that stuck out too far. He was less poised than Robin but he also smiled broadly as he turned and waved to his new department mates. "Alan, who just joined us to cover the paper and forest products stocks, was for three years an associate paper and forest products analyst at Salomon Smith Barney. Welcome, Alan."

Alan smiled at David and mouthed the words "thank you."

"Okay, let's do this alphabetically. Alan, who do you think will take EFS over and at what price? As a reminder, EFS was trading around $21 this morning."

Alan squinted and put his right pointer to his cheek. "I'd say... Bank of America at $38." The analysts and associates cheered. EFS hadn't traded at $38 in many years, and Bank of America was a less menacing potential parent than Merrill Lynch or Morgan Stanley or Goldman Sachs, all of which had highly regarded Research Departments of their own and thus would be more inclined to lay EFS's analysts off.

"And you, Robin?"

Robin, having decided that it was better to "play the game" than to be correct, looked around her and said, "I think, Hong Kong & Shanghai Bank at $60!" The roar was deafening. HKSB, long rumored to be interested in acquiring Merrill Lynch, had no securities operations in the United States that overlapped with EFS's. Thus, everyone in Research would be safe if HKSB became EFS's new parent. And $60 a share... now that was an offer!

"Duly noted," said David as Alan and Robin sat down. "Lisa has recorded your predictions and if, some day, one of you proves to be most correct, I will personally pay you $1,000." David paused and then smiled. "For the record, my favorite prediction remains Ken Lavery's, which was Microsoft at $70." More cheers and hooting from the audience. No one took this stuff seriously, which was exactly why David did it.

Having broken the ice, David got down to business. "Today we're fortunate to have three guest speakers, all of whom you know well... John McLain representing Institutional Sales, Paul Pitcher representing the Private Client Group and Tom Mennymore, who is due momentarily, representing Investment Banking. I've asked each of them to give you a 10–minute update and to allow 10 minutes for Q&A. As it's now about 12:45, we should be able to do all of this and have you out of here by 1:45." Analysts hated working luncheons. They were a waste of time, at least relative to their own personal goals and, luckily for them, because they traveled 40% of the time, they had a 40% chance of being out of town whenever a working luncheon was scheduled.

"John, I know you have another meeting at 1:00 so let's begin with you."

John walked to the podium. "Well, good afternoon, everybody. I want to talk to you today about some important goings-on in Institutional Sales and to ask for your help in getting us to the next level. I brought handouts for everyone, and I'd like you to read along with me." He held up his handout. Most of the analysts, who aren't patient by nature, were already on page 8.

"As you know, we've asked all of you in recent years to focus your marketing efforts on the Target Account List and the Focus List. The Targets are the 100 largest institutional investors in the United States and the Focus accounts are the 25 largest. David, however, has been pushing for us to update and broaden these lists so, over the past eight weeks we've reviewed current and potential business with the 250 largest institutions in the country and, as a result, we're going to make some changes.

"First, we're going to replace the 100–client Target Account List with a new, 175–client Top-Tier Account List. Second, we're going to replace the Focus List with a new Extra-Efforts List and, rather than basing it purely on the size of the accounts, we're going to base it on which accounts are most dependent on research in determining how many commission dollars they pay and which accounts have the greatest incremental revenue and earnings potential for EFS."

Hands were up. "Martin?"

Martin Hogue, EFS's semiconductor analyst, was on his feet. "John, in the past, you asked us only to service the 100 Target accounts and to focus on the 25 Focus accounts."

"That's right."

"But now you're changing the rules and asking us to focus on 175 accounts instead. Where are we supposed to find the time to service those 75 extra accounts?"

"Not all of those 75 accounts will require a lot of your time. Some will call you once a quarter, some once a month. A few will require private meetings with you but most will just be invited to group breakfast or lunch meetings that you're already scheduled to do with larger clients."

The analysts were far from sold, but David had expected that. "More questions for John?" There weren't. "John, thanks for that update. We know you have to run."

"Thanks everyone," John said as he checked his watch, headed for the conference room door, and debated about which local watering hole to patronize until 2:00.

"Paul, you're up," David said. It was 1:00, and Tom Mennymore was still missing. When Paul reached the podium he turned down the lights. "Hi, everyone," he said with a warm and genuine smile. "I too am glad to get some face time with you today. Let me begin with something surprising. Most of you know, I'm sure, that the four largest institutional investors in the U.S. are Fidelity, Barclays, State Street, and the Capital Group. But guess who's bigger than J.P. Morgan, bigger than Bank of America, bigger than Prudential and bigger than American Express."

Paul paused, then smiled. "EFS is. That's right. As the ninth-largest brokerage firm in the country, our branch offices hold roughly $150 billion of equities for EFS clients and that's more than 90% of the 175 institutional accounts on your new Top-Tier list. Just as important, while Fidelity gets your research, it also gets Merrill's and Goldman's and Morgan Stanley's and CSFB's and Salomon's and Bear Stearns's and so on. EFS's retail brokers get your research and yours alone. Thus, you have a much more powerful impact on our retail brokers than on *any* of your institutional clients.

"Currently, we have just over 5,000 financial advisors in 225 branch offices. The Private Client Group generates 60% of EFS's revenues and 50% of its earnings, and pays 40% of your Research budget so we're enormously important to the firm and you're enormously important to us. Here's why.

"First, your ability to make our clients money differentiates us from e*Trade and the other discount brokers, none of which has a Research Department like ours. Second, strong research helps us attract and keep good brokers. Finally, money-making research ideas can be used very effectively in EFS advertising.

"And we are important to you in more ways than simply helping the firm absorb the cost of your department. The senior officers of the firms you cover are often clients of the Private Client Group. Our brokers manage their money, their families' money, their trust accounts and their retirement accounts. Those CEOs and CFOs tell our brokers more about what's going on at their companies than you'd ever imagine and our brokers would gladly share that information with you if you'd only ask. Our brokers build large positions in the stocks you recommend and maintain them for as long as you tell them to.

"Where I need your help right now is in visiting more branches. Some of you have been very good about this, others have been reasonably responsive when asked and the rest of you have avoided visiting branches like the plague, and that's unacceptable. The amount of business that a branch can do in your favorite stocks increases exponentially once the brokers have seen you in person. We need more of you in more branches, and I don't just mean downtown Chicago or Boston or Los Angeles. Many of you go to smaller cities in which we have branches when you do research or investment banking but most of the time you never visit those branches even though they're often only a few minutes away. I cannot tell you how embarrassing and frustrating it is for an FA to learn that you've been in town and that you passed the branch by. It's bad for morale and it's bad for business, so I'm giving you a heads-up right now that I'm going to ask David to make branch visits mandatory when you're on research and investment banking trips, which means you won't be reimbursed for your airline tickets, your hotel rooms and your meals unless you visit the branch as part of your trip.

"Also, I'm going to invite the branches to submit lists of analysts they'd most like to see and to work with David on spreading more of you over more and more branches."

Like clockwork, the eyes in the audience began

rolling and the sighing intensified. Paul knew it was time to wrap up. "So let me conclude first with a heartfelt 'thank you' for all the good work you've done over the past few years. Our brokers are very high on you right now and that's great, but that also creates opportunities for us to do even more together... more meetings, more conference calls and more business in your favorite names. So, if you want to maximize your bonus pool at the end of the year, help us and we'll help you. Questions?" Several hands went up.

"Will?" Will Rivas covered hospital supplies and medical devices.

"Paul, I've had some very positive experiences with your group over the years, but I've also had some very bad ones and most of them involved branch office visits."

"Such as...?"

"Such as lining up branch visits for after the market has closed, when I'd rather be flying home to my family, confirming them before leaving town and then arriving at the branch only to find that the manager is out, the assistant manager didn't know I was coming, and he's only able to corral half of the brokers in the branch into a conference room to meet with me."

"That shouldn't be," Paul confessed.

Arthur Litt, EFS's 55-year-old chemicals analyst, was on his feet. "And Paul, what I object to is this. You know how long I've been at EFS?"

"About 25 years, Arthur, if my memory serves me."

"Twenty-six. Can you imagine how it makes me feel when I go into a branch and some twenty-some-thing-year-old FA says, 'Hi, nice to meet you. What do you follow again?' I follow chemicals, pal. I've followed them for EFS since the 1970s. What are these jokers doing all day long? Do they even read my research? Shouldn't they have some reasonable understanding of what we've been recommending when we walk in the door? Isn't there accountability on both sides?"

"That's absolutely fair, Arthur. We'll have to do a better job of prepping the branches before future visits to ensure good turnouts and insisting that the brokers are fully familiar with your work before you arrive."

"Paul?" It was Nancy Natolio, EFS's young, very blonde oil analyst.

"Nancy?"

"Paul, I agree with you and I'd like to visit more branches but, when I visit Chevron Texaco or Exxon Mobil, I spend all day there. I see the CEO, the COO, the CFO, several division heads, the IR guy, and usually one or two middle managers in areas I need to learn more about. I can easily spend 8 to 10 hours at the company." Many analysts were nodding in agreement. "So, to think that I can ensure that I'm free at 4:15, or 3:15 Texas time, for an after-the-close branch visit is to think the impossible."

Ken Lavery was standing. "David, I have a question for you about this."

"Shoot."

"I have a very good relationship with Retail. Paul and his people have really helped me raise my visibility in the field, and I love visiting the branches. Most of the brokers are smart and seem to know my stuff, they've purchased large blocks of my favorite stocks for their clients and they ask good questions, so my experience has been positive, and I'd like to visit even more branches but I don't know how to find the time."

"Ken," David answered, "analysts always have too many masters and too little time. You need to please me, the Private Client Group, Institutional Sales and institutional clients, the trading desks, Investment Banking, the sales forces in Europe and Asia, Fixed Income, Public Relations, Legal and Compliance, and senior management of the firm. Yet, you're one human being. Even worse, the needs of some of those constituencies are mutually exclusive. So how do you stay sane? It's my job to help you. You can't do more of everything all the time. What I have to do, with help from John and Paul and Tom, is prioritize what's in the firm's best interests for you to do, to tell you what we need, and to provide you with the proper financial incentives to do it."

The analysts were dubious. Luckily for David, the tension of the moment was broken when the conference room door flew open and Thomas C. P. Mennymore III strode in, looking as if he'd just excused himself from an address to the joint houses of Congress in order to keep his date with the Research Department. The wavy, dark hair was slightly askew, the dark blue pinstripe suit was freshly pressed, the shirt and pocket handkerchief were whiter than white and the Gianfranco Ferre tie said, "I'm cool, even for a banker."

"Tom! Perfect timing," said David with relief. "Paul, thank you very much. Let's follow up on the branch visit issue and then circle back to the analysts."

"Absolutely," Paul agreed. "Thanks, everybody."

David fretted. It was already past 1:15 and the analysts were getting fidgety.

"Well, you should feel honored," Tom began as he raised the podium to accommodate his 6'3" frame. He seemed slightly out of breath yet there wasn't a bead of perspiration on his forehead. "I blew off Jack Welch for you, you know." The analysts frowned in disbelief. "That's right. I was lunching with Jack, at his request, because he needed some advice from me, and I told him at 12:45 that I had to get to this meeting, but the guy just wouldn't let me go. He kept asking questions and, as you know, he's a very persuasive guy. So finally, at ten after one, I said 'Jack, look, my most important client is waiting for me and I just have to go' and Jack said, 'Who's that?' and I said, 'Why it's EFS's analysts, of course!' Jack laughed, but you could tell he was impressed, and he asked if he could finish up with me later. I told him I wouldn't need more than an hour with you so he's coming back at 2:30."

The analysts didn't buy a word of it. Why would Jack Welch need advice from Tom Mennymore? "What bullshit," whispered Keith Jackman, the entertainment analyst. "If Jack Welch is less than 1,000 miles from our offices right now I'll donate my next bonus to the charity of Tom's choice." At the dais, David bit his tongue, put on his "Who needs this?" face, turned and said, "Tom, we're running late, I'm afraid, so what we might want to do is have you give us 15 minutes of highlights from investment banking and then give the analysts a chance to ask you some questions."

"Excellent. It's during the Q&A, I always say, that the rubber meets the road, so let me be very brief and just do some stream-of-consciousness with you about what is most important about research and banking. I'm not going to overwhelm you with slides and Powerpoints... let's just talk amongst ourselves, informally and honestly."

"What would Tom know about either?" Keith Jackman asked.

"Maybe how to spell them," answered one of the associates sitting near him.

"First of all, when I told Jack that you are my most important client, that was no lie. EFS aspires to be a bulge-bracket investment bank one day. We've started from ground zero and we've built, objectively, the most successful middle-market bank on The Street in less than five years. Many of you have contributed importantly to our success. Five years ago, 11% of you got bonuses averaging $88,000 each. Three years ago, 25% of you got bonuses averaging $209,000. Last year, 60% of you received bonuses averaging $276,000. This year, *every* analyst with a banker covering his industry will get a bonus, I'm sure. And next year it will be even better, although we'll probably have to disguise what we're doing for the regulators because you're really not supposed to be getting paid by Banking any more.

"But you will, come Hell or high water, because Banking cannot succeed unless you are an active and enthusiastic part of the process. I don't need to tell you how important it is to have, on the banking team, an analyst whom management of the issuing company respects. Issuers always tell me that bankers come and bankers go but analysts stay. Issuers think that bankers pay attention to them when a deal is imminent and then, when the deal is done, they fly off to conquer other lands. But analysts maintain ongoing contact with those companies, researching, writing reports and impacting the price of their shares with their Buys and Sells. We do have Sells, don't we?"

No one laughed.

"So the burden falls on Banking to take your good

work, your reputations as gurus in your fields, and your followings among institutional and individual investors and leverage all of it into investment banking transactions. It's up to us to let you steer us towards areas you like and away from areas that are ugly."

"When's the last time that happened?" whispered semi analyst Martin Hogue.

"It's up to us to do high-quality deals that you are proud to be associated with, deals in which the issuer and the buyer both win, deals that perform well in the aftermarket, deals that enhance your reputations."

"Like W. R. Grace," muttered Arthur Litt, referring to the chemical company for which Tom had pressured Arthur to support a financing shortly before it went bankrupt.

"It's also up to us to get you paid regardless of all this 'separation of Research and Banking' bullshit that's going on in the market place, and we will. You all know that, no matter how many stocks you cover, how many reports you write, how well you pick your stocks and what your ranking is in *Institutional Investor*, there are limits to what David will pay you and there should be. Your market value reflects, in part, how well you endear yourself to institutional clients and how many commission dollars you bring into the firm, and it's our job to pay you that market value. But when you start to max out on your research compensation, you are *not* maxing out on your total compensation because that's when you become most valuable to Banking and when Banking can become most valuable to you." Tom paused for dramatic effect.

"How can you help us help you? First, think like bankers. Ask yourself constantly which companies you follow need to issue stock, to acquire something, to shed a division, to replace 7% debt with 4% debt, to replace their CEOs or to sell themselves because they can't survive stand-alone.

"Tell your bankers this stuff over and over again. Each of you should pitch EFS's investment banking capabilities at the end of every visit you make to your companies, and not to the IR guy or the CFO but to the CEO. Every decision I just mentioned to you, with one exception, is made by the CEO, and that exception is obvious: the decision to replace the CEO." The analysts laughed despite their best efforts not to. "Maybe the regulators won't let you come with us on actual pitches anymore, but that doesn't mean you can't open the door for the pitch team before you adjourn your visits to your companies.

"What else should you do? First, be as upbeat on our clients' stocks as you can without compromising your integrity. If one of our clients misses the quarter by a mile and you have to cut your earnings estimate by 75%, and your target price, you may have to change your rating on the stock. But if you've done some valuation work that suggests that Client XYZ is worth 20 times earnings, and its stock gets to 20 times earnings, be introspective before you downgrade from Buy to Hold on a price basis. How do you know that 20 is exactly the right P/E? What if you're wrong and it's actually 22 or 23? If the fundamentals are good, you have much more to lose by cutting the rating and pissing management off than to gain by being a purist about the P/E of 20. If you downgrade to Hold, all you'll do is knock the stock down so it's once again selling at a P/E of 17, which will force you to go back to a Buy and piss off management even more. Meanwhile, the FAs and their clients will scream that you're churning. So be careful about cutting ratings, especially on our clients, and especially if it's just on a price basis.

"Also, think twice about downgrading clients that are experiencing financial difficulties. It's precisely when companies are most stressed that bankers can add the most value. We can restructure their balance sheets, help them divest money-losing businesses or help them diversify into more profitable businesses. If they're sick enough we can sell them. But guess what? We can't do any of those things for them if their CEOs and CFOs are pissed off at us because you downgraded the stock and knocked it down even more after they announced whatever it was that ailed them.

"Also, never, *never* downgrade one of your companies just before it chooses bankers for an upcoming financing. You're probably wondering who could be so dumb, but two such analysts are in this very room. I cannot tell you how disorganized and uncoordinated we look when our bankers are pitching to do a deal and the CEO looks up at them and says, 'Boys, how on earth are you going to recommend the purchase of these newly issued shares of mine if your analyst just removed the Buy rating on my stock?' What you *should* be doing is looking for excuses to *raise* ratings on companies that look likely to issue stock soon. We can compete for that business if we've got a report of yours with a Buy rating on it. We can't if the report says Hold. Things are changing, and you may know less often from here on out that a stock offering is imminent, but use your heads. Even if you merely *suspect* it, don't downgrade in front of a financing.

"How else can you help us help you? Make *II*. I know there are all sorts of other economic reasons why most of you want to be ranked number one in your field, but the reason I care about is this: Two firms go in and compete for the books on a 10,000,000–share secondary offering for company ABC. One of them has the *II* number-one-ranked analyst in that industry and the other has the *II* number-eight-ranked analyst. Guess who wins? Not every time, but 90% of the time. If I can tell a prospective issuer that I've got the *II* number-one-ranked analyst on my team and that he loves that issuer, I can get the order 90% of the time, but if my analyst is ranked number eight, I've got to jump through all sorts of extra hoops to offset that competitive disadvantage. Issuers want to be blessed by the best analysts covering their industries and, to most issuers, that means the *II*-ranked analysts. So, make your way to the top of the *II* All Star Team as quickly as you can, and stay there."

David looked at his watch. He could see how impatient the analysts had become. "Tom, it's almost 2:00. I'm sorry we've run so late, but we really need to be out of here in five minutes. Can you wrap up or give the analysts a minute for Q&A?"

"Absolutely. Let me finish with the most important point I want to make to all of you today, and that is this: I need more of your time than what I'm getting. There is a direct correlation between the amount of time one of my bankers spends with one of you and the amount of business that banker does. Last year, EFS's analysts spent from 0% to 45% of their time on banking but the average for all senior analysts was 8%. I've got to tell you, ladies and gentlemen, that a banker who only gets 8% of his analyst's time doesn't hunt. Maybe one of these days I will be forced by the regulators to stop picking up 20% of the Research budget each year. Maybe one of these days, our beloved CEO will cut my budget by $20 million and increase yours by that very same amount. Technically, you will no longer be paid part of your compensation by Banking, but make no mistake about it…all that will have changed is that, instead of writing my checks to you, I'll write them to Ed Koster and our CEO will endorse them to you. No matter what accounting rabbits we have to pull out of the stop-paying-analysts-for-doing-deals hat, I will still be funding 20% of your budget when the Spitzer smoke clears, and I will still be entitled to 20% of your blood, sweat and tears.

"So I'm going to send David, starting this week, a summary report showing what I'm getting from each of you and, if it's less than 20%, I'm going to want to know why. Anything other than 'My banker quit' will be stamped 'Unacceptable' and returned to sender. I want 20% of your time this year, not 8%, and when I get it, we're going to do a ton more business, reinvest more of what we make EFS in our investment bank, and pay all of you the biggest-ass banking bonuses you've ever seen no matter how we have to disguise them for the regulators."

Tom paused, looked around the room, and waited for the nods of agreement that didn't come. "Okay," he said, ignoring the analysts, "you've got to get back to work and I've got to finish my foie gras before Jack comes back. So, thank you, you've been great, and I look forward to seeing a lot more of you in the year ahead." With that, Tom held up a water glass, toasted the analysts, didn't take a sip, and raced back to the executive dining room.

David walked quickly to the podium and said, "It's 2:00, thank you for your patience." Half the analysts were already heading for the doors and the rest quickly followed.

"Let's see," said Tim Omori, the bank stock analyst. "I just got 75 more Top-Tier accounts to service, I'm about to get drafted to visit more retail branches than ever before and I'm now going to double or triple the amount of time I devote to banking."

"That shouldn't be a problem," observed Steve Kalagian, the telecom analyst. "I mapped it all out. If you rent an apartment less than three blocks from the office, work 16 hours each weekday instead of 14, work a full day each weekend instead of a half a day, and take no vacations each year instead of a week a year, you can swing it."

"Oh good," said Tim, as the elevator door opened. "They really had me worried for a minute."

* * *

Anna, from her small office in Moscow, called her Merrill Lynch broker in Berlin. "I want to short Yellow Gorge Mining," she said. "There are 100 million shares outstanding. Start slowly and short as much as you can above 17½."

Next she called her Salomon Smith Barney broker in Frankfurt. "I want to short Yellow Gorge Mining," she said. "Down to 17½. Don't be disruptive. Call me back."

Morgan Stanley was next, in London. "Starting in three days, sell Yellow Gorge Mining short for me," she instructed. "Nothing for three days, then up to 250,000 shares. Any time you can get more than 17."

Finally Anna dialed Goldman Sachs's high-net-worth office in Paris. "Simone, starting a week from today, sell short as much Yellow Gorge Mining as you can for me. Don't go below 17."

When she was done, she walked around the corner to Piotr's office. When Piotr looked up, she said, "Yellow's working" softly and turned away when he smiled.

* * *

"I'm sure Ken Lavery needs no introduction," Bob McCarron told the 95 EFS brokers who had packed into his conference room on the 42nd floor of 220 Park Avenue. "He's just seen ImClone's management at the Hyatt, he offered to stop by and see all of you, and I knew you'd welcome the opportunity. Ken, you should know that we're large holders of Amgen and Genentech in the office and we're always looking for new ideas, especially something selling for ten that can go to, oh, fifty?" A few brokers laughed and Bob winked at Ken. "So, we're all yours." With that, Bob joined his brokers in the audience and Ken, having already rewound himself, pressed the Play button in his head.

"Thanks so much, Bob, for having me in today, and thanks to all of you for coming. I know how busy you are so I'm going to run through some things with you quickly so you can get back to more profitable endeavors than listening to me. But I'll be glad to stay as long as any of you have questions and, if anyone wants to ask me something privately at the end, I'll be glad to meet with you one-on-one." Ken danced well. "Let me start with a brief industry overview and then touch quickly on three or four names that I think you should focus on." Ken paused, stared quickly at a half-dozen brokers at random and then he launched into his long-memorized "over-view for brokers."

"Biotechnology is the single most exciting industry on the planet. It will be to the twenty-first century what computers were to the twentieth century. It will cure cancer. It will cure AIDS. It will enable couples to have children with genetic makeups that will guarantee that, unless they're hit by a car or struck by lightning, they'll be between 125 and 150 years old when they die. And it will end world hunger by dramatically increasing the efficiency of all agricultural producers in the developed and developing world. No other industry will more profoundly change our planet for the better. No other industry will impact your life, your spouse's life, your children's lives and your grandchildren's lives more than biotechnology."

Ken watched for brokers with widening eyes and nodding heads. He zoomed in on them and talked to them as if they were the only people in the room. "And one more thing. Biotechnology will create more multi- millionaires and billionaires during the twenty-first century than high technology created in the twentieth. Some of them will be the founders of the biotech companies themselves, but most of them will be investors like you and me who put money into the right names and hold on for what will be a mind-blowing ride. Not every company will succeed, not every recommendation will work, but with some diversification and some patience, smart investors are going to cash in on the miracle of biotechnology to degrees they can barely imagine." More heads nodded. Notepads were opened. There was total silence except for Ken's voice.

"The biotechnology industry is a newborn baby. Technically, it began in 1982 when Genentech and

Lilly introduced Protropin and Humulin, but during the entire decade of the 1980s, only 10 biotechnology products came to the market. A few were blockbusters like Genentech's Activase and Amgen's Epogen but most were relatively minor products. However, almost six times as many products came to the market during the 1990s, and we're now commercializing more products per *year* than we commercialized in all of the 1980s.

"The aging of the baby boomers is creating a huge pool of people who typically need the most health care and spend the most on it. That is why per capita spending on health care should rise more than 50% between now and 2010.

"As if that weren't enough, the sequencing of the human genome in 2000 marked the beginning of a new era in biotechnology, the Era of Genomics. Genomics offers the potential to understand the molecular basis for disease which will facilitate the creation of drugs that directly attack the root of a particular disease without the side effects associated with many of today's pharmaceuticals. Genomics will dwarf all that has been achieved to date in biotechnology. While barely 100 biotechnology products were created over the past 10 years, I believe that genomics alone will foster the creation of 500 new products over the next 20 years.

"Between September 1998 and March 2000, NAS-DAQ's Biotechnology Index increased sevenfold in price. During those 18 months, a typical investor holding NASDAQ biotech stocks turned $1,000 into $7,000, $100,000 into $700,000, $1,000,000 into $7,000,000. From a standing start, the five largest biotechnology companies in the United States reached a combined market capitalization of about $150 billion by the end of 2000, and almost 300 other biotech companies had combined market caps of another $200 billion. That was almost $350 billion of wealth in somebody's pockets. Hopefully, some of it was in yours, but if not, you have *not* missed the boat. In fact, as a result of the bear market that we all lived through between 2000 and 2002, the boat has returned to the pier to board *more* passengers and I'm here with my megaphone: All aboard! All aboard!"

The room erupted with laughter. Lots of big smiles, lots of nodding heads. Seven times your money in 18 months! How could you *not* want a piece of that action? No broker in the room had made anywhere near seven times his or her money in any of the biotech stocks that Ken had recommended to them in the past, but that didn't seem to matter. Maybe they weren't listening hard enough. Maybe they'd picked the wrong names. Maybe they'd tried to trade the group rather than invest for the long term. No one questioned Ken's numbers. Every broker thought, 'These stocks are much better values now than they were when the market peaked in 2000. If I could make even *100%* for my clients when the next bull market gets going, they'd be ecstatic, they'd give me more money to invest for them and I'd do a ton more business. Everyone would win.' So, pens and note-pads in hand, they readied themselves for their marching orders.

"What do you do today?" Ken asked, seemingly reading their minds.

"You buy biotech heavily for your clients and you remind them constantly that biotechs are volatile so they need to hold them for the long term. They're not for widows and orphans, but they're for *many* of your clients and they're also for you.

"Let's start with Genentech, which should be a core holding for any client interested in biotechnology. Genentech pioneered the industry, it generates $2.5 billion of annual revenues and it spends $600 million annually on researching new drugs. Its most important products are Rituxan for non-Hodgkin's lymphoma, Herceptin for breast cancer, Activase which is a thrombolytic agent, growth hormones Protropin and Nutropin, and Pulmozyme for cystic fibrosis. Two of the most promising new products are Raptiva, a psoriasis drug, and Xolair, an asthma medication. The stock is rated Buy based on my 12–month target price of $40, which implies about 30% upside from here. Are there questions on Genentech?"

"What are your earnings estimates?"

"I expect them to make $0.90 a share in 2003 but that doesn't mean anything because Genentech is spending over $0.75 a share on R&D. What you, as a shareholder, should want Genentech to do is plow every penny it can back into research so it maximizes its chances of finding the cure for AIDS or the cure for cancer. Anything else?" A few heads shook.

"Okay, let's move on to Amgen. This is another core holding. I first began recommending Amgen in the spring of 1998. It was around $15 at the time. Two years later it was $80, at which point I down-graded my rating to Hold. During the bear market Amgen got back down to almost $30, and I reestablished my Buy on it late last year around $40. It's now $45. Amgen is a monster. It's got a market cap of $60 billion and nearly $6 billion in annual sales. Prior to its acquisition of Immunex last year, it derived just over 50% of sales from Epogen for anemia associated with chronic kidney failure, and about 33% from Neupogen which counters chemotherapy-induced neutropenia in cancer patients. When it bought Immunex in 2002 for almost $18 billion, it gained ownership of Enbrel, an extremely promising anti-inflammatory that treats rheumatoid arthritis and that should generate well over $1 billion of sales this year.

"Aranesp, a longer-lasting version of Epogen, has cleared the FDA, as have Neulasta, which is a sustained-release version of Neupogen, and Kineret, which is effective against rheumatoid arthritis. Neulasta and Neupogen should generate almost $2 billion of sales this year."

"How much does Amgen spend on R&D?" one broker asked.

"About $0.75 a share."

"What are your estimates?"

"I'm assuming $1.65 for 2003. At $45, Amgen is selling for less than 30 times earnings which is very reasonable for a company growing more than 20% a year."

"What's your target price?"

"It's $55, so upside potential is still about 20% to 25%. Other questions?" There were none.

"Okay. The last name I want to discuss with you is Biogen. To be honest, Biogen is not the strongest company I follow fundamentally. Its flagship product, Avonex for multiple sclerosis, is very mature and will face increased competition in the years ahead. Earnings were down in 2002, and there's no blockbuster introduction on the horizon near term, which explains why I had a Hold on Biogen during most of 2000 and 2001. But the stock, which peaked at almost $130 in 2000, dropped below $40 last year, I got interested again, and I upgraded to Accumulate at $37.

"As things turned out, I was a little early. Biogen got down to $31, but it then recovered to $35, where it is right now. And at $35, down almost 100 points, and with earnings estimated at $1.80 a share, I continue to think the stock can be accumulated. It doesn't have the upside that Amgen and Genentech have, but with a resumption of earnings growth in mid-2003, and with any good news on its Phase III trials of Antegren for multiple sclerosis and Crohn's disease, Biogen should be able to work its way back into the mid-40s.

"Also, one more very important point. None of this will help Biogen near term, but the company is spending like wild on R&D. Its annual budget is over $300 million which, after taxes, is over $200 million, and there are only 150 million shares outstanding, so R&D is north of $1.50 a share. Maybe they'll have a breakthrough in cystic fibrosis, or with new anti-inflammatories, or with drugs that regulate cell development. No one knows. But such a high level of reinvestment in the business adds to my bullishness on Biogen longer term."

The room suddenly got quiet, and Ken looked at his watch. It was almost 5:00. "I know some of you have long commutes and families to see, and I'm sure that some of you workaholics would like to go back to your offices and write some tickets, but I also want to do some Q&A with those of you who'd like to stay. If you want to leave, you won't hurt my feelings, but for those of you who have a few more minutes to spare, let's talk about other stocks that are important to you." How well he sucked up to them. How much they loved it.

As a few of the brokers in the back began heading for the door, a hand went up in the third row. Ken nodded.

"Ken, John Coady. Let me say first that you're doing a great job and we really appreciate it."

"Thank you, John. It's nice to see you again," Ken lied, not recognizing John even slightly. "You're embarrassing me, though."

"No, no, I mean it. Anyway, I like Genentech and Amgen for my more conservative accounts and I've already got some people in Biogen around $36, but what I really want to know is, what would you buy right now in your own personal account? You know, if you could only buy one name, what would it be?"

God bless him. No set-up, no prompting, no hint of how badly Ken had wanted someone to ask "the question," but also no big surprise because Ken was asked this question at 90% of the branch offices he visited. Still, Ken feigned surprise and a touch of indignation. It was all a game. The brokers laughed. Of course they wanted to know what Ken would put his own money into. That was the acid test.

"Well, I don't see any reason why I can't share that with you."

Ken looked at Bob McCarron, knowing that Bob wouldn't stop him.

"Good question, John," Bob said. "I think many of us were thinking the same thing."

"Okay, I'll tell you, but I'll warn you that if you call me two weeks from now and tell me you've put widows and orphans into this stock and that it's down and that you're afraid you're going to get sued, I'll hang up on you." Lots of smiles. "I mean it, I will. This is only for clients who want to gamble, for clients prepared to lose serious money, for clients who don't find 25% returns worth their while. I want your promise."

"We promise," several brokers yelled out. Suddenly, all of the brokers who'd had commuter trains on their minds stopped dead in their tracks and turned around to face Ken.

"Okay then, let me tell you what I just started buying for myself. It's too risky for 99% of your clients and it's too risky for many of you, but if you've got the guts and you want the glory, then back up the truck my friends and buy every share of Regeneron that you can get your hands on."

* * *

"I need 57 East 57th Street," Ken Lavery said to his cabbie the next afternoon. "Hot shit," he said to himself.

In the 22 hours following his presentation to the 220 Park Avenue branch, Regeneron had risen 14%. Granted, the market had been strong throughout the day, but Ken knew how Regeneron traded like the back of his hand, and the volume that day was heavier than normal, the stock had opened strong and it had never looked back. "I can move stocks," Ken told himself.

By 3:00 P.M., Ken had become fully distracted by how well REGN was acting, by the $42,000 he'd made that day on his newly acquired $300,000 block of Regeneron shares and by daydreams of even greater winnings in the future. From the bottom drawer in his desk he'd pulled a stack of articles about Pierce Brosnan as James Bond. Ken considered himself good-looking, not great-looking, but he also recalled several instances in which people to whom he'd been introduced commented that he "had a little Pierce Brosnan in him." He liked that, and sometimes he even thought they were right.

On the top of the pile was a 1999 article from *The Detroit News* that had been timed to coincide with the release of *The World Is Not Enough* and discussed how the film's costume designer, Lindy Hemmings, and Brioni's master tailor, Checcino Fonticoli, had collaborated in designing Brionis for Pierce to wear in the movie. The photo of Brosnan in one of the Brioni suits was breathtaking. The guy was perfect, the suit was perfect, life was perfect. And just what did perfection cost? According to the article, at least $3,000 a suit, which was $2,000 more than Ken had ever spent before. But so what? Life is short, Ken could move stocks, and $42,000 in one day was only the beginning. So, the time had come for Ken to visit Brioni.

Ten minutes later he strode confidently through the front door. Inside were lots of clothes and no customers.

"May I help you?" asked an impeccably dressed salesman with a gold nametag that read "L. Tinelli".

"You sure can." Ken extended his hand. "I'm Ken Lavery, and I need to spend $40,000 in 40 minutes. Do you think you can help me?"

Tinelli took Ken's remark to be a joke but, having been trained to treat all Brioni customers with the utmost respect, he simply smiled and said, "It would be my pleasure, Mr. Lavery," and beckoned Ken deeper into the store. "Would you like to see suits first?"

"That would be great."

"Have you acquired one of our fine suits in the past?"

"No, actually, this is my first time in Brioni."

"May I tell you a little about our company?"

"Of course."

"Brioni has been in business for 57 years. We opened one of the first men's fashion houses in Rome in 1945 and immediately established a reputation as the world's premier men's master tailor. During the 1950s, we were brought to the American eye by Clark Gable, Gary Cooper, Kirk Douglas, John Wayne and Rock Hudson, all of whom became important customers of ours. We employ about 900 tailors. Our suit line comprises 200 models. One-fourth of all the suits we make are made to measure for 25,000 of our customers. Each suit takes at least 18 hours to tailor and is pressed almost 200 times over an eight-week period. Our line comprises 5,000 different fabrics. Needless to say, there is no finer suit to be found anywhere in the world. Feel this... please."

Ken touched the arm of a suit Tinelli had removed from a rack. It was wool, light, soft, easy on the fingertips.

Tinelli looked at Ken closely for a moment and then said, "Forty-two regular."

"That's right." Ken tried on the jacket Tinelli had been holding. It felt wonderful and fit well except in the sleeves, which were long. Tinelli fawned over him, decided that Ken needed a little pad in his right shoulder, which was lower than his left, and suggested that each sleeve be shortened, the right by half an inch and the left by three quarters. "What styles do you prefer? What colors do you like?"

Ken worked his way through the 42's, selecting five different suits in blues and grays, solids, pinstripes and tweeds. Early in the process he snuck a peek at the prices, just to be sure... $2,995, $2,895, $3,195,

$3,025, $2,995. And when he was done, he asked for a tuxedo with which Tinelli promptly returned. It was the most beautiful piece of men's wear Ken had ever seen and had a price tag to match: $3,995. In less than 17 minutes, Ken had exhausted $19,000.

"What else have you got?"

"We have everything a gentleman requires," answered Tinelli. "Perhaps a blazer?" Tinelli escorted Ken across the store to a rack of blazers.

"This is the Brioni Navy Blazer," he said with great pride. "It is an essential part of any gentleman's wardrobe. It is fashioned from the lightest wool serge. It has our two-button front, center vent and signature Brioni buttons." Ken tried it on and liked it. It was $2,195.

"Perhaps next some sport trousers?"

"Why not?" said Ken with glee. This was turning out to be even more fun than he'd imagined. In the sportswear section, Tinelli pointed to some pants on hangers and said, "The Brioni Sport Trouser is hand tailored in Italy, has pleats in front and comes in light and medium gray wool tropical." Ken felt the fabric on a pair in light gray and noticed the sticker… $395. "It also comes in our own 'Vaticano' fabric, a lightweight wool gabardine, in solid gray, bone, beige, medium and dark brown, gold, navy and black." Ken thought they felt better. Not surprisingly, they were $450 each.

"I'll take one of each."

"As you wish. Some shirts next?"

The shirts were disappointing but Ken was not going to let on in front of Tinelli. He was here to be outfitted from head to toe and that was that. The dress shirts, Tinelli explained, were all hand made in Italy, exquisitely stitched and available in white, blue and ecru. They were $275 each. Ken took six in white and six in blue. In neckwear, Ken looked at Brioni's repp stripe, colorful stripe, floral stripe, tonal diamond, mini paisley, paisley with medallion print, honeycomb, geometric print, flower dot and streaked solid woven patterns and took 15 in assorted colors for $135 each. A bow tie and cummerbund set for his new tuxedo was $400.

Elsewhere in the store, Ken selected a reversible brown and black, textured, pebble-grained calfskin belt with a gold Brioni signature buckle ($175), Brioni's classic cotton piqué polo shirts with mother-of-pearl buttons and single patch pocket (two of each in papaya, dusk, lime and marine blue for $165 per shirt), Brioni's tassel slip-ons by Allen Edmonds ($220), Brioni's knitted 100% hemp hosiery (three of each in yellow, bone, denim and tan for $27.50 a pair), and Brioni's cashmere socks (three of each in navy, red, light blue and grey at $39 a pair).

"Perhaps some sleepwear?" suggested Tinelli.

"What would you recommend?"

"For you, Mr. Lavery, I'd make two recommendations. First, our handmade 100% Egyptian cotton pajama and robe set. The pajamas have a classic collar, pure cotton piping, four signature mother-of-pearl buttons, handsewn cuffed sleeves and two chest pockets. The pants have an elasticized waistband and double-button front closure. Complementing the pajamas is a pinstriped blue cotton robe with a classic collar, pure cotton piping, two front pockets and a sash belt. Everything comes in a matching pinstriped travel pouch with separate pockets for each garment. All for only $695."

"Second, you must not go home tonight without our signature hand-crafted cashmere robe, accentuated by the slight contrast of the braided stitching running along the hems and collar, with a medium tie waist and two pockets. Feel it, please."

Ken knew it would be the softest cashmere he'd ever touched and it was. "Sold." It was $1,695.

"And perhaps some leather goods for your home and office?"

"Absolutely."

Tinelli escorted Ken to the leather accessories department. "Let us begin with The Professional, which we make using a traditional technique called 'taglia vivo' where the leather is hand cut on a perfect square to ensure flawless edges and seams, after which it is hand cured and dyed." Ken had no idea what Tinelli was talking about. "The interior is lined with beige leather and divided into two large pockets for your important documents. There are also smaller pockets for cell phones, beepers, business cards and writing instruments. A large, convenient outer pocket for additional documents has a magnetic snap. In black or dark brown, Mr. Lavery?"

"In black, please." Ken noted the price: $1,000.

"Next, you should have our Top Traveler, the ultimate garment bag for the gentleman traveler and made of grained leather. It folds and zips up neatly into a handy carrying bag with a leather top handle and a detachable shoulder strap. The interior is lined with beige leather. It also comes with interior hangers and hooks and a convenient outside zip pocket for documents you'll need to access easily. It comes with a small Brioni padlock and keys, and a detachable strap. Black or dark brown, Mr. Lavery?"

"Black, please." To travel at the top cost $1,550.

"And for your weekend getaways to the Hamptons and Aspen I'd recommend our Weekend Duffle. It is made of elegant grained leather, lined with beige cloth, it zips closed, has a large leather flap that fits over the handles for extra security, two front straps with buckles and the signature Brioni logo. Of course, we provide a mini Brioni padlock and keys. In black?" Ken nodded. A steal at only $1,300.

"May I offer you a passport wallet with our compliments, Mr. Lavery?"

"Oh, that's not necessary," said Ken, protesting appropriately. Tinelli smiled, said that it was his pleasure and added the $450 wallet, in black, to Ken's shopping bag.

Ken looked at his watch. Thirty-six minutes. "Shall we assess where we are?" suggested Tinelli, who had noticed but pretended he hadn't.

"Please." And so, Messrs. Lavery and Tinelli walked slowly, as gentlemen do, to the front of the store. Ken guessed that he was close to $40,000 but still under. Tinelli asked to be excused for a moment but soon returned with this news: $15,105 for five suits, $3,995 for the tuxedo, and $21,063 for everything else. The grand total was $40,163 plus tax.

Ken had done it... $40,000 in 40 minutes. Thank you, 220 Park. As he watched Tinelli get the approval code from American Express, Ken found himself thinking about another pile of clippings in his desk drawer, the ones of men dressed in Brioni at the wheels of their Bentleys. "I too should have a Bentley," he said, half out loud.

Then Ken smiled because he knew exactly what he needed to do to get one.

OCTOBER

"**D**avid? Hi." Tim Omori was standing in David's doorway.

"Timothy! How's my favorite bank stock analyst?"

"Fine, David. I was just wondering if you knew when *II* will be out?"

Every business has its seasons and, with the arrival of October, most Wall Street analysts enter "obsessing about *II* " season, which only lasts two or three weeks but is intense enough to fray nerves, test friendships and goose Tagamet sales in Manhattan and San Francisco. *II*, the be-all and end-all for most Wall Street analysts, stands for *Institutional Investor* magazine, a monthly trade journal that most analysts ignore 11 times a year. But it's also used synonymously with the *All-America Research Team* poll that the magazine conducts each year. The results of that poll are published each October. The *All Star Poll*, as it's best known, is to sell-side analysts what the Academy Awards are to Hollywood. Winning is a ticket to fame and great fortune, but so is finishing second, third, or in a category just below third place called "Runner-Up."

"Making *II* " quickly becomes every hungry, ambitious, competitive sell-side analyst's goal. It dictates how many hours he works, how he allocates his time between researching, writing and marketing his ideas to clients, how much time he devotes to investment banking and to retail (the former only modestly influences and the latter can only hurt how an analyst fares in *II*), how concerned he is about the accuracy of his recommendations (it's quite possible to do well in *II* without being a good stock picker), how much he travels and, in fact, *every* aspect of how he does his job.

Most analysts give lip service to the other priorities that their firms establish for them. "Yes, I'll do more proprietary research; I'll write more detailed, thorough, insightful reports; I'll be more accurate in my Buy/Hold/Sell recommendations; I'll help my bankers do more deals; I'll visit more retail branches and return the biggest producers' phone calls more quickly; I'll see clients in Europe and Asia once a year; I'll help my counterparts in fixed income; blah blah blah." Deep down, though, what almost every honest analyst on Wall Street will tell you if asked is this: "*II*-ranked analysts are coveted by the most firms on The Street, treated the best, provided with the best support and paid *far* more than their unranked peers. Thus, no matter what my present employer believes is in *its* best interests for me to do all day, what *I* will do is figure out how to 'make *II* 'as quickly as I can, to move up as fast as I can and to stay highly ranked as long as I can."

The poll, which has been conducted for over 30 years, includes about 75 industries and other categories such as Economics and Portfolio Strategy. Ballots are believed to be mailed each spring to over 700 leading money management firms, mostly in the United States. *Institutional Investor* keeps the complete list of recipients and respondents a secret. Each participant is asked to name the four "best" analysts in each of the 75–odd categories.

In each category, someone finishes first, second and third, and in many categories one or more analysts are named "Runner-Ups" so, in some categories there may be only three All Stars but in others there could be four, five, six or seven.

David too was curious about *II's* release date. "Let's find out," he said, motioning Tim to come in. "Let's ask Denise." He picked up his phone and dialed her number.

"Denise Murrell." Denise, a very charming woman with a great smile, is Managing Director of Research Products at *II*, and interacts with Research Directors throughout the year regarding All Star Poll results and related topics.

"Denise, it's David Meadows."

"David! I'm so glad you called. I was just thinking of you!" Maybe she wasn't, but Denise could always make you feel as if she was.

"And Andy Melnick and Mike Blumstein, I'm sure," David teased, referring to his counterparts at Goldman Sachs and Morgan Stanley.

"No, really David. I had you on my list to call today so we could run through the logistics of Announcement Day. Is that why you were calling me?"

"Exactly. What's the plan?"

"David, we're going to do things very much as we did last year. On Columbus Day, Monday, October 13th, at 5:00 P.M., we'll tell CNBC, exclusively, who the number-one-ranked analysts are in all categories and they'll spend most of Tuesday the 14th interviewing them live.

"At 4:15 P.M. on Tuesday we'll distribute to each member firm one copy of the October issue and a letter detailing where each analyst at each firm finished. Most firms send a messenger to pick this stuff up but I know you like to do it yourself, so should I assume we'll see you on the 14th?"

"Absolutely."

"And then, as usual, we'll post the All-America Research Team results on our web site, for subscribers only, at 6:00 that evening."

"So I'll have from 4:15 to 6:00 in which to break the news to my analysts before they read about it on your web site."

"That's right."

"Sounds great." David tried not to sound sarcastic. "Thanks, Denise. I'll see you at 4:15 on the 14th if I don't speak with you before."

"Good luck, David."

Before David could hang up, Tim said, "Tuesday the 14th at 4:15?"

"Yup. That's when I'll pick it up. I'll bring it back around 5:00 and meet with everyone and share whatever I've been given, which, for most analysts, will be just how they ranked. If you or anyone else finished in the top three, the article would include a paragraph on you, which I'd Xerox for you."

"Sounds good," Tim said matter-of-factly.

"So what does your belly tell you?"

"I don't know." Tim was pensive. He'd been a Runner-Up the year before in the Midcap Bank category. "It's so competitive. I'd be happy if I stayed Runner-Up."

"You could be number three this year. My fingers and toes are crossed, you know."

"I know they are, David. I just wish the 14th would get here already."

"Me too." David prepared an e-mail for the rest of

the department telling them what to expect and when. EFS might have five All Stars and rank 14th or two All Stars and rank 15th. Either way, it would be pretty pathetic.

* * *

"Joan, does he know we're here?"

"He knows, David," said Tom Mennymore's secretary from outside the conference room adjoining Tom's office. "He's on with Michael Dell."

Inside the conference room, John McLain and Paul Pitcher looked at each other and at David, and smiled. Naturally, this meeting had to be held in Tom's conference room. Naturally, the three of them had come on time. Naturally, Tom would keep them waiting. It was all about turf and power, and Tom acted convincingly as if he had both even though Investment Banking was running deeply enough in the red to more than offset the profits that EFS was able to muster in all of its other businesses combined.

It was 10:12. "Let's start," David suggested, passing out a short memo that John and Paul skimmed. "We've done this before. Budget time is coming and I want to give Ed and Katherine and Carl a budget for next year that incorporates some adds-to-staff." Edwin Allan Koster was EFS's CEO, Katherine Kaye MacMaster its Chief Financial Officer, and Carl Robern its head of Capital Markets and David's boss. "We've got a lot of holes in the senior analyst ranks and, obviously, we'll never get the budget, nor do we have enough office space, to fill all or even most of them. But the first question Ed always asks me is if my wish list reflects your wants and needs so that's what we're here to establish.

"The spreadsheet on the second page shows all of the industries that we aren't covering right now and any *II*-ranked analysts in those categories that we might have a prayer of hiring. What we need to do is look this list over and see if there are certain senior analyst hires that we, as a group, can recommend that EFS undertake next year."

"How did you decide which analysts we had a prayer of hiring?" asked Paul.

"The usual. We're not going to get anyone out of Goldman, Merrill, Morgan, Salomon Smith Barney, CSFB or Lehman. Their analysts have strong investment bankers working with them every day, and we aren't competitive with those firms on any investment banking front. Those analysts also have global counterparts who are important to them. They like coming in each morning and finding overnight e-mails from teammates in London or Tokyo summarizing what's going on in their markets and helping them understand their groups on a global basis. So, the odds of us hiring from those firms, or from Bear Stearns or J.P. Morgan, approach zero.

"Then you get down into the foreigners, UBS and Deutsche Bank, which are not well established but are spending aggressively to build and thus are tough for us to hire from. Bernstein has analysts who are hard to budge, Prudential and Bank of America each has only a handful of analysts we'd want to hire, and the regionals have analysts who definitely don't want to work in New York City.

"So we probably can't hire anyone is what you're saying," said Paul.

"No, I'm saying that we can recruit in 10 industries and hire 10 analysts, but the odds are that one of them will be a good analyst from a good firm who was pissed off for whatever reason and got a call from us at exactly the right moment, two will be damaged goods from top-notch firms that we couldn't initially tell were damaged, three will be good analysts at small firms who'll use us until they can trade up to Goldman or Morgan Stanley, two will come from institutional clients of ours (only one of whom will make the transition successfully), and two will come out of industry but neither will succeed as a sell-side analyst. That doesn't mean you don't give it your best shot, but it does mean that we have to continue developing our own analysts internally because we just don't have what it takes, meaning a real investment bank, global counterparts and competitive pay packages, to land the best analysts on The Street."

"And takeover risk probably doesn't help either," added John.

"That's right. No one can guarantee these analysts that we won't be taken over and that they won't lose their jobs involuntarily as a result."

David paused. Neither John nor Paul said anything. They'd heard all this before and knew it was true, so why waste even more time wringing hands about it?

"Should we start at the top and work down?" asked Paul.

"Brokers and Asset Managers?"

"Retail doesn't care."

"Pass," John agreed.

"Cosmetics and Household Products?"

"Wait... you skipped chemicals," Paul said. "What about Van Trudell as an upgrade for Arthur Litt?"

"Don't know him," John answered, "but he'd have to be an improvement."

"I've got to do something there," David acknowledged, "and Prudential is a firm we should be able to recruit out of." John and Paul nodded.

"Cosmetics?"

"Limited interest," said Paul.

"What about William Steele at Bank of America?" asked John.

"He's worth a call," David noted. "If we can't take someone out of BofA, I don't think we can hire anyone from anywhere."

"Data Networking?"

"Who's Nikos Theoblahblahblahblahblah?" asked John.

"Theodosopoulos. He's supposedly very good. He's been at UBS for a long time and he's been top-three ranked for quite a while, which suggests to me that UBS must be paying him so much that Goldman and Morgan can't afford him. That means that we certainly can't, but I'll call him anyway."

"Electrical Equipment?"

"Retail doesn't care."

"How long do you see Nick Heymann staying at Prudential?" asked John.

"I don't know, but he's definitely worth a call."

"I'd support Nick," said Paul.

"Electronics Manufacturing Services?"

"Pass," Paul voted.

"I'd call Christopher Whitmore," John suggested. "I've heard a few positive things about him from clients, he's at Deutsche Bank and he's ranked number three."

"I agree," said David. "Food?"

"Hire John McMillin." McLain was waving his hands wildly. "He's one of the best analysts on The Street. I've never heard a bad word about the guy. He's been number one forever, he works at a shitty firm and he probably only has a few years left before he starts living the good life, so offer him $5 million a year for three years and get it over with. He's worth it, and it would be a feather in all of our caps."

"He's probably had a dozen offers over the last dozen years but he's still at Prudential. He's loyal, so money alone won't do it. He also loves to tell it like it is and, surprise, surprise, he hates investment bankers. So, the good news is that we don't have a bank, and the bad news is that Mennymore pretends that we do and will veto any offer for McMillin."

"Ask Koster what he thinks," said Paul, calmly. "But I agree, we're not going to get the green light to offer $5 million and, without an offer like that, we're not going to get McMillin. Who's this guy Don Pinkel at UBS?"

"No idea," David confessed, "but if he's at UBS, I should call him and I will. Gaming and Lodging?"

"Pass."

"Pass."

"Imaging Technology?"

"Alex Henderson," said John.

"Gave it up," David sighed. "He's now number one in networking at Salomon. But Ben Reitzes is a possibility. He went from nowhere to *II* number one in 36 months. He's some one worth calling, and I'll also try Kurt Coviello at Bear Stearns even though hiring from The Bear has been tough."

"What about the Internet?"

"Oh sure." Now John was rolling his eyes. "Let's lay off 15 of our analysts and see if Mary Meeker will come for a 50% pay cut."

"Anyone know Daniel Roe at UBS?"

John and Paul shook their heads.

"I could give him a try," David said. "Life Insurance?"

"Grow someone, probably," said John, "unless you can get this chick, Vanessa Wilson, out of Deutsche Bank."

"I don't know her, but her numbers are very good. I'll call her. Leisure?"

"Robin Farley," John bellowed. "I worked with her a couple of years ago, and she's hot. She's also pretty good."

"Are you recommending her because she's good or she's hot?" David asked.

"Mostly because she's good, but…"

"I'll call her," said David, not wanting to hear the rest of the sentence. It was 10:40 and there was still no sign of Tom Mennymore. "Natural Gas?"

"Call Ron Barone," John suggested. "The guy's a beast. I worked with him at Kidder 20 years ago. By now he must be 55 going on 18. He's a health nut, you know, a vegetarian or some shit, but he has biceps like my thighs, he has more energy sleeping than I have awake, and he's been ranked 30 straight times. You think you can hire him?"

"No, but he's at UBS," said David, "and UBS isn't Goldman Sachs. Is he worth a phone call? Yes. Is UBS going to let him go easily? No. Packaging?"

"The only reason to hire Dan Khoshaba," said John, "is to get the *II* vote. We don't bank his space, and retail, if I'm not mistaken, doesn't give a shit about it."

"You're right," Paul confirmed.

"Well, it's Deutsche Bank," said David, "which means there would be a chance, but my suspicion is that it's going through exactly the same exercise right now, and that as long as Khoshaba is ranked, he's going to be treated well and made impossible to hire."

John and Paul nodded.

"PC Hardware?"

"Now that's an important group to cover," said John, and Paul agreed. "Kim Alexy is a girl?"

"She used to be Don Young's junior," David said, "and she got the group at Pru when Don followed Culp to PaineWebber. Within a couple of years, she got ranked in her own right. I'm sure Prudential is treating her well, but we should be able to pry her loose. Don is strong and, from what I've heard, very demanding. Any junior who cuts the mustard with him has to be good, and getting ranked herself confirms that. Restaurants?"

"Not much left there that's worth covering" Paul answered. "We don't have much interest."

"Janice Meyer is the best of the bunch," said John. "Culp had Deb Bronston train her when they were all at Pru. She's been number one or number two forever but you'll never get her out of CSFB."

"In Retailing—Hardlines, I would've gone after Aram Rubinson but he just left UBS for BofA so there's nothing to be done there" David sighed. "What about Satellite?"

"Limited interest," Paul sighed.

"I'd pass," said John.

"Textiles and Apparel?"

"Wait!" said Paul, banging his fist on the table. "What about semiconductors?"

"Martin Hogue does semis."

"I know. What I mean is, let's fire Hogue and hire Mark Edelstone."

David was irritated. "Oh, of course. Mark Edelstone of Morgan Stanley? Mark Edelstone, top-three-ranked semi analyst for years on end? Mark Edelstone with counterparts in 23 different countries? Mark Edelstone with 14 Managing-Director-level investment bankers, one to call on each of the 14 companies he follows? And what, exactly, do we have to offer Mark that Morgan Stanley doesn't?"

"Make him Director of Technology Research. Make him an Associate Director of the entire Research Department. Pay him $10 million a year for five years, after which he can retire. He's just like McMillin. Cut from the same cloth. I'd trade six of our analysts in a heartbeat for an Edelstone." Paul seemed serious.

"I'm not going to call him," said David. "It's a complete waste of time. He's not going to leave Morgan Stanley for EFS. I'm not going to get $10 million to pay him, and I don't need more than one Associate Director of Research."

"Okay, okay," Paul relented. "But do this: Propose it to Koster, and when he blows a gasket, come back with the McMillin for $5 million idea. He'll look like a bargain and maybe Ed'll go for it."

"I'll think about it," said David, who had already decided to propose neither. "Where were we? Textiles and Apparel?"

"Nope," Paul voted.

"Pass," John agreed.

"Tobacco?"

"Is that a full-time job?" Paul asked.

"If you can't hire someone who's already ranked in this space there's no reason to cover it," John said, yawning. Paul nodded.

"Do you know Liz Tytus at Prudential?"

Neither did but both were amenable when David offered to call her.

"Wireline equipment?"

"We could try Grace Flagler at Prudential," Paul suggested. "We hired a few Pru brokers recently who mentioned her positively, I think."

"Last two. Quantitative Research?"

"Retail could use it if packaged properly."

"Hard to get paid for," answered John. "The only person I always heard good things about in Quant was Melinda Brown when she worked at Pru years ago."

"Melissa," David corrected. "You're right. She was extremely good but she's on the buy side now at Goldman and I'm sure the last thing she'd want to do is come back to the sell side at EFS."

"Linda wouldn't let you hire a quant any way," laughed John, referring to Linda Anne Logan, EFS's chief investment strategist. "Her toes are very, very long, and you know how much she *hates* in-house competition!"

David sighed and shook his head slowly. Linda was almost always a thorn in his side. For a woman of Anglo-Irish descent, she was remarkably plebeian and radiated more testosterone than most of the men who surrounded her. "Little Napoleon" the analysts called her, referring to her five-foot-two-inch frame and "charming" personality.

"You could probably say the same thing about Small Caps," Paul added.

"Who's Steve DeSanctis?" John asked.

"Don't know. He's number one, he's at Prudential, and it looks like he assumed the slot when Claudia Mott retired from Pru. You remember Claudia?"

"I do." John nodding. "She was the number one analyst in small caps for years."

"I do," said Paul. "Some of the brokers that we hired from Pru swore by her."

"It's hard to believe that Prudential once had Claudia Mott and Melissa Brown sitting side by side doing quant together. Melissa did big picture and large caps, I think, and Claudia did small caps. That was some team," said David, wistfully. "But Claudia retired so that isn't a call worth making. Maybe DeSanctis inherited her franchise. No matter what, he's *II* number one now and he's at Prudential, which adds up to 'call him.'"

"Call who?" Tom Mennymore was through the door and racing for an open seat, hair slightly disheveled but pinstripes neatly pressed. He picked up his copy of the memo, looked at it for five seconds and said, "Let me tell you exactly what needs to be done here. We don't bank cosmetics. We don't bank GE in any way that Nick Heymann could help me with…if we ever bank GE it will be because of my relationship with Jack and the ties he still has with GE's board. We don't bank Electronics Manufacturing Services, whatever that is, we don't bank gaming, we don't bank life insurance or packaging or restaurants or textiles.

"So, I could use Nikos but you'll never get him, I could probably use Reitzes, I'd be okay with Barone but you'll never get him, and I could take Kim Alexy or leave him."

"Kim's not a boy, Tom," said John, grinning broadly.

"Leave *her*. It doesn't matter. What you're doing here is playing *II* and nothing more. You're going after votes wherever you can find them, regardless of whether the firm can do business in their names or not. And, when it comes to banking, we can't, so let me tell you what's on my wish list.

"First, I don't need any more *II*-ranked analysts who

don't like banking. I don't need analysts who want to campaign for votes all day long and blow off bankers looking to do deals. I don't need coverage of the S&P 500 because those companies don't need our banking services. They've used Goldman and Morgan Stanley since 1900 and that isn't going to change. I need analysts willing to spend half their time on banking and to cover lots of small-and mid-cap names that we *can* bank. Small computer software companies, small semiconductor companies that Mr. Hogue won't touch, small wireless names that are not *interesting* enough to Mr. Kalagian, small biotech names that could fatten up Mr. Lavery's universe, and small energy companies that Ms. Natolio is too *busy* to pay attention to. I don't need any basic industry analysts, I don't need transportation and I don't need your entire consumer group because the deals we do there are few and far between.

"If you want to help me, get me technology analysts, health care analysts, energy analysts and financial services analysts who are glad to cover the second-string names, glad to spend half of their time on banking, glad to support the name-brand analysts as they go after *II*, and that's it. I've told Koster this a thousand times and I'll tell him again tonight at Traviata. Name-brand analysts help us land business, but what would really make a difference would be teams of analysts covering 50 to 60 names in a given sector, not one *II* -aspiring analyst covering 10 large-cap names that I can't bank. Do you read me?"

David, John and Paul sat silently. They'd seen this kind of performance many times before but it still intimidated them.

"What I read, Tom," David said at last, "is this. At the rate EFS is losing money, I may very well get a flat-to-down budget for next year, but should a miracle occur, I'll get the green light for, at most, four or five new hires. If I do, I'll call all of the above-named analysts and succeed in hiring one of them. The other hires will come from somewhere else, and hopefully they'll be good, but 80% of what John and Paul would love to see me do won't get done and 95% of what you just rattled off won't get done.

"We can't get *II* votes out of small-cap analysts covering names we can bank and we can't get a lot of new banking business out of Liz Tytus's tobacco universe so, as usual, at the end of the day, everyone will be pissed off at me."

"I can't speak for Messrs. Pitcher and McLain," said Tom, "but *I* am unprepared to be disappointed." With one last stare at David and a half-raised eyebrow, Tom stood, swept from the conference room and headed to the men's room for a pit stop before the lunch he claimed he was having with Steven Jobs about which Joan Atwell, Tom's secretary, was clueless.

* * *

Thirteen days after Volkov had called Piotr in Moscow and asked for Yevgeny, Nick Denisovich signed up to speak on EFS's Morning Call. Every Wall Street firm has a Morning Call that typically runs for 45 minutes or so beginning at 7:15 or 7:30 A.M. Typically, the institutional sales-people sit in or listen in remotely and can interact with the analysts in a Q&A format. Retail brokers, however, are only allowed to listen. It is on the Morning Call that analysts formally begin coverage of new companies, change their recommendations and/or earnings estimates on companies they already cover, and generally make their "most actionable" calls. A good call predicts what will be in the news a week or a month before it happens; a bad call reacts to news that's already out. The analysts are typically given three minutes or less in which to speak but many run longer because, insecure by nature, they feel compelled to demonstrate how much they know to the salesmen by padding their basic message with nonessential information.

Generally, analysts sign up for The Call by alerting the moderator of The Call the afternoon or night before that they want air time, and by submitting to the moderator a summary of their most important points that is distributed electronically to all institutional salespeople and retail brokers prior to the start of the next Morning Call and posted on a variety of electronic research services such as *First Call, Research Direct, Multex* and *Bloomberg* for institutional investors who subscribe to them. When he signed up, Nick had told Paula Hainsworth, who moderated EFS's Morning Call, that he had a ratings change and an earnings estimate change to make, and Paula scheduled Nick to speak third.

At about 7:20 the next morning, Nick walked quietly into the conference room and grabbed one of the chairs along the side of the room, near the head table where Paula was sitting with two other analysts, one of whom was speaking. At 7:25, Paula turned towards Nick and said to the salespeople, "Nick is next with a ratings downgrade and an earnings estimate reduction."

Nick took his place at the head table, watched as the salespeople leafed through their Morning Meeting packets to find the *First Call* note that he'd written the night before, and then began. "Thanks Paula, and good morning everybody. I'm downgrading Yellow Gorge Mining this morning, ticker YLL on the Big Board, from Hold to Sell. The stock closed yesterday at $16.98. The reason for the downgrade is that I spoke with management last night and came away convinced that it will take Yellow Gorge longer to return to profitability than I'd been assuming, and longer than the rest of The Street is assuming.

"As you know, Yellow Gorge lost $0.25 a share in 2002, its fourth straight down year. Earnings had peaked at $1.55 a share in 1997. Yellow is a much purer gold play than most of the other companies I follow so its earnings ebb and flow much more closely with the price of gold than do the earnings of most of its competitors. As a result, depressed gold prices in recent years have taken their toll on Yellow's earnings and its stock price.

"I had hoped that a gradual uptick in gold prices, coupled with substantial cost savings associated with its recent acquisition of Black Hills Mining Corp., would push Yellow back into the black this year, albeit modestly. I no longer think this will happen. Until today, my model had assumed $0.20 a share of cost savings and synergies this year from the Black Hills acquisition. But my conversations with management last night led me to conclude that the cost cutting is proceeding far more slowly than planned, that synergies are proving harder to realize, and that there may be no cost savings at all over the next 12 months. As a result, I'm cutting my earnings estimate from a profit of $0.05 a share to a loss of $0.15.

"I suspect that other analysts will have to cut their numbers as well, and this will put downward pressure on the shares at least over the near term, until Yellow

Gorge moves back into the black. As a result, I'm cutting my target price on Yellow from $17 to $13.50, which would still be about 1.5 times book value. That target price suggests about 20% downside risk from current levels, and that requires me to change my rating from Hold to Sell. Are there any questions?"

Herb Hirschorn, an institutional salesman, asked, "Nick, you were already below the rest of The Street. First Call says the consensus among all analysts was $0.20. What are your competitors assuming to get to that number?"

"Obviously, Herb, I don't see their models, but management has been guiding analysts to $0.20 based on $0.30 a share of cost savings associated with Black Hills and an average gold price for the year of $330 to $340. I was below that number already because my average gold price assumption for the year was only $325 and, now, if I have to assume lower cost savings, my estimate has to go even lower."

Barbara Malek, a young saleswoman who was sitting close to Nick, asked, "Why should the stock sell at 1.5 times book value if it can't make any money and Yellow Gorge isn't a takeover candidate?"

"Good question, Barbara. There really isn't any magic about that 1.5 times multiple. Gold stocks don't typically sell at prices based on book value, but the company has no earnings so a price-to-earnings-multiple discussion is irrelevant. I don't consider Yellow Gorge a takeover candidate, but it's hard to imagine Yellow getting down to book value, which is only about $9 a share, given how substantial its remaining gold reserves are." Nick paused for a second longer than he needed to. "But it could, under the wrong circumstances, if investors get more pessimistic about gold prices and/or the Black Hills acquisition starts to look like a mistake."

The salespeople looked up from their notebooks. They wanted to measure Nick's level of conviction with respect to the $13.50 target price and Nick knew it.

"I guess what I want to convey to clients is this: If I'm right about the gold price and I'm right about the absence of cost savings, then $13.50 is a reasonable target. But if I'm wrong, it is more likely that gold prices will be lower than I expect than higher, and that Black Hills winds up being a drag on Yellow than a big boost to earnings, and that means that, if I'm going to be wrong about the target price, it will probably be because $13.50 is too high, not too low."

"Other questions for Nick?" Paula Hainsworth asked. There were none.

Nick walked quickly out of the conference room, as if he had 100 institutional clients to call right away, but when he returned to his office he didn't touch the phone. Instead he glued his eyes to CNBC. Shortly after 7:30, he watched and listened as David Faber reviewed EFS's downgrade of Yellow Gorge Mining to Sell and noted how refreshing it was to see an analyst use "the S word." By 9:15, as the market was readying to open, Maria Bartiromo had highlighted EFS's downgrade to Sell on Yellow Gorge twice and David Faber had referenced his prior report on the downgrade once.

Maria, from the floor of the NYSE, indicated that there was an order imbalance in Yellow Gorge's shares, that there were far more sellers than buyers at the moment, and that the indication was that YLL would open between $14 and $15 versus the prior-night's close of $16.98.

Nick finally picked up the phone, but not to call any of his clients. He needed to place a "courtesy call" to Robert Robasco, the Director of Investor Relations at Yellow Gorge. Robasco almost certainly already knew from watching CNBC or from distressed YLL shareholders who had been watching CNBC and then called him, that Nick had cut his numbers and his rating on the shares even though he'd told Nick the night before that the cost savings, while slow in coming, should still reach $30 million this year. It would be a strained conversation, but Nick would keep it short.

As Robasco answered his phone and Nick began talking to him, two things happened. First, Linda Chute began waving and yelled out to Nick that Mark Haines of CNBC was on the line and wanted to interview Nick live (using the CNBC camera that had been placed on EFS's trading floor two years before) in 10 minutes. Nick nodded. "Get the okay from Public Relations," he whispered to Linda.

The other thing that happened was that Maria Bartiromo was back on TV reporting that "sources were telling her" that EFS was out telling clients that, it was *possible* that Yellow Gorge, if it didn't return to profitability soon, could drop towards book value, which was estimated to be $9 a share, barely half the price at which it had closed the night before. "What's noteworthy about this call," Maria was telling her audience, "is that most Wall Street analysts won't go to a Sell unless fundamentals are really deteriorating out there. Most are much more comfortable using Market Performer or Hold, and $13.50 isn't really all that far from $16.98, where it closed last night, so some traders may be reading something far worse than simply a $0.20 earnings estimate reduction into EFS's downgrade to Sell this morning.

"And by the way, Mark," Maria concluded ominously, "the new indication on YLL is $11 to $13. Yellow Gorge, it appears, is going to get crushed today."

* * *

David's phone was ringing. It was Linda Logan, his chief strategist. Linda rarely called David, but, whenever she did, it was with something unpleasant. David hesitated for a moment and then reluctantly picked her up.

"Hi."

"David, who's this idiot Robin Lomax that you just hired?"

"She's a top-ranked retail trade analyst from CIBC. Why?"

"She's a moron. She's totally incompetent. She doesn't understand the first thing about retailing. My kids know more about retailing than she does."-

"What did she do?"

"Did you hear her on the Morning Call today?"

"No."

"You should ask Paula about her. The sales force hates her."

"What did she do?"

"She downgraded Federated because she thinks the October quarter is going to be a penny light."

"And…?"

"David, October is history. Do you think the stock's price over the next six to 12 months is going to be dictated by whether October was a penny too high or too low? Does this woman have any vision? Does she understand the first thing about what makes stocks go up and down?"

"Do you have Federated on your Recommended List?"

"Of course I do, and I'm not selling it no matter what she says. She's an idiot. The only reason you hired her is because she's *II*-ranked, and I'm going to tell all of the brokers who call me to complain about her exactly that."

To play kindergarten teacher or not to play. David decided not to play and hung up without saying another word. ·

* * *

"I loved you in *Road to Perdition*," Ken Lavery said when his broker picked him up.

"I hope you're calling with some business," Tom Hanks the broker said, "because I'm taking my family cruising in the South Pacific next week and I need the dough."

"Tahiti?"

"Tahiti, Bora Bora and Moorea on the Paul Gauguin."

"When are you leaving?"

"Tomorrow night."

"Well have a great time. Listen, just a quick question before you go?"

"Shoot."

"How do margin accounts work?"

"Let's see what your account looks like." Tom keystroked and then waited for Ken's account to come up on his PC monitor. "You've got $1,200,000 of stocks and $200,000 of cash in your account, or equity of $1,400,000. That means that you have borrowing power, initially, of $1,400,000. We'd charge you the broker loan rate, which is now 4%, on anything you borrowed."

"I have to have equity that's equal to 50% of the total value of my portfolio?"

"Fifty percent initially but 30% on an ongoing basis. So, if you borrowed $1,400,000, you'd have, initially, $2,800,000 of stocks and cash. If the value of your stocks and cash dropped to, say, $2,500,000, your equity would fall to $1,100,000 or 44% of $2,500,000, so you'd be okay, but if your stocks and cash fell to $1,800,000, your equity would dwindle to only $400,000 or 22% of that $1,800,000 and you'd get a margin call requiring you to add enough funds to your account to get your equity back up to 30%."

"And if my $2,800,000 turned into $4,000,000?"

"At $4,000,000, your equity would have increased to $2,600,000 or by $1,200,000. At a minimum, you'd be able to borrow that much more, which would then increase the size of your portfolio to $5,200,000. In truth, though, if you were handling your account responsibly, which you always do, I could probably get permission from my manager to lend you another $2,000,000. You always want your equity to be more than 30% of your portfolio's value and your borrowings to be less than 70%."

"I get it. And how much paperwork is involved in switching my regular account to a margin account?"

"Almost nothing. Just say go."

"And if I did that, I'd be able to borrow $1,400,000 immediately?"

"Correct."

"Go," said Ken. "I'll call you before you leave and tell you how to invest it."

* * *

"Why?" asked Nancy Natolio, the oil and gas analyst, of her investment banker.

"Because we landed the IPO mandate completely unbeknownst to you," said George Sherva defensively.

"I made the introduction, George! You didn't know anyone at CPM before I put you in front of them at our conference." Nancy was referring to CPM Oil & Gas, a small refiner that had been privately owned when invited to EFS's last Energy Conference and that had given EFS the mandate to manage its initial public offering soon after Nancy had introduced George to CPM's top brass at the conference.

"You did, and that's why you're in for 10% of the management fee and not 5%. You didn't pitch for the business. You made the introduction, which makes you "the finder" on the transaction, and you're following the stock now that the deal is done, which would always be the case. So, if we'd have recommended 15% had you pitched for the business, we feel very comfortable recommending 10% because you didn't."

"How many dollars are we talking about here?" asked Nancy with irritation. "The difference between 10% and 15% is a rounding error to you. It costs The Bank nothing. On the other hand, it's the difference between making me feel appreciated and pissing me off. It's ludicrous that I have to get on my hands and knees and beg for this!"

George liked the image of Nancy on her knees. "You know exactly what the difference is. It was a $60 million IPO. Our management fee was $240,000, and you're getting 10% of it, which is $24,000, not 15% which would be $36,000."

"Exactly what I said. Twelve fucking thousand dollars. We shouldn't even be having this conversation!"

"That's all I can do, Nancy. Talk to Tom about it if you want to."

Nancy silently rejected the idea. Tom Mennymore loved to stiff analysts on their banking bonuses. It was an obvious turn-on for him and she wasn't going to give him the satisfaction. There was another path. "I'll do what I have to," she told George, and hung up. "Shanna?" she yelled in the direction of her research assistant. "Shanna, find out when Carl can see me."

A moment later, Shanna Pender poked her head into Nancy's office and said, "Carl has a lunch meeting in 20 minutes but he said to tell you that you can come right now if you want to."

"Tell him, please, that I'm on my way." Nancy headed for the executive suite on the 75th floor, which Carl Robern called home. Carl, who was President of Capital Markets and part of the firm's four-member Operating Committee, was a nineteen-year EFS veteran with a background heavy in investment banking. He had risen through the ranks, to almost everyone's surprise, to a perch from which he now oversaw not only investment banking, but equity research; institutional equity sales and trading; fixed income research, sales and trading; and all international operations. Carl was viewed internally as of average intelligence, an ass-kisser and an uninspiring, truly mediocre manager. He was also one other thing.

"Come in, Nancy," said Carl, waving and smiling. As Nancy entered his large, walnut-paneled office and admired the fabrics and carpets and furnishings that were much too classy for Carl, she heard him ask, "Open- door or closed?"

Nancy closed the door behind her and sat down in one of the two large Chippendale-style chairs facing Carl's desk and looked at Carl directly and angrily.

"Did Shanna tell you that I have a lunch in 15 minutes?"

"Yes. This won't take that long."

"I'm listening."

"Carl, I need your help in getting me paid fairly on the CPM deal. I'm sure you recall it. It was a $60 million IPO that we did with Morgan Stanley." Carl admired Nancy as she talked. He liked blondes, and Nancy was very blonde. He also liked women who weren't too tall, because Carl was only 5'8", and thin, which made him look even smaller. Nancy was 5'7".

"I was the finder on the deal. I introduced George Sherva to the company. We had not called on them previously. I invited them to our conference expressly to get George in front of them. After the conference, George and his team held several follow-up meetings with CPM and, before you knew it, CPM told Morgan Stanley that it wanted us to be the co-lead on its IPO."

"That was good work, Nancy."

"Yes it was, and it entitles me to a good payout, meaning 15%."

"How much are they proposing to pay you?"

"Ten percent."

"So we're talking about what? Five percent of..."

"Five percent of $240,000, or an extra $12,000. It's not the $12,000 that's bugging me. After taxes, that's $6,000, which is what Tom Mennymore spends on a couple of bottles of Chateau Petrus Pomerol when he takes clients out for dinner most nights. It's about paying me the max because I earned it, not paying me what they think they can get away with. I didn't pitch for the deal because I didn't *have* to. CPM knew me and knew my abilities."

"So you want me to override George and Tom and give you $36,000."

"That's right."

"You know, Nancy, that we're not supposed to pay analysts for banking any more" Carl said as seriously as he could.

"Bullshit, Carl. We've always paid analysts for banking and we always will, even if it's masked as a bonus from the firm instead of a bonus from the bank."

"Well, we're *definitely* not supposed to pay analysts specific amounts for specific deals."

"Why are we pretending here? Each year, you give me my bonus and tell me it's for my overall effort to support the firm. I know that we did two deals during the year and that 10% of the management fees on those deals equals $120,000. I open the envelope and find inside a check for whatever my Research guarantee was plus $120,000, from which I conclude that I got paid 10% on the two deals and zippo for all of my other efforts."

"Maybe you got 8% on the two deals and $24,000 for everything else."

"I don't think so, Carl, nor does any other analyst in our department."

Carl rocked back in his burgundy leather chair. He looked at Nancy slowly, smiled in a slightly contemptuous way and shook his head slowly from side to side.

"What?" she asked.

"Twelve thousand dollars. Twelve thousand dollars." Carl turned and looked out his window for a minute, seemingly deep in thought, and then turned back to Nancy, leaned forward and said, "I'll tell you what I'll do." Nancy returned his stare and concentrated, listening for the words "I'll do it."

"I'll do it," Carl said. As Nancy started to sit back in her chair, victorious, Carl added, "if you'll suck my cock."

Nancy was startled but knew well enough not to say a word.

"Just once. I'll be quick about it."

Nancy's eyes widened and her cheeks flushed. She stood up and started walking towards the door.

"Nancy," said Carl, firmly. Nancy turned as she wrapped one hand around the doorknob and looked over her shoulder. "Think about it. I bet even Xaviera Hollander never made $12,000 for a blow job, and you'll never have another chance to earn $1,000 a minute having the time of your life."

Nancy swung open the door and slammed it behind her. Carl smiled and checked his clock to see how long he had to tame his erection before his lunch meeting was slated to begin.

* * *

"Jim Molloy."

"Jim, Ken Lavery."

"Hi, Ken, what's up?"

"I want to buy some more Regeneron and two small names that I don't follow."

"How much Regeneron?" Ken could hear Jim pulling up Ken's account.

"$300,000."

"You just bought $300,000 Regeneron. You're buying more?"

"That's right."

"Any plans to change ratings or estimates any time soon?"

"No."

"Any reports you're planning on publishing on it any time soon?"

"No."

"Okay, you're clear but you have to buy it within 24 hours."

"Thanks."

"What else?"

"The other two stocks I want to buy are small, OTC names that I don't cover and don't intend to cover any time soon. They're too small and too speculative for me to follow at EFS. I just can't cut 5,000 brokers loose on them."

"And they are…?"

"The G-NOME Company and Genomic Innovators. GNOM and GINV."

Molloy checked his Watch List and Restricted List and found neither name. "These stocks are both selling around $6?"

"Yes. They're early-stage genomics companies with no established products."

"How much are you going to buy?"

"About 100,000 shares of each."

"What's the market cap of these companies?"

"G-NOME has 14 million shares outstanding so its market cap is about $85 million. Innovators has 11 million shares outstanding so its market cap is about $65 million."

"So you're talking about buying 1% of each company?"

"Less." This was true, but barely.

"How do they trade?"

"Actively…as much as 500,000 shares a day. I can do this in one block without being disruptive."

There was a long pause at the other end of the line. Finally, Molloy said, "Okay, you're approved, but only for 48 hours."

Ken thanked him and immediately called Tom Hanks. "Put $300,000 more into Regeneron," he told him, "and buy me 100,000 shares each of The G-NOME Company, ticker GNOM, and Genomic Innovators, ticker GINV. They're both trading at around $5.90 right now. I'm willing to go up to $6.50 if I need to."

"Double up in Regeneron and buy 100,000 GNOM and 100,000 GINV up to $6.50. Consider it done."

"Fly safely," said Ken, "and remember your sun block."

* * *

On Tuesday morning, October 14th, David Meadows went to work and watched TV. He'd intentionally kept his calendar free of appointments as much as he could so he wouldn't be interrupted. By the time he settled in with CNBC at 8:15, Mark Haines was already on his second interview of the morning with just-announced, number-one-ranked analysts in *II's* new All-America Research Poll. David watched not because he expected to see any of his own analysts on CNBC but to see other analysts whom he knew or with whom he'd worked in prior incarnations on The Street and to watch how differently each analyst dealt with his long-established or new-found stardom.

Ben Reitzes of UBS Warburg, who had just finished first in the Imaging Technology group, came on, looking very young and talking about how Xerox had gone down and then back up, up a little more and then back down. While he obviously understood the significance of these moves, Mark Haines appeared puzzled. Later in the hour, a second UBS Warburg analyst appeared and was interviewed by David Faber. She was Robin Farley, who had won in the Leisure category and who discussed some of her successful calls on the cruise ship companies and the importance of doing "anecdotal" research.

During a break in the interviewing action, Meadows perused his e-mails and found nothing requiring immediate attention. Before long, Maria Bartiromo was on with John McMillin, Prudential's veteran food-stock analyst who had ranked number one consistently over the past decade. John rarely smiled and today was no exception, his re-crowning notwithstanding. "I'd like to thank my clients for voting for me," he said, "but I have to admit that I come to work every-day to make my clients money and I didn't make them very much money over the past year." The food group had been an underperformer of late and, even though John's recommendations had beaten those of his competitors, they were up only slightly in absolute terms and John couldn't hide his disappointment.

Towards the end of "Squawk Box," Mark Haines returned with the perennial winner in the Brokers and Asset Managers category, Henry McVey. Henry was exceedingly young, and just as bright and articulate. He was humble and gracious and very forthcoming about what he liked and didn't like in his group. Mark obviously knew Henry's work well and reminded Henry of several predictions he'd made on CNBC that had all played out well. Haines doesn't impress easily but he clearly liked Henry.

During a long break between interviews, David had Lisa reconfirm his expected arrival time at *II's* offices that afternoon, looked quickly through his mail and returned a few important calls. But everything ground to a halt when Sam Buttrick's face appeared on David's Mitsubishi screen. Sam was the longstanding number-one-ranked airline analyst who now worked at UBS Warburg. David began smiling even before Sam said a word. Co- anchor Ted David congratulated Sam on winning top honors in his category again and asked him which of his calls he was most proud of.

"I'd like to thank all of my clients for voting for me," said Sam.

Ted tried again. "I know Sam that you've had some success with your Southwest Airlines recommendation of late, but do you really think investors should still buy it?"

"I have a Buy on Southwest," said Sam, deadpan.

"And why is that?" asked Ted, thinking he was now making headway with Sam.

"Why? Well, basically, I think Southwest will be selling at a higher price in the future than it is today."

Ted couldn't tell if Sam was toying with him or merely stating the obvious. "You mean to say that that's why you have a Buy rating on Southwest?"

"Well, that's right," answered Sam. "You see, because I think it's more likely that Southwest will move higher over the next year than lower, it would be inappropriate for me to put a Hold or a Sell on it. Stocks that are heading higher are supposed to be rated Buy."

Ted decided he'd had enough of Sam, congratulated him again and then quickly got the camera refocused on himself.

Throughout the remainder of the morning and the early afternoon, Ted, Martha MacCallum, Michelle Caruso-Cabrera and Bill Griffeth kept the interviews flowing at a rapid rate. Rick Sherlund, the longstanding top-ranked computer software analyst and the "axe" on Microsoft, extended his record to 837 consecutive CNBC appearances without smiling. In contrast, Dana Telsey of Bear Stearns, who won again in Retailing/Specialty Stores, flashed her trademark ear-to-ear grin that made her look 17 again as she accepted a "brava" from Bill Griffeth.

Around 3:15, Ed Hyman, who had ranked number one in Economics for more than two decades, appeared to accept his kudos from Maria Bartiromo for winning once again. As Hyman finished up, Lisa came into David's office sporting her "What are you waiting for?" look and pointed towards the elevator banks.

"I'm going, I'm going. If you don't hear from me, e-mail everyone at 4:30 and ask them to join me on 74 at 5:00 for *II* results. Okay?"

"You got it."

David arrived at 225 Park Avenue South at 4:15 sharp, just as three women carried two dozen large manila envelopes into the conference room where everyone had been herded. Each envelope had the name of a firm written on it. David signed for his envelope, waved hi/bye to Denise and dashed for the car service that was waiting for him downstairs.

Once inside the car, David opened the envelope, skimmed through the magazine and the letter about EFS's analysts and then placed all the paperwork on the seat beside him. At 5:05 P.M., he raced for the elevators to the 74th floor and found, in Conference Rooms A&B, about 40 of his analysts and twice as many associates, all of whom watched him intently for signs that they'd done well or badly. David, as usual, remained poker-faced until he reached the front of the room.

"Good news and a few surprises," he began. "We ranked 14th, same as last year, with five All Stars, up from four. All four Runner-Ups from last year repeated: Keith Jackman in Entertainment, Nancy Natolio in Oils, Tim Omori in Banks and Will Rivas in Medical Supplies and Devices. And because Robin Lomax joined us 48 hours before *II's* "job-hoppers' deadline" in August, we were credited with her ranking as a Runner-Up in Retailing-Department Stores." David could hear sighs of disappointment both from the five All Stars who had hoped to move up in the rankings and from analysts who had thought they'd had legitimate shots at making *II* for the first time this year but hadn't.

"I mentioned a few surprises," David continued. "These are surprises only because of how quickly these analysts garnered recognition. First, as you know, *II* typically identifies about a dozen analysts each year who are singled out by our clients either for their accessibility and responsiveness, the accuracy of their earnings estimates, their industry knowledge, their phone calling, their stock picking or the quality of their written reports. This year, Laura Payden was singled out for her industry knowledge, Phil Suprano for frequent and helpful phone calls, and Donald Ferber for his written reports. Let's give them a hand." Everyone applauded enthusiastically and several associates called out their analysts' names.

"Second, two of our analysts made *II's* "Next Generation" list of the best "Up and Comers" in the eyes of our clients. If you hear your name, please stand up." Suddenly, the silence in the room was deafening. "Mark Noel in Enterprise Hardware." Mark, a 32-year-old with a mop of dark brown hair, glasses and a nerdy look, even for a computer analyst, jumped to his feet, clenched his right fist and yelled "Yeah!" in a way that made everyone around him laugh and smile. "And Matt Burlingame in Managed Care." Matt, 33 and almost bald, stood up slowly and shook his head as if in disbelief. The cheers for Matt were even louder because Matt had done, in the eyes of his peers and the sales force, an almost flawless job over the last 12 months in a tough group.

"Finally, I haven't had a chance to look at the letter from *II* closely yet, but it appears that at least 10 of you were close to making Runner-Up this year and have excellent shots at making it 12 months from now. Matt and I are going to work closely with each of you to maximize your chances of making *II* next year. In any event, I'm very proud of all of you who did well, whether you made the team or just came close, and there'll be champagne and hors d'oeuvres outside my office at 5:30 with which we can celebrate how well we did. Please come and join me.

"Complete results will be up on *II's* web site at 6:00 tonight. Keith, Robin, Nancy, Tim, Will, Mark and Matt, bravo and brava!" David said loudly.

"What an embarrassment," he whispered to himself. Carl Robern called the following morning and told David that Ed Koster and Katherine MacMaster wanted to meet with them at 10:30 to discuss the upcoming semiannual analysts' reviews and October bonus payments. As usual, Carl asked David to pick him up on the way. As David approached Carl's office at 10:25, he could see Carl standing outside, talking to Heather Hope Weeks, his new secretary. Carl looked up briefly as David neared and then refocused his attention on Heather.

"So this department head is told by his boss that business is bad and he has to let one of his employees go. The choice is Mary, who has lots of kids, or Jack, who has been with the company for many years. That evening he talks to his wife about his dilemma and, after a sleepless night, he decides to get the evil deed over with by laying off whoever arrives at work first. At 7:30, Mary arrives and the department head calls her into his office. 'I've got a tough choice,' he tells her. 'I either have to lay you or Jack off.' And Mary says 'Well, I guess you'll have to jack off 'cause you sure as shit aren't fucking me.'"

Heather smiled, slightly uncomfortably. Carl looked at David and held up his right pointer. Then he turned back to Heather.

"So, this man steps into an elevator in the lobby of a fancy Chicago hotel. He pushes 16, turns around, and accidentally elbows a woman who'd been standing near him in the breast. 'I'm so sorry,' he says to her, 'but if your heart is as soft as your breast is, I'm sure you'll forgive me.' And the woman turns to the guy and says, 'Yes I will, and if your dick is as hard as your elbow is, I'm in Room 725.'"

"Cute," Heather said uneasily.

"David, let's go," barked Carl. As they walked, Carl shared what little he'd been told by Barbara Summerville, Ed Koster's secretary. The purpose of the meeting was to finalize the size of the October bonus pool for the analysts. Barbara had led Carl to believe that David's bonus recommendations, which had been submitted a week earlier, were deemed excessive in the current, soft business environment and that they were going to be cut. This surprised neither

David nor Carl, who had gone through this charade many times in the past and who understood that if you need $1 you don't ask for $1. The question was, had David, in asking for $40 million, requested just enough so that, if it was cut back to $37 million, the pool would still be adequate, or had Ed and Katherine considered $40 million way too high and chopped it to $35 million, leaving David with a bonus pool from Hell.

Ed Koster's conference room was large and extremely luxurious. It had dark cherry wood paneling, a 40–foot-long table made from four 10–footers, several dozen oversized, burgundy leather armchairs, an endless assortment of audio/video paraphernalia, a large bar and the most stunning French area rugs. It was good to be the king. Surprisingly, Katherine was already there. Ed joined the group 30 seconds later. "Good morning," he said unenthusiastically.

"Good morning, Ed!" Carl boomed. David just nodded silently. Katherine passed out copies of the memo that David had sent to Ed, Katherine and Carl the week before in which each analyst's compensation was identified, including his or her salary, last two bonuses and proposed October bonus. David had also provided a sentence or two summarizing how each analyst was performing, why the bonus recommendation was up or down considerably if it was, and which bonuses were contractually guaranteed. David could see that certain numbers had been circled, probably by Katherine, and that handwritten comments were scribbled in the margins on each page.

"David, you did a nice job with this, as usual," Ed began, "but the numbers have to come down because of how much money we're currently losing. The third quarter was far below plan, John's business has been shitty for months, Banking is bleeding badly and now, suddenly, Private Client is doing half of what it's supposed to be doing. I'm sure you and your analysts can appreciate these facts so let's cut to the chase here. Your total budget for this year was about $130 million. Of that, compensation was $105 million and everything else was $25 million. Is that right?"

"That's right."

"And of the $105 million of compensation that you budgeted, $25 million was for salaries and $80 million was your bonus pool. You were approved for $35 million of bonus payments in April and you've asked for the remaining $45 million now, presumably because you have more analysts in the department."

"Actually, Ed, I've asked for $40 million, leaving $5 million for all the associates, secretaries and others who are in the year-end bonus pool." Ed nodded. "Regarding the increase from $35 million to $40 million for the senior analysts, it isn't because I have more analysts but because certain analysts who've performed extremely well this year were underpaid in April. To a lesser extent, the Robin Lomax hire was expensive, as you'll recall." David was sure Ed didn't.

"David, here's our situation," Katherine interrupted. You allocate it as you see best, but if you got $35 million in April, when the firm was making money, you can't expect to get $40 million when we're in the red. It just doesn't work that way. We understand that your pool can't fluctuate wildly because the analysts derive so much of their comp from bonuses as opposed to salary and because you have guarantees you have to honor. So we've never cut your bonus pool sharply in any one bonus period no matter how badly the firm was doing."

And you never increased it sharply when times were really good, David thought.

"But Ed and I are of one mind that $30 million is the right number, which would be down about 15% from April's level. That would give you $35 million in April plus $30 million in October plus, presumably, $5 million for the year-end pool, versus the $80 million you budgeted, so your total pool would be $70 million, down only 12%."

"Katherine," David answered impatiently, "did you look closely at the breakdown between those with guarantees and those who are not under contract?"

"I did. You have a lot of people under contract. I understand that contracts keep turnover down, but we've told you repeatedly that, when the shit hits the fan, if you have lots of contracts, you have far less flexibility in allocating a smaller bonus pool than you would if everyone was on a level playing field."

"Katherine, we can argue the pros and cons of contracts some other time. What's at issue right now is this: I have contracts outstanding that obligate us to pay bonuses of $18 million, versus $17 million in April. When you approved $35 million in April, that left me $18 million for people without contracts. If you approve $30 million now, after guarantees I'll have only $12 million for people without contracts. That's a 33% cut. It will kill me."

"It's not going to kill you, David," said Ed. "It's just a challenge, and maybe it will motivate you to use fewer contracts in the future. The world isn't going to come to an end. Presumably, the analysts you most want to keep are already under contract and the analysts whose bonuses will be down are those you didn't feel compelled to lock up in the first place, analysts who are less marketable and less likely to leave even if they're disappointed this time around."

David looked to Carl for help. Carl, as usual, said nothing. David could never believe that Carl held the position he held, and he resented having to report to him.

"Don't be ridiculous, David," Katherine concluded. "If an analyst gets 80% of his comp from bonuses and 20% from salary, if his bonus is up 5% in April and down 30% in October, his full-year bonus will only be down 11% and his total comp down 9% in a year in which we lost money. Excuse me? The four of us should be so lucky!"

David wondered if this meant that Ed would only pay himself $20 million this year, down from $25 million.

"You've got $30 million, David," said Ed, who stood up and headed for the door.

"Sorry, David," said Katherine, close on Koster's heels.

* * *

When David returned to his office, he found a memo from Katherine setting November 1 as the deadline for submitting budgets for the following year. Knowing that he'd be tied up in reviews for most of the rest of October, he summoned Matt Speiser, Heidi Sitko who headed Finance inside the Research Department, and Lisa, and told them the topic was next year's Research budget. Within minutes the three were huddling with David around the coffee table in his office, the door closed.

"Surprise, surprise," David began. We've just gotten our 'you've got two weeks to put your new budget together' memo from Katherine. So, we'll rush to assemble it, get it to Katherine a day or two early, and then sit for four months waiting for it to be approved or disapproved."

Everyone laughed.

"Why we always have to get almost entirely through the first quarter before we find out what the full-year budget is never ceases to amaze me," said Heidi. But it never failed. If business was good, this was not a problem, but if business turned bad, and your budget was cut after 25% of the year had come and gone, you had to make up that 12–month cutback in nine months which was never pretty.

"Let's not have a nervous breakdown over this," David suggested. "Our budget had been $130 million, including an $80 million bonus pool, $25 million of salaries and $25 million of everything else. Correct?"

"Correct," said Heidi.

"So now it's $120 million because the bonus pool has been cut from $80 million to $70 million." Six eyes widened. "That's right. Ed and Katherine just cut the analysts' October bonus pool from $40 million to $30 million."

"But it's really only $115 million going forward," Heidi said.

"That's right. It's only $120 million for this year because we got $35 million for the analysts in April. If we assume we'll be stuck at this new $30 million semiannual level for a while, then $60 million for the seniors and $5 million for everyone else only equals $65 million, plus $25 million for salaries and $25 million for all non-compensation-related expenses."

Everyone agreed.

"So, let's inflate salaries and benefits by 3%. That gets us to about $26 million. We'll keep the bonus pool flat at $65 million, assuming that business remains soft, which gets us to $91 million of compensation-related expenses for next year. Subscriptions, printing, stationery and postage is $7 million, rent is $3.5 million, communications is $2.5 million, computers are $2.5 million, the portion of travel and entertainment that Sales doesn't pay for is $2.5 million, depreciation and amortization is $2 million, and professional services and all other expenses are $3 million. Those non-compensation categories normally equal about 20% of our budget. Do they now?"

"They're $23 million or 20% of $115 million," said Heidi casually.

"Okay, so we're still at 80% comp, 20% everything else. Let's inflate that $23 million by 5%, which will take us to $24 million, add in the $91 million for comp and give Ed and Katherine a $115 million budget for next year. I'll include the wish lists that I just got from Mennymore and McLain and Pitcher, and tell Ed and Katherine that none of those hires can be made with $115 million. I'll also ballpark the incremental cost for them. What should I tell them? A good senior is $2,000,000, two associates are $200,000 each and a research assistant or secretary is $50,000 so what's that... $2,450,000?"

No one answered but Heidi nodded.

"And if comp is 80% of all the expenses we incur, then that team probably has another $600,000 of rent and computers and T&E and so forth associated with them so let's just call it $3 million per team to keep life simple. I'll tell them $115 million plus $3 million per analyst you'd like me to hire. You want me to hire five analysts? I'll need $130 million. Ten analysts? $145 million. Zero analysts? Sold for $115 million. Heidi, can you make these numbers work?"

"Of course, David, but keep in mind that you're not allowing for the hiring of any additional associates, research assistants or secretaries for existing analysts, for any promotions or any increases that are contractually mandated."

"There aren't many… maybe $700,000 to $800,000…but you're right. Let's add those in. So, $116 million, down from the $130 million that was originally approved for this year and down about 80% from what Merrill, Morgan and Goldman must spend."

"That's true," Heidi agreed.

"Okay?" David asked, giving everyone the body language that he'd had enough.

"Okay," they answered and beat a hasty retreat.

* * *

Review Week arrived. During Review Week, David and Matt sat in David's office all day long and did almost nothing but conduct 30–minute semiannual reviews with each of EFS's 50–odd analysts, strategists and economists. Review Week was grueling because it was hard to summarize how each analyst had performed over the preceding six months and discuss his or her Business Plan for the next six months in only 30 minutes, and also because David and Matt had to constantly shift gears between veterans and rookies, analysts who were performing superbly and analysts within inches of being fired, analysts with guarantees and analysts without. There was no cruise control button the reviewers could press as the day wore on and their energy waned, and this was especially true for David who did 75% of the talking.

Will Rivas's review was quite typical. First David discussed what Will's October bonus would be. Will's contract called for total compensation of $2,400,000, including a base salary of $200,000 and semiannual bonuses of $1,100,000 each, so there was no bad news to break here regarding the bonus pool. Bonuses were 80% cash and 20% restricted shares of EFS that vested in equal installments over three years.

Next, David and Matt walked Will through his Progress Report, in which he received grades or scores from institutional clients, institutional salespeople, the international institutional sales force, the Private Client Group, his traders, Paula Hainsworth and his investment bankers.

"I'm going to kill Claus," Will said when he saw his scores from Banking. "He refuses to call on the firms I ask him to focus on and keeps jamming the crappiest companies down my throat and threatening me if I don't pick up coverage on them."

"Such as?"

"Such as Retinal Microvision! Ever hear of them?"

"No," David admitted.

"What a surprise. This is Claus's newest 'must cover' stock. It had revenues of $70 million in 2002, lost $5 a share between 1997 and 2002, and saw its stock drop from $70 to $7 during the bear market and its market cap plunge from $250 million to $25 million. Am I unwilling to initiate coverage on it in the hope that they'll do banking business with us one day? Guilty as charged."

"Will, ignore him, and if he squeezes you too hard, come to me and I'll deal with him. We really don't have any serious bankers in your space."

"It really pisses me off."

"I know," said David, shooting a knowing glance at Matt.

Next, David and Matt reviewed Will's accomplishments over the preceding six months, including how many stocks he covered, the accuracy of his recommendations, the frequency with which he spoke with his institutional clients, the quantity and quality of his written research, his visibility on the Morning Call, and how well he kept the ratings and target prices for each of his stocks up to date.

One thing that drove David crazy was Buy-rated stocks selling for $20 that had $18 target prices, or Hold-rated $20 stocks with $30 target prices. Target prices were serious business in David's eyes, and his weekly "Exception Report," lovingly known as the "Green Sheets," flagged for each analyst the stocks that he or she covered whose ratings and target prices just didn't make sense.

Near the end of each Progress Report, David listed how each analyst had ranked in the most recent *II* and *Greenwich* polls, and any "broken promises"–commitments that the analyst had made during the preceding review but failed to keep.

All told, Will was doing very well with the institutional salespeople and clients, and with the European sales force, marketing aggressively, picking stocks well and writing some good, longer, more detailed and thoughtful research. He'd gotten lower scores from the retail brokers in the Private Client Group, with whom he promised to work more closely, and poor scores from Banking which David had urged him to ignore.

The remainder of the half hour was devoted to a review of Will's Business Plan for the following six months, in which he listed new companies he planned to cover, reports he would write, the level of institutional client contact he'd maintain, help he'd provide to the retail brokers, and any steps he'd take to address areas of weakness in his Progress Report.

When they were done, David asked if there was anything that he or Matt could do that would be helpful to Will.

"Kill Claus," Will said, trying to laugh.

"We'll keep him away from you," David said reassuringly.

After the three had shaken hands and Will had left, David and Matt looked at each other, rolled their eyes and shook their heads.

"When's his contract up?" Matt asked.

"December 31st. This whole exercise may have been a waste of time. He's not going to Merrill, Morgan Stanley, J.P. Morgan, CSFB or Bear Stearns, but my guess is that Goldman has already spoken to him, and that Lehman and Salomon may have, too."

"Not much we can do, is there?" Matt hoped David would disagree.

"Nope. If I were Goldman, I'd just have my 11 MD-level investment bankers who are focused on medical supplies and devices take him out to lunch and recount the last 75 transactions they've done in his space. By dessert time they'd have convinced him that, even for a 50% pay cut, he should be panting at the chance to join them. He's a goner."

"Banking is killing us," Matt sighed.

David nodded. "Banking is killing us."

* * *

"Oh no! That can't be right," Arthur Litt protested. "Say it again?"

"Last time your bonus was $70,000 but this time it's $35,000."

"David, my salary has been $200,000 forever, so my total compensation is now below $300,000 a year. We have associates who make more than that!"

"Arthur, no one is happy about this, but your numbers are awful. We'll run through them in a minute, but one of the first ones you'll see is the Institutional Salesmen's Poll, where you ranked dead last in the department. They've washed their hands of you, Arthur. They're paying no attention to you, they aren't selling you and, frankly, some of them are squeezing me pretty hard to replace you."

Arthur had jumped ahead in his report card to find the Sales Vote. "Forty-eighth out of forty-eight? Impossible! When I'm out with the salesmen, they all tell me that I'm doing a very good job, that they have much more confidence in me than in many of those hotshot rookies you've been bringing in lately, so I don't buy this. I see here that I got 3.8 for industry knowledge. That's not bad."

"Arthur," David said, growing impatient, "you got 1.6 out of 5 in how effectively you present to the sales force, 1.7 for how well you market to buy-side analysts and 1.8 for your marketing skills with portfolio managers. You got 1.5 for your ability to generate new ideas, 1.3 for your ability to anticipate rather than report, and 1.5 for your importance to the typical salesman's franchise."

"They never tell me that they're unhappy with me."

"They won't, Arthur. Salesmen won't criticize analysts to their faces for fear that the analysts will stop calling their clients. Analysts won't criticize salesmen to their faces for fear that the salesmen will stop marketing the analysts to their clients. Everyone walks on eggshells with everyone else in public, but offer any of them a confidential questionnaire and all Hell breaks loose."

"And why should my bonus be down 50%?"

"Because the bonus pool is down from April and so are your vital signs."

"How much is the bonus pool down?"

"About 15%." David knew he shouldn't be saying that, but he had always been forthcoming with his analysts about changes in the bonus pool, whether up or down.

"So I'm down more than three times as much as the average analyst?"

"That's true. If your numbers were better, your bonus would've been better."

"This is an outrage!" Arthur stormed.

What's an outrage, David thought, is that you don't have a clue how badly you're performing and how lucky you are to still have a job.

* * *

"Forty-five client contacts a month isn't nearly enough." David Meadows was reviewing Donald Ferber, his wireline telecommunications services analyst. "The department average, as you can see, is about 120 a month."

"That number means nothing to me," Donald snapped. "Analysts make mindless client calls with nothing new to say and no value added just so they can tell you that they made 100 calls a month or 150 or 200. I call when I have something important to say, and my calls aren't 30–second voicemail messages either. I can be on the phone with one of my clients for an hour or more. When clients hear that it's me, they drop what they're doing, think of all the important questions they have on their minds and ask them, including tons of questions that have nothing to do with what I'm calling them about. I've provided a lot of value-added by the time we hang up. I'd stack my 45 calls against anyone else's 120 calls seven days a week with respect to their quality and their impact."

"Donald, you're in the middle of the department in both the Client Vote and the Sales Vote. You want to know how to move higher, and I'm telling you that you need to market much more than you have been."

"Clients don't pay me for mindless phone calls, David, they pay me for the quality of my research. You yourself pointed out when you announced *II* that I was singled out by clients for outstanding written reports."

"No one is questioning the quality of your print. I've told you on many occasions that it's among the most thorough, insightful, thought-provoking work on The Street, and it explains much of the progress you've made to date with your clients and with Sales. What I'm saying is that analysts who spend most of their time writing cap their impact on the Buy Side because they have tons of competitors who write 75% as well and market 300% as much. Guess what? All of those analysts finished above you in *II* this year."

"Did you see what *II* said clients want from the Sell Side?" Ferber asked. "What they said they value most is industry knowledge, integrity, professionalism, accessibility and responsiveness. Phone calling was farther down the list and stock picking was close to the bottom. They do their own stock picking so they don't care what we think, and they're busy so they don't want to be bothered with mindless, it's-been-28–days-since-we-last-spoke phone calls."

"Useful and timely phone calls and visits ranked fourth while written reports and financial models ranked eighth and ninth," David argued. "Analysts who don't write but who market like wild only get so far on the Sell Side and analysts who don't market much but who write like wild only get so far. If you want to get out of the middle of the department, write less and market more. If you don't, then stick to your knitting."

* * *

"If I had a contract, this wouldn't be happening to me, right?" James Brell was asking in something close to a yell.

"What wouldn't be happening to you?" David knew exactly what Brell meant.

"I'm 21st in the Client Vote, up from 25th. I'm 18th in the Sales Vote, unchanged from last time. I make my 100–plus calls a month. I write good reports. My stock picking is pretty good. Paula Hainsworth says I make good Morning Calls. My traders like me. I try to help The Bank even though they don't have a senior banker in my space. Even Retail likes me, but my bonus is still down 25% from $600,000 to $450,000."

"It's down not because of your performance but because the bonus pool is down." "How much is the bonus pool down?"

"About 15%."

"Exactly my point. The pool is down 15% but all the analysts with guarantees are down zero so the suckers like me who don't have contracts have to be down more than 15% in order to get the average decline for the entire department to 15%!"

"That's true."

"How come I don't have a guarantee, David?"

"Because the whole department can't be under contract, James. That's just not how it works. If you're *II*-ranked, or you're a new hire, or you're high up in the Client Vote and Sales Vote but haven't yet made *II*, you're probably under contract. You're none of those things right now so you aren't under contract."

"And loyalty? Where does loyalty come into play?"

"Meaning…?"

"… that analysts with contracts are here because they signed the non-compete agreements in those contracts and are legally precluded from going anywhere, but analysts who never signed non-competes but who stay are staying because they want to."

"Look, James, I value loyalty more than anyone but I can't pay bonuses simply based on how loyal you are. You're doing a good job. You've got a bright future. You've been here a while and you're loyal. All of these things explain why your bonus is down 25% and not the 40%-50% that other analysts without contracts are seeing. That may be small comfort to you, but those are today's realities. I kept you as close to flat as I could but with all the guarantees, there were limits on what I could do."

"It's a caste system, David. We both know it. And guess what. I'm one of the untouchables."

* * *

"Eight stocks is not a real universe, Keith," said David in the middle of his next review. "I need you to go higher and you should want to go higher."

Keith Jackman had heard this before and he was armed for a duel. "David, let me explain some things

to you. I do AOL Time Warner, I do Disney and I
do Viacom. Guess what fraction of the time I spend
with clients is devoted to talking about those three
names."

"Seventy-five percent."

"Ninety percent. Those three names *are* entertainment. They're huge companies, they're enormously
complex, they're global and they're very, very time-
consuming to do right. I won't cover a company
unless I can cover it right. I'm not like most of the
other analysts in this department. I dig. I have the
best sources in Hollywood of any analyst on Wall
Street. I spend countless hours with the 'Who's Who'
of Hollywood and TV and radio. I respect those guys
and they respect me, and I'm *II*- ranked because clients
know that I know my companies and my industry
better than anyone else on The Street today."

"I understand this," said David, trying not to be
defensive, "and your rankings suggest that you're
doing a very good job with the big three, but I did
some research on this and I found that your principal
competitors cover, on average, 13 names each yet
still manage to rank in *II* despite the dilution that
those five extra names cost them."

"Who cares about those five other names? They're
flies on AOL Time Warner's ass. They carry no clout,
they make no headlines and they're crappy investments."

"What about Vivendi?"

"No time."

"What about International Speedway?"

"Hire a leisure analyst."

"What about IMAX?"

"The stock was $5 and book value was *negative*
$100 million the last time I checked. David, I guess

I'm not making myself clear. My job is to cover AOL, Disney and Viacom. If you want me to do a whole bunch of shitty little third-rate film studios, get me another associate and I'll have him do them. Otherwise, if I make any changes in the breadth of my universe, expect them to be the dropping of some of the five names I already cover that are wasting my time. The last thing I'm going to do, as long as I'm at EFS, is pick up anything new."

* * *

"Why didn't you pay me above my guarantee, David?" asked Nancy Natolio 60 seconds into her review.

David was surprised by how brazen she'd become. As he watched her leaf through her report card before he could even begin discussing it with her, he answered, "Nancy, you're the highest-paid analyst in the department, and you've got a contract that protects you. The bonus pool is down, and it's not exactly the environment in which I can pay people above their guarantees."

"David, I was number two in the Client Vote. Only Linda Logan beat me, I'm sure. I was top 10 with the institutional sales force, I'm *II*- ranked in one helluva tough group and I do deals. What else could you possibly want from me?"

"We're getting off on the wrong foot here, Nancy. I would've preferred to walk through your Progress Report slowly, carefully, thoughtfully, looking at how you did and placing your bonus in that context but, since we're jumping ahead, let me say this. As you scanned the report and noticed how well you did in the Client Vote and the Sales Vote, you may have missed the fact that you ranked third from last in the department in stock picking and that the retail brokers want to kill you. You're doing a terrific job in most respects, but that's not to say that there aren't a few areas in which you can improve."

"These stock picking numbers are wrong. I wasn't that bad this year. I had a couple of bad calls for sure, but I could never have been third worst in the whole department. Any way, the good news is that institutional clients don't pay us to pick stocks. They do their own stock picking. They pay me for what I know, for my reports, for how well I service them, for bringing my managements to see them or bringing them to see my companies, for the Energy Conference, blah blah blah. I wouldn't be number two in the Client Vote and an *II* Runner-Up in Oils if stock picking mattered. Institutionally, it doesn't, as we both know. Retail hates me because I bagged them with one or two bad ideas. That'll turn around. Who gives a shit about Retail anyway? You know, overall, my numbers look pretty good to me."

"Overall, I agree with you, and that's why $3,000,000 a year plus banking bonuses for the deals you do is fair."

"It was fair a year ago, when I signed that contract, but it isn't fair now."

"How do you know?"

"I know. I'm not exactly undiscovered. I'll grant you that Salomon is, I'm sure, very happy with Paul Ting and that Morgan won't part with Doug Terreson. Prudential has Mike Mayer, but who'd work there anyway? Merrill has Steve Pfeifer, who's quite good. Did I mention UBS? UBS offered me $6 million a year for three years," she lied. "Over the phone. Never even met me and they were prepared to pay me that kind of money. They would've bought me out of all my EFS stock, too, I'm sure. I don't want to sound ungrateful, David, because I do enjoy working with you. You're the only decent guy in this place."

"What does that mean?"

"It means that, beyond the fact that EFS can only afford to pay me half my market value, I'm pretty tired of all the shit I have to put up with around here. You'd think that, given that EFS isn't exactly Goldman Sachs or Morgan Stanley, there would be some offsets aimed at attracting and keeping good people who could just as easily work at better firms. You know? Above-average pay instead of below-average, more support rather than less or, at least, a friendly environment in which people aren't always trying to screw you."

David was befuddled and Nancy could tell.

"I'm tired of this. Tom Mennymore can't wait to screw me out of every dollar of banking bonuses he possibly can, and Carl just can't wait to screw me, as in *screw* me."

"Did something happen?"

"Did something happen? Is the Pope Catholic? Do leap years have an extra day? Of course something happened. Nothing physical, just verbal abuse that I don't need, that no one needs. It's not the first time. It's not even worth talking about. He's a fucking pig, that's all. He's got this boyish, preppie, almost *cherubic* look to him. You know? So you feel as if you can put your guard down, and you do, and before you know it, he's negotiating to stick his hand down your blouse or his dick in your mouth."

Nancy shrugged and shook her head. "It's just symptomatic of what's wrong with EFS. And you know what, David? No matter how hard you try, and how well-intentioned you are, there's absolutely *nothing* you can do about it."

* * *

Six days after it had started, Review Week ended, not with a bang but a whimper. There had been no shootings or stabbings, but almost every review had been stressful. Maybe it had been the undercurrent of nervousness about the firm's red ink. Maybe it had been fear that there would be layoffs, which there weren't because David knew that anyone he'd have laid off would've gotten more in severance pay than in a drastically reduced bonus, and that would've pushed him over budget at a time when no manager wanted to be over budget. Maybe it had been the caste system that pitted those with contracts against those without. Maybe it was all these things.

All David knew was that this undercurrent of unease raised substantial risks with respect to the stability of the department. One of these days, he thought, someone will challenge those non-compete provisions and unshackle not just himself but everyone worth keeping inside EFS's Research Department.

NOVEMBER

David reread the e-mail one last time. In it, Carl Robern congratulated all of the EFS employees who had just run with him in the New York City Marathon. At last count, Carl wrote, some 23 people from Capital Markets had completed the course, a new divisional record. And speaking of records, Carl noted that he had run his first sub-3:30 marathon, beating his prior personal best of 3:38 by eleven minutes.

Can you spell "self-serving?" David wondered.

* * *

At 6:30 on Election Night, Ed Koster prepared to head home. As always, he planned to stop at the public school near his prewar co-op on 76th Street and Park Avenue and vote before going upstairs. Once each year, Ed opened up his apartment, which comprised 16 rooms and 5,600 square feet, to his seniormost managers for an off-site meeting, and "Koster's Place" had become legendary inside the walls of EFS.

"Getting ready to vote?" Barbara Summerville asked.

"Unenthusiastically, Barbara, but you know me.

Not voting is voting, so why not assume responsibility?"

"You know you have breakfast with John Mack tomorrow."

"At the Harvard Club."

"At the Harvard Club." The phone rang and, as Barbara reached for it, Ed grabbed his tan cashmere overcoat from the closet in his office, and his hat. As he was putting them on, Barbara walked back in. "It's Larry Cohn."

"Hmmmm," Ed grunted. He'd had his annual physical two weeks earlier and all the initial test results had been fine. But Dr. Cohn didn't normally call him. "I'll take it," he told Barbara, who closed the door without asking.

"Dr. Cohn! Did you vote yet?"

"This morning, Ed. How are you?"

"Very well, very well, I think. Any news?"

"Ed... you may have prostate cancer." There was a long, very silent pause.

"Prostate cancer," Ed repeated. "How bad is it?"

"It's bad and it's not so bad. Many men get prostate cancer in their 60s and 70s. You're 61 so this isn't unusual. Many men live with prostate cancer for twenty years or more and die of completely unrelated causes. Some prostate cancer grow slowly, but some are very aggressive and that creates all sorts of issues relating to how and when to treat it. One patient will say, 'I want it out and I want you to operate tomorrow.' Another will say, 'I don't want to deal with the side effects of surgery. I'm sixty years old and I'm just going to ride it out.' Everyone is different. But I want to see you so we can talk about the options in person. Can you come in tomorrow morning around 9:00?"

"I've got a breakfast at the Harvard Club at 7:30, so 9:00 will be fine. I'll see you then."

"Bye," Cohn whispered.

Outwardly Koster looked composed, but inside a tempest raged, and in the corners of both eyes Ed felt the tiniest teardrops form. "Cancer," he said to himself. "How do you like that?"

* * *

"He's got a bug up his ass about Jessie Jackson," Carl told David as the two sat in Carl's office 10 days later. "He's terrified that Jessie is going to walk in here one of these days and ask how many blacks we now have in Research, Sales, Trading and Banking and that, when he finds out that we *still* don't have any, he's going to publicly humiliate us or worse."

"I've gone through this with Ed before, you know," said David.

"He asked you about this before?"

"A couple of years ago, when Jackson had... what was it called? The Wall Street Project? That freaked Ed out."

"What did you tell him?"

"I told him then what I'd tell him now. I don't have a single black analyst in the department and it's not because I'm a racist. It's because there are virtually no black analysts on The Street for me to hire away from other firms. If I could have hired some really solid black analysts from other firms over the years I would have in a heartbeat, but when I recruit I never see a black candidate. Never. I don't like the makeup of the department any better than Jessie would. I've got plenty of black research assistants and some black associates, and I'm painfully aware that, when they look around, they see no black seniors.

"So what's the solution?"

"The solution is to go on to some business school campuses and hire a bunch of black graduate students whom I can grow into sell-side analysts. But that requires a budget for home-growns that I never get. McLain wants me to hire senior, established analysts for whom his salesmen can get instantly paid. Mennymore also wants every recruiting dollar spent on established talent who can ring his bankers' cash registers on day one.

"And that's not all. To create a bullpen of graduate students of any color requires office space and I don't have it. I've asked for it repeatedly and been denied it, and I'm certainly not expecting to get it over the next 12 months the way our business is going. Even if I did, there are other problems. If I go and hire three black graduates from Stanford or Wharton or Harvard and seek to develop them into seniors, one of two things must happen. Either they'll have to follow the same path as all other newly hired graduate students, meaning working as an associate analyst supporting a senior for three years before getting promoted, or they'll have to be hired with the understanding that they're going to skip that step entirely and be trained from day one as seniors."

"So?" Carl asked.

"So if they go down the traditional path, it'll be three years or more before they become black senior analysts in the department, and if we accelerate them, every white associate in the department who's now putting in three years of 80– to 90–hour workweeks in the faint hope that there just *might* be a senior analyst slot for him or her at the end will feel discriminated against because he or she is *not* black. And every institutional salesman will look at those three young, black, newly minted seniors and think, 'well well well, I know exactly what's going on here, and I'm certainly not going to sell any rookies who were hired because of the color of their skin.'"

"You know what, David? If you want to tell Koster all of this, feel free, but don't expect to move him with your logic. He's terrified of Jessie. I mean it. And what he's going to come back at you with is something one of my old high school teachers used to say to us all the time: 'No excuses, just results.' He wants black analysts and he wants them now. That's what he asked me to convey to you 'in the strongest terms' so I've conveyed it. You obviously think there's a problem here, so get the fuck out of my office and go solve it."

* * *

When David returned later that day, after having interviewed an institutional salesman that John McLain wanted to hire, Lisa told him that Carl had called.

"Did he say why?"

"Nope, just that it was important."

David quickly checked some stock prices on his PC screen, glanced at his e-mail in-box for urgent correspondence and then called Carl. A minute later, he poked his head into Lisa's office. "What do I have this afternoon?" It was already 3:30.

"You've got a Commitment Committee meeting at 4:00, and Arthur Litt wants to follow up with you about his review. He says he talked to a lot of the salespeople, they all said they gave him high marks and you must have made a mistake."

"Okay. Ask Matt, please, to do the Commitment Committee meeting for me and bump Arthur to tomorrow. Ed Koster needs some budget numbers from me ASAP."

"Got it."

David returned to his office, closed the door and sat down at his coffee table with the brand-new *Institutional Investor*. According to Carl, Koster wanted to know how much bigger a budget David would need to get EFS into the top 5 in *II*.

The starting point was the $116–million budget that David had submitted on November 1 for the following calendar year. For $116 million, EFS could have five ranked analysts and a number fourteen ranking in *II*. How many analysts did a firm need to be top five? David guessed 40, and then checked The Leaders table in the October issue. He was close …42. To be number one you needed 53.

What would hiring 37 *II* All Stars cost? David knew it would vary enormously from category to category and from industry to industry. Technology analysts would be, by far, the most expensive. Technology was the most difficult sector to analyze well because of the pace at which fundamentals changed and because of the complexity of the products and services that those companies provided. Anyone could explain what McDonald's does, but almost no one could understand, discuss in everyday English, and accurately anticipate trends in the computer, semiconductor and software sectors. The other big variable was relative rankings. The number-one-ranked analyst in a given field might earn twice what a Runner-Up in the same category earned, so it made more economic sense to hire Runner-Ups because *II* gave just as much credit to a firm for Runner-Ups as for number-one-ranked analysts when it ranked all the firms. To *II*, an All Star was an All Star.

But not knowing in exactly which sectors he'd be able to hire, and which analysts, David was forced to make some general assumptions, and they were these. First he assumed that EFS would have to pay, at least initially, a substantial premium over market value to convince ranked analysts at "good" firms to come to EFS. As he had no global counterparts and almost no real investment bankers, the only offset would be a much bigger paycheck. Second he assumed that he'd be able to hire only Runner-Ups at least until EFS had cracked the top 10 (which would require 12 ranked-analyst hires). Third he assumed that each analyst would come as a package with two associate analysts and one research assistant or secretary. Fourth he assumed that, whatever the compensation costs were for those analytical teams, their non-compensation-related costs would equal 25% of their compensation. Finally he assumed that he'd have to buy some of his new hires out of hand-cuffs at their old firms. Out came the calculator.

He'd need to hire 37 All Stars. Assuming they weren't technology analysts, David felt that $3,500,000 apiece was safe because, at better firms, they'd be scarcely making half of that. But given EFS's mediocre reputation, he might even have to pay $4,000,000 each for the first few new hires so, to get the ball rolling, he assumed $3,750,000 per senior hire. Each associate might cost $200,000 but David used $250,000 just to be safe, so that was another $500,000, and the research assistant/secretary would probably cost $50,000 but David used $75,000 instead. So, all told, the salaries and bonuses for each team of four would be $4,325,000. Another 25% for rent, phones, computers, subscriptions, travel, entertainment and all other expenses would bring the total cost of each team up to $5,406,250. And doing this 37 times would require an additional $200,031,250.

David had no idea how to estimate handcuffs but he knew they'd be substantial, probably between $1,000,000 and $2,000,000 per hire. To be safe, he assumed $1,750,000 in handcuff buyouts per All Star, or $64,750,000. In fairness though, those costs probably could be spread out over the first two or three years that the new analysts worked at EFS so he cut it in half and added $32,375,000 to his incremental budget, which now stood at $232,406,250.

Not all of the 37 new hires would be true adds-to-staff. Maybe half would be and the other half would replace existing, unranked analysts. What would that mean? David assumed that the analysts who'd be replaced cost EFS $1,250,000 each. From that figure he deducted estimated severance payments of $500,000 and settled on net savings of $750,000 per laid-off analyst or $13,500,000 in total, which cut his incremental budget to $218,906,250.

Over the next two hours, David double-and triple-checked his math and challenged his assumptions repeatedly. After sleeping on it, he called Carl early the next morning and told him to "tell Ed that if he wants a top-5 Research Department, beyond the extra salespeople and traders he'll need to hire, he'll need to take the Research Department budget alone from the $116 million that we just proposed for next year to $350 million."

* * *

After delivering the news to Carl, David went through his in-box. Most of the mail was junk, but the November issue of *Institutional Investor* did catch his eye, and David opened it to the Table of Contents. Under "Research" he found what he was looking for: "The Best of the Buy Side." David quickly scanned the article, saw a few people he recognized like Gordon Crawford at Capital Research and Norm Fidel at Alliance, and then tore it out.

"Lisa, come get this from me and make me 200 copies please, ASAP?"

Then he dashed off an e-mail to all his seniors and associates telling them that a copy of the article was heading their way. "In this poll," he wrote, "every analyst who received votes in last year's *II* All Star balloting was asked to name the Buy-Side analysts and portfolio managers whom they considered the best. Many of you probably participated in that poll. In any event, when you get your copy of the article, scan it for names and faces you know, pick up your phones and call and congratulate those Buy-Side All Stars right away. If you voted for them, tell them so. If you didn't, just tell them how happy you are that they got the recognition they so clearly deserve."

Buy-Siders have egos too, David thought but didn't write. If you want these guys to vote for you every May and June you make sure you do some serious sucking up each November.

* * *

A week later, David's corn-chowder-at-his-desk lunch was interrupted by a call from Ed Koster. "David, you aren't serious about needing $350 million now are you?"

"I don't need $350 million, Ed, unless you need us to be top 5 in *II.* "

"I've been thinking about that a lot in fact," said Ed to David's surprise, "because I feel like we're stuck in Never Never Land between the regionals and the bulge-bracket firms and I don't like it. I don't want to go out and buy an investment bank because our stock price is too low and we don't have the currency to buy someone with, and when you're the buyer you wind up writing the check and then watching a lot of the talent you thought you were buying walk out the door. Remember Prudential and Volpe? What a disaster that was!"

"I agree."

"So I was thinking about how to go about building an investment bank from the ground up and everyone told me that you'd have to build a top-5 Research Department in concert with the banking build-up or we wouldn't land the mandates needed to fund the cost of the bankers." Ed paused, seemingly deep in thought.

"But I've got to tell you, David, that your $350 million budget really threw me for a loop, and you can only imagine how much Mr. Mennymore wanted to hire the bankers he said he'd need, so I've scrapped the idea."

David listened in silence. He was hardly surprised.

"Now David, let me ask you something in complete confidence, all right?"

"Of course."

"Suppose I decided to gut the Investment Bank, to get out of banking all together and just revert to being an investment house that served the institutional and retail marketplace with good, solid research and money-making investment advice, untarnished by the conflicts of interest that banking always creates. How much would I save on your end?"

"Save?"

"Yes, save. How much lower a Research budget could we get away with?"

"God, Ed, I haven't thought about it." David's mind raced through his roster. "But I've got to tell you that my belly is saying that you wouldn't save much. There might be one or two analysts in the department who are here principally to accommodate banking and who could be laid off, but you're talking about less than $2 million of annual savings.

"That's it? Two million dollars?"

"Not even."

"Why's that?"

"Because even though we have a pretty shitty investment bank, several dozen of our analysts still get small banking bonuses each year. They like doing banking and they count on banking for part of their annual compensation. If you take their banking bonuses away from them you'll have to make it up to them in higher research comp or they'll start walking. If 'A' is research comp and 'B' is banking comp, 'A' plus 'B' have to add up to an analyst's market value or you won't hold on to him. We've held on to good analysts by making 'A' bigger than it should be because 'B' was smaller than it should be, but if 'B' becomes zero, 'A' has to absorb the shortfall."

"So if I decide to pull the plug on The Bank, the Research budget won't go down at all and might even have to go up."

"Correct."

"Thank you, David," Ed sighed and hung up.

Build a top-5 research effort? Kill The Bank? What major strategic initiative would Koster ask about next? He's flailing, David thought, and it frightened him.

* * *

Ken Lavery had been busy. Earnings season, which had spanned the second half of October and the first week of November, had included several company announcements of earnings disappointments that had sent those stocks plunging. On top of that, Ken had advised on a hostile takeover bid by one of his companies for another that had fizzled at the eleventh hour. He'd been out of the office 75% of the time and his body was tired, but his mind was still sharp and full of energy.

Aside from the companies that had preannounced earnings shortfalls, his stocks had been down and up, up and down, and flat overall. So were G-NOME and Genomic Innovators, Ken's two newest holdings. Both stocks had moved up quickly to $6.50 during the 48 hours in which Tom Hanks had purchased 100,000 shares of each for Ken, pushing Ken's average acquisition cost over $6.25 a share. They'd both pulled back as soon as Ken stopped buying, to just under $6, and then traded between $5.80 and $6.30 for a month on heavy volume. All of this had been fine with Ken.

But it was Bentley time now, and Ken knew what he needed to do. In the back of his EFS phone directory was a listing of all EFS retail branches by city. Ken checked Boston, Cambridge, Brookline, Somerville, Watertown and Chelsea. He found the two downtown Boston branches that he knew well, a branch in Cambridge and another in Brookline. Then he dialed Charles Willing's number in Boston. Charles picked him up on the first ring.

"Charles, it's Ken Lavery. How are you?"

"Excellent, Ken. Long time no see!"

"And that's exactly why I'm calling. I have to see Millennium in mid-December, and I know the timing isn't ideal with everyone out Christmas shopping and going to parties, but since I'll be in the neighborhood any way, I wanted to offer to stop by and see you."

"We'd love it, Ken. You know that. How much time can you give us?"

Ken smiled. "Well, I can be flexible. Why?" he asked innocently.

"Oh, I don't know, I just thought if you had the time, we could probably use you in several offices, not just here where we know you well. We've actually got two branches downtown, one in Cambridge, one in Brookline and two on Cape Cod, but that's too far I think. Maybe we could focus on the four in and near Boston."

"I'd be glad to do that if you think it makes sense. I could stay overnight, hit one or two after I see Millennium and the rest the following day."

"Would you be willing to have dinner with some of my best brokers on the night you stay over? We could get a private room somewhere and have a very nice time."

Ken normally would've looked for any excuse to avoid getting trapped with 10–15 brokers who'd probably listen and ask good questions for 30 minutes, and then spend two hours drunkenly complaining about all of the other analysts in the department and everything else that bugged them, but this time he agreed. "I'd love to."

"Terrific. You let my secretary know exactly which dates we're talking about and she'll set it up. All right?"

"Done deal. Thanks, Charles."

As soon as Ken hung up, he called his Investor Relations contact at Millennium Pharmaceuticals in Cambridge and told him that, as fate would have it, he had to be up in Boston doing some retail branch visits in mid-December and was wondering if he could stop by for an hour or two. Of course he could, Millennium told him.

The last step in the process was to give Charles's secretary the dates, which he did. "Good!" Ken said with a smile. "Now to more serious matters."

It was 11:40, the perfect time for a different kind of "working" lunch, so Ken grabbed his raincoat and a cab downstairs and asked the driver to take him to 437 Madison Avenue at 49th Street. A half hour later, Ken stood outside of Bentley Manhattan, the sole Bentley dealership in New York City. For a moment he enjoyed watching passers by check him out as he looked in the showroom window. Then, slowly, he opened the heavy glass doors and went inside.

As the sales desk in the middle of the showroom was unoccupied, Ken felt free to wander around. The first three cars he saw were all Rolls Royces and thus of little interest. They were stuffy looking, and the men in the Brioni ads never drove them, so Ken sized them up quickly and then moved on to the Bentleys, of which there were four. His heart beat faster. There were three hard-tops, and a convertible towards which Ken had begun walking when a voice behind him chimed, "Good afternoon!"

Ken turned and saw a nicely dressed but jacketless young man walking towards him. "I'm Matt Stocklin. May I help you?"

Ken shook his hand. "I'm Ken Lavery and I want to buy a Bentley."

"Delighted, Ken. May I?" Matt raised his right arm in the direction of the first of the sedans, a black one, and escorted Ken to the front of the car on the driver's side. "Bentley only makes four cars, and you're looking at them. By far our most popular model is the Arnage Red Label Long Wheel-base sedan. This particular car is finished in black sapphire and has Autumn hides. It has a 6.75–liter, turbocharged V8 engine, and 400 horsepower, and can go from zero to 60 in 5.9 seconds. Where laws permit, it can cruise at 155 miles per hour.

"While it's obviously breathtaking to look at, this automobile is actually more impressive under the hood. The Arnage comes with an electro-hydraulic, four-speed automatic gearbox, adaptive shift control, engine intervention assistance, double wishbone independent suspension, ASC traction control, and an electronic, anti-lock braking system that can take you from 60 to zero in 2.85 seconds.

"The body is of hand-polished stainless steel, and each car comes with grade 'A' hide upholstery, handcrafted burr walnut, bur oak, bird's eye maple or black lacquer woodwork, independently adjustable front and rear seats, climate control with separate front and rear temperature regulation, and a GPS satellite navigation system."

Ken recognized the Arnage's beauty and craftsmanship, and he was intrigued by the red leather steering wheel and the red label with that unmistakable "B" at the front of the hood, just above the grill. But the

Arnage was not for him. "It's very beautiful," he said to Matt, "but I think I'm looking for something sportier."

"Perhaps our Continental Coupe," Matt suggested, pointing towards the two cars sitting next to the Arnage. "Bentley's two-door coupe comes in two flavors, the classic 'R' and the unique 'T.' The Continental R, which you see here in red, performs virtually identically to the Arnage. Same acceleration, same horsepower, same maximum cruising speed. It is also finished very much as is the Arnage. But something tells me that the Continental T might be more suitable for you, and here it is, in silver." Matt walked Ken around to the driver's side and opened the driver's door.

"The Continental T is a rear-wheel drive, V8 turbocharged coupe. This car is a monster. While it has the same 6.75–liter turbocharged engine as the Arnage and the Continental R, it delivers 420 horsepower, can accelerate from zero to 60 in 5.7 seconds, can cruise at 170 miles per hour, and delivers the greatest peak torque output of any production car in the world. It brakes from 100 to zero in less than five seconds. *Car* magazine said in its review that the Continental T had 'huge performance, tireless brakes, formidable roadholding, staggering handling... and drop-jaw presence.'

"Inside, instead of burled wood, the 'T' has an aluminum fascia and trim, and a single-color dark hide, very much as did the early racing Bentleys. An aluminum dash isn't for everyone, but then, the handful of people who buy a Continental T each year are hardly 'everyone.'"

Ken smiled. "This is closer." Then, turning towards the convertible, he added, "But this, I think, is it."

"Ahhhhhhhhhhhh, the Azure. I should've known. Isn't this the most breathtaking car you've ever seen?"

It was, and Ken knew that he and his Brioni suit looked straight out of *GQ* magazine standing next to it. The Azure was a deep blue that Ken had never seen before. It thrilled him and distracted him as Matt rambled on.

"The Azure was Bentley's first entirely new convertible in almost 30 years. It gets 385 horsepower from its 6.75–liter V8 with an exhaust-driven turbo-charger and liquid-based charge cooler. It incorporates a digital boost-control system, and it can go from zero to 60 in 6.3 seconds and cruise at 150 miles per hour, laws permitting." Ken saw himself in his new Azure at Nick & Toni's in East Hampton.

"Automatic ride control provides computer control of the suspension dampers to ensure perfect handling and the most comfortable of rides." Ken saw himself driving his new Azure through Bernardsville, Far Hills and Mendham, New Jersey during fall foliage season.

"Dynamic shift pattern modifies the gear change points in 'normal' mode according to your unique driving style. Our Zytek EMS3 engine management system uses high-density, 32 by 32 site bit-maps for fueling and ignition to provide maximum efficiency and power and virtually instant throttle response. And the air conditioning system is CFC-free." Ken saw himself parked outside 3 New York Plaza, pretending he was waiting for a date but actually just enjoying having everyone who knew him notice his newest acquisition on their way home from work.

In truth, Matt could have been describing a Yugo for all Ken cared. It wasn't the size of the engine or the efficiency of the brakes or the lack of CFC that was prompting him to buy. It was the "package," the look, the status, the experience. He was James Bond, outfitted in Brioni from head to toe, and this was his Bentley Azure convertible. He sat down in the driver's seat and let his head spin. The smell of the hides, the touch of his fingers wrapping around the knob atop the gear-shifting lever, that big, winged, "B" staring at him from atop the steering wheel where the airbag was undoubtedly hidden, everything, intoxicated him. We fit like hand and glove, he said to himself. "It's me," he told Matt.

"We have eight in stock. We're the largest Bentley dealership in the United States, and we'd be delighted to provide you with references should you require them."

"It won't be necessary," said Ken as he stepped reluctantly out of the car.

"Would you like me to arrange a test drive for you?"

"It won't be necessary. This is my baby. What other colors does it come in?"

Matt showed Ken all of his options. The dark blue remained Ken's favorite, and Matt agreed to check his inventory and call him that afternoon to discuss availability. Ken and Matt exchanged business cards and shook hands. Ken thanked Matt for his help and headed for the door on Madison Avenue. As he reached it, he paused, turned back towards the sales desk and said, "Matt, I forgot to ask. How much is it?"

Matt had been waiting and wondering. "It lists for $349,900 plus options and an $800 destination charge." He was about to add, "but we're competitive," but never got the chance.

"Later," Ken said, connecting his thumb and pointer in a small circle and hoping he'd be noticed as he walked once more through the heavy glass doors.

* * *

At 3:15 P.M. on the Monday following the long Thanksgiving weekend, Lisa told David that he'd been asked to come see Ed Koster when the market closed at 4:00.

"Any details?"

"No, just to be sure to come on time."

"I always come on time." David dialed Carl but was only able to reach Heather.

"He's not here, David. He's been locked away with Ed Koster all day."

"Do you know what the 4:00 meeting is about?"

"Nope, but Carl asked me to call a bunch of people, including you and John and Billy," she answered, referring to Billy Lynch, the head of trading.

David thanked her and then checked with Paul Pitcher, who had also been summoned and who thought the meeting might be related to a mandated round of layoffs. Convinced that nobody knew, David let it go and turned for half an hour to a stack of phone messages needing attention.

At 3:55 P.M., David took the elevator to 74 and walked to the conference room in which Ed always held his meetings with his department heads. The room, which had been set up classroom style with chairs and tables to write on, filled quickly. Having been warned, no one was late and, at 4:02, Ed and Katherine walked in, closed the door behind them and took their seats on the dais. Ed shuffled some papers, whispered back and forth with Katherine for a minute and then stood up and stepped down in front of the dais. Everyone studied his face for hints but none was forthcoming.

"It's so quiet," Ed said with a grin. David and his neighbors sat silently. They'd all seen Ed's grin before, knew it meant nothing and braced themselves for bad news.

"About three weeks ago I received a visit from Herr Vilhelm Josef Drews, the CEO of BC Holdings, which owns Bonnberg Commerzbank, the 10th-largest bank in Germany. I'd called on Herr Drews when I'd made my last swing through Germany, in May. We had a very pleasant meeting, but nothing special. He told me about BC Holdings and I told him about EFS, all pretty routine stuff if you ask me, so I'd assumed the meeting three weeks ago was going to be a courtesy call and nothing more when Barbara put it on my calendar."

David could feel his heart racing and hear his pulse in his eardrums.

"In truth, something very different happened. Herr Drews came with a proposal in hand involving the merger of EFS and BC Bank. He'd clearly done his homework, I could see that, and frankly I was impressed with how *much* research he'd done on us since our meeting in May. So, over the past three weeks, he and I spent, oh, close to 100 hours together wading through the myriad of issues that such a proposal presents. Katherine was brought into the negotiations about a week ago.

"Last Wednesday night we reached what I considered a definitive agreement, subject to BC Bank's due diligence and the approval of both firms' boards. We gave them 96 hours in which to conduct their due diligence, and they completed it, thanks to a Herculean effort by Katherine and her team, on Saturday evening, just before midnight. Yesterday, BC Bank's board held a special meeting and approved the transaction and, tonight at 6:00 P.M., our board will meet and vote on it as well. Assuming that our board approves the merger, we will issue a press release at 7:30 or 8:00 this evening and hold a conference call for all of the analysts who cover us tomorrow at 9:00 A.M. You'll be able to access the press release on our web site tonight."

Everyone in the room except Ed and Katherine was thinking the same thing: "Tell us the *price*, Ed, tell us the *price!*"

"Now let me tell you about the price," he said with a grin. "I'm sure most of you don't care about that, but in the interest of full disclosure, I'm obligated to tell you." He paused for five seconds. "When things started to look serious between EFS and BC Bank, I enlisted two firms to act as our financial advisors, Wasserstein and Morgan Stanley. I go back a long way with both of those firms and I consider them especially smart about M&A in financial services."

"Tell us, Ed," 60 managers whispered in unison.

"Interestingly enough, those firms reached almost identical conclusions about our value to a prospective acquirer. Morgan Stanley came in at $38.50 and Wasserstein came in at $41." That was a double from where the stock has been mired in recent months. Everyone in the room recalculated his net worth in his head using a $40 takeover price.

"So that's why I feel especially pleased to tell you that the price at which I convinced Bonnberg Commerzbank to acquire EFS is... $50 a share, 70% in cash and 30% in stock."

The room erupted in yelling and applause. For everyone except EFS's most recent arrivals, who hadn't been on board long enough to amass any holdings of consequence of EFS stock or options, Ed Koster had parted the seas. He'd sold a firm that had slumped into unprofitability and whose stock had been stuck near $20 for what felt like an eternity, for $50 a share. Just as importantly, he'd sold it not to Goldman or Morgan or Merrill or CS First Boston but to a large German Bank with no U.S. securities businesses that would require EFS employees to be thrown out on the sidewalk.

David, having recalculated his net worth using $50 instead of $40, now turned to the issue of how much BC Bank was actually paying for EFS. The firm had 130 million shares outstanding so, at $50 a share, it was paying $6.5 billion. In a good year, EFS made about $150 million after taxes, which meant that BC Bank had agreed to pay more than 40 times bull-market earnings for EFS. Why? Why hadn't it been Deutsche Bank or Dresdner, Hong Kong Shanghai Bank or ABN-AMRO, Societe Generale or ING? What did BC Bank see in EFS? What did it want?

"Now what I'd like all of you to do, with the exception of those of you who are board members, is to leave the building immediately, talk to no one, and lie low until the board votes tonight. Tomorrow morning you can meet with your people and tell them what I've told you and anything else that's in the press release, but until then I want you out of sight and I want no leaks. Okay?" Everyone agreed, and everyone headed for the exits, trying not to smile or in any way acknowledge publicly the giddiness he felt inside.

At the EFS board meeting that began at 6:00 P.M., David learned little beyond what Ed had already revealed. BC Holding was the parent company of Bonnberg Commerzbank, Germany's 10th-largest bank with assets of $120 billion. It was venerable, profitable, and its stock price had gone nowhere for three years. It aspired to become a dominant investment banking concern on a global basis and that meant acquiring or building an investment bank in the United States. Its plan was to take all that was good at EFS and build upon it, leveraging BC's success in Europe into America. It also professed to want to keep EFS's management team in place, which made sense since it lacked the knowledge and experience that would be essential to its success on U.S. soil. EFS's outside directors asked the bulk of the questions but even they didn't ask many.

At 6:15 P.M., while EFS's Board of Directors was meeting, the story broke on CNBC. At 6:16 P.M. David's office phone and home phone both began to ring incessantly. So did his cell phone, although David had muted it before the board meeting had begun. At 6:35 P.M. the board voted unanimously to accept the offer and at 7:20 P.M. the press release announcing the merger of EFS with Bonnberg Commerzbank for $50 a share in cash and stock hit *Dow Jones, Reuters* and *Bloomberg*. David slept not a wink that night, rehearsing endlessly in his head what he'd say to his analysts the next morning.

He knew his world was changing but was clueless how much.

* * *

Ed Koster addressed the firm about the "merger" with BC Bank on the Morning Call, after which David had scheduled back-to-back special meetings, first with his senior and associate analysts and then with the research assistants, secretaries and other support people. When the conference room on 74 seemed ready to split with analysts and sidekicks, David said only how optimistic he was that the "merger," as Koster had instructed everyone in management to call it, would lead to a substantially bigger Research budget, access to global counterparts in Europe and Asia and, hopefully, a much better investment banking effort in the United States. Then he asked for questions. As usual, the analysts weren't shy.

"What do we know about BC Bank?" asked Steven Kalagian, the wireless telecom analyst.

"I don't know much more than I've already told you. It's the 10th-largest bank in Germany, it has total assets of $120 billion, it's quite old, quite successful in Europe, consistently profitable, it has no U.S. operations that conflict with ours, it has relatively minor market shares in Asia and Latin America, and it professes to aspire to become a major, global investment bank a la Deutsche Bank and UBS, largely by building on the existing EFS platform."

"Have you met them?" asked Tim Omori.

"I only met Vilhelm Drews, briefly, at the board meeting last night. I understand that I may meet others later today."

"What analytical staffs do they have outside the U.S.?" asked Robin Lomax.

"Don't know. I'm sure I'll find out today or tomorrow."

"Is everyone getting 70% cash and 30% stock?" asked Arthur Litt.

"I'm not sure. I was led to believe last night that you may be able to request all cash or all stock but that, when the smoke clears, no more than 70% of the purchase price will be paid in cash no matter what people ask for."

"Why hasn't their stock done anything for three years?" asked Keith Jackman.

"I have no idea."

"David, when is the deal supposed to close?" asked Martin Hogue.

"I'm told that everyone wants it to close very quickly, in the first quarter."

"Are we going to do anything differently between now and then?" Martin asked.

"Not that I'm aware of, but remember... I've known about this for a half a day longer than you, so I have just as many unanswered questions at this point as you do."

"Are you going to stay on?" asked Matt Burlingame. Suddenly, all the whispering in the room stopped and all eyes focused on David. "I honestly don't know. I'd like to. I may or may not be offered the opportunity. I've been told that BC Bank wants to keep as much of EFS's existing management team as possible, which sounds good to me, but it's also possible that they might want to put one of their own in my position. I have no idea what the mission for Research will be, whether it will make sense to me or not, whether my job description will change for the better or worse with this change of control and so on. I'm sure all of these things will become clear to me in the days and weeks ahead, and I'll keep you posted along the way. What I'd like you to assume for the moment is that it's business as usual, and that you're stuck with me."

The room erupted with clapping and hooting. A few analysts yelled "Oh no!" with big smiles on their faces. David motioned for quiet. "Ken?"

Ken Lavery stood. "Do you know what their plans are for building The Bank?"

"No, although I understand that they aspire for us to be much bigger in banking."

"David, everything vests as a result of this merger?"

"Everything vests when the deal closes."

"What about contracts?" asked Will Rivas.

"That I can't answer for certain, but a few things seem obvious. One is that they will remain in force, at a minimum, until the deal closes. Another is that, as they're now worded, unless some of you are laid off as a result of this merger, you're still bound to remain with the firm. Change of control, in and of itself, doesn't free analysts from their obligations under the contract. Third, what usually happens in situations like this is that BC Bank might seek to sign those of you who are now under contract, and perhaps others, to new contracts. Existing contracts speak of compensation in cash and EFS stock. Well, there won't be any EFS stock after the deal closes, so BC Bank might seek to substitute its own stock for the EFS stock, but I don't know about that from a legal standpoint. Also, I don't know how they compensate their own analysts in Germany and whether or not they'd want to do something similar with us."

"Their analysts in Germany probably make a lot less than we do," said Nancy Natolio. "I hope they aren't thinking that's the way they should start paying us!"

"Anyone who understands our business," David said reassuringly "understands that U.S. analysts are by far the most experienced, the most sophisticated, the most accomplished, the greatest revenue generators and therefore deserving of the highest compensation. I'm not saying that there aren't some extraordinarily capable analysts in London and, to a lesser extent, in Europe and Asia because there are, but those analysts' pay is limited by the markets in which they work, and that's a choice they've made. I'd like to assume that BC Bank wants to keep as much of what's good about EFS in place as it can, which means that it won't be proposing to pay all of you, and me, the same way it's paying our counterparts in Germany."

"I hear that they pay their analysts 50% of their total compensation in stock," said Keith Jackman.

"It wouldn't surprise me. CSFB, UBS and Deutsche Bank have typically paid more of total compensation in paper than have their U.S. competitors, but I don't know for sure and I'd stop worrying about things you don't know you need to worry about."

There was silence for a moment. "What else?" David asked.

"Are we going to go to annual bonuses from twice a year?" asked James Brell.

"I have no idea. It's possible, but no one has said a word to me about it."

"Could we exchange our EFS options for options in BC Bank instead of exercising them if we want to?" asked Nancy Natolio.

"I don't know. I'll find out as soon as I can."

"Do you know what all the various tax implications are of taking stock versus cash or exercising options versus swapping them?" Nancy followed up.

"No, but I'm sure all of this will be explained, graphically, in written memos, long before any of us has to decide what to do."

David was getting impatient. "Anything else?" There were no other questions. "All right, then. I will update you daily, via e-mail, with what I know that's new and important. In the interim, assume the best and give this a little time. Over the next week or two, I'm sure all your questions will be answered and that you'll like what you hear."

"You better stay, David," yelled someone from the back of the room.

"I love you too. Now let's get back to work."

David remained, awaiting the research assistants, secretaries and the rest of the support team with whom he planned to go through a quicker and simpler version of his meeting with the analysts. Everyone else rose and moved slowly towards the doors. Dozens of small groups conversed in whispers and asides. No one, it seemed, noticed the first person out the door, a thin, wiry man, 5'10" it seemed, with a blue dress shirt, no tie, black pinstriped suit pants and great urgency in his strides towards the elevator banks.

* * *

Lisa was waiting for David when he returned to his office 20 minutes later. "Pretty wild," she said with a smile.

"Are you okay?" David asked.

"I don't know. Am I?"

"Of course you are."

"Are you staying?" Lisa asked with considerable concern.

"Are you holding a job offer for me that no one told me about?"

"No."

"I'm staying and you're staying and everything is going to work out fine."

"You really think so?"

"I do. Now what's my schedule look like for this morning?"

"You've got back-to-back Commitment Committee meetings and I just got a call from Barbara Summerville saying that you're having lunch today with their Director of Global Research. His name is Dieter Gustav Schmidt."

"Good. Where?"

"The private dining room at Fraunces. He'll pick you up at 11:45."

* * *

The private dining room at Fraunces was convenient for EFS executives who wanted to be "away from the office" but only a block away. Dieter and David were escorted, seated, asked for beverage orders, provided with menus and then left alone.

"So, great excitement," said Dieter, smiling.

"It's all a little unreal, but I must say that it was a very well-kept secret."

"It had to be, so Ed did almost all the work himself. He only brought Katherine in at the last minute, and her people are used to dealing with highly confidential matters and large sums of money. Both firms were great models of efficiency."

David noticed Dieter's accent, which was not pronounced, and the fluidity of his speech. He also recalled how badly he'd done in foreign languages in high school. Whenever he'd been called on to translate aloud one of the French books his class had been reading he'd stumble along for a minute or two and then his teacher would tell him, in French, "That's enough, David... David, this was not one of your better days." David tried to recall if he'd ever had a better day and concluded that he hadn't.

"I think this is a great opportunity for both firms," David said, partly because he believed it and partly because he knew what was expected of him. "The potential for us domestically is still enormous, and the ability to leverage BC globally is very exciting."

"Oh, I agree. This is a bold step for us to take. I'm sure our friends at Deutsche and Dresdner and UBS are wondering what on earth we're up to. And maybe they're kicking themselves for letting you get away from them. We aren't as big as they are, but we're still quite large, with deep, deep roots throughout Europe and an excellent reputation. Also, we haven't had some of the bad publicity that our friends have had." David wondered what that meant. Probably Holocaust-related, probably better left alone. The waiter returned with their drinks, took their orders and closed the door behind him.

"So, David, I know a little about you from the research that we did on EFS these past few months, but I'd love to know more. You're 45, I believe." David nodded. "And you've been on Wall Street for 17 years?" Another nod. "And if I remember correctly, you were an analyst for 10 years and have been a research director for seven."

"That's right. My last three years as an analyst were at EFS. Then I became Director of Research.

"And you are married?"

"Divorced. Devin and I were married for eight years."

"She's in the business?"

"Oh no, she owns a small art gallery in SoHo."

"Children?"

"None, luckily for them. Do you have children?"

"Yes, I have three sons, Otto who is 20, Heinrich who is 17 and Ernst who is 12."

"Hard work."

"Hard work, but mostly for my wife. I, at least, get to go off to work every morning," confessed Dieter. He closed his eyes for a moment, and then asked, "So, David, have you enjoyed your work at EFS?"

"On balance, it's been very rewarding. We've made some good progress over the past seven years. It's been, at times, a little frustrating because we're not where we should be in investment banking and we haven't had, until now, any global capabilities. That has really hurt me competitively both in hiring and keeping good analysts." Dieter nodded enthusiastically. "We really were caught in the middle between the global, bulge-bracket firms and the regional boutiques. It didn't feel good sometimes."

"Yes, yes, we saw that right away, and that's what got us excited because we now have the foundation in place on which to build something very powerful in the United States. Very good people, lots of branches, a good retail business, a good institutional business and, if I may say so, a not-so-good investment bank, but overall, a good name, a good franchise, a good starting point from which to build a world-class investment banking and securities firm. That's what got us excited about this merger.

"I don't know how much you know about European banking, David, but it's a very, very competitive business with frightfully low profit margins. Our return on assets is very low, our return on equity is low, and it's not because we are a badly managed firm. It's because everyone's margins are low. There are just too many banks with too much money to lend. And it's a business that has been growing slowly and will continue to grow slowly. So, even though you might say the same thing about the investment banking business, investment banking, globally, is much more profitable and much faster growing than commercial banking is in Europe. That's why we 'want in.'

"We believe there is room in the world for five true global investment banking powerhouses. That's a word? Powerhouses?"

"That's a word."

"Goldman Sachs and Morgan Stanley will be two of them. Merrill Lynch may or may not. It's floundering, in our judgment, and coasting on its reputation, which has been tarnished. That's very dangerous. If it sells itself to Hong Kong Shanghai Bank, it will be the third powerhouse. Let's assume that it will. That leaves two spots. Who will get them? Citigroup could get one. CSFB keeps shooting itself in the foot. Frank Quattrone comes, Frank Quattrone can go. Five years from now, CSFB will be back where it was before, an also-ran, despite Mr. Mack's best efforts. Deutsche Bank is definitely spinning its wheels in the United States. It had its chance and it's blown it. Lehman is too small. UBS could do it. That's the list. So what am I saying? We think that Citigroup and UBS and BC Bank will slug it out for the last two spots and we believe that we will be one of the two winners. This buildup, near term, will hurt our earnings and the price of our stock, but 10 years from now, if we execute, we will be making far, far more than we have been of late, and our stock price will be a large multiple of what it's been for the past three years. Our margins will widen, our P/E multiple will expand, and we will have shocked, and I mean *shocked*, the global financial community."

"That's very ambitious," David said, but it came out sounding as if he doubted that BC could succeed so he added, "and very exciting."

"Very exciting is right. It's going to be great fun, and very hard work, but we are 100% committed to doing this and we want you to be part of it."

Here it comes, David thought.

"David, what we want from you is your commitment to build for us a top-5 U.S. Research Department. We will build investment banking in the United States in concert with your buildup of research. We want to be viewed, with respect to Research, as in the same league as Goldman and Morgan and Merrill. So, ideally, we'd like to be number four. But number five will do just fine too. That's a huge jump from where EFS has been, but we're convinced that you are the man to take us there."

"Do you have any idea what it will cost to take us there?"

"We do. We think it will take, at a minimum, a doubling of your budget. Your budget has been, I believe, just shy of $120 million recently. Is that correct?"

"Correct."

"What we think it will take is an increase to $200 million next year and to between $250 million and $300 million the year after. Obviously, even if we yelled 'Go!' right now, and you went out recruiting with our checkbook in your hand, you wouldn't be able to hire everyone you wanted to right away. Analysts would come on board gradually throughout the next 12 months, and hopefully you'd have made a lot of progress by the time a year had gone by. We'd expect that of you, and we'd expect you to finish the job during your second 12 months, which obviously would include a full year of pay for each analyst you hire next year. That is why you probably only need to spend $200 million next year but $250 million to $300 million the year after that."

"And you're prepared to commit to that?"

"Yes."

"How much are you going to build The Bank?"

"We've told Tom Mennymore that we want him to go from 150 bankers to 500 bankers over three to five years. We're less precise with him because we want to build The Bank as we build Research. You can't hire good bankers unless you have good analysts so you must build Research first and let those new analysts act as magnets to attract good bankers. We want to rival Goldman and Morgan in the United States. We cannot do that with 150 bankers."

"How will you measure me? What does top five mean to you?"

"It means top 5 in the *II* All Star Poll. We are now number fourteen. It will take a Herculean effort to get us to number five or number four, and that's why we want you to lead it. You understand the business better than we do. You know all the analysts on The Street. You know what motivates them and what turns them off. From all accounts, you know how to hire good people and keep good people. You are the one to take us from number fourteen to number five.

"To motivate you particularly in this direction, David, we've crafted a special compensation plan for you."

"Special?"

"Yes and secret. You must never breathe a word of it to anyone. Are you ready?"

"I'm ready."

"All right, here it is. Most recently, according to

Katherine, you've been earning about $2,500,000 annually including stock options. What we want to do is sign you to a two-year employment contract, effective the day the merger closes, with guaranteed annual compensation of 2,500,000. So, no downside to you under any circumstances. But beyond that $2,500,000 we will pay you, each year, a "supplemental bonus" based on BC Bank's ranking in *II* each October. Here's how it would work. Our starting point is your current ranking, which is number fourteen. Correct?"

"Correct."

"Beyond your $2,500,000 guarantee, we will pay you $500,000 for each rung up the ladder that we move between number fourteen and number ten, $750,000 for each of the next two rungs, $1,000,000 for each of the two rungs after that, and $2,000,000 for each rung after that. So, if we're number ten you make $4,500,000, if we're number eight you make $6,000,000, if we're number six you make $8,000,000 and if we're number four you make $12,000,000."

David tried to look unimpressed. He was sure he failed miserably, but as calmly as he could, he asked, "So if, hypothetically, I was able to get BC Bank to number six next year and to number four in my second year…"

"…we would pay you $20,000,000 over two years," said Dieter without blinking, "and with great pleasure."

Lunch arrived, but David never lifted his fork. Less than 48 hours later, he had convinced Dieter to up his annual budget commitment to $250 million the day the merger closed and to $350 million 12 months later, to put the terms of his "secret" compensation plan in writing, and to find David substantial, unused office space on a floor close to 63 where EFS could house all the new analysts it would need to hire.

"May I take you to dinner tonight to celebrate?" he'd asked as they shook hands.

"That would be great. Where would you like to go?"

"Let's see. David, Dieter, destiny, done deal." He closed his eyes, puckered his lips slightly and then smiled. "Why, to Daniel, of course."

DECEMBER

The next morning, David and Dieter met in David's office and mapped out plans to ensure the stability of the Research Department following the completion of the deal.

"I can't allow us to turn into Prudential/Volpe Brown," Dieter was saying. "You always lose some good people in situations like this. It can't be helped. But if you put some serious thought into it, and some creativity, you can avoid seeing when the smoke has cleared that all your newly enriched talent has kicked you in the ass and said goodbye, leaving you only with egg to wipe from your face."

"I agree. How Prudential thought it could keep all the good Volpe people without signing them to contracts with non-compete agreements in them will always mystify me," David mused. "NationsBank did the same thing with Montgomery, but we're smarter than that and we can have a much happier ending than they did."

"Good, so let me tell you what we've planned and tell me if it makes sense. First, we cannot do anything formally until the merger closes. You must conduct business as usual, and all existing contracts must continue to be honored by both sides."

David nodded.

"Next, we should go to each analyst with a new contract that would become effective once the merger has been completed and that would supersede all now-existing contracts. The new contracts would cover next year, during which we should be merged for, say, 10 months, and the following calendar year. We would give one to each analyst you feel it would be important to keep during the first 24 months following the merger. Obviously, the five *II*-ranked analysts must get them. Also, any of your analysts who is doing very good work and who could make *II* within the next two years should get one, and any other analyst who, for other reasons, should be kept should get one.

"We'd prefer not to extend new contracts to analysts who are perceived to be expendable, and we recognize the need to offer them to some of your most recent hires who haven't yet proven themselves."

All of this made sense to David who was relieved by Dieter's thought process.

"Some of the All Stars that you hire over the next year or two will fill holes in the department, but some will also be upgrades of weaker analysts and we'd like to minimize the amount of severance we must pay those weaker analysts by ensuring that they are not under contract when we tell them the bad news."

"I assume that we'd still offer them severance packages in keeping with EFS standards prior to the merger?"

"Of course, but that's very different than having to pay them the last 18 months of a 24–month contract" Dieter laughed. "I presume that you didn't typically give poorly performing analysts 18 months of total compensation as severance when you fired them!"

"Obviously not."

"Good. So, if I recall correctly, you have almost 20 analysts under contract now."

"That's right."

"And perhaps there are 12 to15 others that we'd like to put under contract, so my thought was that we'd extend new contracts to between 35 and 40 of our 50 analysts…"

"…and strategists and economists."

"And strategists and economists. I understand that Linda is very good."

"She's very good, but she's unmanageable and very labor-intensive, and she'll make a big stink before she signs any new contract."

"Perhaps I should deal with her directly?"

"That's an excellent idea!"

"She's not *II*-ranked, is she?"

"No, but she's close, and that merely encourages her to continue acting like she's been number one forever. She just missed ranking this year. She'll be a Runner-Up next year."

"Okay then, with your blessing, I will invite Linda out for lunch or dinner and begin the process of romancing her into signing a new contract."

"Good. Now, with respect to the other three dozen contracts that we'll be extending, what thoughts have you had about compensation levels and handcuffs?"

"Unless there are a handful of analysts whom you feel are seriously under-compensated at the moment, and we'd make adjustments there, we'd like to offer each analyst a two-year guarantee at the rate of pay he has most recently experienced…"

David felt his first twang of concern.

"…plus a block of BC Holdings common stock equal in value to one year's total compensation that would vest after 36 months."

136

"So, if I'm an analyst now making $2,100,000, I'd get a new, two-year contract at $2,100,000 per year plus $2,100,000 of BC Holdings stock that would vest after three years."

"That's right. Notionally, it could be viewed as vesting $700,000 per year for analysts who stay for 36 months, which we obviously want them to do. And that would represent a 33% raise. It's similar to re-inking that $2,100,000 analyst at $2,800,000."

"You don't want to offer three-year contracts to the analysts?"

"No. We don't see the need and we doubt that most analysts would want to commit themselves for that long."

"They sort of have to if they want their BC shares to vest."

"Well that's right. You want that $2,100,000? You have to be loyal for three years and you have to gamble a little bit on your third year of compensation which wouldn't be addressed in the new contracts. But David, let's be real about this. BC Holdings is about to spend billions of dollars buying EFS. Do you really think we'd be shortsighted enough to destabilize the best analysts in our new Research Department by shafting them on compensation 24 months after buying you?"

"I'm sure you wouldn't."

"Of course we wouldn't. Just as you would've done, we'd go to the strong analysts several months before those two-year contracts were to expire and seek to negotiate new contracts with those analysts. While it's true that we'd have the upper hand to some extent because they'd all, presumably, want to stick around for at least the 12 additional months needed to see their stock vest, one of the keys to making this merger work is keeping the best employees happy for many years, not just two or three, so the analysts will have to trust that if they perform well they'll be treated well."

"And the analysts who aren't offered contracts?"

"They will be compensated fairly, just as we compensate fairly our non-U.S. analysts, none of whom is under contract."

"What about the mix of cash versus stock?"

"We have a sliding scale that is similar to yours but skewed somewhat more towards stock than yours is. Our highest-paid analysts get 45% of all bonuses in stock."

David gulped. He'd expected that kind of cash/stock mix for members of management but not for the analysts.

"But we won't ask your analysts to go there cold turkey. We'll phase them in over three years, starting at 35% next year, 40% in year two and 45% in year three."

David thought it all through. The good news was that everyone he'd want to keep would be put, hopefully, under contract with non-compete provisions, and that they'd get instant 33% raises. The bad news was that they'd be at BC's mercy in year three and get almost twice as much stock as they were used to receiving. Then again, many of them would've fared very well selling their shares to BC for $50 each in February.

Finally, David realized, the market for analysts was crappy at the moment because business was slow, and the analysts' ability to reject the new contracts and find more lucrative offers with less stock in them elsewhere was limited at best, which meant that most of them would probably sign.

"Shall I tell them?" David asked.

"Tell them that this is our intention but that none of it can happen until the merger closes." Dieter paused for a moment. "You know, David, that they'll immediately want to know if they're in the getting-a-new-contract camp or not."

"Of course. I'll just tell them that each of their situations will be reviewed individually with you in coming weeks, that you'll probably want to meet many of them…"

Dieter nodded.

"…and that, if they're sure they will, they probably will, and if they're worried that they won't, they probably won't."

"Exactly right and nicely put," said Dieter. "So let's tell them."

* * *

Carl Robern and Maryanne Miles were finishing their desserts and sipping cappuccinos at 14 Wall Street, an elegant, French, rooftop restauranton Wall Street just east of Broadway. To Maryanne's surprise, Carl had invited her out for lunch "to discuss her promising career in institutional sales."

Maryanne had only been with EFS for about four months. She was 28 years old, 5'7", blonde and slim. Maryanne had a lot of sex appeal, and it hadn't taken her long to catch the eye of half the traders at EFS and plenty of others who had begun frequenting Sales more often soon after she'd touched down. Maryanne also used it well with clients, trading the pleasure of her company for orders to buy 100,000 shares of this or that.

Lunch had gone well. Carl had seemed genuinely

interested in hearing about her initial impressions of EFS, her early efforts to build relationships with several mid-sized institutional accounts that she'd been offered by EFS as an inducement to leave Lehman Brothers, her recent marriage and honeymoon in Maui, and her plans not to have children any time soon. Carl, in turn, had told her about his condo in Maui, the use of which he'd offered her the next time she vacationed there, and some high points of his years long ago as a budding investment banker. He'd also given her a few words of advice about how to "manage" John McLain. As expected, Carl had tried out one of his 3,000 dirty jokes on Maryanne, and he'd been delighted to find that she'd appreciated it. In fact, she'd told him one of her own, which prompted him to tell two more and Maryanne to tell one more, after which the entrees had arrived and the conversation had returned to more work-like topics.

"Maryanne," said Carl as he filled out the credit card voucher, "if there was one account that you really coveted, that you most wished you could do if one of the other salesmen wasn't already doing it, what would it be?"

"Wow, that's an interesting question." She hesitated and then said, "You know, Carl, I haven't really thought about it much. I was doing all small accounts at Lehman. Now I've got some larger accounts, and I feel as if my hands are full, at least for now. But some time soon, I guess what I've been thinking a little about is co-covering a real, top-tier account like Alliance with someone else in the office. You know, not being one of five salesmen on the account but one of two or, at most, three."

Carl was nodding. "Did you ever mention that to John?"

"No, it's too soon. I don't want anyone thinking I'm out to steal their accounts after four months at the firm."

"Do you mind if I plant that idea in the back of John's head?" Carl was smiling, knowingly. "With the BC merger, you know, I'm sure John will be hiring additional salespeople and moving accounts around. This would be the moment if you want it."

"I'd love for you to mention it, if you think it's appropriate."

"Good, then I will." Carl smiled and gave Maryanne a little wink. "Shall we?" At the coat check stand, Carl extended his right arm over Maryanne's right shoulder and surrendered two claim checks and a ten dollar bill. Maryanne, her back to Carl, was reading a note on the counter about what the restaurant would and wouldn't be responsible for. She heard the coat check woman pass coats over her right shoulder and sensed Carl grabbing them behind her. As she finished reading, she felt Carl drape her coat over her shoulders and got ready to step away from the counter and put it on.

But before she could, Carl's powerful hands grabbed her firmly at the top of both arms and spun her around so she was facing him and, in a flash, his left arm encircled her back, his lips were on hers, his tongue was inside her mouth and his right hand was on her left breast, squeezing it and rubbing it in a circular motion. Frightened and embarrassed, Maryanne recoiled, and tried to pull her head back and to grab Carl's right hand with her own. To her surprise, Carl pressed even harder against her mouth, and his right hand darted under her skirt, up her left thigh and between her legs.

"Jesus!" Maryanne screamed and, with all her might, she pushed Carl away.

"Pretty tasty," Carl smirked with satisfaction.

"Jesus," Maryanne gasped again and, sensing how disheveled she suddenly looked, she added, "I need to stop."

After five minutes in the ladies room regaining her composure, Maryanne, still frightened and confused, walked back to the office, in silence, with Carl.

* * *

"This will be quick," David told the analysts who had gathered in the conference rooms on the 74th floor after the market had closed. "Rather than do it in an e-mail, I want to do today's update in person." The analysts could tell from David's demeanor that the news was good and they hoped that some of it had to do with them.

"There are just three points I'd like to make and then I'll answer questions. First, I'm staying." The room erupted with applause and with laughter of relief. The prospect of getting a new, German boss was not appealing to most of the analysts and David, while not universally adored, was genuinely liked by most of the people he managed.

"Second, it is BC's intention to develop us into one of the five highest- ranking Research Departments on Wall Street, and it has committed the funding necessary to get us there." For a second, the analysts and associates seemed stunned, but then someone whistled loudly from the back of the room, triggering a second round of enthusiastic applause. Top five had been unimaginable to most of EFS's analysts, but David's commitment to stay and his disclosure that the

Research budget was about to go up a lot suddenly made the prospect less surrealistic. Most liked the idea.

"Finally, a little about all of you. Until the merger closes in February or March, it will be business as usual. All existing contracts will remain in place and must be honored by all parties involved, but when the deal closes it is BC's intention to offer new, two-year contracts to everyone who is performing well, and that's almost all of you. The contracts would, I'm told, guarantee each of you two additional years of compensation at the rate at which you've been earning most recently, plus a special bonus equal to one full year's total compensation that would be paid to you in BC Holdings stock 36 months after the deal closes."

"Say that again, David," asked Matt Burlingame, the managed care analyst.

"If you've been making $1,000,000 most recently, you'd get a new, two-year contract at $1,000,000 per year plus $1,000,000 of BC Holdings common stock that would vest after 36 months."

Two dozen hands went up and David could see yellow lights flashing everywhere. He decided not to allow himself to say things he shouldn't and to stick to generalities.

"I don't have any more details to share with you, and I don't want to get into technicalities that could change later, but let me just answer a couple of questions that I'm sure you want to ask. First, the decision about who will be offered a new contract and who won't will be made by me and by Dieter Schmidt, who will be, along with Carl, my post-merger boss, and who heads BC's global research effort. If I had to guess, I'd wager that 80% of you will be offered new contracts. If you're worried that you might not qualify, you probably won't. Second, BC is unwilling to do three-year contracts, although it has said it might seek to extend or negotiate new contracts two years from now with those of you who are doing well and whom we wouldn't want to lose. Third, all contracts will contain non-competes. Fourth, total compensation going forward will be a blend of cash and BC stock on terms that I don't yet know, but the fraction of total comp that will be paid in stock will creep higher over the next two or three years from where it is now, but not beyond 40%-45%. Finally, this approach is fair, it reflects BC's desire to keep everyone who's doing really good work for many years to come, I want you to sign up and help me build the department into something to be reckoned with and I will get you answers to every other question you may have over the next week or two."

The analysts, not surprisingly, were confused and far from elated as they filed out of the conference rooms and headed back to their offices.

As David brought up the rear, Linda Logan approached him and, with a pout, whispered "David, just two things. First, two more years at my current, pitiful rate of compensation is a complete nonstarter. Second, if, when you go out looking for All Stars to hire, you even *call* anyone doing quant, small caps or technical analysis, I'm out of here." Then she smiled as insincerely as she could and walked away.

* * *

Winter had arrived in Boston. It was snowing and 11 degrees outside, and Ken Lavery found the warmth of Charles Willing's branch office welcoming. It was 7:15 A.M., and the RX branch, as it was known, was the first of four stops that Charles had arranged for Ken to make during the day. Second would be a pre-opening meeting at EFS's other downtown Boston branch, third would be a lunch meeting at the Cambridge branch, after which Ken would drive to Brookline for a 4:15 meeting there. All told, he expected to see 150 brokers. Luckily, no one wanted to have a group dinner with him.

Here in the RX branch, Ken and Charles were standing at the front of a large conference room that had been catered with donuts, croissants and coffee, and most of the financial advisors, or "FAs", were in their seats. "I'm sorry about the weather, Ken," said Charles. "I fear that a few of our guys with longer commutes won't make it in on time, but we've got everyone here that matters, right Bob?" Bob McGruder, a President's Club member sitting in the front row and finishing the second of his four donuts, nodded and shrugged, indicating that he was ill-prepared to speak.

"Good morning everyone," Charles boomed, "and thanks for being so punctual on such a meteorologically challenging day!" Ken and many of the brokers smiled. "I'm sure that Ken Lavery needs no introduction from me. He's a longstanding friend of the branch's, he's been here many times, and we're delighted to have him back again. I'm sure he'll talk about Genentech, Amgen and Biogen and, of course, we have a lot of interest locally in Millennium which, I understand, Ken, you'll be visiting tomorrow."

"Correct!" said Ken, nodding enthusiastically.

"So, without further ado, let's welcome back Ken Lavery." There was a smattering of applause, limited by the hands needed to hold coffee and donuts.

"Thanks so much, Charles, for having me in today, and thanks to all of you for coming. I know how busy you are so I'm going to run through some things with you quickly so you can return to more profitable endeavors. But I don't have to be down the street until 8:30 so, if some of you want to do a little Q&A with me or ask me something privately after I'm done, it would be my pleasure. Let me start with a brief industry overview and then I'll touch quickly on three or four names that you should focus on.

"Biotechnology is the single most exciting industry on the planet…"

By 8:05, Ken had completed his industry overview and his discussions of Genentech, Amgen, Millennium and Regeneron.

"Any other questions about anything else?" Ken asked.

After a moment, Bob McGruder raised his hand.

"Ken, do you have any new names you're working on?"

"Any new names…," Ken pondered and squinted. "Not really, Bob."

"Anything you're planning to pick up coverage on that would be new?"

"Well you know, I couldn't really tell you that even if I wanted to for Compliance reasons, but the answer is no, I'm not planning to expand my universe any time soon."

"Ken, I think what Bob is really asking is if, over and above the four names you reviewed, and we know you still like Biogen, is that right?…"

"That's right."

"… if there's anything new we could go out to clients with. Business is, as you know, pretty slow of late, and going out again and saying how much we like Amgen and Genentech is fine, but something with a little more sizzle would be much more helpful."

"More sizzle. I'm drawing a blank."

"Well, what do you own in your personal account?" Bob asked. All eyes zoomed in on Ken.

Ken looked long and hard at Bob and then seemed to scan the entire room. "I'm not sure this is a brilliant idea, but you know me... if you ask, I'll tell. I own Genentech, Amgen, Regeneron and two stocks that I don't cover and won't be covering. They're $6 names." Notebooks were opening everywhere. "They would be suitable only for your highest-risk accounts because, frankly, they could be worthless a year from now." He paused, just long enough. "But they could also be ten-baggers, and that's what I'm hoping for." The room was silent except for brokers breathing.

"I've warned you, so now I'll answer you. They're The G-NOME Company and Genomic Innovators. Let me tell you a little bit about them."

* * *

Barely an hour later, Ken had made it across town to EFS's other downtown Boston branch, been introduced, done his industry overview, reviewed Millennium, Genentech, Amgen and Regeneron, and just completed his quick take on Biogen. Attendance was down but Ken still counted 40 FAs whose ears were wide open.

"Other questions?"

Initially, there were none. Ken pushed harder.

"Anything beyond the big five that you'd like me to talk about?"

Still nothing.

"Who owns other names in the group?" Ken looked at branch manager Tom Tenser for help and got it.

"Ken, do you know a little outfit called Gandalf Genomics?"

Close enough, Ken thought. "I do, Tom," he answered. "It's a penny stock, it has a couple of founding partners with good research reputations and it got a lot of publicity when UBS Warburg brought it public last year and it shot up initially in the aftermarket. But it's come down quite hard since then and, from what I recall from the last time I looked at it, it's probably five years away from introducing its first product."

"There's nothing that you cover right now that's like Gandalf?"

"You mean with respect to products and markets or to selling under $10?"

The brokers laughed. "The latter, of course," Tom answered, smiling broadly.

"Unfortunately, Tom, there isn't." Dramatic pause. Look of hesitation. Quick scan of the room. "But I'd feel, frankly, as if I'd misled you if I didn't disclose that I own two stocks like that in my personal account." Notebooks opened.

"And they are…?"

"One's called The G-NOME Company and the other's Genomic Innovators. Do we have time for me to give you 60 seconds on each of them?" he asked innocently.

"By all means," Tom answered, "tell us."

* * *

It was 1:10 P.M., and Ken was happy. His morning meetings in downtown Boston had gone very well, and lunch in Cambridge had been just as successful, albeit with a smaller audience of 30 brokers. The meeting room was cramped and the presentation much less formal, everyone ate sandwiches and Fritos as Ken talked, and the FAs frequently interrupted his canned remarks with questions that sidetracked him. But Ken, the master of broker presentations, was always able to steer himself back on track.

In 55 minutes he'd covered Genentech, Millennium, Regeneron and Amgen and answered questions about several other stocks selling between $25 and $40 that he didn't cover. Ken was also, to his surprise, asked questions about conflicts between research and investment banking, about the different priorities that a banker and an analyst should have when they bring a new company public, about analysts' integrity and about how analysts got paid. These broader questions made Ken nervous, and he danced around them a little bit while making sure to underscore his complete objectivity in the work he did, his loyalty first and foremost to the brokers and their clients, and how relatively inconsequential investment banking bonuses were to most EFS analysts.

"Isn't that going to change once BC buys us?" one seasoned broker had asked.

"It could," Ken admitted. "We may become bigger in investment banking than we've been, and I may spend more time on deals than I have, but what won't change is the fact that, at the end of the day, all I take home with me is my reputation and I would never do *anything* to tarnish it no matter what the economics of a deal might be."

"Do you own the stocks you recommend to us yourself?" asked a young FA.

"Not all of them, but I almost always have most of my liquid assets invested in biotech names. I know them the best, I like them, I'm convinced I'll make money in them over time, and I think that analysts who tell you day after day what to buy but don't have the guts to put their own money into those names shouldn't be taken seriously."

Lots of nodding.

"Doesn't that cloud your objectivity?"

"Hopefully not. We have all sorts of Compliance regulations designed to ensure that I handle my account appropriately relative to the advice that I dispense. I'm not going to make the rounds in Boston telling you to buy Regeneron as I sell it short in my personal account, and I'm always very straightforward when brokers ask me what I own personally which, interestingly, no one here has done today."

"So what's in your personal account, Ken?"

"Thank you for asking. I've got some Genentech, some Amgen and some Regeneron. I don't own Millennium." Long pause. "And I own two low-priced stocks that I don't cover."

"Why not?"

"Because they're very-high-risk/very-high-reward names that I just think are inappropriate for the vast majority of our clients, and I can't see cutting 5,000 of you loose on them, given how small they are."

"You could cut 30 of us loose on them." The room filled with laughter.

"I won't cut *anyone* loose on them," Ken said, putting on his most somber face.

"Well, could you at least tell us what they are?"

"Of course," Ken obliged, "with the understanding that I don't follow them, I won't be following them and they're unsuitable for the vast majority of your clients."

"Understood."

"OK, in that light, one name is The G-NOME Company, the other's Genomic Innovators."

* * *

"I own Genentech, Regeneron, Amgen and two penny stocks I don't cover."

He was batting a thousand and he was almost done. It was Brookline, it was 4:55 P.M., and Ken was about to tell a group of brokers about G-NOME and Genomic Innovators for the fourth and final time.

His only concern was that both stocks had traded up $0.50–$0.60 during the day in a flat market. Those were almost 10% moves in seven hours, and only three of the four branches he'd hit had been told about the two names while the market had been open. What Ken wanted and needed was steady but slower progress from $6 to $10 to $15 to wherever but he knew he couldn't orchestrate things that well and that he'd have to lie low for a while after this Boston swing before lighting fires under FAs in other markets.

"Thank God there's no dinner," he thought as he left Brookline for the Ritz in downtown Boston. "I haven't done anything to prepare for my Millennium meeting tomorrow." But Ken wasn't worried. He'd planned just a 45–minute drive-by, and how many questions could an analyst ask in 45 minutes, anyway?

He'd be fine, he thought… and 10 minutes late.

* * *

That Thursday afternoon, as Ken had pulled into

Brookline, Nick Denisovich had stopped as he was packing his attache case and said to Linda Chute, his secretary, "You know I'm out tomorrow, right?"

"I do indeed. Vacation day."

"Any plans for the weekend?"

"Nothing special," Linda sighed. "My brother and sister-in-law and their kids are coming over on Sunday. That's about it. What are you doing?"

"I'll be around," Nick replied, matter-of-factly. I haven't done any Christmas shopping yet, so I will, assuming there's anything left in the stores."

"I finished mine a month ago. I hate the last-minute pressure. You know?"

"Well, Linda, some of us plan better than others. Have a good one."

"You too."

Downstairs, Nick grabbed a cab and asked to be dropped off at his apartment at 622 Greenwich Street. As the cab pulled up, Nick could see the Elite Limousine awaiting him. "I'll be back in 60 seconds," he told the Elite driver and, true to his word, he returned a minute later still carrying his attache case.

"JFK?" the driver asked.

"That's right. As fast as you can."

* * *

"Are we still going to do this?" David asked.

"As far as I know, we're doing it," answered Carl, helpful as usual.

David was reviewing a memo describing the year-end promotion process that he knew well but had somehow assumed might look different this year.

"Am I supposed to involve Dieter in this?"

"Not according to Koster. He said to just do it the

way we always did it. You know, part of that 'business as usual until the merger closes' bullshit."

"Okay," David said and hung up.

"Lisa?" She was through his door like a bullet. "Did you see the promotions memo?"

"I've got it right here."

"Good. I'll give you the names of the seniors who should be made Managing Directors in a minute. I think there are six of them."

"Seven."

"Okay, but I'll double-check them before we submit them."

"And for all other categories?"

"We'll do what we always do. We'll promote everyone we can possibly promote. You've got the hurdles with respect to income and years of service, right?"

"Right."

"Well then, just go through the list and anyone who got a positive writeup from his or her boss and who can be promoted from Assistant VP to VP or from VP to First VP or from First VP to Senior VP should be promoted. And more importantly, look carefully at all the associate analysts and research assistants and see who can be promoted to Assistant VP or Associate VP."

"It's going to be a pretty long list."

"That's fine," David replied. "If these titles meant anything, if there were any benefits that accrued to you at one level that didn't at a lower one, I'd be more selective about this. But as it turns out, these titles mean absolutely nothing…no extra vacation, no health club memberships, no improvement in health care coverage, nothing but something a little nicer looking on a note pad or business card. So, if it costs the firm not a penny and it makes 100 people in the department feel a little better about themselves, why not? They'll show off to their families and their friends. It's a little thing that means a lot so let's do it until someone tells us we have to stop."

* * *

At exactly 10:15 Friday morning, Nick Denisovich wound his way through customs and to the taxi stand. A small, white Mercedes was next in line, and Nick jumped in, smiling at the driver. "I need to go to Boulevard Georges-Favon, number 29," he said.

The driver nodded. "First time in Geneva?" he asked, lighting a cigarette.

"Yes it is," Nick said, resolving to be quiet and pretending he wanted to sleep. Behind closed eyes, he recalled meeting Anna for the first time in a discotheque in Frankfurt three years earlier. She'd been talking with a guy and two teenage girls at the bar when he'd first noticed her, and Nick had waited, watching, trying to determine who the guy was. As time passed, it had become clear that the guy was more interested in one of the teens than in Anna, and when he asked the young girl to dance, Nick had made his move. He remembered buying Anna the first drink, telling her a little about himself, trying to hear her over the din of the disco, taking her to two other bars later that night, and then returning to his hotel with her, arm in arm, around 3:00 A.M.

Over the next few months, Nick and Anna had met four more times, once in Frankfurt and thrice in New York. Each time, Anna had shown him great affection. They'd dined together and talked at length about many things but most of all about Nick and his work.

Anna had said that she was a model and aspiring actress, but that she'd found it hard to make a living at it and was contemplating a career in finance. She'd demonstrated strong mathematical skills to Nick on several occasions and also spoken surprisingly well about global economic issues. This had made Nick increasingly comfortable discussing his work with Anna, which he'd done on each night they'd shared.

It was after they'd made love on the fourth night that Anna had asked if Nick might like to meet a friend of hers who had an investment idea that might make them both rich. Two weeks later, after the three of them had dined at The Four Seasons on 57th Street, Nick and Anna and Piotr had returned to The Plaza, to Piotr's room, to sip nightcaps and talk business.

"I have a lot of money to invest," Piotr had told Nick. "What I need are ideas, and I need to hear them before others hear them so I can build positions and sell when everyone else starts to buy or buy from everyone who's dying to sell."

Nick was sure he misunderstood.

"What I'd need from you, Nick, is this. I'd need to be told several weeks in advance about ratings changes that you'd make on stocks that were thin enough to move substantially as a result of those changes. If you planned to upgrade a stock to Buy, I'd buy it first and sell it right after you upgraded. If you were going to downgrade to Sell, I'd sell the stock short during the two or three weeks leading up to your announcement and then buy it back as soon as the stock declined on your downgrade."

Nick looked at Anna, who was smiling and nodding enthusiastically. "You're insane," he told Piotr. "I could go to jail for this. Why should I even *think* of taking a risk like that?"

"How much money does Equitable Finance pay you, Nick?"

Nick recalled having told Anna that he made over $1 million a year, early on, in an effort to impress her.

"About $1,500,000," he exaggerated.

"So, after taxes, you take home $900,000."

"That's right."

"So, it would take you 11 years to bring home $10 million."

Nick nodded.

"What if I could make you that $10 million in three years, or perhaps even two?"

Nick frowned. "How?"

"By sharing some of the profits I make on front-running your ratings changes with you."

"Share how much?"

"Ten percent."

"You can't move enough stock to make those numbers work."

"I believe I can."

Nick looked again at Anna. She winked long and hard at him. He could feel the wine in his head, and how dangerous his infatuation had become. To his surprise, part of him liked that danger, a lot.

"I'd want 50% of the profits."

"Out of the question."

"I'd be taking an enormous risk."

"Twenty percent."

"Forty percent."

"Twenty is all that I'll do."

"Then 30%."

Stalemate. Nick and Piotr stared at each other in silence. Each looked at Anna, but Anna said nothing.

Ten minutes later, Nick and Piotr had agreed on

25% or $5 million a year, whichever was more. Nothing could be written, so they simply shook hands to seal their accord.

"You must open a Swiss bank account," Piotr had told him, "into which we'll wire your share."

"No," Nick said, surprising everyone. "No wires. No paper trail. Nothing that ties you to me. Nothing."

"It would be perfectly safe," Piotr protested. We'd wire from our account to your account. We'd use the same bank. The confidentiality of both accounts would be protected."

"No, Piotr, no paper trail. I will open the Swiss bank account, but there must be no trace of anyone wiring funds into it. Wires can become evidence. Nothing must connect us."

"Then how am I going to pay you? Send shirt boxes of money to Mailboxes Etc.? This isn't Get Shorty, you know."

"You could."

"And what will you do with those shirt boxes when you receive them? Stuff them in a suitcase and fly with them to Geneva, hoping no one from Security stops you and asks you to open your bags?"

Nick knew Piotr was right. Even before 9/11, the risk of being stopped was too high; after 9/11 it had increased exponentially. So, reluctantly, he'd agreed to go the Swiss bank account route, with funds to be wired only from Piotr's account to Nick's.

"I can't believe I'm doing this," Nick had said when all their negotiating was done.

"You're going to be a very wealthy man," Piotr had reassured him.

Nick's cab lurched and the driver honked loudly. Instinctively, Nick jumped and grabbed wildly around him for his attache case. When he found it, he sighed, closed his eyes again and went back to sleep.

* * *

In New York City, at 4:15 A.M., Will Rivas was wide awake. He'd stayed up late watching David Letterman and Craig Kilbourne and hoping that eventually he'd fade, but he hadn't so he switched to CNN with the mute button pressed.

"Claus is such an ass," he thought. "No, it's more than that…he's dangerous. There's no deal he won't do." Once more Will replayed, in his mind, portions of the meeting he'd had in his office the prior afternoon with clueless Claus Abner. As always, Claus had dropped by without warning or invitation and interrupted a series of phone calls that Will had begun making to his most important institutional clients about his outlook for December-quarter earnings for his companies. These were important calls, and they became much easier to make after he had done a few and gotten into the rhythm of it, but Claus seemed Hell-bent on denying Will his rhythm. Before Will could utter a word, Claus had entered the office, closed the door and made himself at home.

"Did you look at Dominus?"

"I looked at it." Will shook his head. "No interest."

Dominus Dent-L Care was a tiny, three-year-old manufacturer of X-ray machines, computer imaging systems, artificial teeth, root canal instruments, sealants and impression materials, all of which were sold to dentists in the U.S. and Europe. It had sales of $80 million and had not turned a profit since being founded. It was privately owned, contemplating an IPO and soliciting expressions of interest from Wall Street firms that wanted to do the deal. Claus, naturally, wanted the mandate.

"Why, Will?"

"Why? Because it's barely three years old, it doesn't even do $100 million in sales and it can't turn a profit."

"It'll be profitable 24 months from now. You've seen the projections."

"I don't believe them," said Will defiantly. "And Dentsply can kill them if it wants to." Dentsply International, the dominant manufacturer of dental products around the world, has sales of about $1.5 billion and earnings of about $150 million annually.

"It could also buy them."

"I'm not going to do it, Claus. It's a rotten use of my time."

"Why is that?"

"It's a $50 million, four-handed IPO: UBS, Cowen, and two other firms. The management fee is $700,000, of which we'd get, at most, $187,500. Let's say you give me 10%. So what this deal means to me is $18,750 minus taxes, or $10,000."

"That's not nothing," Claus snorted.

"It *is* nothing, because I'll have to have a Buy on the stock when it starts to trade, otherwise no one will understand how I could have supported the IPO. And guess what. Six months after the deal is done, when Dominus misses the quarter and drops 45% on the news, it will be *my* face that has the egg on it, *my* fingers that will have to dial to apologize, and *my* reputation that will have been damaged. You'll be gone, off to your next conquest, but I'll be stuck with this piece of shit."

"I'll talk to David," Claus had snarled, leaving and slamming the door behind him. Will had looked at his calendar. In six weeks he'd get his banking bonus and in 10 weeks BC Holdings would buy EFS and his restricted stock and options would vest. Then he'd be gone. Yet, even with job offers in hand from Goldman, Lehman and Salomon Smith Barney, Will couldn't sleep. He pulled his feet up on the sofa, put HBO on low, and listened to *The Bridges of Madison County* with his eyes closed. Maybe, he thought, the softness of Meryl Streep's voice would help. Within 20 minutes, it did.

* * *

"I'm Mr. Denisovich and I have an appointment with Francois de Rousseau," Nick told the receptionist.

"At what time?"

"At 11:00."

"Please wait," the receptionist said, pointing Nick towards one of the Louis XV originals sitting on the real Aubusson carpet in the waiting room. "Let me tell him you've arrived."

But as she picked up her phone, her second line began to ring, and she answered it. "Pictet et Cie, *bonjour*."

Nick sat and listened as the receptionist spoke in rapid-fire French to the mystery caller. Then she called Francois de Rousseau and, after listening three times and whispering twice, escorted Nick to one of Pictet's private conference rooms where he drank black coffee, nibbled on little breakfast cakes and opened his attaché while waiting for his private banker to arrive.

* * *

As Nick waited, one time zone to the west, Robin Lomax, having slept soundly at London's Dorchester

Hotel, prepared for her first client meeting. She'd showered and dressed and was skimming the morning papers when her cell phone rang.

"It's Robin."

"Robin, hi, it's Nelson." Nelson Yule ran aggressive money at a hedge fund called Eastport Capital Management. Robin had met him two years earlier on a marketing trip. He'd become a good client of hers and he'd always made a point of showing her a Xerox copy of the *II* ballot he'd submitted with her name written in as number one in her category. Robin liked that, and she liked Nelson.

"Nelson! How are you?"

"Wonderful, wonderful. Did I call at a bad time?"

"No, but I'm in London and I'm about to go into a client meeting."

"Do you have 60 seconds?"

"Always. What's up?"

"Listen, Robin, I hate to impose but I need a favor from you."

"What?"

"I've had a touch-and-go year and I'm under the market by a half of one percent. I've never underperformed the market since opening shop in 1992. I need your help."

"What can I do?" asked Robin warily.

"Just this, love, if you can. I'm up to my eyeballs in Polo, and you're the axe on Polo. You won't admit it but you are." Robin just listened.

"I need you to push it hard between now and year end. The difference between $25 and $28 could be the difference between me beating the market and lagging it. You still love it, don't you?"

"It's rated Accumulate and my target price is $30."

"Any chance you could you raise your target price or go to a Buy on it?"

Robin began to squirm.

"I don't know, Nelson, I'd need to raise my earnings estimates in all likelihood."

There was an uncomfortable silence between them that Nelson finally broke. "Listen, Robin, I don't want to keep you from your client meeting, and I definitely don't want you to feel pressured over this."

"I know," said Robin, who was not at all sure she believed him.

"It's just that, if you *were* inclined in such a direction, the difference between doing it in late December and early January could be very, very substantial to me."

"I understand, Nelson. Let me see what I can do."

After hanging up with Robin, Nelson Yule dialed Dana Telsey at Bear Stearns. He was sure she'd say no, but The Gap was an even bigger holding for him than Ralph Lauren was, and he just had to try.

* * *

My timing is perfect, Nick thought as he shook hands with Monsieur de Rousseau and wished him good day. It was just after 11:30 A.M., and British Air's flight #727 from Geneva to JFK was scheduled to depart at 1:25. With no luggage to check, Nick could get to the airport as late as 12:15 and still be home by 7:30.

" *Au revoir, monsieur,* " said the receptionist with a smile.

" *Au revoir, madame.* "

Nick could see the private car service that Rousseau had arranged for him right out front. As Nick exited

Pictet, the driver jumped out of the car and ran around to open Nick's door.

"The airport, please."

"My pleasure, *monsieur*."

En route to the British Air terminal, Nick reached into his attache case and pulled out an 8" x 11" grey envelope with "Pictet & Cie, Founded 1805" and its address in the upper lefthand corner. Inside were a half-dozen sheets of heavy, white Pictet stationery, the first of which had Nick's name and the date on it. Underneath was his newly updated financial statement that included entries dating back three years. While everything had looked as it should have during his meeting with Rousseau, Nick couldn't resist the urge to triple-check the numbers.

First, Nick looked under Recent Activity and saw that, indeed, he'd been credited with a $550,000 (U.S.) deposit that morning. Then he checked his balance... $15,167,034.75.

For $2,167,034.75 he thanked David Meadows and EFS.

And for $13,000,000 Nick thanked Piotr.

* * *

The day after Christmas, always one of the slowest days of the year, Robin Lomax went to the Morning Meeting, said she believed that Ralph Lauren had enjoyed a stronger finish to the Christmas selling season than she and others had anticipated, raised her earnings estimate by a nickel, raised her target price by 10% to $32, and raised her rating on Polo Ralph Lauren from Accumulate to Buy.

With trading as thin as it was that day, it didn't take many buyers to push the stock higher and, with a dearth of other news to report, CNBC mentioned the upgrade four times that morning and interviewed Robin once. The stock finished at $27.50, up $2.50 on the day, on very low volume.

Three days later, Nelson Yule was relieved to find that, no thanks to Dana Telsey, who had blown him off in disgust, he'd beaten the market for the year by two-tenths of one percent.

JANUARY

The new year began inauspiciously for David with a call from an angry broker.

"David," the voice snarled, "this is Richard Raman. I'm a President's Club member. You and I have spoken before."

"Hi, Richard."

"David, I've counted to 10 a bunch of times before placing this call, but I'm up over 100 now and I'm sick and fucking tired of counting."

David decided just to listen.

"I'm calling about Martin Hogue. Have you seen his latest report on QLogic?"

"No, I haven't."

"Well, it's remarkable for at least two reasons. First, as I'm sure you know, Martin has had a Buy rating on QLogic for quite some time, and he still does. But suddenly, last week, he decided to cut his target price on the stock from $70 to $40. Not a rounding error, I'm sure you'd agree."

"Agreed."

"And then, for reasons that only you may understand, there's no reference to this target price reduction on the cover of the report. There *is* a sentence on page four of the report that references the $40 target price and the reiteration of the Buy rating, but there isn't even a *hint* that the target price has been reduced, let alone cut in half."

"Not good," David admitted.

"Pardon me for asking, David, but how do you let this stuff go out?"

"Richard, we publish 30,000 pages of research every year. I hope you don't think that I personally read every page of it before it's published because I can't and I don't. That's what Supervisory Analysts and editors are for. But someone should have caught this. Give me your number, let me do a little research and I'll circle back to you."

"Fair enough." Richard left his number and expressed his appreciation.

"Lisa," David called, "if Martin Hogue is around, ask him to come see me for a minute and to bring his most recent QLogic report with him, please."

Target prices, the prices at which analysts expect their stocks to sell 12–18 months out, remained a sticky problem for David. While they are usually ignored by institutional investors who use their own sophisticated valuation models or "black boxes" to determine what stocks are worth, they're relied on heavily by retail brokers and their clients, individual investors. Without them, an analyst with seven Buy-rated stocks would have trouble flagging which of those seven he liked best and which seventh best.

The most serious problem that David faced on this front was getting the analysts to take target prices seriously and to ensure that their rating on each stock and their target price were logically consistent. According to the guidelines that David had created, Buy-rated stocks were supposed to be able to rise in price by at least 20% over the next 12 months in a flat market, while stocks rated Accumulate were expected to rise 10%–20%, stocks rated Hold were likely to be roughly unchanged, and stocks rated Sell were expected to decline in price by 10% or more.

While he waited, David grabbed a copy of Martin's current universe and found that over half of his stocks had ratings and target prices that were inconsistent. The ratings and target prices on semiconductors, because they are so volatile, are tougher to manage than are those of other stocks, but 50% was still too high, much too high. David had warned Martin before about this, but clearly he'd have to warn him again.

Hiding a change in a target price on page 4 of a report was almost as bad as getting the target price wrong. Hiding was the gasoline, misjudging was the fire.

"Were you looking for me?" Martin asked, poking his head in.

"Martin, come in." David could see the report in his hand. Martin was 52, grey, and long past his prime, if he'd ever had a prime.

"Is that QLogic?"

Martin handed it to David, who looked quickly at page 4. Raman was right.

"Martin, I'm getting complaints from brokers about the huge cut in your target price and the fact that it's hidden on page 4 of the report. I have to tell you...I understand where they're coming from."

"I wouldn't say it's hidden, David, but I'll admit that I didn't make a point of calling attention to it on the cover."

"Martin, it's on the last page of a four-page report, and the target price is merely stated as being $40. There's no reference to the old target price of $70 at all!"

"Well, I'm sure you can understand that a change

of that magnitude is something you'd prefer to downplay," Martin said sheepishly.

"Why did you have to cut the target price so drastically? It doesn't look as if you changed your earnings estimates very much."

"Well, the stock had plunged from $55 to $25 before bouncing back a little and it just didn't make sense to use a $70 target price on a $30 stock."

David could feel his belly knotting. "How did you get to $70 in the first place?"

"Well, QLogic is a great company. It has a highly diversified product line, it's well positioned in storage area networks and it's going to be a big beneficiary when storage spending recovers. When the stock was at $55, I needed to use $70 as the target price because I wanted to keep my Buy rating on the stock and any lower target price would have forced me to use Accumulate instead."

"Wait a minute, wait a minute. You picked a target price that suggested enough appreciation potential to justify a Buy rating?"

"That's right. If I'd used $65, I'd have gotten a note from you saying there was less than 20% upside potential from $55 and that the Buy rating was inconsistent with that so I used $70 instead."

"How on earth can you do that, Martin? You're treating the rating as the chicken and the target price as the egg. You're deciding first that you want to have a Buy on the stock and then you're arbitrarily picking a target price that justifies that rating?"

"Well, I wouldn't say it's arbitrary, but you're right about the order of things."

"What happened to Securities Analysis 101, in which an analyst first determines what a stock is worth or where it should sell at some point in the future and then rates it based on how much upside potential or downside risk it appears to have?"

"It doesn't work that way in semiconductors, David."

"Why?"

"Because they're just too volatile. You can't be a purist. You can't know with any precision at all what the earnings will be or where the stock will be selling. All you can do is identify the relative appeal of each stock and use your ratings to steer investors towards certain names and away from others."

"I don't buy it and I think your clients would be very surprised to learn that that's your methodology."

"Not true. They know it and they understand it. Only Retail doesn't understand it and that's because they don't know anything about semiconductor stocks."

"Martin, half your universe has ratings and target prices that don't make sense. You've got Buy-rated stocks with target prices that are below where those stocks are now selling, Hold-rated stocks with target prices that are 50% above where those stocks are now selling, and Accumulates with 75% appreciation potential that should be Buys. What on earth is going on here?"

"David, David... the Buys that are above their target prices were up 25% last week. How many analysts in the department have stocks that can move 25% in five trading sessions? I know I've got to raise the target prices on them and I will. The Accumulates and Holds with 50%–75% upside can't be rated Buy because they're too risky. They're not suitable for most investors and I don't want us to burn anyone."

"That's not how the rating system works, Martin. You can't take a stock selling at $50 and tell me that, in your best judgment, it will be selling for $80 a year from now but that no one should buy it because it's risky. That stock is a Buy, and it should be flagged as high risk or suitable only for risk-tolerant investors. It's not a Hold."

Stalemate. Silence.

"Martin, when we did your review, I told you three things about this: first, that your stock picking had been terrible of late; second, that you had the highest number of mismatched ratings and target prices in the department and that it had to stop; and third, that those mismatches were going to hurt your next bonus, and not inconsequentially. I don't know how much clearer I can be with you. I don't like the way you're picking your target prices, that you're hiding the fact that you were wrong on the last page of your reports, and that you're unwilling to incorporate EFS's ratings system into your work on the semis. What I *would* like, though, is for you to go back to your office and rework all of your ratings and target prices, and then to come back to me when you're done so we can discuss them."

"Will do," said Martin, quietly.

As he left, David made a note to talk to his head of Editorial and his overseer of the Supervisory Analysts about letting this kind of nonsense fall through the cracks, and he thought about one other aspect of the target price problem that he still hadn't solved. Some of his worst stock pickers and worst target price abusers were his *II*-ranked analysts and his almost-ranked analysts and, as they were all under contract, with compensation guarantees, there was absolutely nothing he could do to punish them.

* * *

Carl had asked David to come see him at 11:00 the following morning, but when David arrived he was surprised to find Billy Lynch sitting in Carl's office, looking very relaxed and joking with Carl about something.

"Grab a chair," Carl instructed, and David took one next to Billy.

"How's business, Billy?" David asked.

"Slow, slower than it should be."

"David, the reason I asked you to come up was that Billy has been talking with me over the past week or so about a couple of ideas he has for ways in which to get the analysts to help him do more business and I thought he should share them with you."

"Sounds good," David said distractedly. It's always the analysts' fault, he thought.

"Billy, why don't you tell David what you told me?"

Billy swung his chair farther towards David. "David, what I was telling Carl is that, as far as most of my traders are concerned, the analysts don't spend nearly enough time on the trading desk, they don't spend nearly enough time talking to the traders and, in many cases, they don't even know who their traders are. I don't sense a high level of comfort between the analysts and the traders. They should be working hand-and-glove and they're not."

David was going to protest but he opted instead to wait.

"The young ones in particular seem clueless. They just don't know what traders want or how to give traders what they need. They don't understand what traders do."

Here it comes, David surmised.

"So, what I proposed to Carl was two things. First, we thought it would be a good idea if you required all of your younger analysts to spend a full day sitting on the trading floor with the traders and learning about trading by watching them work close-up."

"We'd have each of them sit with his block trader for a half day and with several OTC traders for the other half of the day," Carl added.

"Sounds fine to me."

"And second, we thought you should require every analyst to take his traders out for drinks and dinner during the first half of this year. That way, they'd get to know each other better and figure out ways to work better together, away from the office and while the markets were closed."

"I wish we had talked about this sooner. We could have folded it into everyone's first-half business plans."

"It's not too late," said Carl, always the one to minimize the amount of work someone else had to do.

"It's not, but it would have been easier. Anyway, I can ask the analysts to do this, but I'll need someone on your side to come up with the invitation lists."

"Why can't you do it?" Carl asked.

"Because, as the analysts always complain, they've each got one trader for their NYSE-listed stocks but, when it comes to their NASDAQ stocks, they've each got five or seven or 10 or 12 different traders. Even worse, according to the analysts, you two change the OTC traders' assignments constantly so the analysts never really know whom to talk to on their OTC names."

"That's bullshit," said Billy.

"That *is* bullshit," said Carl.

"Maybe it's an exaggeration," David backpedaled,

"but you know full well that you split trading responsibilities for a particular industry among several traders rather than giving the group to one guy."

"That's right. You have to do it that way," said Billy. "Otherwise, when a group is hot, you have one guy who is totally overwhelmed."

"I'm not questioning the strategy. I'm merely saying that it creates uncertainties in the analysts' minds."

"Which is all the more reason why we should get these assholes out together," Carl bellowed. For a little guy, Carl could pack a verbal wallop when he wanted to.

"I'm fine with it, Carl. I just need someone who knows all the traders and their current assignments to assemble the invitation list."

"I'll take care of it," Billy volunteered.

Carl turned to Billy and, without missing a beat, changed the subject. "So this hippie is hitchhiking through Alabama and he gets picked up by this tough-looking red neck truck driver. They're sitting there together, driving along, not saying anything. So after an hour, the kid looks at the truck driver and says, 'So, mister, don't yuh wanna know?' And the truck driver looks at the kid, dumbfounded, and says, 'Know what?' And the kid says, 'If I'm a guy or a girl.' And the truck driver laughs and says, 'Don't matter none 'cause you're gettin' it in the ass either way.'"

Billy burst out laughing.

"Are we done?" David asked.

"You're done," Carl said. "Billy, you stick around though. I've got more."

* * *

It was, for sure, a Kodak moment.

Gathered around a table in one of EFS's private dining rooms on the 74th floor were six of David's favorite headhunters: Larry Fraser, Richard Lipstein, Bob Taylor, Dave Hart, Les Carter and Julia Harris. While Richard worked at Gilbert Tweed and Julia was ensconced at The Whitney Group, Larry, Bob, Dave and Les had all started their own firms.

"I don't need to introduce you to each other, do I?" David asked rhetorically. Everyone laughed. They were archrivals, and they weren't necessarily crazy about each other, but they were also professionals so they were courteous and civil. As David was their client, they aimed to please him. If he wanted to meet with them as a group, they'd meet as a group. David shook hands with each of his guests, thanked Julia for not being another white male, and invited everyone to sit and order lunch. Once the formalities were out of the way, he launched into the business at hand.

"The reason I asked all of you to lunch with me today is that I've been given a mandate from our new parent that I will need your help in fulfilling." Notepads were out. "Nothing can be done officially until the deal closes, which should be at the end of February, but we all know that recruiting takes months and months of hard work and that almost every analyst on The Street is going to sit tight until year-end bonuses are distributed so we're not going to hire anyone before the end of February anyway."

Everyone nodded.

"The mandate, simply put, is to turn EFS, or whatever we'll be called after the merger is completed, into an *II* top-5 research organization, and to do it in the 17 months between March 1st of this year and August 1st of next year."

"Why August 1st?" Bob Taylor asked.

"Because that's about when the *II* job-hoppers' deadline always is. Any progress we make after that deadline won't be reflected in that year's All Star Team so we have to hire as many good All Stars as we can by August 1st of this year, and then make a second big push that would end around August 1st of next year."

"That timing is right," said Les Carter.

"There are several reasons why you're all here together. First, it's much easier for me to go through this once than six times. Second, it eliminates the risk that I inadvertently tell some of you certain things and others of you other things. You'll all get exactly the same message at the same time. Third, and perhaps most important, you're all going to get more than enough business to keep you happy and that means that I want in-house competition among you to be eliminated. We have to work as a team here if we're going to succeed and that means that if you, Julia, stumble upon someone, or some information, that Larry could use, I'm going to expect you to tell Larry, and vice versa. I need 100% cooperation on this. Are you with me?"

Six heads nodded in unison.

"The economics are going to be identical for each of you so none of you can feel resentful that someone else at the table cut a better deal. We'll pay you a mutually agreed-upon percentage of first-year comp for each candidate you help us land, subject to a cap which we'll all agree on. If one of you can't work at the rate with which the other five are peaceful, you'll force me to find a different sixth player."

"I'm sure we can find a scheme that works for everyone," said Les.

"I am too. We'll also ask each of you to agree not to recruit any EFS analysts between now and two years after this assignment ends," David added.

"Are you going to call any candidates directly?" Dave Hart asked.

"Probably not. I know that some ranked analysts prefer being called by Research Directors but I'm going to have you do most of the initial screening because it'll be faster and more discreet. You can just tell candidates when they ask why I'm not calling them directly that I'm worried that my name is too well-known inside the walls of their fine organizations and that I don't want to embarrass them by having their bosses discover early on that David Meadows has left them messages. They'll understand and some of them will actually appreciate it."

"How many analysts do you want to hire?" Richard Lipstein asked.

"In round numbers, 30. I will give each of you five searches. I have almost 30 holes in the department and I have a few badly performing analysts who can be upgraded. I will tell them in advance that we're recruiting in their space because I've never believed in recruiting behind my analysts' backs and that has served me well over time. It fosters the kind of trust that many of them complained that they lacked in their old bosses. So, no secrets here."

"Realistically, David," said Julia Harris, "we're not going to be able to land an All Star in every category for you, no matter how hard we try. In some categories there are only three ranked analysts."

"That's right. If I give you 30 searches, you may turn up 15 to 20 All Stars for me, maybe a few more if we're really lucky. But if I need 37 more All Stars to get to top-5, I'll also have to get some by pushing my almost-ranked analysts over the finish line. That will be my job. The fresh blood will be yours."

"Are you going to talk about aspiring to be top-five publicly?" Julia asked.

"Probably. I'm less interested in covering my ass than in succeeding, and it will be important for candidates we're recruiting to understand that we're not looking to add a half dozen ranked analysts to a base of five and then call it quits. They have to believe that we're shooting to look like Merrill and Morgan and Goldman, at least rankings-wise. So, yes, I think it'll come out in the press at some point that we're aspiring to become a top-5 player in the U.S. research ranks."

Lunch arrived, and David drank a lot of water. His throat was dry and his voice was hoarse.

"What I'd also like to do today, though, is brainstorm with all of you a little about strategies we might employ and obstacles that we should expect to encounter, and about particular industries or sectors in which each of you has been active and has expertise I can tap."

"With respect to strategy, David," Larry Fraser said, "we need to find and hit hard the analysts at the good firms who got shafted on their bonuses, did no banking last year but wanted to, did too much banking last year and now want to do less, want global counterparts but don't have them, and want to be under contract for the next two years."

"We will probably have to pay materially above the market initially," said Julia.

"At least for the first half dozen to dozen hires," David agreed, "but if we're successful, the battle pay for the fifteenth hire should be far less than for the first."

"That's correct," Larry confirmed, "but I'd also recommend putting our five now-ranked analysts under new, much higher contracts so they don't feel jealous when stories start swirling about new hires coming in at much higher compensation levels."

"Good point." David had already realized that.

With lunch plates cleaned and coffee (but no dessert) ordered, David turned to his last goal. "Let's run through the areas in which I'd want to recruit, and tell me who's been active where and who'd be interested in focusing where."

"Everywhere," said Les.

"Just for that, Les, you get the coal industry search!" David threatened with a smile. No one else said a word, but everyone readied to take notes.

"Where do I have holes? In electrical equipment and packaging, and I'd consider upgrading in chemicals and multi-industry. I have no one doing cosmetics and household products, food, gaming and lodging, leisure, restaurants, hardlines retailing, textiles/apparel/footwear and tobacco. I'd also consider upgrading in autos and auto parts. In energy, I need Ron Barone or someone else in natural gas if we can't get him. In financial services, I have holes in brokers and asset managers, and in life insurance, and I might be willing to upgrade in property/casualty insurance.

"In health care, I need a specialty pharmaceuticals analyst. In technology I need someone to do contract manufacturing, imaging, PC hardware and Internet. I would also upgrade in semis. In telecom and media, I have no one doing data networking and wireline equipment. In transportation, I have a hole in airfreight, and in other areas I could use someone in small caps but I'm sure Linda won't let me hire anyone, and I have no coverage at all in accounting, converts, derivatives, quant (which Linda will also claim she's doing), technical analysis and Washington research.

"So, who knows what?"

"I'll do whatever you want me to," said Larry.

"Ohhhhhhhhhhhhhhhh," his fellow recruiters whispered, giving Larry their best "you're such a Goody Two-Shoes" looks and clapping softly.

"I know Consumer well," said Richard.

"We know Financial Services well," said Bob.

"I've done a lot in Energy," Dave Hart volunteered.

"I know everyone in Technology," Les said humbly.

"I'll do whatever you'd like," said Julia.

"Okay then." David looked around the table. "Are we ready to do this?" Six heads nodded again in unison. "I've got some homework to do. Then we'll reconvene. In the meantime, this must be our secret."

"When can we start?" Bob asked.

"Soon, Bob, soon."

* * *

Two mornings later, after the Morning Call, David was grabbed outside Lisa's office by Jim Molloy, his head of Compliance. "Got a second?"

"Of course." David was relieved. He knew Jim's "we've got a problem" look and didn't see it. Jim walked into his office and David followed, closing the door behind him. They both grabbed chairs by Jim's coffee table.

"What?"

"George Schuler came to see me last night. It seems that a friend of his co-founded a small software company in Palo Alto that's developing pretty nicely and that's out raising a round of private money at the moment. This friend offered George the chance to buy 100,000 shares at $1 each and George wants to do it."

"What's the company?"

"It's Saruman Software. Saruman, I'm told, is a character in Tolkien's *Lord of the Rings,* which the other co-founder is a big fan of."

"Like Gandalf Genomics," said David with a smile. "Is this the kind of company that George would follow if it ever went public?"

"I asked him about that and he said it could be but might not be. It seems to make add-on software that's used in Palms, Blackberries and other handheld devices, so it's definitely software, and it certainly isn't enterprise software."

"Why did he say not necessarily?"

"Because it would probably be too small for him to cover, at least at EFS."

"They're not planning to come public next week and generate a juicy six-day profit for him, are they?"

"No. I asked him that too and he showed me the offering materials indicating that the company did not, at this time, intend to come public over the next 12 months."

"We've let other analysts do this from time to time, haven't we?"

"I think we've done it four times before and, as far as I can recall, none of those companies ever went public."

"Is there any reason you can think of to deny him?"

"No. He can update us quarterly, and we can watch it, but there's no reason to prohibit him from putting money into it."

"Okay. Do I need to talk with him about this?"

"You know what I know, so only if anything I've told you makes you wary."

"These *all* make me wary, but this one is no worse than the rest." David hesitated for a moment and then refocused on Molloy. "Tell him he's approved."

* * *

"Dieter, it's David."

"David, how are you? What news?"

"Dieter, I had lunch today with some headhunters that I'm going to enlist when it's safe..."

"It's not safe yet."

"I know, but *when* it's safe. Anyway, they suggested that we give our five existing All Stars bigger blocks of restricted stock than all our other analysts so that, when we start paying up for new hires, they don't get jealous."

"Why would they know what we pay new hires?"

"They shouldn't but, somehow, too much of this stuff finds its way into the press or becomes common knowledge in other ways."

"How much more stock?"

"Twice as much."

A long pause followed. "How much money is that?"

"Well, those five analysts are making about $13 million among them, so it would mean an extra $13 million, spread over three years."

"So, if Nancy Natolio is making $3 million now, she'd get $6 million of stock instead of $3 million, and she'd effectively make $5 million a year over the next three years instead of $4 million a year."

"That's correct."

Dieter thought about it in silence and then answered, "No, David. I don't want to do that. Let's take our chances. If one of them quits, we'll deal with it then."

"Then could be too late."

"Could be, but the answer is still no."

* * *

"Four lunches a week, no more. I'd like one lunch a week during which to breathe." David was sitting with Lisa, mapping out his first-half lunch schedule.

"You can do that," Lisa said reassuringly. "I've got you having lunch with two analysts a week all year so that leaves two lunches each week for other people. Who do you want me to schedule?"

"I'm not sure, given all the BC stuff that's going on, but let's start with Katherine. I'm pretty sure she'll be sticking around. Then I'd add you, Matt, Jim Molloy, Heidi…she should be in a private dining room so we can discuss the budget part of the time…Carl, John McLain, Paula, one New York institutional salesperson per week, Mennymore, probably a half-dozen MDs in Banking like Claus Abner and Clayton Kiernan and George Sherva but I'll get you the exact names, Paul Pitcher, a group lunch with several people from the Equity Research marketing desk, and Billy Lynch."

"What about Jennifer?" Jennifer Von Moos, pronounced like "most" without the "t", headed Public Relations.

"Yup. She should be on the list too."

"You're almost up to four days a week now."

"Well, I still need to allow for several lunches with Dieter, I'm sure, so let's put two or three of them in, even though we don't know exactly when they'll be."

"Anyone else?"

"Not that I can think of, but I'm sure we're forgetting people. We'll just add them later."

As Lisa returned to her office to call all of those lunch guests, David realized that, should he have to go traveling to see institutional clients or people in Germany or analysts he wanted to hire who worked outside New York, or for any other reason, he'd have to reschedule the lunch guests he'd be bouncing and thus eat up those fifth lunch hours that he'd reserved for himself.

One, nice, quiet, peaceful lunch each week, during which he could think, during which he could breathe? Out of the question, it seemed, always out of the question.

* * *

"She's an idiot, David!" Linda Logan was screaming. Once again, Robin Lomax was stuck in Linda's claw.

"Why?"

"Did you hear her on the Morning Call today?"

"No."

"Did you know she was going to downgrade Annapurna to a Sell?"

"No."

"Well, she did, and the salespeople hated it!"

"How could you tell?"

"They all called me right after the meeting and told me. They think she's an idiot."

David pulled up a copy of Robin's Morning Meeting handout on Annapurna as he listened to Linda shrieking and scanned it quickly. "She seems to have good reasons for going to a Sell."

"Good reasons! This company's earnings are rising 40% a year, it's got fabulous products, teenagers and outdoorsy twenty something types can't get enough of them, and have you heard, David, that trekking in Nepal is now one of the five most popular 'next destinations' among people who read *Conde Nast Traveler* magazine?"

"No, I haven't," said David sarcastically. "What about the fact that their inventories are too high, or that last quarter was two cents below what most analysts were estimating, or that the company, over the next six months, will go up against quarters in which earnings were up 70% and 80%, year to year, respectively? Those are very tough comparisons."

"They're going to make the numbers, David."

"And what about the fact that the stock is now selling at 55 times earnings?"

"That's cheap for a 40%-growth company!" Linda snapped.

David paused for a minute and then asked, slowly, "And what about all the criticism from you and clients and CNBC about analysts who won't use the 'S' word? Robin thinks the risk of an earnings disappointment is high over the next few quarters. She thinks inventories are too high and that they're vulnerable to markdowns that would pressure margins. She also thinks that, at 55 times earnings, nothing can go wrong without popping a balloon under the stock. If she's right, and they guide the analysts' earnings estimates down over the next quarter or two, this stock could easily drop 25%, maybe more, and that's Sell material in my book."

"Think what you want, David, but you don't know anything about this company or its management or the smart money that's sticking with it. All I'm telling you is what the salespeople are telling me. They *hated* going out with that call. Clients think Robin is an idiot and they told the salespeople so. Just because you're *II*-ranked doesn't mean you're smart."

"It doesn't necessarily mean you're an idiot, either," said David. He hung up and called Herb Hirschorn, the seniormost institutional salesman.

"Tough call, David," Herb critiqued. "I respect the thought process, and we never say Sell enough around here, but this is a very popular stock. The clients who own it have been in it for a long time and have made tons of money in it. They're grateful and they're loyal. And they don't like us 'trashing' it, as one client said." Herb paused and David could hear him keystroking in the background. "It isn't trading yet, but it closed at 57 and the indication is 50 to 52, so it's going to be down 10% on the opening. Clients are going to be even more upset when they start taking their lumps than they were listening to us passing on Robin's downgrade."

"You know, Herb, if Robin is right, the stock is going to 40 to 45, with or without us. Had she kept a Buy on it from 57 to 40, you'd all have nailed her for being bullish all the way down. At least she took a stand. Now she just needs to be right."

"I'm crossing my fingers for her, David. Just keep her off of CNBC on this one. We don't need to be higher profile on Annapurna than we already are."

David hung the phone up, then picked it up again with great urgency and dialed Jennifer Van Moos.

"Has CNBC asked for her?"

"Yes, but we haven't agreed to it yet. I wanted to ask you about it first but I've been in Ed's office all morning."

"Good," David said, relieved. "The answer is no."

* * *

At 11:30 that morning, Ed Koster called. "David, do you know who Patrick Firth is?"

"No, I don't."

"Neither did I until five minutes ago. He's the Chairman and CEO of Annapurna Apparel and he just called me, all in a lather, over us issuing a Sell on him today. Did we?"

"Yes."

"Why?"

"Because Robin Lomax, who has covered Annapurna since it went public and who knows it well, and who, by the way, had a Buy on it from 10 to 57, is now afraid that they're going to have an earnings shortfall over the next six months and that the stock, at 55 times earnings, had nothing built into it to allow for such a shortfall."

"You know how much the stock is down?"

"It's 48, down 9."

"Do you know how much stock Mr. Firth owns?"

"No, and I don't think it matters, but how much?"

"Three million shares."

"So he's had a very bad morning."

"I'd say losing $27 million is having a bad morning."

"You know, Ed, I'm sorry about that, but we don't rate stocks on the basis of how much the CEO is going to make or lose on the recommendation. What else did he say?"

"Not much. Just that he was going to ask the NYSE to investigate reports that he'd received that we were selling his stock short, big-time, yesterday, and that our real motivation was to make $10 million on our trading desk, thanks to Robin's dirty work."

David gulped. He was sure this hadn't happened, but Koster had blind-sided him and the slim chance that Patrick Firth was right made him queasy.

"Oh… and one other thing, David. Did you know that Suzanne Considine had been calling on him?" Suzanne was the MD-level banker who ran the Retail Trade Group.

"No."

"Well apparently she'd been pitching them on a $400 million acquisition and a $300 million convertible bond offering that they would have used to fund most of it."

David knew what was coming.

"According to Mr. Firth, his board was expected to approve both of these transactions next week, as well as the hiring of EFS to handle them."

"And we're fired."

"Oh, we're fired all right. We're 'fired for life.'"

"Does Suzanne know?"

"I have no idea. I understand she's on vacation in the Caribbean."

"Well," David sighed, "I'm sorry that we lost that business, but this is what happens when an analyst is on the right side of the Chinese Wall."

"Find out more about what happened, exactly, will you, and then call me back?"

"Will do."

* * *

"Tough day?"

"Not pleasant," Robin answered. She'd been out for some fresh air when David first called her, and it wasn't until 1:10 P.M. that they connected telephonically.

"Who's unhappy?" David asked.

"Who isn't? The Investor Relations guy at Annapurna has been all over me. I think he's afraid he's going to lose his job over this. He said Pat Firth was going to call Ed Koster."

"He did."

"Great. I called 18 institutional clients who were holders of the stock to go through my analysis with them. Two were supportive. Of the remaining 16, and I kept a record of this, six were cool and noncommital, and seven were argumentative and angry."

"That's only 13." David looked at his PC. Annapurna was 46, down 11.

"Oh yeah. Two of the last three made a point of telling me that I could kiss my *II* vote from them goodbye, and the third told me never to call him again on anything other than news that I was leaving the business, preferably involuntarily."

"Nice to know who your friends are."

"Yup. I've got Paul Pitcher and the marketing desk guys up in arms. They've been swamped with calls from unhappy brokers including some who, I guess, bought the stock as recently as last week and can't believe that I could go from Buy to Sell 'out of the blue' like this. They don't understand that one day you can come upon key information that you were lacking the day before and that forces you to change your mind about a stock. They don't want logic any way. They want to give their clients their money back."

"I love that one," David mused. "If only I could remember the last time we called up clients and asked them to share with us the profits that they'd made on one of our recommendations."

"I know. If the recommendation works, the brokers

and the clients are geniuses. If the recommendation doesn't work, we refund the clients' money. Great system."

"Did you alert Suzanne that this was coming?"

"I told her before she went on vacation that I was getting worried about the P/E on the stock and about how tough their comparisons were going to be over the next two quarters. She didn't agree with me, but then she's always upbeat on Annapurna."

"Did you know she'd been calling on them?"

"She said she'd been out pitching to them but she didn't say anything else and I didn't ask. I figured when I needed to know she'd bring me over The Wall."

"Do you think she sensed that you were close to pulling the plug?"

"Not really, because I wasn't, but when the 'spot checks' that I always do indicated some slowdown in their sales over the past few weeks, and with the bulge in inventories and the spike in the stock from 50 to 57 last week, I just felt I had to do it."

"But did you tell Suzanne last night that you were going to do it this morning?"

"First I checked with Compliance and they said no problem, which told me that we had no mandate from Annapurna to do any banking business for them. So, I assumed that nothing was imminent on that front. When I tried to reach Suzanne, her assistant said she was on a catamaran in the Caribbean and that she'd try to get her on her cell or leave her a message if no one answered."

"Which she did." David had checked. "Last night."

"Has anyone heard from her?"

"I haven't, but I'm sure I will because, as things turned out, she'd pitched them on M&A business and a convertible offering that would've made the firm between $5 million and $10 million, and Mr. Firth fired us today when he spoke to Ed."

Robin was quiet for minute. Then, in almost a whisper she said, "Management is going to cut me off cold, my clients are furious with me, Retail wants to kill me, $10 million of banking fees are up in smoke, and the stock opened down so much that no one could get out anywhere near 57 even if they'd wanted to."

"You did the right thing, Robin."

"I should've gone to Hold."

* * *

"She should be fired." So spoke Suzanne after she'd stopped in St. Bart's, replaced the cell phone that had slipped overboard while she'd snorkeled at sunset the night before, and called her office and learned the terrible news. It was now 1:45.

"Why didn't you bring her over The Wall?" David asked.

"We didn't have the mandate yet, and she'd given me no reason to think that she was going to go from Buy to Sell on the stock while I was away. If she'd called the boat to tell me that she was going to cut her rating from Buy to Accumulate on a price basis, it wouldn't have surprised me and, deep down, I wouldn't have disagreed with her. But from Buy to Sell? David, this is the height of unprofessionalism, and it's why life as a banker at EFS is so unbearable. It's a nightmare," she said, "but one from which EFS bankers never awaken."

* * *

David heard Michelle Caruso-Cabrera say, around 2:15, that Annapurna was continuing to trade sharply lower at 48, down 9 points, on the downgrade to Sell by EFS, that despite repeated requests, EFS analyst Robin Lomax was not being made available for interviews, and that Annapurna CEO Patrick Firth would be interviewed live by Michelle at 2:35 P.M. David called Carl, Ed Koster and Jennifer Van Moos to let them know and then busied himself with odds and ends until the appointed hour.

"With us now," said Michelle at 2:35 sharp, "is Patrick Firth, Chairman and CEO of Annapurna Apparel, whose stock has been hammered today following a Sell rating issued by EFS analyst Robin Lomax. Mr. Firth, nice to have you with us on what I know must be a difficult day for you."

"Thank you for having me, Michelle," said an obviously weary and stressed Patrick Firth.

"So let me ask you straight away, is EFS justified in recommending the sale of Annapurna's stock?"

"Michelle, let me be as direct with you as I can. We came public at $10 a share four years ago. We'd increased almost sixfold in price since the offering. We've had consistent earnings growth in excess of 50% per year throughout the period, and we've never missed a quarter."

"What about last quarter, when you missed by $0.02?" Michelle interrupted.

"We didn't miss at all last quarter. The First Call consensus was $0.16, and we reported $0.16. Only EFS was at $0.18 and we'd warned Robin she was too high."

Michelle knew this wasn't true, that the First Call consensus had indeed been $0.18, but she also knew she had a lot of ground to cover in 75 seconds and that she couldn't allow herself to get bogged down on this one point.

"What about your inventories, Mr. Firth? Is it true that sales have been below plan recently and that your inventories are rising?"

"Not true, Michelle, not true. Our sales are fine and our inventories are fine. We're anticipating no material increase in markdowns and no margin pressure, this quarter or next."

"What about the very difficult comparisons you're up against, Mr. Firth? Your earnings were up very sharply in the first half of last year."

"They were, Michelle, but we're right on plan, as I said before."

"EFS is saying that your guidance for the January and April quarters of $0.30 and $0.08 could be too high. What do you say to that?"

"We say that's baloney. We'll do $0.30 this quarter and more than $0.08 in April. Obviously, we do much more business in the October and January quarters than we do in April and July, but that's true of all outdoor apparel retailers."

"And you're still comfortable with full-year guidance of $1.00 to $1.10 for this year?"

"I am, Michelle."

"So, Mr. Firth, let me ask you, if your sales are on plan and your inventories are all right and your earnings guidance hasn't changed, why is EFS out recommending that your stock be sold today?"

"I was hoping you'd tell me, Michelle, 'cause I sure as Hell don't understand it. It seems to me that this analyst is just trying to make a name for herself. We've got Buy recommendations from 12 other analysts who follow us. I guess if you want to call attention to yourself, and you're one of 13 analysts with a Buy on Annapurna, the best way to do it is to go to a Sell, but it's an extraordinarily irresponsible thing to do if you ask me, and I hope your viewers will see it clearly for what it is."

Michelle thanked Patrick Firth, indicated that CNBC would continue pushing for an interview with Robin Lomax, and then went to a commercial break.

David called Jennifer. "The answer is still no and it's not going to change."

* * *

Too bad it was January. The sun had set early and it was cold outside, but that didn't bother Ken Lavery as much as it could have. True, he would have preferred to have been sitting, parked in his new dark blue Bentley Azure, in the warm sunlight of summer, with the top down rather than up, but everything in life couldn't always be exactly the way you wanted it to be, and this was close enough.

As hundreds of people who had toiled all day inside 3 New York Plaza made their way through the revolving doors, out on to the sidewalk and towards their subway stations or express bus stops, Ken sat with the heater on, listening to Vivaldi's *Four Seasons* and pretending that he was waiting to pick someone up after work. The dual thermometers told him that it was 9 degrees outside and 71 degrees inside. Cranking the heat up had enabled him to roll down his window so that, without freezing, he could see and be seen most clearly.

Strange, beautiful women in long fur coats stopped and stared at him... blondes, redheads and brunettes. Those who knew a Bentley when they saw one paid him the most attention. Some looked like models. All must have wondered who he was.

Did you see my movie? he imagined asking them. Did you come to my concert? Did you like my fielding at Yankee Stadium? Did you like the suits I modeled in *GQ* last month?

What a tickle. "I'm no movie star," Ken said out loud. "I'm no rock star. I'm no Yankee and I'm no model. All I am is a little old biotechnology analyst with 100,000 shares of G-NOME that I paid $6.25 for and that are now worth $9, and 100,000 shares of Innovators that I paid $6.25 for and that are now worth $11."

What does that mean, Mr. Lavery? he imagined the fur-coated models cooing.

Why girls, it means that, thanks to my extraordinary selling skills and the gullibility of 150 brokers in and around Boston, Massachusetts, U.S. of A., the $1,250,000 that I invested in those two worthless heaps of genomic junk is now worth $2,000,000, and that $750,000 profit, even after Uncle Sam manhandles me, covers the cost of my $339,800 Bentley Azure that you see right here and a lifetime's supply of gas.

Why, you're a genius! he imagined the fur-coated models whispering.

Maybe you girls would like to see my house in the Hamptons when the weather warms up a little.

Oh, may we? May we?

I think so, thought Ken Lavery. I think I'd like that very much.

* * *

Despite the darkness inside the topless bar that

occupied the basement of an office building across the street from the Ed Sullivan Theater where David Letterman taped each evening, Alexander Volkov was able to see that it was 3:45 P.M. The bar was almost devoid of patrons, and two women "danced" listlessly on stage to a near-deafening rendition of Van Halen's "Panama." Volkov had been wasting time, drinking and ogling. He'd offered to buy one of the dancers her favorite libation when she'd finished her stint on stage but, when she'd tried to squeeze him for $30 for a private dance in one of the back rooms, he'd passed. Maybe for $20 but not more. So the minutes had passed slowly, the music had begun to give him a headache, and he was relieved to find that it was time to place his call.

Upstairs and outside in the cold and near darkness of a New York winter afternoon at 4:00, Volkov walked slowly to the pay phone on the corner of 52nd Street and Broadway, paid his 25 cents and dialed.

"Mr. Denisovich's office."

"Is Nick there?"

Linda's eyes were glued to her PC monitor, watching the final trades of the day in the three stocks she owned.

"May I say who's calling?"

"Jim from the FT office."

"Please hold." Volkov checked his watch again. He was two minutes early but he doubted that would make a difference. It didn't.

"Denisovich."

"Hi Nick, this is Jim from the FT office. How yuh doing?"

"Very well, Jim, very well, and you?"

"I'm good. You must be busy, but my client wants

to do something in your group. Could you tell me what you're recommending?"

"I'd be glad to," said Nick, closing his door. "We're still basically pretty cautious on most of the gold stocks we cover at this juncture. Demand is relatively stable and so is supply. This has led to a stabilization in gold prices just above $300 an ounce. Our estimate is that gold prices will average around $325 an ounce in 2003, up from $310 in 2002 and $271 in 2001. Our preliminary estimate for 2004 is $335, so the price should trend 3% to 5% higher annually in this environment. Demand ebbs and flows a little bit with the level of economic activity around the world, especially from jewelry manufacturers and electronics companies, but it doesn't change materially from year to year. With no major new mines coming on stream, neither will supply. So, unless we get some much higher level of terrorist activity in the United States or a major, negative financial 'event' of some kind, there's no reason to expect gold prices to move up much from here. Inflation expectations remain relatively low, and I don't see any reason why people should begin fearing a reacceleration of inflation in major financial markets this year.

"So, this is a less than ideal operating environment for most gold companies. They tend to be very capital intensive, they have high fixed costs, and they really need to see gold prices moving up faster than 3% to 5% a year to do well. We don't expect them to, so we're not recommending most of the stocks we cover. We think investors should have only modest exposure to gold at this time."

Nick waited. He knew Volkov wouldn't say anything, but it would be perfectly natural to pause and give a "real" broker a chance to ask a question, so he did. After a moment of silence, he continued.

"The only stock in my group that looks fundamentally interesting to me right now is ASA Ltd., which is a closed-end investment company with substantial holdings of South African and other gold stocks that would move up if the price of the metal moved up. The net asset value of the fund's gold holdings is around $35 a share and any time you can buy the stock at a meaningful discount to net asset value you should. Most recently, ASA has been trading around $30 and, while I don't see it moving up to $40, it could get into the mid-30s, which is enough to justify my Accumulate rating." He paused again.

"Anything else?" Volkov asked.

"Not much," Nick sighed. "Since the Homestake acquisition last year, I've gotten more calls than usual about other takeout candidates in the group, and the economics of the gold business certainly suggest that more consolidation would make sense, but takeovers are very hard to predict and I wouldn't buy Billings, for instance, or any of my other names simply to gamble on a takeover." For the third time, Nick paused.

"Great, Nick. Thanks."

"My pleasure."

When they hung up, Nick opened his Palm Pilot and wrote "Birthday" in his calendar exactly six weeks later.

At 6:00 P.M. that evening, from his Stratolounger behind his triple-locked door on Brighton 5th Street, Volkov dialed Moscow and got "Piotr" on the phone.

"Is Boris there?" he asked.

"No Boris," Piotr told him and hung up.

Anna took another sip from one of the Bellinis

she'd fixed for them and gave the old man a puzzled look. "We're buying Billings Butte?" she asked.

"He's never given us that one before," mused Piotr. "I hope he knows what he's doing."

"Oh stop fretting," Anna scolded. "The way you carry on, you'd never know he's nine for nine."

"Right as always, my love," said Piotr, raising his Bellini glass. "To our next $50 million," he said with a smile and clinked her glass.

* * *

On Friday morning, January 31, a huge stack of year-end bonus checks arrived on Lisa's desk. First she found her own check and tucked it safely in her purse. Then she sorted the rest by type, separating David's and Matt's from those of the senior analysts (who got Research bonuses in April and October but Banking bonuses at year-end), the associate analysts, the research assistants and others, and by location so she could walk around and hand them out most efficiently if asked.

Lisa waited 15 minutes for Matt to emerge from David's office but, when he didn't, she poked her head in and asked David if he wanted to hand out the senior analysts' checks or not.

"I don't think so," David answered after a moment of deliberation. When business was good and the bonuses were high, David liked hand-delivering bonus checks to the analysts because it reminded them of who was paying them or, at least, determining their bonuses, and it made the analysts associate him with something important and very positive in their lives. But when the checks were disappointing, as they'd been most recently, especially for the analysts who lacked employment-contract protection, or when the bonuses were from Banking rather than from Research, David preferred to simply have Lisa e-mail the analysts to come and get them, which she said she'd do.

"They can't go anywhere yet," mused Matt after Lisa had closed David's door.

"Not if they want their stock and options to vest."

"I suppose someone could buy them out," said Matt.

"Theoretically yes, but who on earth would write an analyst a check for $1 million or more if, by simply waiting 30 days for the merger to close, they didn't have to?"

"How many do you think we'll lose?"

"A few," David answered. "None now under contract, but a few who aren't and who wished they had been."

"Early March is going to be very interesting around here," Matt predicted.

"I can wait."

FEBRUARY

Through the grapevine David heard, less than a week later, that all of the necessary regulatory approvals surrounding BC's purchase of EFS had been secured and that the EFS shareholders' meeting would be held at the end of the month.

"Is it safe?" he'd asked Dieter.

"What do you want to do?"

"Give the headhunters their assignments and begin recruiting."

"You'd normally do some recruiting at this time of year anyway, wouldn't you?"

"Yes. The best time to get people is right after they've been paid, especially if the checks were disappointing."

"So this would be business as usual for you."

"Well, the scale is different but the act of going out and looking for people is the same."

"Then it's safe, David, but be discreet about it."

"I will. And Dieter, I need the space you promised me."

"I will get it for you," Dieter said. "I know it doesn't come easily for you, David, but just be patient."

* * *

David reassembled his six headhunters the next

afternoon and gave them their assignments. Of the 30–odd searches that David intended to undertake, 10 or more were in consumer sectors where EFS's coverage was most spotty. "Larry, you take autos and auto parts, cosmetics and personal care products, gaming and lodging, electronic imaging and leisure. Richard, you take food, restaurants, hardlines retailing, textiles/apparel/ footwear, and tobacco."

Dave Hart had asked for energy, but with only one hole to fill there, in natural gas, he also was given the four basic industry searches: electrical equipment, packaging, chemicals and multi-industry stocks. Bob had expressed the greatest interest in financial services, so David gave him brokers and asset managers, life insurance and property casualty insurance, and also threw in the only health care search he needed someone to do, specialty pharmaceuticals. Les had flagged technology, so David gave him contract manufacturing, PC hardware, Internet and, after having resigned himself to replacing Martin Hogue, semis. That left, for Julia, data networking, wireline equipment, satellite communications, airfreight and ground transportation, and the macro searches: accounting, convertibles, quantitative research, derivatives, small caps, technical analysis and Washington research.

"That's a lot to put on one person's plate," Les said innocently. He'd counted 10 searches for Julia versus the five in technology for himself.

"Don't kid yourself," David answered. "Julia will have to deal with Linda on all of the macro searches, and I can guarantee you that Linda will try to kill small caps, quant and technical analysis. So Julia, realistically, I think you've got four plus anything you can do in macro land. Linda will tell you that we need none of those hires and will threaten to quit if we make any of them but, once she's expressed her opinion, you and I will go forward as planned. I just don't want you thinking this is really 10 searches because, unless Linda quits, it isn't."

"Are you signing Linda to a long-term contract?" Larry asked.

"I'm not, but Dieter is going to try to," David said gleefully. "He doesn't have a clue. What I'd give to be a fly on the wall at *those* meetings. Anyway, you can tell candidates that we aspire to become *II* top-5 over the next few years."

"What does few mean?" Les asked.

"Two or three. You should tell candidates that I'll go into as much detail as they want about compensation schemes…you know, stock versus cash and the like, but that, as you understand it, BC will be paying bonuses that are 35%-40% stock and 60%-65% cash. This won't be terribly different from what those analysts are already getting so I don't expect it to be an issue.

"You can tell them we'll be doing two-year deals, no three-year deals, that all contracts will have change of control protection in them, meaning that they'd be paid out in full if we undergo another change of control during their first two years with us that costs them their job, and that the non-competes will preclude them from quitting and joining any competitor of ours during the term of the contract."

"Has anyone tested the enforceability of the non-compete, David?" Larry asked.

"Thank God, no. Why?"

"Because I don't think you'll have an easy time defending it." Five heads flanking Larry's nodded.

"I know," David sighed. "One of these days, someone will test it and the chances are that we'll lose."

"But you're still going to include them?" Julia asked.

"Yes. They do scare some firms away, firms that don't want the messiness of litigation even if they're sure they can win. They also change the mindset of most analysts who sign them. It's as if they make peace with staying put for two years and stop thinking every waking moment about who might call them and how much they might be offered."

"That's the real benefit," Richard suggested.

"I agree." David looked around his office, which was cramped and getting warm. "What else?"

"When do we start?"

"Give me 24 hours. I want to tell Wes Persico that Dave is going to be talking to Wes's fellow multi-industry analysts who don't insist on 'working' at home every Friday, to tell Mitch Potvan and Alan Loparco that Larry is going to be active in autos and auto parts, to tell Martin Hogue that he's no longer safe in semiconductors and, while I dread it, to tell Arthur Litt, with an HR person by my side, that he's at risk in chemicals."

"How old is Arthur?" Dave Hart asked.

"He's almost 56, I think, and he's been at EFS for 26 years. I hope you can find an old All Star for me to replace him with."

"A lot of the chemical guys are older," Hart reassured David. "I think we'll be okay here."

"Do you have someone doing property casualty insurance?" Bob asked.

"John Henriksen. Not terrible, but so pompous and pretentious that it drives people crazy. I've got to talk to him too."

"Do you want to alert Linda that I'll be calling her?" Julia asked.

"No, but I will, and I'll make sure Dieter knows so when Linda has him take her to dinner at Alain Ducasse so she can rail about the idiocy of recruiting in some of these categories, at least he'll be prepared."

No one could think of anything else to cover, so David thanked them and adjourned their meeting.

"Breakfasts rather than dinners, please," he told them as they walked towards the elevators. "I don't want to weigh 800 pounds by the time this is over."

* * *

"David Meadows."

"Hold please, David, for Mr. Koster?" It was Barbara Summerville, Koster's secretary.

After 20 seconds, Koster picked up. "David, do we follow an outfit called Rivington Resources?"

"I don't think so. It doesn't sound familiar."

"Could you look into it for me?"

"Sure. What do you need?"

"David, do you know John Carlton in our Houston office? Chairman's Club, good guy, does four and a half million a year for us."

"Yes I do," answered David, not at all convinced that was true but wanting to sound well-connected to EFS's biggest producers.

"Well, you see, John is very close to the Chairman of Rivington, who has about $25 million of his own money with John, and there's another $15 million of other family money with us, so $40 million all told. And this guy, I think his name is Billy Bob something or other, is pressing John pretty hard for coverage of his company. Now I have no idea whether Rivington is a good company or not, but it seems to me that we have enough analysts around here making untold millions of dollars to get Billy Bob some coverage of his company in return for that $40 million, don't you think?"

"Let me do some research, Ed, and see what I can find. Do you know what they do for a living?"

"I don't know shit about them. All I know is that John Carlton is busting my ass over this and that he and I will be really pissed off if Billy Bob takes his $40 million to Merrill Lynch because we couldn't get an analyst to pay him a little attention."

"Let me look at it, Ed. I'll come right back to you."

"Please." Koster hung up.

Shit, David thought. Probably a piece of crap, probably losing money, probably has a Board of Directors with all of Billy Bob's retarded siblings on it, probably selling for a song and probably followed by no one on The Street with any credibility.

"You're joking, right?" David could hear the analyst to whom he assigned Rivington asking in disbelief.

"Do you want me to tell Koster no on your behalf or do you want to tell him yourself?" he heard himself answering.

David picked up a Stock Guide and began looking for information on Rivington. Not that it mattered. David could never allow himself to be responsible for the loss of a $40 million account, nor would he.

* * *

David's recruiting-breakfast venue of choice was Adrienne, on the second floor in the Peninsula Hotel on 55th Street and 5th Avenue. His table in the back, in the corner, felt like home to him. It was quiet, private and ideal for conversations that shouldn't be heard.

At 7:06 A.M., Kurt Coviello, the imaging technologies analyst at Bear Stearns, arrived. After learning that Kurt, who lived in Rumson, hated working in midtown, and after ordering some breakfast, David got down to work.

"So, did Larry fill you in on what we're interested in doing?"

"Only a little. He said the acquisition by BC Holdings was shaking a lot of things up, and that one of the areas in which BC was going to invest the most was Research. He said you want to be *II* top-5 in two years?"

"Well, within the next two or three years. It may not be possible to get all the way there between now and next October," David hedged.

"That would still be pretty awesome if you could pull it off."

"You're right. It *will* be." David paused before shifting gears. "So you've been at Bear Stearns for three years?"

"That's right. Kay hired me out of Wharton, gave me the imaging group and said, 'Go!' She gave me a lot of support and encouragement, all the resources I needed and a lot of leeway about how to maximize my chances for success."

"And you became successful very quickly!"

"I guess so. I was named to *II's* Next Generation list in my second year and was a Runner-Up in my third year, so that's not bad."

"Not bad at all. What do you like and not like about Bear Stearns?"

"I like a lot of things. Kay is terrific. It's a very

entrepreneurial shop where everyone does what he thinks will help the firm the most. *II* is important. They make that pretty clear. But so is banking and I spend a lot of time on it as well."

"How much time?"

"Maybe 40%?"

"That's pretty high. I'm surprised you were able to make *II* so quickly if you were only spending 60% of your time on research."

"Well, the banking involvement helps me with clients too. I have the inside track at companies I wouldn't be an axe on if we weren't their bankers. I see clients when we do road shows and I have more to talk with them about on the phone. I'm in the flow and clients know it."

"Do you feel pressure from your bankers to pick up companies you don't want to follow or to stay positive on stocks when you want to cut your ratings?"

"There's always an undercurrent of that, but I think that's true at all firms, and Kay really protects us well when the bankers want us to do things that we aren't comfortable with. I like banking, though. It's intellectually stimulating in ways that writing up another 'earnings-in-line' quarter can't be. It also pays well."

"What else is good or bad about Bear Stearns?"

"Well, we've got a great analyst in Tokyo."

"Anyone in Europe?"

"It's not as important. What impacts Kodak is Fuji, and I've got great sources on Fuji thanks to our analyst there. He e-mails me overnight, several times a week, and I do the same for him. We work pretty well together."

"How's your trading desk?"

"It's awesome. Our market shares in many of my stocks are in the top five. Trading is what Bear Stearns was known for before Kay built up the Research Department and before banking became such a lucrative business for us, and we're still huge in trading. I talk to my trader sometimes five times a day. I visit the trading floor every day. I give them what they need. It usually takes 15 seconds. They tell me what they're seeing or hearing. A lot of the time I can't do anything with that information but, once in a while, it really gives me a leg up."

"So it sounds as if you're pretty happy," David sighed.

"On balance, I'd say I'm very happy, and I told Larry that, but he said you should always invest the time when a Research Director wants to meet you, so here I am."

"Are you under contract?"

"No."

"Where are you, comp-wise?"

"I made $2,300,000 last year, which I was disappointed with."

"That's not bad for your third year in the business."

"It's not, but my client vote is higher, I understand, than a number of other analysts in the department who are earning $3,000,000 to $4,000,000, and I shouldn't be punished just because I'm young or haven't been in the business for 10 years."

"So you think you'll clear $3,000,000 this year?" David asked, thinking that it would take $4,000,000 at least to land him.

"I better."

Breakfast was served and David gulped down several bites, knowing that it was Kurt's turn to ask questions and David's turn to do most of the talking. "So what can I tell you about EFS or BC Holdings or me?"

Kurt laughed. "I've heard good things about you, David, from analysts who used to work for you."

"I pay them each a dollar to say something nice but it's money well spent."

"I'm sure you don't need to, so I guess I'm not really worried about you, but I *would* like to know what life is like for analysts in your department, how the BC acquisition might change that, and what reasons you think I might have for changing firms."

"Fair enough. Let's start with everything except money. Obviously, we would try to put something together for you, economically, that would motivate you, but moving just for money is a bad idea and, frankly, I can never hire anyone just for more money. If an analyst I meet is happy, and I offer him more money, he just goes back to his boss who matches the offer or comes close and the analyst stays put. So, what I need to do is try to find non-financial reasons for moving you that make sense and, if I can, couple them with a raise."

"Sounds logical."

"So… life at EFS…I think that, in many ways we're quite similar to Bear Stearns. We have about 40 institutional salespeople and a travel schedule that guarantees that all of our analysts will visit every institutional market at least once a year to see clients. I don't know how we'll manage that as the department gets bigger, but I don't like the idea of allowing the salesmen to play favorites and only use, for instance, the analysts who have 'hot' groups."

"I agree."

"We also have about 5,000 retail brokers, many of whom are very seasoned, very smart and very active in the stocks we're recommending. When one of our analysts speaks on the Morning Call and raises a rating from Hold to Buy, that stock may open up 10% or 15% at 9:30 because those retail brokers push it up. It's a lot of fun being that influential when you're raising your rating or your estimates but it also works in the other direction which can be quite painful."

"Bear Stearns has retail brokers, but nowhere near 5,000. Don't they drive your analysts crazy?"

"No, because we only allow the Chairman's and President's Club members, who are the biggest producers, to call the analysts directly. All the other brokers must work through our Equity Research Marketing Desk, which includes 20 very smart youngsters who act as middlemen between the analysts and most brokers all day long."

"That's a relief."

"On the banking side, until now we've been pretty spotty. We've had analysts who've spent 40% of their time on banking and analysts who spent no time. With the BC acquisition, The Bank will be expanded considerably, in concert with the buildup of Research, and most of our analysts will have much more banking involvement in the future than they've had in recent years."

"Do you let your analysts veto deals that they don't like?"

"Yes. When they don't, it's because they've been seduced by the size of the banking bonus they expect to receive and there isn't much I can do about that."

"You do reviews annually?"

"No, in April and October. It gives the analysts a fresh read every six months on how they're doing, and it gives me a chance every six months to catch problems and work with the analysts on fixing them."

"Are your analysts free to change ratings whenever they want to?"

"Yes. The analysts can change ratings whenever they want to without worrying about anyone overruling them. I always say, you can't judge an analyst's stock-picking skills, and pay him in part on the basis of those skills, if you don't let him rate his stocks the way he wants to." The waiter had cleared the table and was pouring coffee. "What else can I tell you?" David asked.

"I don't really know," Kurt said thoughtfully. "Everything sounds pretty good, but not that different from what I've got at The Bear right now. I probably have better bankers than you have, and better traders. Retail scares me a little, but it sounds as if you've got that under control. I've got the potential to make some money if Bear Stearns is ever sold, which has been rumored for a long time but still not happened, but EFS *has* been sold and I missed my chance there, and I guess I'd be worried that, if BC decided after a year that it didn't want to spend all that money building EFS up and opted instead to sell it, I could be out on the sidewalk. I love Kay, and I love my sales force. They really did right by me. I would never have made *II* this quickly without them."

"So, you're happy" David concluded. He watched Kurt smile. "That's good. Given how many waking hours you spend working, if you can't love your job, you should at least like it."

"I do, David. It's not that I wouldn't love to work for you, and it's probably pretty dumb of me not to play along and pretend I'm interested so I could get a $4 million offer out of you and force Kay to match it, but I just can't bring myself to do that. It wouldn't be fair to you."

"Well that's refreshing."

"So I'll just tell Larry that I enjoyed meeting you

and that, if anything changes at The Bear, I'll certainly call you first. But you'll probably have hired Ben Reitzes by then so the window may be closed."

"You never know," sighed David. "Once it took me five years to hire an analyst I'd had my eye on. It's all about being in the right place at the right time. If I've left you with a good impression, then mission accomplished."

"You have, David. I've enjoyed meeting you." The two rose and shook hands, and Kurt left David at the table awaiting his check.

It's going to be a long 18 months, he told himself. One meal down, 149 to go.

* * *

Up on the 74th floor, David convened his annual "How to Make *II* " meeting with his analysts. David moderated from the podium, his five ranked analysts shared the dais with Matt, and all of the remaining seniors and some curious associates sat in the audience, notebooks in hand.

"It's that time again," David explained. "Not *II* season, but 'getting ready for *II* season,' and that means that each of you should take very specific steps in the weeks ahead to maximize your chances of making the team or moving up in the rankings. I have my own ideas about what you should do, and I'm going to share those with you in a minute, but first I've asked each of our current All Stars to give you a couple of observations about the poll, the process and how he or she got the recognition that all of you crave. Let's do this in reverse alphabetical order, starting with Will and following with Tim, Nancy, Robin and Keith."

"Thanks, David. For me, beyond doing original research and providing a high level of service to my clients, meaning frequent phone calling, one of the keys has been the sales force. I can't tell you how much they can leverage you. If you treat the salesmen well, they'll keep your name in front of clients during May and June when the ballots are sitting on those clients' desks. I've never been comfortable with salesmen who ask clients to vote for particular analysts but I know it's done at other firms and I guess that means that we should do it too. But even if they don't ask for the vote, the salesmen can keep gently reminding clients about what you did for them over the past year, some of your best calls or some disasters you avoided, and that can make the clients think warm, fuzzy things about you when it's time to fill out the ballot. Tim?"

"For me, it's all about client service. I'm pretty good as a stock picker, but I'm not great, and many of my clients do their own stock picking so that skill set doesn't usually help you win votes during *II* season. What *does* help is being all over the clients with worthwhile information on the companies they care about. I'm not talking about calling up with nothing new to say but about creating valid excuses to call clients and calling them constantly in the two months before, and throughout, *II* season. The more you call them, and the more they hear your voice and converse with you, the more they'll associate your name with your industry when they see the *II* ballot. Nancy?"

"I agree with Tim about stock picking. It matters a lot less than people think and, if any of you plan to try to make *II* based on stock picking, God bless you. It's been done but not by many. Most analysts have their fair share of winners and losers each year. We've all heard David talk about aspiring to be right 60% of the time while cutting our losses early when we're wrong, and that's what I try to do. But many analysts on The Street are right 51% to 52% of the time and wrong 48% to 49% of the time, which means that, unless you had a huge winner or an unmitigated disaster, clients probably won't remember you or vote for you on the basis of your stock picks.

"What they will remember, though, is how much truly insightful industry-and company-specific knowledge you shared with them, your ability to tailor your calls to the areas that interested them the most, providing them with access to your managements, inviting them to conferences and, in general, the intensity and professionalism with which you serviced them. Service is what separates All Stars from also-rans. Robin?"

"As the new kid on the block, I don't know all of you well enough to know how valuable my experiences will be to you, but here's what I've found. The Buy Side is awash in reports, phone calls, e-mails, conferences and so forth. It's very hard for analysts on the Buy Side to remember who said what to them and when because there's so much noise out there, so it's important to develop, a few times each year, a clearly non-consensus view on something... anything that will be viewed as controversial and materially different from what your competitors are saying. Just as important is to be right. Taking extreme stands just to make headlines is analytical suicide but working really hard to find a few big calls each year can pay off in spades. Clients remember them and, if you're right on most of those calls, they will associate you with digging, with unique insights and with real value-added, and they'll vote for you on that basis.

"The best way to unearth those calls is by talking with customers and competitors of your companies, suppliers, private companies, trade journal reporters, anyone other than management who can confirm what management is telling you or challenge it. Every truly controversial call I've made has had, at its root, information gleaned in this manner. It's still important to visit your companies regularly, to sit next to management, ask tough questions and watch their body language. Smiling, blushing and twitching all tell you things that you'd never catch by talking to management on the phone. Keith?"

"I guess I'm last but hopefully not least. I've been talking to portfolio managers for more years than I can remember, and I always try to put myself in their shoes when I do. It seems to me that what I *wouldn't* want, as a PM, is endless critiques of just-announced earnings or recent news developments that have been written up in *The Times* and *The Wall Street Journal*. Rather, what could really help me are two other things: the view from 35,000 feet, and deep, deep knowledge about a short list of companies that matter the most to me. That's what I try to do. I try to take time each weekend to think very big picture and very long term, and to provide a context that spans more than the next 90 days for all the work that I do.

"Some Buy Side clients are responsible for 100 companies or more. They can't possibly learn anything in detail about those companies so they count on The Street for the in-depth work. That's what I provide. My job is to know how far over budget each of the films Disney is now producing is running, and why theme park attendance is better on Tuesdays this year than it was a year ago but worse on Thursdays and Fridays. I don't need to follow 15 stocks to be valuable to my clients. I need to follow AOL Time Warner, Disney and Viacom better than anyone else on The Street, and I do."

"Thank you All Stars," David said from the podium. "Obviously there are many different ways to 'make *II*.' There's no one path that everyone must follow, and that's good because you don't all have the same skill set. Some of you are great stock pickers, some service clients exceedingly well, some write great reports and so on. It's my job to help each of you figure out what you're good at and bad at, and how to leverage your strengths in ways that best help our clients make money.

"Trying to make or rise in *II* on the basis of one or two skills is risky business; trying to do three or four things well in the months leading up to voting time makes more sense for most of you.

"You don't have to be a good stock picker to make *II*. As perverse as it sounds, your ability to pick stocks is *not* the key to becoming an All Star. In fact, *some of the highest-ranked analysts in* II *are Wall Street's worst stock pickers*. The top-ranked analyst in any category is most often the one who had the best industry-and company-specific insights, provided the best client service (which means phoning and phoning and phoning), got the best support from his or her sales force and/or wrote the best reports.

"Let's start with written reports. What I'd like each of you to do ASAP is two things. First, think about something especially insightful, topical or, as Robin said, controversial that you can write a report on in March and distribute widely to clients in April, just before the ballots hit their desks. I'm talking about something that will make some waves, something that the media will quote from and something that clients might respond to by saying, 'Thanks, Robin, I really couldn't have done that research myself.' Second, go back and find all of the reports you wrote over the past six months that made you look smart and bring them to Matt who'll have them reprinted, packaged in a snazzy EFS binder and mailed to clients around April 1st. Inside that binder you'll include a letter that doesn't ask specifically for an *II* vote but gently reminds clients about some of your best work over the past two quarters in the hope that they'll look at it, be impressed and become more inclined to vote for you."

"Can we do some nice artwork for the cover of the binder?" asked Mark Noel.

"Yes, as long as it's in good taste." David sensed that the analysts liked this idea. "Next is marketing. Everyone wants to go to visit clients in key *II* -voting markets like New York, Boston and Chicago during April and May. Clients see right through this, especially if you were in Boston in November and now it's April and you're back. But having said that, it's better to be more visible in these key markets during voting season than less. Unfortunately, we can't send the entire department to those cities during those eight weeks, so, I've made sure that the travel schedule will get all ranked analysts and those who were close to making *II* last year into all key *II* territories between February and May, and I will pick up the tab for any travel that the rest of you undertake in key *II* markets that you weren't scheduled for. The catch is that you will have to line up these trips yourself because the salesmen will only focus on the analysts who are on the travel schedule to be in their markets during those months. But that's no big deal. Just call your clients, invite yourself in to see them and then let the salesmen know that you'll be visiting in case they have time to come along."

"Any markets?" asked Matt Burlingame.

"Any markets. Determine where you haven't been in a while, or where you have clients who aren't fully sold on you yet, and schedule trips there yourself in March through May. And remember, once you've scheduled those client visits, to bring along and hand out your 'Am I Not Smart?' research binders.

"Will Rivas mentioned marshaling help from the sales force. We're also going to do two things here, one of which is a necessary evil. First, each of you will tee up with John McLain and Paula a big Morning Meeting call during *II* season that the sales force will use as the excuse to ask clients to vote for you. Hopefully each of you will come up with one special call that the salesmen will go out with, clients will respond positively to and the salesmen will use as the excuse to say, 'I know *II* doesn't mean much to you but it means a lot to Keith and, if you think he's done good work this year, please remember him when the ballots arrive.'"

"Why don't you like this, David?" Keith asked.

"It's a little too aggressive for my blood, but most of our competitors have sales forces that will be doing it and I don't want to place any of you at a competitive disadvantage by being a purist about it.

"Also during March and early April we'll hold a steady stream of 4:15 teach-ins for Institutional Sales where you'll be able to give them fresh material to go out and talk with clients about just before the ballots arrive.

"And I've asked Jennifer Von Moos to work with each of you on a big media push during *II* voting season that would include CNBC, *The Wall Street*

Journal, The New York Times, Fortune, Forbes, Business Week and *Barrons.* Again, think about special reports or big calls that Jennifer can use to get you that extra attention from the media. More visibility, if you have worthwhile things to say, is better than less.

"Finally, please remember this. You can pretend that *II* doesn't exist, and that you don't know it's voting season when it's voting season. You can try to be 'above it all,' assume that good work will get rewarded, and do nothing out of the ordinary during *II* season. But let me warn you… each of your competitors is obsessing right now about how to keep you *off* of *II* this year and, if you don't adopt the same attitude towards them, they'll all be in the magazine in October and you won't.

"Don't let it happen. Matt and I will do everything we can to help you but, at the end of the day, you're either going to do what it takes to make *II* or you aren't. And if I'm going to deliver a top-5 department to BC Holdings within two years, I'm going to need every one of you to be an All Star within the next 18 months. Do we understand each other?"

Everyone in the room nodded.

"Good," David said. "Make it happen."

* * *

"Meadows."

"David, it's Michael Piccardi, manager of Beverly Hills."

"Hi Michael, what's doing?"

"David, I know you're busy and I hate to make calls like this but I wanted to pass on something to you that really upset me and that I thought you should know."

"Shoot."

"Did you know we had one of our regional broker gatherings here last week?"

"I knew it was coming up but I didn't realize it had come and gone already."

"Well, it did. We had about 300 brokers in a ballroom at the Ritz at Laguna Niguel on Thursday and Friday. Big producers, you know, serious guys, very influential in their offices."

"Did one of the analysts fuck up?"

"No, they were great. Steve Kalagian did a nice job on wireless telecom, Laura Payden had a couple of special situations in specialty chemicals that sounded pretty interesting, and Mark Noel did a great job as always on the computer stocks."

"So what went wrong?"

"What went wrong was Linda's Q&A session. She did her normal, big-picture strategy call, which was fine. She was very entertaining as always. The brokers really love her, and she was relatively harmless during her canned spiel. She came down pretty hard on Bruce and his 'always safely in the consensus' economic forecasts but she always does. But what really shocked me was her Q&A session with the brokers. It began when an FA complained about one of Nancy Natolio's disasters in the oil group. Linda said that Nancy was a perfect contrary indicator, that if you had your clients do exactly the opposite of everything Nancy recommended you'd make them very rich."

"Nice," David sighed.

"That's just the beginning. She called Robin Lomax an idiot, said that Arthur Litt was senile and that Martin Hogue should've been fired a long time ago…"

"I bet she got a standing ovation on that one."

"…and some pretty mean things about James Brell, Jackman and Omori."

"Really. I'm surprised."

"She said that Tim Omori typified everything that's wrong with our business, meaning that it's full of analysts who focus exclusively on making *II* and spend far too little time trying to make clients money. She said that most of our All Stars are terrible stock pickers and that, with our new parent seemingly interested in employing many more All Stars than we've had in the past, our stock picking, which is abysmal already, is only going to get worse. This really upset the brokers, as you can imagine."

"Then what happened?"

"One of the brokers asked Linda why you, David, didn't do something about it?"

"And what did she say?"

"She said that you were firmly on board with BC's plan to hire ranked analysts, regardless of their money-making skills, and that you were largely insensitive to the needs of the brokers."

"Jesus."

"I'm really sorry to call you about this," Piccardi said, "but I feared that no one else would tell you and I didn't think it was healthy for Linda to be walking around badmouthing our own analysts and you in front of 300 highly influential brokers."

"I'm sorry you had to call, but I appreciate it," David said. "Let me check this out and see what I come up with."

As soon as Piccardi hung up, David called Linda and asked her to come see him.

"Did you actually say all of those things?" he asked after she'd grabbed a chair.

"Most of them."

"Why?"

"Because they're true. Your analysts stink, David, and I can't defend them. They're making me look bad and they're making the firm look bad. All you care about is if they're *II-* ranked or not. All the brokers care about is making their clients money."

"I can't tolerate you badmouthing our own analysts in front of a huge ballroom of brokers. You're entitled to your opinions, and to air them privately if asked, but what you did was so disloyal and counterproductive to all of my efforts to build some team spirit around here that it just blows my mind."

"I'm going to keep saying how I feel, David, as long as I work here. No one can force me to call terrible analysts good just for the sake of team spirit."

"I'm not going to tolerate it, Linda. Consider yourself warned."

"You'll tolerate what you need to, David. Your boyfriend Dieter is wetting his pants trying to get me to sign up with them at $6 million per. We'll be at $10 million before it's over, and I can guarantee you that, if I tell Dieter that I'm refusing to sign because you're trying to force me to lie to brokers about the ineptness of our Research Department, he's going to be one unhappy boyfriend."

David and Linda stared at each other in silence. Finally, Linda stood and headed for the door. "In fact, I'm going to call my lawyer right now and insist that wording be added to my contract guaranteeing me the right to be honest about the relative strengths and weaknesses of our analysts if I am asked to express my viewpoints by brokers and/or their clients."

"Make it 'our analysts and their boss' while you're at it," said David in disgust.

"Good idea," Linda replied. "Very good idea."

* * *

David played good listener. He was sitting at Adrienne, breakfasting with Liz Tytus, a tobacco analyst who worked at Prudential Securities.

"She's a head case," Richard Lipstein had warned. "She's furious over her bonus. I'm sure you can hire her right now if you make her a good offer."

"I'm definitely leaving Prudential," she was saying. "I've gotten several calls since the beginning of the year, and I know my market value. Prudential knows it too. Why they're playing chicken with me I don't understand but they'll be the losers."

"How far off were they?" David asked innocently.

"A million dollars."

"Meaning?"

"Meaning they paid me two million last year and my market value is easily three."

"Did they explain how they came up with $2 million?"

"No, they made some flimsy excuse about the number of stocks I follow and the relative importance of the group but no valid explanation."

"And you follow how many stocks again?"

"Five... Philip Morris, R.J. Reynolds, Universal, UST and British American."

"How did you conclude that being a Runner-Up in tobacco and covering five stocks is worth $3 million a year?"

"I've been offered it."

David nodded. "Do you think you have a chance to move up this year?"

"I do. Feldman will be tough," she said, referring

to her competitor at Merrill Lynch, "but the others could be beatable."

As Liz continued to rail against Prudential and the indignity of being paid only $400,000 per stock, David ran the numbers in his head. He'd have to offer her over $3 million to get her, she'd only cover five stocks that are influenced much more by litigation news than by sales and earnings, and she was barely Runner-Up material, having finished in a dead heat with Marc Cohen of Goldman. Then again, she worked at Prudential, and David's recruiting prospects were much brighter there than at most other firms on The Street.

After listening politely for 15 more minutes to Liz drone on about how wonderful she was and how disgracefully she'd been treated, David smiled as genuinely as he could and said, "Liz, I think we can offer you a much better platform than the one you're now on, which you'll need if you want to be number one in tobacco some time soon, and I'm sure we can work out the economics in a way that you'll like."

"That would be nice," Liz said, unimpressed.

"I'd like you to come in and meet a short list of people in research, sales, trading and banking."

"Fine. When?"

"I'll get your availability from Richard Lipstein, if you'll get it to him."

Liz stood up, extended her hand, said, "I'll call Richard," and stormed out of the restaurant.

"You're welcome," David said half out loud. "I enjoyed meeting you too."

* * *

On Valentine's Day, after the market had closed,

Annapurna Apparel "preannounced" that January sales had been materially below plan and inventories had ballooned, forcing the company to mark them down heavily during the final weeks of the quarter. As a result, Annapurna said, earnings for the January quarter now appeared likely to come in materially below the $0.30 a share that management had been anticipating. The new guidance for the quarter was $0.22–$0.24.

Further, management expressed concerns about how strong Annapurna's business had been 12 months earlier and how difficult the year-to-year comparisons were going to be over the next few quarters. Finally, the press release quoted CEO Patrick Firth as "being comfortable" with earnings estimates for the coming year in the range of $0.80–$0.85 a share, rather than in the $1.00–$1.10 that he'd blessed before.

Rather than picking up the phone and calling Robin Lomax to congratulate her, which he'd do before he went home, or Ed Koster whom he'd reach the next morning, David just decided to sit back in his leather rocker, relax, and watch the fireworks. Annapurna, he checked, had closed at $50, down from the $57 at which Robin had gone to a Sell last month but up from the $46 at which it had bottomed that day.

Within 15 minutes, CNBC had picked up the story, and during the 4:00 to 5:00 segment of "Market Wrap," Tyler Mathisen had checked with Kathleen Tanzy on extended-hours trading in general and trading in Annapurna in particular. At 4:25 it was selling at 47, down 3, at 4:40 it was at 44, down 6, and at 4:55 it had reached 39, down 11.

Feeling keenly satisfied, David headed for the men's

room inside of which he found Alan Gildersleeve, his paper and forest products analyst, and Phil Suprano, his supermarket and drug store analyst, brushing their teeth and combing their hair.

"So, young warriors, big dates tonight?" David laughed.

"Thank you, David!" said Phil. "I've been feeling like 28 going on 50 lately."

"No more dates for me," Alan said, holding up his six-month-old wedding band. Then Alan turned to Phil, said somberly, "I hope I look better than you do when *I* get to be 28," and punched Phil in the belly.

"Fuck you," Phil answered. "You're so immature."

"You look happy," Alan observed, turning back towards David.

"I am. Did you see the Annapurna preannouncement?" Neither had.

"Did they miss the quarter?" Phil guessed.

"They missed, they cited poor sales, high inventories, markdowns, worries about near-term comparisons, *everything* Robin flagged when she went to Sell last month."

"Where's the stock?" Phil asked.

"At 39, down 11."

"Jesus!" Phil was stunned. Alan seemed to be as well but he didn't say a word.

"This isn't pretty but it's what we get paid to do every day, and when you see an analyst nail a story like this a month before it happens, all alone, you have to feel pretty good about it." David paused and then added, "She really did her homework."

"She really did," Phil agreed.

David washed his hands, said goodnight, and returned to his office.

"Wow. She *did* nail that one!" Alan said, nodding and smiling.

"It's true, but I've got to tell you that I'd never do what she did," Phil said.

"How come?"

"Are you crazy? Management hates her, her institutional clients hated the call, even though she was right they'll be so pissed off selling the stock at 39 that they'll never give her the credit she deserves, all Retail will remember is that she had a Buy on the stock at 57 the day before she went to a Sell on it at 57, and her bankers are trying to get her fired for costing us an M&A deal and a convertible bond offering that would've made the firm $10 million."

"Shit. So what would you do?"

"I'd never go to Sell unless I thought the company was going bankrupt. If one of your companies is going to miss the quarter and its P/E is high, you go to a Hold. Everyone knows what that means. Management isn't thrilled but they aren't rip-shit over it; clients remember that you pulled in your horns and they'll sell anyway if their style is to sell whenever someone downgrades to Hold; and Retail, which knows what Hold means, will give you no more credit for a Sell than a Hold so why bother?"

"You might still lose the banking business."

"You might, but with a Hold, management looks pettier and more like assholes if they boot you from a deal. With a Sell, it's like asking to be fired."

"Have you ever had a Sell?" Alan asked.

"Nope, and don't hold your breath either. When you go to a Sell, you'd better be right, and not down-5–points right... down-25–points right. How often do you really think you can be that smart? If you go to a Hold, you're fine if the stock is up a little, it's flat or it's down a little. You're only really wrong if it craters or soars, which almost never happens. And almost never is exactly how often you should use the 'S' word."

"What if my valuation work comes up with a target price that's 25% below where the stock is selling?" Alan asked.

"Make your target price down 15% and use Hold. Read *II*. There were writeups last October on the top three finishers in 75 categories. Do you know how many of those 225 analysts were cited for using Sells effectively?"

"None?"

"None."

* * *

"Lisa, did you get me the Rivington 10Q?" David owed Ed Koster an answer. There was no reply because Lisa was not in her office.

"I'll do it myself," David said to no one in particular.

The 10Q, the financial report that all publicly traded companies file quarterly with the SEC, was easily attainable in EFS's library on the 66th floor and that's where David headed. David normally didn't visit the library himself, nor did most of the analysts who sent their associates and RAs instead. The library was an invaluable repository of annual and interim reports to shareholders, trade journals, financial publications and other source materials that helped the analysts do their jobs. When David had first come to Wall Street, almost all of these documents had been stored in such libraries in hard copy or on microfilm or microfiche. Now, most were stored on CDs that the analysts could access using their desktop or notebook computers. Many were also available on line.

The library had banks and banks of CD cabinets, plus dozens of more traditional-looking shelves that housed books, magazines and other bound periodicals. A long counter, four feet off the floor, separated users from a staff of librarians who did the retrieving and kept records of who had borrowed what and when. Kathy Delbridge, EFS's head librarian, was a pleasant-looking 35-year-old with a reputation for sternness with her underlings and ambitions to expand her empire.

"David! To what do we owe the pleasure of a visit from someone so busy?"

"I need Rivington Resources' most recent Q, Kathy, please."

"You could've pulled it down yourself from Free Edgar, you know."

"From the Internet?"

"Freeedgar.com, David." Kathy smiled. "You're so low-tech. Are you going to wait or shall I have someone bring it down to you?"

"I'll wait if it won't be long." David needed to resolve this ASAP.

"Samantha? Samantha, can you help me please?"

From behind a row of bookshelves to David's far right an unfamiliar woman emerged. She seemed very young, 20–ish, with a huge head of dark brown hair that was puffed high and flowed halfway down her back. She was heavily made up, especially for a librarian, and she was physically striking owing both to her build and how she dressed to flaunt it. Samantha was an hourglass. Her shoulders were broad, but it was the size of her breasts when compared with the minuteness of her waist that demanded attention.

"Samantha Smeralda, this is David Meadows, the Director of Research," Kathy explained as Samantha approached the counter. "Samantha's new."

"It's nice to meet you." David extended his hand, maintaining his best air of indifference.

"You too," said Samantha with a smile. "I've heard a lot about you."

Her work done, Kathy excused herself. "Samantha will get you that Q."

When Kathy left the counter, Samantha looked very directly at David and asked, "What do you need?" She leaned slightly forward on the counter. Her perfume was palpable. Armani, David guessed. Most of her sheer white silk blouse remained visible, but her short pink leather skirt did not. As she leaned forward slightly, David could see that Samantha had undone three buttons. He could also tell, because of the sheerness of the silk, that her bra was very wide at the sides and that it scooped low across her chest.

"I need the most recent $10Q$ for Rivington Resources." David made sure to look at her eyes as he spoke.

"That's easy. I'll be back in a jiffy."

David watched her vanish in the $10K/10Q$ section. In half a minute she returned. "Here you go," she said with a smile as she handed David the $10Q$. "Is there anything else I can do for you?" As she asked, Samantha turned unexpectedly to her right to ensure that David noticed the fourth newly unbuttoned button, the way in which the right side of her blouse had moved away from the left and away from her chest, just how low that wide-at-the-sides bra really scooped, and the substantial amount of her large right breast that it failed to contain. She looked unblinkingly at David, innocently. "Do you like the view?" she asked.

David was surprised by Samantha's directness. "Excuse me?"

"I bet you have a great view from your office," she said without missing a beat. "Aren't you in the corner with the best view of the Statue of Liberty and the harbor?"

David was sure Samantha was toying with him but wasn't going to let on. "Yes I am, and you're right, the view is very beautiful." He paused, added, "You should stop by some time so I can show you," and then headed, with thanks and a smile, towards the elevator bank.

* * *

"Barbara, is Ed around?"

"He's got Tom Mennymore in with him but they're just BS'ing, I think. Should I slip him a note?"

"I promised to get back to him on a stock he asked about."

"Let me see if he'll pick up."

Almost immediately, Koster was on the line. "What?"

"Ed, I looked into Rivington Resources."

"It's no Exxon Mobil, is it?" David got the feeling that Ed knew more about Rivington than he'd let on during their last conversation.

"No, it's not. It's a pretty sad story from all I can tell. Its earnings have been flat over the past three years, its stock price has fallen 60% from its high, its Board is dominated by Wheeler family members, and it's only covered by two firms, Petrie Parkman and Simmons & Co., both of which brought Rivington public. Its market cap is down to $110 million from almost $300 million. The family owns half of the stock."

"Can you get someone to cover it?"

"I can get one of Nancy Natolio's juniors to follow it but it would be a complete waste of time for Nancy."

"They want Nancy, David. They don't want a no-name."

David hesitated. He knew there was no way out.

"David?"

"I'll have Nancy do it, Ed, but what if she can't put a positive rating on it? Wouldn't they be better off with no coverage than negative coverage?"

"They don't need to receive negative coverage," Koster said firmly. "At worst they're a Hold at these levels, and maybe, just maybe, Nancy can put an Accumulate on them so she and Mr. Mennymore can go down there and meet with Billy Bob and get the mandate to sell them to someone bigger. Hell, 2% of $250 million, if we could get that for them, is $5 million. That's even more than *you* make in a year."

"I'll talk to Nancy."

"I knew you would. Barbara, get me John Carlton in Houston. Thanks for your help, David."

* * *

Answering the phone when you don't recognize the caller's ID is always risky business.

"David, it's Tom Waring in Boston. Do you have a minute?"

"Of course, Tom, what's up?"

"I don't know what's up, but I can tell you for sure what's down and that's Back Bay Semiconductor."

"Are you in it?"

"Up to my eyeballs, unfortunately, and so are three of my best clients."

"It's been a bad call, I know. Have you spoken with Martin about it recently?"

"I spoke with him a week ago but I haven't been able to bring myself to call him since then because I'm just so steamed up about it. He's had an Accumulate on it from 52 to 31. I did most of my buying in the 40s. It was down 8 points last week alone. I'm getting killed here."

"Should I ask Martin to call you?"

"No, and I'll tell you why. All the way from 52 to 31, every time I spoke to him he told me it was still rated Accumulate and that I should put more money into it. But yesterday afternoon I was speaking with a friend of mine who's a portfolio manager at Fidelity, and he told me that Martin had visited with them about a month ago and told them, off the record, that Back Bay Semi was really a Hold, not an Accumulate, that he didn't see any upside in the stock and that he'd stuck with the Accumulate because, and I quote, 'Retail would kill me if I downgraded it now.'"

"Well, that's not good."

"Wait, there's more. My buddy told me that Fidelity began selling the stock soon after Martin's visit and that they got out at an average price of $38, just before it cratered."

"I don't like this at all."

"I'm not finished. As soon as I heard this, I called the Equity Research Marketing Desk and asked them what Martin was saying about Back Bay Semi, and they told me he was still solidly positive, that the Accumulate stood and that I should be averaging down for my clients."

"Let me look into it," said David, "and I'll call you back."

"Don't bother, David. This happens all the time and it's never going to change. The only purpose Retail serves in this firm is to provide buyers when the institutions need someone to sell to. And you know what? It works every time."

* * *

Ron Vargo feared he was babbling. He knew he was in the middle of his first sit-down with the newly hired head of Investor Relations at one of the advertising agencies he followed, Milbanks Media, that he'd come prepared with his standard list of questions plus a few special ones aimed at learning more about Claire O'Daniel's pre-Milbanks background, and that he'd brought her some samples of his recent reports on other agencies he followed including WPP Group, Interpublic and Omnicom.

But he was disoriented. His heart raced, and he could feel his pulse in his neck and along the inside of his wrists. He felt flushed and foolish and vulnerable.

Claire's beauty had disarmed him. She was slim but not skinny and tall but not too. She had huge brown eyes and brunette bangs. There was a directness about her that was totally disarming and, when they'd shaken hands and she'd held on longer than she should have, Ron had tried hard not to notice and failed.

For what could've been 15 minutes or two hours Ron worked through his list of questions. He asked them, hoping his voice wouldn't betray him, and she answered them smoothly and confidently, her eyes darting back and forth as she stared at Ron. She also seemed to be using her hands a lot, but Ron was mesmerized by her lips and her eyes. Everything else was a blur.

He wrote down her answers in handwriting he didn't recognize. At times he felt as if he'd left his body and was watching their exchanges from high above. Claire's energy seemed overwhelming to him. He battled for concentration and self-control.

Could she tell? Did she know? Was this all in his head? Ron wasn't sure. All he wanted to do was finish his list of questions and depart gracefully without making more of a fool of himself than he feared he already had, but still Claire talked and still her smile blinded him. How could she seem so perfectly at ease when he was so unnerved and unrecognizable to himself?

Finally, his list of questions exhausted, Ron saw Claire rising from behind her desk, walking around it, extending her hand and shaking his. This time she let go more quickly, making Ron think that, perhaps, he'd been wrong. But as she walked him to the door of her office, Ron could feel her hand, first on his elbow and then high on his back, just below his neck. And while her words seemed innocent enough, he was sure as he stepped into the hall outside her office that he could feel her fingertips touch his hair, just above his shirt collar, ever so softly.

"Call me," she whispered, "or come visit whenever you want."

* * *

"Matt's on the line," Lisa yelled. David picked him up.

"What's doing?"

"David, I'm in the middle of a fairly heated Commitment Committee meeting and I have to step out to see a portfolio manager from the Government of Singapore who's waiting in my office. Can you relieve me?"

David checked his calendar and saw that he was free for the next hour. "I'll be right there." It took him less than a minute to make his way to the Commitment Committee conference room on the 66th floor, where he found, around a large table, Matt, Eva Wrightsman who headed the Syndicate Department, entertainment analyst Keith Jackman and his banker Barry Seels, two of Barry's assistants whom David didn't know, Carl Robern, John McLain, Paula Hainsworth, Paul Pitcher and Dennis Domolky from Compliance. Matt thanked David, handed him a thick stack of papers and left.

"David," Eva began, "what we're discussing here is an IPO for a small movie theater operator called Primo Theaters. They have about 600 movie theaters in the South and Southwest. The mandate was landed by Barry and his team with a last-minute assist from Keith. We gave them an offering price range of $10 to $13. We think that institutional interest will be pretty high, especially under $12. Barry says the company will be disappointed with $12 and very unhappy with anything below that."

"We told them we were sure we'd be able to do this deal at the top end of the range," Barry piped in.

" *You* told them," Keith corrected.

Eva continued. "Keith, on the other hand, thinks the stock is only worth $12 and wouldn't be able to have a Buy on it unless we did the deal at $10 so we've been $2 apart for the past 90 minutes and we need to go back to the company and tell them what we're planning to do today."

"Can I add something?" Barry asked. Eva nodded. "We worked very hard to land this deal. We had to beat out Merrill and Goldman for the lead, which we did. This is a very successful company, with earnings that should reach $0.40 a share this year and $0.50 next year. Our institutional clients, I'm told, love it, and Retail, I'm told, will also love it. We promised them $13 if market conditions were good and $12 if they weren't, so we gave ourselves a little wiggle room, but we didn't promise them $10 and they'll certainly feel that we lied if we go back to them today and tell them $10."

"Keith, where are you on this?" David asked.

"David, it's a good company. It's small, it doesn't have serious competition, it can probably do $0.40 this year and $0.47 to $0.48 next year. I have no problem telling clients that it should sell for 25 times earnings, but 25 times $0.48 is $12, and if my target price is $12, I can't have a Buy on it if it's selling above $10."

"If it's worth $12, we should do the deal at $12," yelled Barry.

"If it's worth $12, we should do the deal at $10," John McLain disagreed. "You've got to price this thing so that it moves up in the after-market once the offering is over, Barry. Our clients pay us for access to 'hot' deals and what makes a deal 'hot' is strong after-market performance. You get that by pricing the deal below where you expect it to trade, guaranteeing clients an instant profit."

Barry's eyes were rolling. He's clearly overpromised, David thought.

"Why should we kiss $50,000 of management fees goodbye?" Barry growled.

"Because we can make that back in a heartbeat by being the number one trader of Primo after the deal has closed," explained Carl. "The lead manager always gets the bulk of the after-market trading in an IPO."

"All of our happy clients who got in at $10 and want to take their instant 20% profits will have to sell through someone," McLain added, "and if that someone is us, the management fee give-up will be dwarfed by the commissions our trading desk will take in during the first 24 to 48 hours after the deal closes."

"You can't flip the stock for an instant 20% if there's no 20%," Carl mused.

"I didn't say it would go to $12 now," Keith protested, "I said my 12–month target price would be $12."

"It'll go to $12 as soon as the deal is done," Carl disagreed. "Just make sure you don't downgrade it to Hold as soon as the 'quiet period' has ended."

"What should I do instead, Carl, raise my target price to $15?"

"I'm just telling you, Keith, that you can't bless this deal when we're out peddling at $10 and then downgrade it 40 days later with the stock at $11.75."

"Then we should do the deal at $8," Keith bellowed, pounding his right fist on the table top. "Let's do it at $8, let it run up to $10 in the aftermarket and then I can still have a Buy on it and I can still use a $12 target."

"That's bullshit," Barry yelled back. "No one's going back to them and telling them that we're doing the deal at $8 even though our clients are happy to pay $12 for it just because Keith would only be willing to buy it at $10 in his own account. Fidelity must know something that Keith doesn't."

"I taught Fidelity everything it knows about this industry," Keith said pompously.

"I agree with Keith," David volunteered. "One of the principal reasons why returns are crappy on so many banking clients is that the analysts don't apply the same standards to banking clients as to the other stocks they cover. It sounds as if Keith would rate Primo a Buy at $10 and a Hold at $12 yet we're asking him to keep the Buy on it at $12. What if it trades at $12.50 or $13 in the after-market? To keep the Buy on it, Keith would have to use a target price of $15 to $16 instead of $12."

"You just don't want to do this deal, Keith," Barry snarled. "You didn't find it, you won't make much money on it, you'll still have to follow it and we all know how much you love adding new names to your universe."

"Absolutely baseless," Keith snapped. "If it's priced at $10 or less, I'll bless it and follow it and you can pay me my pathetic little $23,000 pretax bonus for it. But at $12, you'll force me to tell clients that it's fairly valued and you can expect a Hold on it if it trades at or above $12 in the aftermarket."

Ten minutes later the Commitment Committee, of which neither Keith nor Barry was a member, voted unanimously to price the Primo IPO at $10 a share and to instruct Barry to go back to the company and break the bad news.

* * *

Will Rivas thought he could see the paper yellowing. It had been white when his secretary had taken the message to call Claus Abner, his banker, but after having procrastinated for longer than he should have, Will could now see what too much sunlight could do. Reluctantly, he dialed Claus's number.

"Abner."

"Claus, it's Will."

"How was your vacation, Will?"

"What vacation?"

"Weren't you on vacation the past two weeks? When I didn't hear back from you I assumed you'd gone off to some exotic island that had no cell phone service."

"Sorry. I've been out of the office a lot, but not on vacation. What's doing?"

"Are you close to picking up Retinal Microvision?"

Will sighed as loudly as he could. "No."

"Will, what's the problem here? This company is landing new contracts, its losses are narrowing, and the stock fell 90% during the bear market. The stock is cheap, and this is a great company! What are you waiting for?"

I'm waiting to sell my shares to BCH and to exercise my options, Will thought.

"We can do business with them," Claus continued. "Believe me. I'm not asking you to help me, I'm merely asking you not to hurt me. Management likes me and they like the firm. The only thing they don't like is that we aren't covering them."

"You mean recommending them."

"I'm going to talk to David about this."

"Talk to whoever you want to. David already told me I didn't have to do it."

"Really! And when was that?"

"During my review."

"You complained about me to David during your review?"

"Yup."

"And David said you didn't have to do it?"

"Yup."

"Fine. David isn't God, you know. David has a boss just the way you and I do, and Carl is much more interested in generating revenues for this firm than David is. Luckily for me, Carl tells David what to do and not vice versa."

"Talk to Carl, talk to Koster, talk to the Germans for all I care," Will said, raising his voice. "This isn't the only place on The Street I can work, and if I need to go somewhere else to avoid being your whore I will."

* * *

Carl's ears should've been burning as Claus squabbled with Will but they weren't, perhaps because they were 5,000 miles away.

As he sat in EFS's London institutional sales office at 55 Bishopsgate, he was vaguely aware of a seemingly endless stream of institutional salespeople, all of whom sold EFS's U.S. research to money managers in London and Edinburgh and all of whom were complaining about their lack of vocational visibility, thanks to BC Holdings.

"When is someone going to tell us who's a keeper and who's getting canned?"

"I hope you're helping them figure out how much stronger we are than their sales guys in London are."

"Why can't we have contracts like the analysts?"

All the while, Carl just nodded, smiled, acted as if he cared and watched the time. He never took a note or intended to do anything with any of the feedback the salesmen were giving him. In fact, Carl didn't care one bit about any of the salespeople or their futures. He merely viewed them as an excuse for a first-class vacation at The Ritz, at EFS's expense, whenever he found himself twiddling his thumbs in New York. And no one in London ever criticized Carl's lack of follow-up because, when it came right down to it, Carl was President of International.

It was already 2:30 and Carl was growing impatient. He hurried the last two salespeople along, listening seemingly with great concern to their problems and making certain to be done by 3:00. When the last salesman had departed, Michael Millington, who headed the London sales force, poked his head in. "So, did you survive for five hours without me?"

"Oh sure, no big deal. They just needed to complain a little. That's my job, you know… complainee."

"I didn't know such a word existed," said Michael, seriously.

"Well I figure that, in life, there are complainers and complainees, and I'm sure not a complainer so I must be the other thing."

Michael didn't know whether to even bother pursuing this or not, so he changed the subject. "Was lunch all right?"

"It was fine." Carl started to move slowly towards the office door.

"Excellent!" Michael looked at his watch. "I thought what we'd do now is trot you over to Mercury for a few minutes and visit with their chief investment officer and several of the portfolio managers."

"Oh, I don't think so," Carl said.

"It really won't take long," Michael insisted. "They're our largest account, you know, and we can probably still do twice or thrice the business with them that we've been doing lately."

"Oh, I don't think so," Carl repeated. "I think I'm done here for today."

"Really. I'm... well, surprised. I thought we had you for the full day."

"You've had plenty of me," Carl said sternly. "Now what I really want is for you to tell me where to go for some sex around here."

Michael was dumbfounded. He'd booked five hours of one-on-one meetings with the key institutional salespeople followed by client meetings at Mercury and two other key accounts, but it was clear now that his boss was going to pass on the client meetings.

"I'm not really certain, Carl, what you're asking."

"I'm asking where to go for some sex around here, and I'm not talking about standing in a topless bar watching some ugly cunts dance."

Michael's mind raced. "I can't vouch for any of them personally," he said, "but there are several clubs behind Shaftesbury between Regent Street and Charing Cross Road that you might try."

"Good. Drive me, would you, Michael?

"Of course."

Twenty-five minutes later, Michael deposited Carl on the corner of Old Compton Street and Charing Cross Road, thanked him politely for having spent the time with the salespeople, and said how much he looked forward to meeting him back at EFS's offices the following morning. "I'll rework the schedule a little bit if you don't mind, Carl, to get Mercury on your dance card for tomorrow."

"Sure, sure. Whatever." Carl looked down Old Compton Street. "This way?"

"Yes, straight down towards Regent. I'm sure you'll find something you'll like."

"Okay, thanks," said Carl dismissively. "See you tomorrow."

Carl wound his way down the quiet side streets of SoHo, past Greek Street and Frith, past Dean Street to Wardour. After rejecting a few topless bars that were seedy even to Carl, he selected one near the corner of Wardour and Peter Street called "Wardour Werks" and walked through the narrow doorway into the dimly lit club. Two young women, topless but wearing G-strings, danced to Billy Idol's "Rebel Yell" on the small stage. Six men sat at four tables drinking beer and looking bored. Carl cased the room for other women and noticed a waitress with very long, platinum blonde hair and enormous, substantially implanted breasts who was standing at the far end of the bar. Carl watched her bring two patrons a basket of pretzels before seating herself at a table for two near the register. He joined her.

"Hi there," the woman said, smiling broadly, eyes widening. "How are you?"

"Oh, swell," Carl answered, staring long and very hard at her breasts and then making a little eye contact. "I'm Carl."

"Hi Carl," the woman said, placing a hand on Carl's forearm. "I'm Felicity. Would you like something to drink?"

"I don't think so."

Felicity didn't miss a beat. "Would you like to have a private dance with me?"

"How much for a blow job?"

"Twenty-five pounds with a condom, fifty without."

"No condom. Let's go."

Felicity smiled, took Carl by the hand and walked

him down a narrow flight of stairs to a private room with two chairs, a king-sized bed and a bathroom with a sink, a shower, a toilet and a bidet. Carl guessed that, behind the closed door across the hall, another private room had been similarly outfitted. He thought for a second that he heard a chair move inside, but Felicity closed their door behind her and reached to remove Carl's jacket. In the background, an old U2 album softly played. Felicity took Carl's jacket and the 50 pounds that he'd removed from his wallet, placed them carefully on one of the chairs and sat Carl down in the other chair, facing her and the bed.

To the beat of songs that Carl recognized but couldn't name, Felicity undulated, swaying from side to side, clasping her hands behind her head so her breasts rose before him and staring at him to heighten the sense of intimacy. She turned to face the bed and bent over, peering back between her legs at Carl and touching herself. She turned back towards him, fell back on the bed, spread her legs wide and ran her hand under her G-string as she stared deeply into his eyes. Then, before Carl even realized, she was up again, sitting on one of his legs, pushing the other leg apart with her knees and rubbing his penis through the fabric of his suit pants with the palm of her right hand. Carl closed his eyes and sighed.

Felicity let her hand linger there a moment longer and then stood, removing her G-string, lifting her right leg and resting it on Carl's left shoulder. She leaned in towards him, far enough to brush her closely cropped pubic hair against his face. As she felt Carl start to lean towards her, she backed away, undulating, lifting her breasts and licking each nipple as she held his gaze. Carl reached out for her but Felicity kept her distance. Only when he'd dropped his hands to his sides did she return to him, backing in at first and rubbing her bottom against his groin, up and down, then in circles. Carl grabbed her hips and moved with her.

Then she swung around and straddled him in the chair, rubbing herself against him, slightly faster each time, arching backwards and touching the floor with the palms of her hands, then lifting her upper body all the way and pressing it forward until she could bury Carl's face between her breasts. He tried to suck on her left nipple but Felicity was too fast for him. "No touching, you bad boy," she whispered, "only I get to touch!"

Felicity, feeling how hard Carl had become, stood once again and led Carl by one hand to the bed, where she pushed him down, quickly removed his shoes and socks, and then ever so slowly disposed of his pants and boxers. Then she began working Carl's penis with her hand and, after what seemed like an eternity, her mouth.

"She's okay," Carl thought to himself. For a few minutes, he just lay still, reveling in the feelings, holding Felicity's head with the back of his right hand and guiding her pace. As he felt himself getting close, he pulled Felicity's head up and said, "Say you're Nancy Natolio, and thank me for letting you blow me."

Felicity sucked on Carl twice and then said "I'm Nancy Natolio. Thank you for letting me blow you."

"No, no. Say thank you, Carl, for letting me blow you."

Felicity continued to suck away and, after several seconds, stopped and said, "I'm Nancy Natolio. Thank you, Carl, for letting me blow you."

Carl seemed pleased. "Tell me how much you always wanted to suck my cock."

"Oh, Carl, I've wanted to suck your cock for so long... from the first time I saw you."

"Tell me you're Nancy, and that the only reason you stayed around at EFS was in the hope that I'd let you suck my cock."

"It's me, Carl, it's Nancy. I've wanted to suck your cock from the minute I saw you. The only reason why I'm still at EFS is because I hoped you'd let me suck you and suck you and suck you and suck you."

Carl grabbed Felicity's head and wrapped her lips around his penis. "You're Nancy, you cunt, and letting you blow me is the biggest favor I've ever done *anyone!*" Carl could feel Felicity nodding and, as she did, he came, shaking violently. "Jesus!" he yelled. "Nancy, you fucking slut."

Felicity, who had no idea what mini-drama she'd been acting out with Carl, just stretched out beside him on the bed and rested for a minute. Carl's breathing slowed and the room grew still but, when Carl showed no inclination to move, Felicity hopped off the bed, replaced her G-string, tucked inside it the 50 pounds that had been resting on Carl's jacket, and then walked to the side of the bed.

"You were delicious," she whispered in Carl's ear. Then she kissed him on the cheek and went back upstairs. Carl lingered for a moment, decided not to avail himself of the shower, washed up quickly at the sink and got dressed. Then he mounted the stairs and returned to the bar.

It was 5:10. "Can I walk to the Ritz from here?" he asked Felicity.

"Of course. It'll take you twenty minutes. Tops."

"Swell. Thanks." Carl took one last gander at Felicity's mammaries, stepped out into the cold and dark of a February night in London and headed for Piccadilly.

* * *

"You're joking, right?" asked Nancy Natolio from behind her desk.

David, having acted in this play before, knew everyone's lines cold. Now it was time for him to explain why the analyst needed to cover a stock that she had no interest, desire or plans to cover.

"I know this doesn't make a lot of sense, Nancy."

"A lot of sense? It makes no sense, David, and you know that full well. Rivington is a piece of garbage. It's what the Wheelers do when they aren't committing incest or competing on *Half-Wit Family Feud*. The stock is down 90% from its high."

"Sixty percent."

"No one on The Street covers it."

"Petrie Parkman and Simmons do."

"They're Rivington's bankers!"

"That's not no one."

"It is, in the eyes of most clients. You know what they do with research from a company's bankers. Do the words 'recycling bin' mean anything to you?"

"I know it's not major league material."

"Its market cap is $50 million."

"It's $110 million."

"It's 99% family owned."

"Only 50%."

"Is there a deal here?"

"Not necessarily, but there's a retail branch that's got its grubbies on $40 million of Billy Bob's life savings and Billy's threatening to drive the pickup truck to Merrill Lynch with it if we don't give him some coverage."

"I'll have Shanna do it," said Nancy, referring to her research assistant.

"It has to be you, Nancy."

"Says who?"

"Koster."

This set Nancy back for a moment. "What if it's a Sell?"

David almost laughed. Nancy never used Sell. "It needs to be a Hold at worst, preferably Accumulate. If you do the work and you won't be able to sleep at night with an Accumulate, come back to me and we'll sit down with Koster and tell him why, but we can't do that until you've done your homework and have airtight reasons."

"There must be a deal here."

"Koster joked that maybe you and Mennymore could sell them to one of your larger companies for, say, $250 million and that we could charge them 2% for doing it."

"Oh sure, and I can already see what my share of that $5 million fee would be. What's 1%, $50,000?

"You know we pay analysts more than 1% on M&A."

"Well, you sure as Hell won't pay me 10%. Even if it's 5%, that's $125,000 after taxes. Barely worth my while. And selling it is still a long shot. More likely, I do all this work and we don't do a stitch of banking business with them, which means *nada* for Nancy." Nancy looked long and hard at David who was sitting in one of her guest chairs. "You're ordering me to do this."

"I'm not ordering you. I'm telling you that Ed Koster has specifically asked you to do it and that either you do it or we go back to him after you've given them a serious once over and tell him why you can't."

"This is so typical," Nancy mused. "Crappy employer with crappy CEO and crappy broker pressured by crappy CEO at a different crappy firm. What's wrong with this picture, David?"

"I give up."

"It's simple," Nancy said, smirking. "You and I are in it."

* * *

"I have good news," Dieter said as he strode into David's office.

"What?"

"I have found more space for you."

"Close to 63 I hope."

"Yes yes, very close. On 65, one floor from sales and trading."

"And banking?"

"It's staying on 66 for now but we're also trying to get 67."

"We should put in a staircase connecting 63 with 64 and 64 with 65."

"We'll see." Dieter obviously cared not at all about staircases.

"When will I get it?"

"It's being vacated at the end of the month. Renovation will begin in April and you should be able to use it by September."

"I'm going to run out of space before September."

"We'll see what we can do." Dieter placed a blueprint of the 65th floor on David's coffee table. "I'd start laying out your offices right away," he said.

"How much of it can I have?"

"As much as you need."

"Thanks, Dieter," said David, gathering his roster and hiring plans and heading for Lisa's office next door.

* * *

After the market closed on February 28, a press release was distributed internally via e-mail and externally to all of the media announcing the consummation of the merger between BC Holdings and Equitable Finance Securities.

The new management team was outlined and the retiring of the words Equitable and Finance was announced. Newly christened BC Securities, "one of the world's leading investment banking and brokerage firms," would open for business bright and early the following morning.

MARCH

For three straight mornings David breakfasted with potential recruits at Adrienne.

On Tuesday, Prudential's chemicals analyst, Van Trudell, told David how upset he was that his firm had fired all of its investment bankers, preventing him from doing any deals and earning any banking bonuses. When David told him that BC had a number of bankers devoted to basic industries like chemicals, Van seemed interested, and when breakfast ended, he agreed to come in to interview.

On Wednesday morning, Credit Suisse First Boston's small-cap analyst, James Sephton, insisted that he'd only consider joining BC Securities if he was granted 10-year options to purchase at least 500,000 shares of BC Holdings at a 10% discount to its current market price and if the options vested on his first day on the job. David smiled politely and wished James a nice life.

And on Thursday, David met Louis Liddy, Goldman Sachs's restaurant analyst who was furious that his firm had fired both of his overseas counterparts without warning him and refused to extend a new contract to Louis when his old one expired. David pointed out that BC had restaurant analysts in both Europe and Asia, and that it would be delighted to write him a new contract. Not surprisingly, Louis agreed to come in and meet more people.

As the weekend neared, David reviewed the early days of his recruiting campaign. He was batting .600 when it came to getting analysts in the door for a look-see. When he thought of how many more breakfasts awaited him he began to feel his suit pants tightening at the waist and to imagine his thighs ballooning. David suddenly felt tired, but he knew there'd be no coasting for many months to come.

* * *

Exactly five weeks and six days after Nick Denisovich's last conversation with Volkov, Nick placed a call to Billings Butte Mining for a quick update on current operations and then called Paula Hainsworth and signed up for the next Morning Call. The following morning, he walked leisurely to the Morning Meeting Room, seated himself along the side of the room and waited patiently for his turn. Paula had scheduled him to speak ninth which bothered Nick not at all and, at 28 minutes into The Call, Paula motioned him to the head of the table and introduced him as the next speaker.

"Good morning everyone," Nick began, smiling slightly and looking relaxed. "I'm raising my rating this morning on Billings Butte Mining from Hold to Buy and my earnings per share estimate for this year from $0.05 to $0.10. Billings lost $0.05 a share last year and made $0.08 in 2001.

"This is not a truly fundamental call. The nickel-a-share increase in this year's estimate was driven by a 2% increase in estimated production from the company's Black Hills #7 mine in South Dakota as well as by a slightly lower tax rate but, in and of itself, that increase would not have justified upgrading the rating. In truth, Billings Butte has made a few cents a share or lost a few cents a share in each of the past five years.

"What I've found myself thinking recently about Billings is that it's begun to look more and more like Homestake did before it was acquired, and that means that the likelihood of a sale of the company to a larger firm has increased in my judgment, especially with prospects as dim as they are for a spike in gold prices this year or next. Now normally I wouldn't allow takeover prospects to color my ratings as much as I appear to be today, but the math is pretty compelling so let me run through it with you.

"When Homestake agreed to be acquired by Barrick Gold, it was trading at $6.65, and shareholders were offered 0.53 of a Barrick share for each Homestake share they held. With Barrick trading near $16.50, that meant about $8.70 worth of Barrick per Homestake share, or about a 30% premium to Homestake's pre-acquisition price. Homestake's book value at the time was about $2.30 a share so the takeover price was equal to about 3.8 times book value.

"Billings, like Homestake, has made little if any money over the past five years. Its reserves are obviously much smaller but, in its favor, its stock price is more depressed. Specifically, Billings' book value is roughly $4.50 per share. Four times book would be $18 a share, and let me say as clearly as I can that I don't expect anyone to pay four times book for Billings simply because Barrick paid four times book for Homestake. But three times book would be $13.50, and a 30% premium to the midpoint of

Billings' recent price range of $9 to $11 would be $13, so something south of $18 and north of $13 would be a reasonable guess in my mind.

"With respect to the rating, last night Billings closed at $9.25, down $0.25. If I were to use $14 as a possible takeover price, I'd get upside potential from here of more than 50%. And if I considered a takeover a 50/50 proposition, then I'd get a weighted target price of almost $12. With the stock near $9, that's enough upside to justify the Buy."

"Nick, is this really something our clients could do?" asked Maryanne Miles.

"Probably not if they're very large," Nick answered, pursing his lips and trying to look thoughtful. "This isn't a terribly large company and the shares aren't liquid enough for some of our biggest clients to invest in, but for smaller institutions and for Retail, as I see it, buying Billings Butte right, meaning around $9, makes sense if you can be patient. Worst case is probably that it's dead money. Maybe the stock drops to $8, but more likely, if nothing happens, it holds where it is right now. Best case is that someone comes along and offers *them* four times book which, again, would be $18, but let me repeat that that's best case, not expected case.

"And the expected case, again…," said Maryanne.

"… is the midpoint between where the stock is now, meaning $9, and Billings getting $18 a share from someone."

"Who'd buy them?" asked Paula.

"Actually, I'd consider Barrick the most likely buyer. It's already the dominant gold company in North America, and its acquisition of Homestake has probably gone well enough to open management up to the idea of doing something similar again although probably on a much smaller scale."

Most of the salesmen looked disinterested in this call which surprised Nick not at all. Paula asked if there were more questions, which there weren't, and thanked Nick who returned to his office. As usual, he turned on CNBC and began listening for coverage. For quite some time he heard nothing but finally, around 9:05, Maria Bartiromo mentioned an upgrade of Billings Butte Mining by BC Securities from Hold to Buy on the basis that the company could be taken over for from $14 to perhaps as much as $18 a share. "That's 50% to 100% above where the stock closed last night, Mark," Maria said as she passed the baton back to anchor Mark Haines.

At 9:30, Billings Butte failed to open. Nick thought at one point that he heard Maria say that the indication was $10–$11 but he wasn't sure because he was dialing Billings to let them know what he'd said. At 9:51, the stock finally did begin trading at $10.75, up $1.50.

Not enough, Nick thought. He checked the opening volume, which was slightly more than 1,000,000 shares. "They need more," he whispered. "They can't get out."

Throughout the day, Nick behaved reservedly. He responded to requests from The Desk to repeat his comments for Retail, once in the morning and once in the early afternoon. He did a short interview with CNBC around 11:30, in which he repeated the importance of buying Billings right, and he responded to calls from some smaller institutions looking for body language or other telltale signs that Nick knew something that he wasn't saying about how soon a deal might happen. He gave none.

Still, interest in Billings Butte built as the day wore on and, at 4:00, when the closing bell rang, Nick sighed for what seemed like 30 seconds. Billings Butte had closed at $12.25, up $3, after having traded as high as $13 in mid-afternoon. Volume was over 7,000,000 shares. Many people had come in as buyers throughout the day, but the fact that the stock hadn't risen more suggested that there'd also been a lot of sellers around.

Or one big one, Nick mused, with a signed wire-transfer form in hand.

* * *

"Can you believe this?" asked Rebecca Suess, the environmental services analyst.

"What is it?" Her secretary looked concerned.

"It's an e-mail from Kathleen Drakos at Kingston Investment Management."

"What does it say?"

"You won't believe it. It says 'To Rebecca Suess from Kathleen Drakos. Confidential. Re: Waste Connections. Rebecca, your coverage of Waste Connections is a poor excuse for securities analysis. You are relentlessly negative on a stock of which Kingston recently purchased 2,000,000 shares, and a stock that has performed far better of late than your rating and target price would have led a beginning investor to expect. I would be grateful if you would stop calling me, e-mailing me, faxing me and sending me your reports unless and until you have turned materially more positive on my stock. You should also know that you can kiss this year's *II* vote goodbye. I'm certain that Leone Young or Alan Pavese will be happy to have your vote recast for one of them. Regretfully yours, Cheryl."

"Sounds like blackmail."

"Push my stock or I'll vote in *II* for someone else who does." Rebecca debated for a minute about whether or not to answer Cheryl and decided not to.

"I think David should see this," she said and headed down the hall to show him.

* * *

Will Rivas had prepared himself to resist the onslaught.

"Don't you think Goldman's bankers are going to make just as many demands on you, if not more?" David asked.

"They'll make demands but they won't push me to follow crap. Goldman has real clients that make real products and earn real profits. They get the first call when a company wants to finance in my space. They don't chase the companies that have been rejected by everyone else like Claus does."

"How much did they offer you?"

"It's not about the money, David, it's about the quality of life."

"Okay, but I'd still like to know."

"Three."

"For two years?"

"No, just for this year."

"You've got a contract from BCS that you haven't signed that says $2,400,000 per year for two years plus $2,400,000 of restricted stock. That's equivalent to $3,200,000 per year assuming you stay at $2,400,000 in year three."

"And putting up with Claus isn't worth $200,000 pretax to me each year."

"Is Claus really the only issue?"

"He's the principal one."

"But you'd give up all the goodwill you've built with Institutional Sales."

"And I'd be the new kid on the block, and a smaller fish in a bigger pond."

David's mind raced. "Give me 24 hours. Please. I'm entitled to that."

"David, you're entitled to it, and I'll give it to you, but don't jump through a ton of hoops trying to keep me because you probably can't and I don't want you being more embarrassed over this than you need to be. They're not going to fire Claus to keep me, and I wouldn't want them to."

"Twenty-four hours." Will agreed.

The following day, after David had wheeled and dealt with his U.S. and German bosses well into the night, Will signed a new BCS contract. He'd been upped to $3 million per year for two years, and given $6 million of restricted stock, meaning that he'd make $5 million per year over the next three years if his ongoing comp remained $3 million in year three.

More importantly to Will, David had agreed that every single request from Claus Abner or anyone else in Banking for Will's time and attention would have to be preapproved by David, and David had promised to veto requests involving any company that Will didn't want to involve himself with, whether Will knew the company or not.

Later that day, David asked Dieter again about offering two years worth of stock to the other four ranked analysts. Dieter had said he'd think about it and he called back late in the afternoon. "David, here's the deal. These blocks of stock will not become compensation to the analysts until three years after the merger closed, nor will they have to be expensed by us until then. But if you want to do this, I'm going to charge that extra $10 million against your budget over those three years rather than have to take that hit all at once in the fourth year."

"So I'll have to absorb $3.3 million this year and next year out of the $250 million and $350 million you committed to spend on Research in those two years."

"That's right."

"And if I'm willing to do that?"

"Then go ahead."

David did.

* * *

Back on the Atkins Diet, David breakfasted on a ham omelette and a side of bacon with Tim Parish, an auto analyst at SG Cowen whom Larry Fraser had unearthed. David had experienced great difficulty hiring analysts from Cowen over the years and he wasn't optimistic as he listened to Tim ask about BCS's financial advisors.

"It's not that it scares me or bothers me, David, but I'm completely unfamiliar with the retail side of the business. How many brokers did you say you have?"

"About 5,000."

"And how do you keep the analysts from being overwhelmed by them?"

David launched into his spiel about the pluses (many) and minuses (few) of having 5,000 retail brokers there to follow the analysts' recommenda-

tions, and about the importance of The Desk and its members to leveraging the analysts' work in the field.
· Tim seemed to soak it all up well and not to be put off by it, but he also manifested a high level of satisfaction with where he was. He asked a series of questions about investment banking at BCS and expressed the kind of interest and curiosity that gave David a little hope. Still, as the waiter arrived, check in hand, David felt that he'd struck out.

"As much as I hate to admit it, Tim, you sound pretty happy where you are. I've been listening for hooks that would justify a change of venue for you but I don't hear them. You like Cowen, you think it's full of really smart people, you love the institutional side of the business, you haven't missed dealing with retail brokers, you've been focusing on research and thus haven't missed investment banking until now, and you feel fairly paid."

"All true, fortunately and unfortunately," Tim joked. "I told Larry all of this but he still felt it would be worthwhile for us to meet."

David nodded and sighed. "I wish that, other than helping you do some deals that you can't do now at Cowen, I had more to offer you that Cowen lacks."

David and Tim sipped their coffee refills. Tim could see David's mind racing, but for a long moment the table was silent. Finally, David asked about auto parts.

"Oh I wouldn't want to do those, David," said Tim, surprised. "It's a much less important group that's pretty well followed on The Street already."

"I didn't mean trading autos for auto parts, I meant doing both."

Tim's eyes widened a little. "Wow... that's interesting."

"It's been done before," David pressed. "Girsky was number one in both categories when *II* separated them, David Bradley was number three in both and Wendy Needham was top-five in both, if I remember correctly. I'm sure you could rank in both if *II* ever split them into separate categories again, and I'd promise to lobby them to do that if you came on board."

"That's interesting," Tim repeated. "Cowen has no interest in auto parts so it wouldn't make any sense for me to do them where I am, but it could be stimulating to do and I presume my market value would be higher if I ranked in two categories than one."

"Much higher."

"But I thought you said you were recruiting in both categories."

"I am. I would have to give up the second search to do this."

"You'd be willing to do that?"

"Yes," David said. "If you're as good as I think you are, and you come in and interview well, and if the biggest hook to get you to BCS is your ability to cover both autos and auto parts, then I'd do it."

"Let me think about it," Tim said.

Perhaps he did but, to David's surprise and Larry's, Tim never called back.

* * *

As David waded through his in-box, he noticed the *II* logo sticking out of one corner and, when he lifted the paper above it, he found the magazine's March issue. As usual, most of the articles were of little interest to him, but one, "The Home-Run Hitters of 2002," was quite important. Every March, *II* publishes its annual list of the prior year's "home run hitters," the analysts who were first and most vociferous in identifying the five best-performing small-cap growth stocks and the five best-performing mid-cap or large-cap stocks during the prior calendar year. Each stock is identified, its percentage gain for the prior year is displayed prominently, and a photo and short writeup on the analyst who recommended it first and most prominently takes up the rest of the space. Analysts working for firms that brought any of those companies public within the preceding four years are excluded from consideration.

Not surprisingly, at least half of the list usually comprises analysts who followed some of the hottest groups during the prior calendar year, but each year, several of the 10 best performers are "special situations," stocks that did well for unique reasons, and this is what enables *II* to avoid having, for example, 10 biotech analysts in the article because biotech had been the best-performing group on the NYSE and NASDAQ the year before.

From time to time, an *II* All Star would make the list but, much more often it seemed to David, the analysts who were recognized as home run hitters were less well known and employed by smaller firms. More evidence, he thought, that picking stocks and ranking well in *II*, while not mutually exclusive, were far from synonymous.

David scanned the new list. He saw no EFS/BCS analysts and, in fact, only four analysts he recognized. Thus, as there were no flowers to send or champagne bottles to order, he closed the magazine and returned it, disappointedly, to his in-box.

* * *

Farther down in David's pile of mail was an inter-office memo clipped to a blueprint. As it looked much more interesting than most of the memos above and below it, David pulled it out and read it. The cover memo was addressed to a half-dozen people including David, Carl, John McLain, Billy Lynch and Tom Mennymore and its topic was a proposed layout for the newly acquired 65th floor.

"Wow, that was fast!" David had submitted his requisition 48 hours after Dieter had broken the news to him in February about the availability of the 65th floor. He had asked for about half of the floor, had included a proposed layout of offices and additional conference rooms, and had suggested that it might make sense for Investment Banking to take the balance of 65, at least temporarily, given that it had already consumed most of 66 and obviously would need additional space soon. David had warned, though, that if Banking and Research were to share 65, it would be necessary to house them at opposite ends of the floor, with big walls and doors between them to preclude any Chinese-Wall-breaching issues.

Let's see how they did, he thought as he unfolded the blueprint. At first David couldn't get his bearings but, after twisting and turning the plans in several directions, he came to recognize what had been drawn. Fully half of the floor had been earmarked for Banking. Several dozen offices were drawn in, as were four large conference rooms and six smaller, private meeting rooms. All of this space was to the northwest of the reception desk in the middle of the floor. David wasn't sure that Banking and Research should share a receptionist, and he made a note to ask about it from a compliance standpoint later. Otherwise, the northwestern half of the floor looked fine.

At first, so did the southeastern half. All along the perimeter, offices had been drawn in using almost the exact mix of larger and smaller spaces that David had requested. He saw two large conference rooms, adequate rest rooms, a fair number of workstations for associate analysts, research assistants and secretaries, and quite a bit of the filing space that he'd requested. But overall the space looked smaller than what he'd recalled in his requisition, and what David didn't recognize was a large square in the middle of the southeastern half of the floor that was raw and had the words "The Market" written on it.

"What the hell is that?" he whispered. "Lisa?" In seconds, Lisa stood at David's door.

"What's The Market?"

"I think it's a cafeteria."

"A cafeteria?" David was incredulous. "In the middle of the Research Department?"

"That's what Facilities told me this morning. I called them when I saw the blueprints and they said that Carl and Katherine had approved it."

David called Carl. "Are you aware that Facilities is planning to build a cafeteria right smack in the middle of the Research Department?" he asked.

"I heard that it's going to be somewhere on 65, but I haven't seen any plans."

"Well I have, Carl, and it's right in the middle of my department!"

"I didn't put it there," Carl said defensively. "If you don't like it tell Katherine."

"Carl, why the hell do we need a cafeteria on 65 at all?"

"Because the traders never leave the building

between 9:00 and 4:00 and they need some place to get a snack during the trading day. They're on 64 but there's no place on 64 for a cafeteria, and you're on 63 so there's no place there, but 65 is opening up and better it should go there than 10 floors away."

"You didn't pick the location?"

"No, I guess Katherine did."

"Who's going to be allowed to use it?"

"Fuck if I know. I guess Research, Sales, Trading and Banking."

"So all day long I'm going to have salesmen and traders and bankers traipsing through the Research Department."

"Katherine said it would be confined to only a small part of the floor."

"It's not. It's huge, it's in the core of my half of the floor, and it's going to be nothing but disruptive. It's going to be noisy and it's going to smell."

"So the analysts will close their doors," said Carl.

"Carl, has anyone considered the Compliance-related problems this could cause?"

"What problems?"

"The problems, for instance, of having salesmen and traders and bankers walking past the analysts' secretaries' desks, on which are sitting, quite possibly, soon-to-be-published reports with ratings changes in them that we haven't yet announced?"

"I doubt that would happen."

"Really. Who's going to proof everyone coming to 65 to get a cup of coffee?"

"What do you mean 'proof'?"

"I mean who's going to determine that the nicely dressed man with *The Journal* tucked under his arm is actually a BCS analyst, salesman, trader or banker?"

"The doors will be locked and you'll need an ID to unlock them."

"Oh, of course, and when a dozen people exit the elevator on 65, talking and laughing and heading for the cafeteria, and when one of them unlocks the door with her ID, who's going to proof the other 11 people to make sure they're all BCS employees?"

"That could happen right now, David. Nothing's different."

"What's different, Carl, is that right now, Research is on 63, and the only people who typically walk through the glass doors on 63 are members of my department and a small number of salesmen, bankers and others who visit us during the day. What we're talking about here is hundreds of additional people each day who suddenly need to visit the Research floor, never having needed to before. We're talking about an exponential increase in both the amount of foot traffic and the potential for someone who has no business being in Research being in Research."

"I think you're being paranoid, David."

"I think I'm doing my job, Carl."

"Well then, do it with Katherine," Carl snapped. "This is a non-issue, and you and I both know it."

* * *

The hiring of new analysts at BCS comprised three acts. The first involved the whetting of the candidates' appetites by David at Adrienne. In Act II, the candidates visited BCS's offices and met with a cross section of analysts, salesmen, bankers and management members who split their time between sizing them up and selling them on joining the firm. If the candidates did well in Act II, it was then up to David to complete the negotiations and get them across the finish line.

Liz Tytus was ready for Act II, which was normally performed in a centrally located but hopefully discreet conference room in which candidates were planted for one to eight hours and to which a steady stream of interviewers came for 30-to 60-minute sessions. All interviewers were prepped with a memo from David describing the candidates' backgrounds, hot buttons that shouldn't be pressed, key selling points to be made and other information designed to maximize the success of the interview. Attached to each memo was a one-page form on which each interviewer voted yes or no on the candidate and explained why. Almost always, David scheduled himself last so he could discuss open issues that had come up at any of the preceding sessions and answer any questions that other interviewers might have been ill-equipped to address. Unanimity was rarely achieved. All David hoped for was a solid consensus one way or the other.

Liz Tytus's schedule looked quite typical. Liz had called in sick at Prudential so she could devote the entire day to interviewing, which David took as a sign she needed to make a decision soon. As a result, her dance card comprised 11 partners: Carl, David and Matt, John McLain, Paula Hainsworth and Herb Hirschorn, Paul Pitcher, investment banker Andrew Biddle Bivens, and three fellow consumer analysts: Joe Altschuler who did beverages, Robin Lomax, and Richard Geyer, the apparel retailing analyst.

Years before, David had also included Linda Logan in the process but, after she'd nixed 10 recruits in a row, six of whom were ranked and nine of whom had gotten overwhelmingly positive feedback from everyone else they'd seen, David concluded that Linda would never vote Yes on any analyst and relieved her of all interviewing responsibilities. Linda loved this because, every time new analysts fouled up, she could say that David had never given her the chance to interview them.

When David collected Liz from the conference room at 4:00, she looked very tired. "So, how did we do?"

"You did well, David, I have to admit. I knew that BCS was a better platform than Prudential but the people I met today were just as sharp as the people I've seen at some of the bulge-bracket firms."

Make sure I know that hiring you won't be easy, David thought.

"Matt had lots of good ideas about ways to leverage my tobacco litigation contacts that I hadn't thought about before. He knows a lot about the trials!"

"That's Matt. And he was very high on you," David said. He had, in truth, no idea what Matt thought about Liz but his mission at the moment was to send her home as high on BCS as possible. If Matt didn't like her he could let her down later without ever revealing how Matt had really voted.

"Herb Hirschorn's very, very sharp and pretty blunt, which I appreciate in my salespeople. Same for Paul Pitcher. He was excellent."

"And Paula?"

"She was tough," Liz said, wincing slightly. "She had me pitch her one idea after another until I thought I was going to faint but she seemed satisfied when we were done."

"And your meeting with Banking?"

"It went fine. Andrew knows tobacco but he hasn't spent much time on it lately because he hasn't had an analyst to work with and there hasn't been much financing in my space. I'm sure I could work with him and teach him what he needs to know."

"And my consumer analysts?"

"I loved Robin. She's very detail-oriented which I relate to. She's very professional, very client-focused like me and very competitive in a healthy kind of way. Joe just talked about Consumer Conferences that we could do and about the need to get food covered too, which reminds me …where do you stand in your food search?"

"It's under way. My hope is that we can get you on board quickly and then enlist your help in landing a really good food analyst. I'm sure you know all of them."

"I know most of them. Obviously, no one can touch John, and he and I have worked well together, but he isn't going anywhere. Nomi's gone, Erika's joined the buy side, David's pretty good but, if you can't get John, the one to get is Jaine Mehring at Salomon. She's done amazing work since she picked up the group a few years ago. At least that's what clients tell me. John respects her too, I think."

"Could you be helpful?"

"I could try. She knows me but not well. We'd need to spend more time together but I bet we'd hit it off pretty well."

"That would be great, but first things first. Tell me more about your meetings."

"That's about it. Carl was a little creepy."

David tried to look blase. "Creepy?"

"Yeah, you know. He kept looking me over. No big deal. I've seen his type before. He doesn't look his age, even though that black hair of his is turning salt-and-pepper, and he's obviously in great shape…I wish

I could do a three-twenty-seven marathon... but he's also sensitive about being, you know, short and skinny? So he tries to cover those insecurities by playing the ladies' man."

"Ladies' man?" David winced.

"He didn't say or do anything bad. It was just the way he kept looking at me."

David shook his head and Liz smiled.

"Did he really go to the London School of Economics? He must have mentioned it five times in thirty minutes."

David shrugged his shoulders. "That's what they tell me."

"It's hard to believe. He's not that smart. But anyway, I'd give everyone but Carl a thumbs up. I hope you didn't show me the only ten people at BCS who are any good."

"Hardly," David laughed. "We've got nothing to hide here. In fact I always say that the closer you look at us the better we appear. My toughest job is getting analysts in the door to check us out. Once they do we always more than hold our own. So what yellow lights are flashing?"

"Not many. I like the focus on the institutional business, the power of your retail system, which is much better than Prudential's from what I've heard, and the way you buffer the analysts with the Equity Desk. And banking looks better than nothing which is what I have at Pru now."

"Did the analysts talk about how we run things and how they like working here?"

"I asked them a lot about that. They all seem to really like and respect you and Matt. They like that you let them do their jobs in the way they think makes the most sense, they think your reviews are fair and objective, and they get a lot of good information out of them, and they like that they can change their ratings and estimates whenever they want to without having to jump through a lot of bureaucratic hoops."

Liz sighed. She was fading. "I'm pooped. This is worse than an institutional marketing trip!"

David laughed. "How about this. Think about it overnight and let's talk tomorrow. I'll get the feedback from everyone you saw today and, assuming it's good, which I'm sure it will be, I'll work through Richard on getting us back together next week so we can talk some more and I can put an offer together for you. Does that sound okay?"

"Perfect, David. I appreciate all the time. I hope everyone liked me."

Liz headed home and David returned to his office. He liked Liz a lot better this time than he had at Adrienne but there was no getting around it. She covered a relatively unimportant group, she was barely *II*-ranked, and she was going to be very, very expensive.

* * *

"How did she do?" Richard Lipstein asked that evening.

"She got six solid Yes's, four Okay-not-greats, and one No."

"Who voted No?"

"Paula. She said: 'Incapable of pitching cohesive stories. Thinks she's much better than she is. Condescending. Will be tough for Sales to work with.'"

"And who was lukewarm?"

"Richard Geyer, my apparel retailing analyst whose vote I don't weight heavily, Herb Hirschorn more

272

because of her coverage than her capabilities, Banking, and Carl."

"Is Carl's vote a problem?"

"I doubt it. Let me see what his objections were again." Richard could hear paper shuffling. "Here it is. Carl's comments were 'Tits kind of small, otherwise fine.'"

Richard laughed. "What did he really say?"

"He said 'Okay not great. Would rather our first hire be in a more important group.'"

"And your response to that would be…"

"I'd rather that too but we'll take what we can get, at least at the beginning of this process. Almost any All Star hire is better than no All Star hire."

"So how shall we proceed?"

"Tell her she did fabulously and that I want to make her an offer next week. See what you can learn about our competition for her services. There's at least one bulge-bracket firm on the scene I'm sure. Find out about the timing of any move she's planning to make, about handcuffs and about how much she's looking for."

"Let me also see what she thought about how her meetings went," said Richard.

"Call me back."

* * *

"David Meadows."

"David, it's George Sherva. How are you doing?"

"Still employed," David joked. "At least I didn't see any mention of my termination in *The Wall Street Letter* this week."

"Oh stop," George protested insincerely.

"What's doing?"

"David, I need to talk to you about Great Prairie Oil & Gas. I don't know if you know it at all, but it's a small exploration and production company that Nancy follows and has had an Accumulate on for over a year now. The stock is down a little from a year ago but it's held up reasonably well, and I've been working with them on a convert offering that they're close to signing us up to do.

"Well, the company just announced that they're going to miss the quarter by about a nickel, and Nancy is all in a tizzy over it. She's reading much too much into this, and she's threatening to cut her rating to Hold."

"When did you speak with her?"

"Five minutes ago. We had a long talk about it and I gave her a bunch of good reasons why this is a one-quarter problem and why she should keep the Accumulate on it, but she said something really stupid like… earnings disappointments are like cockroaches."

"Meaning?"

"Meaning that if you see one, you're probably going to see more."

David smiled. He remembered the first time he heard that theory. It was in a report that Melissa Brown, who had been an *II*-ranked quantitative analyst before moving into money management, had published, probably in the 1980s. David wasn't sure if Melissa had coined the phrase or not, but she'd been closely associated with it for many years. It was the kind of quote you never forgot.

"And she wants to downgrade to Hold?"

"I think so. She said she'll have to cut estimates and that the rating is at risk."

"And you want from me…what?"

"To block the downgrade."

"On what basis?"

"On the basis that we'll lose the convert deal for sure if she does."

"Do we have a mandate?"

"We're close."

"So you can't bring her over The Wall."

"Not until we get the mandate."

"And the timing of that is…?"

"Probably within the next two weeks."

"So the company just preannounced that it's going to miss the quarter, Nancy must react immediately and cut her estimates, but you want her to reiterate her Accumulate in the face of that for two more weeks until you can bring her over The Wall, restrict her and preclude her from changing her rating."

"That's right."

"That's wrong," David said, "and the answer is no."

* * *

Alan Bellone's spine was starting to ache. His high-back leather desk chair provided lots of support but, when you sat in it for six straight hours and left it only to retrieve the lunch you'd had delivered and for two quick trips to the men's room, you just couldn't avoid the pain. Alan's eyes were also getting tired from looking at his computer monitor. After six hours they'd begun to glaze.

Alan's secretary, who had taken messages whenever the phone had rung, as instructed, hoped her boss had made some serious progress on his REIT Industry Outlook but he hadn't. In fact, he'd made no progress at all on it because, rather than writing about real estate investment trusts, his specialty, Alan instead had spent six uninterrupted hours, from 10:45 A.M. to 4:45 P.M., surfing the Internet for porn.

It was a pastime that Alan had first undertaken several months earlier. Initially, he'd stayed late after work and surfed in the darkness and quiet of his office after everyone else had gone home. He'd have to cover his web browser with an Excel spreadsheet whenever the cleaning people came by but, once they'd collected his trash, he almost always had smooth sailing. Only twice had fellow analysts come unexpectedly into his office and, in both cases, Alan had been more than fast enough using Excel to mask his growing obsession.

As the weeks and months passed, however, Alan had found himself starting his surfing earlier and earlier, first at 5:00 when his secretary went home, then at 4:00 when the market closed, then at 2:00 after having worked until 1:30 and lunched for 30 minutes and, most recently, at 11:00 when he'd begun locking himself away "to write reports." His secretary seemed puzzled at times over the dearth of reports that Alan produced but she never questioned him about it.

All afternoon he'd surfed hardcore sites that could be accessed without a "membership fee." Alan was careful about those. The last thing he wanted was porn site memberships associated with a BCS phone number. Now, as 5:00 neared, he changed gears and accessed Danni Ashe's web site, where he could look with great pleasure at dozens of nude photographs of "the world's most downloaded woman." Alan looked to see if any new photos had been added to her gallery and, finding none, hunted down his old favorites on pages he'd memorized long ago, said goodbye to his secretary, rubbed his aching lower back and soaked Danni up.

* * *

As promised, Louis Liddy also made his way to 3 New York Plaza to meet and be meeted but, unlike Liz Tytus, Louis was only available after 3:00 P.M. so David only scheduled him to see six people.

"We're going to start with Robin Lomax," David explained as he set Louis up in one of the conference rooms on the Sales and Trading floor.

"Robin's our broadlines analyst. She's very good and she joined us fairly recently so she should have some interesting perspectives on transitioning to BCS from another firm. After Robin you'll see Craigson Lucie who's an MD in Banking and who specializes in the restaurant industry. Then, Paul Pitcher from Retail, Matt Speiser who's my Associate Director of Research, Joe Altschuler who does beverages and John McLain who heads Institutional Sales."

"Sounds good."

"Can I get you something to drink?"

"No thanks David, I'm fine."

"Good. Well, I'm going to run but I'm sure Robin will be here in a minute so make yourself at home. If you need to dial out just hit '9' first."

"I've got my cell phone," Louis said, holding up his right hand and shaking his head quickly.

"Okay then. When you and Robin are done, Robin will call Craig and tell him you're ready for him, Craig will call Paul and so forth. So I may not see you again today but I'll check back with you tomorrow, through Richard, to see how things went and to talk about round two."

The two shook hands and David left, closing the door behind him to minimize the risk that someone who shouldn't see Louis saw him. As he did he could hear Louis opening his cell phone, probably to check for voicemails.

* * *

At 4:45 P.M., David's phone rang and Paul Pitcher's number flashed in Caller ID.

"Where's Louis Liddy?"

"What do you mean? He's in Conference Room B on 64."

"No he's not."

"Weren't you supposed to see him at 4:00?"

"That's what my memo says."

"I don't know. He had Craig Lucie at 3:30 and you at 4:00. Craig never called?"

"Nope, and I just called Conference Room B and there was no answer."

"I'll call you back."

David called Robin Lomax. "Yes," she said, "I passed Louis on to Craig at 3:30 and reminded him to call Paul at 4:00."

"Well, he didn't. Thanks, Robin. I'm sorry I bothered you with this."

David next called Craig Lucie's office. "He's behind closed doors," his secretary told David.

"I need to interrupt him. Would you slip him a note please?"

David was placed on Hold. A moment later someone picked him up.

"Lucie."

"Craig, it's David Meadows. Do you know where Louis Liddy went?"

"I certainly do. He's right here with me. We've been having a great time comparing notes on all the nut jobs running restaurant chains we've gotten to know over the years. As it turns out, we're close to a lot of the same companies. I know we could do a lot of business together and I think Louis agrees."

"Well, that's great, Craig, but do you know what time it is?"

"Jesus, it's ten to five."

"That's right, and Louis was supposed to see Paul Pitcher at 4:00 and Matt at 4:30."

"I'm really sorry, David. Can he see them now?"

"Why didn't you stay in the conference room?"

"Oh, I just thought it would be more comfortable up here," Craig said, clueless.

"You thought it would be more comfortable. Look, take Louis, please, right back to Conference Room B, have your secretary let Joe Altschuler know that he's ready for him, and call Paul and Matt and explain what happened. I'll have to reschedule them."

"Done, David. Sorry."

David hung up, shaking his head slowly and rolling his eyes. Why was it, he wondered, that the only people who couldn't simply interview a candidate for 30 minutes in a conference room on 64 or, in fact, *ever* play by anyone else's rules, were the bankers?

* * *

Ken Lavery was bored and it was time to do something about it so he speed-dialed his broker.

"The other Tom Hanks."

"Tom, Ken Lavery."

"Ken! Where've you been? I haven't heard from you in ages. How are you?"

279

"Good, but very busy. So busy in fact that I haven't paid much attention to my account until today. I'd like to do something, I think."

"Let's pull it up." Ken waited as Tom accessed his account summary. "Let's see. You've got 100,000 Genomic Innovators at 11, 100,000 G-NOME at 9, and $1,500,000 of Regeneron, Amgen and Genentech. So you've got $3,500,000 of stocks, about $50,000 of cash, and a margin loan totaling $1,400,000."

"So my equity is now…"

"$3,550,000 minus $1,400,000 or $2,150,000."

"And that gives me additional borrowing power of $750,000?"

"At least."

"Good. Let's do this. Let's increase the margin loan to $2,150,000 and let's use that $750,000 of additional borrowings plus the $50,000 of cash to buy another 40,000 shares each of G-NOME and Genomic Innovators."

"I may have to push both prices up a little to get you the 40,000 shares."

"That's okay. Up to 9½ and 11½ is fine. That means I'll probably spend a little more than the $800,000 I've got, including commissions, so let me know what the final damages are and I'll send you a check for the difference."

"Consider it done. I'll call you back to confirm."

As soon as Tom hung up, Ken called Jim Molloy.

"I'd like to buy some more G-NOME and Genomic Innovators," he told Jim.

"How much?"

"Forty thousand shares of each."

"You don't cover either of them, do you Ken?"

"No."

"Do you plan to initiate coverage within the next six months?"

"No."

"Are you involved in any investment banking transactions relating to either of those companies?"

"No." There was a long pause.

"Okay, you're clear, but only for 48 hours."

Two hours later, Tom Hanks called back. "You got the G-NOME at an average price of $9.25, so you now have 140,000 shares at an average cost of just over $7, and you got the Genomic Innovators at $11.25, so you now have 140,000 shares at an average cost of just over $7.50. Send me a check for $25,000 and we're even."

Next Ken opened his calendar and looked for the first two consecutive days on which he had relatively few appointments. He found them: April 17 and 18. Then he picked up his phone, found Martin Gool's phone number and dialed it. To his surprise, Martin answered his own phone.

"Martin, it's Ken Lavery."

"Ken Lavery, Ken Lavery, I know that name from somewhere."

"Fuck you, Martin, you know I pay more attention to your region than anyone else in the Research Department so don't bust my balls."

"Lavery, did you say? And you're an analyst?"

"Yes, you asshole, I'm your biotech analyst. You know, the one you said was the best analyst at EFS the last time I visited your branches?"

"That's so long ago. I can't really get that in focus."

"Oh, really! Well, focus on this! How about two days of nothing but branch visits of your choosing in April?"

"Am I paying for another of your Florida vacations

that you're tacking some branch visits before or behind?"

"No, I'd come down just to visit your branches."

"Which days?"

"Thursday and Friday the 17th and 18th."

"That should be fine. You can do St. Pete, Sarasota, Naples and Ft. Lauderdale on the 17th, and Palm Beach, Boca and the two branches in Miami on the 18th."

"Eight offices?"

"You can do it if you fly into Tampa/St. Pete on the night of the 16th and fly out of Miami on the evening of the 18th. You'll be driving about 400 miles over two days but it's doable."

"You'll put the schedule together?"

"I'll do the schedule and e-mail it to you. What are you pushing these days?"

"Mostly the same names... especially Regeneron."

"Your group's been sort of flat lately."

"That's true but it'll pick up again."

"You have enough stuff you like to get these guys excited?"

"Yup."

"Good. It'll be great to see you again. Watch your e-mail."

"Thanks, Martin. You too. See you."

Ken hung up, marked his calendar, asked his secretary to reschedule the handful of appointments that were conflicts, kicked back in his chair and wondered just how big a hurricane he'd create in GNOM and GINV by the time he finished branch number eight.

* * *

Thankfully, March was going out like a lamb. Ten days into spring, New York had turned sunny and quite mild, lifting David's spirits. He whistled Andrew Lloyd Webber and checked for voicemails. There were two, both from James Brell.

"Do you have a minute?" James asked when David reached him.

"Sure. Come on over."

David could feel his heartbeat accelerating. His belly recognized the tone in Brell's voice. It was somber-sounding and strained. When James arrived, looking grave, David became even more convinced. Perhaps his father had suffered a heart attack. Perhaps he'd gotten a margin call that he couldn't meet. Maybe his wife had asked for a divorce. Selfishly, David hoped for any of them but, deep down, he knew it was door number four.

"I have an offer," James said as he closed David's door behind him.

"Who?"

"Lehman. Two years. I signed it last night."

"Beyond being pissed that I didn't offer you a contract, what else is going on here? How much did they offer you?"

"I'd rather not discuss economics, David. It really isn't about the money."

"What can I do to keep you from leaving?"

"Nothing, David. Don't ask all the salespeople to call and tell me how much they love me, and don't have every Lehman alumnus call and tell me what a rat hole Lehman is. Just let me go."

As David stood up, extending his hand and wishing James well, Lisa knocked on David's door and told him that Carl was calling and needed to interrupt him.

"James is going to Lehman," David told her.

"Really! Are you taking all your people with you?" Lisa asked. James nodded.

David held up a finger, walked to his desk and picked up his phone. "Carl?"

"What took you so long?"

"I had James Brell in my office, resigning."

"Where's he going?"

"To Lehman."

"That little prick."

"So why were you calling me?"

"I forgot," Carl admitted. "I guess it wasn't important."

What a surprise, David thought as he jotted himself a note to call Julia Harris. He *must* have photos of *someone*.

APRIL

$\mathbf{B}$ack at his table at Adrienne, David began April Fools' Day by breakfasting with Tom Batchelder, a packaging analyst at Merrill Lynch whom Dave Hart had convinced, after much hemming and hawing, to invest an hour in BCS. Packaging, which included companies like Sealed Air, Avery Dennison, Crown Cork & Seal and Owens-Illinois, was far from the most important industry that *II* measured, and throwing a lot of money at it would be, under normal circumstances, indefensible in most clients' eyes. But David needed to hire so many All Stars that he'd err by hiring in, rather than passing up, too many less important industries.

David liked Tom a lot. He found him cerebral, soft-spoken and reserved, not at all typical of most sell side personalities. His written product looked deep and thorough, and his ability to verbalize his analytical approach and investment philosophy was first-rate. Not surprisingly, Tom also manifested great satisfaction with Merrill Lynch, although he expressed discomfort with following a less important group inside a very large department and frustration getting his fair share of the salesmen's attention. At times, he said, he'd found it hard to set up marketing trips to see his institutional clients because the sales force was too busy selling deals or marketing analysts with more important groups.

After David had done his song and dance for Tom, and Tom had asked about the pros and cons of analysts appearing all the time on CNBC, David said, "What else didn't we talk about that's important to you?"

"I don't know, David. We covered a lot. Maybe I should think about it a little and then call you."

"I'd love to get you in to meet some people."

"I know. I just don't want to waste your time."

"Investing a day in you would never be a waste of time," David said, meaning it. He'd lost count of the analysts with whom he'd struck out initially but who later joined his ranks, and he knew that, unless he at least got them through the door now, his chances of hiring them later approached zero.

Tom nodded. "I'll think about it, seriously, and call Dave Hart."

David nodded, understanding. He wasn't optimistic, but it was better than a "no."

* * *

"I'm such a Lame-O," the voice in the background kept repeating. David knew it well and, whenever he heard it, his eyes moved involuntarily to his TV screen to see who CNBC was going to ding next.

"That's right, Mark," David Faber was saying, "I have a Lame-O to award today, and it goes to BC Securities, which demonstrated unique insights and timing in downgrading semiconductor manufacturer D-RAM Designs today from Buy to Hold." Faber paused, being forced to wait slightly too long for the chart of D-RAM to come up on the screen. The chart was ugly. "D-RAM, as you can see here, Mark, peaked 10 months ago at 79, and over the past 10 months, even longer in fact, BCS maintained a Buy rating on the stock. However, today, for reasons that only *he* may fully understand, analyst Martin Hogue has decided to downgrade D-RAM from Buy to Hold. D-RAM, as you can see ever so clearly here, closed last night at $8.25.

"Mr. Hogue, my records indicate, had previously reduced his target price on D-RAM on four occasions, from $110 to $70, then to $52, later to $37 and most recently to $21. But today he cut it again, to $9 which, he says, and I quote, 'provides insufficient upside potential to justify maintaining the Buy at this time' unquote."

"Lisa, ask Martin Hogue to come see me right away if he's around," David called out, having seen and heard enough from CNBC. "If he's out, ask that he call me ASAP."

A minute later, Lisa reported that Martin was traveling and that she'd left word asking him to call. About 25 minutes later, he did.

"You went to Hold on D-RAM at 8, down from 80?"

"I had to," Martin answered. "I don't see it trading above 10 any time soon."

"Martin, I'm not asking about that, I'm asking how you could've maintained the Buy on the stock from 80 to 8."

"Well, we're obviously late."

"That's putting it mildly. Why?"

"Well, we really couldn't have done it sooner because, when the stock first started falling, the selloff seemed to be based more on changes in market psychology than on deteriorating fundamentals."

"What does that mean?"

"That the company's business was holding up all right as far as we could tell and that investors just seemed to be souring on the group and seemed unwilling to pay as high a P/E for D-RAM as they had before."

"Then what happened?"

"Then bookings began to soften but, by the time this became clear, the stock was already down from 80 to 25. We reduced our target price when we needed to, but it wasn't until our most recent cut in our earnings estimates that the stock actually stopped looking undervalued."

"So you took the decline from 80 to 25 as nothing more than a change in market psychology?"

"Yes, that's how it looked to us."

David was speechless. "Do you know that you got a Lame-O today?"

"I heard. I really don't think CNBC is being fair about this. Is someone going to call and explain things to them?"

"You can if you want to, Martin, but I wouldn't know where to begin."

* * *

"So where do we stand?"

"She appears ready for your offer," said Richard Lipstein. "She's been very coy about her other opportunities but she's hinted that they exist often enough to make me think she has at least one real offer from someone else that she's prepared to accept."

"Handcuffs?"

"$550,000."

"And timing?"

"If you're interested you should make your offer now. That's all she'd say."

"And her feelings about us?"

"She liked you, liked the people she met and could see herself working at BCS…"

"… if the price is right."

"Exactly."

"And you think, Richard, that we need to offer her what?"

"Well, she's intimated on more than one occasion that she considers her market value something starting with a three."

"She said that to me too when I met her."

"I don't know that she actually has an offer that high in hand but she's clearly angling for one."

"Let's say she has an offer of, oh, $2,750,000 from someone. If I offered her $3,750,000, that would look materially better to her, wouldn't it?"

"It should," Richard agreed, although not as emphatically as David had hoped.

"She thinks her market value is $3,000,000."

"If you want to know what would deliver her, without question, it's $4,000,000."

"Jesus, $4,000,000 for a tobacco analyst?"

"It's not just for a tobacco analyst, David. You know that."

"It's for my first All Star hire of this new campaign."

"Exactly. The first analyst to say yes assumes a much higher degree of vocational risk than does the tenth or twentieth, so he or she gets the most battle pay for assuming that risk. What if you fail to build up as quickly as you want to? What if BC Holdings changes its mind? What if your budget is reduced?"

"All unlikely."

"You and I know that but Liz Tytus doesn't."

David was quiet for a minute. "Hold on for a second," he said. "Let me get the green light from Dieter."

"You want to call me back?"

"No, just hold on." David called Dieter who, everyone had agreed, would be the one to approve specific job offers for new analysts. He explained the situation to Dieter, told him that Liz had an offer believed to be in the low threes, and that BCS would have to offer her four plus the handcuff buyout to get her.

"She interviewed well?"

"Very well," David lied, "but we'd still make her offer subject to a client check."

"I hope all your new hires won't cost $4 million, David," Dieter said, predictably. "Otherwise, you're going to run out of money very quickly."

"They won't," David said, reassuringly. "It's hardest at the beginning."

"Then do it."

"Ask her to come see me ASAP," David said to Richard. "Tell her that her offer is ready. You don't know how much it is, but you know that I know that she believes her market value is $3 million."

"Will do. Any time today?"

"Whenever she can get here."

"I'll be back to you."

David summoned Lisa. "Write me a contract for Liz Tytus," he said when she arrived. "Managing Director, Senior Tobacco Analyst, salary of $200,000, guaranteed bonuses of $3,800,000 this year and next, plus $550,000 of restricted BC Holdings stock to vest 33% a year for three years. All the usual stuff beyond that, including change of control protection and subject to a client check."

"When am I doing the client check?"

"As soon as she approves it, probably tomorrow."

"When is she going to take her drug test?"

"Don't know, probably tomorrow too."

"Cool," Lisa said. "This will be fun."

* * *

David told Liz at 6:00 that evening that BCS would pay her $4,000,000 a year for two years and would make her whole on her $550,000 of Prudential Securities handcuffs. Liz seemed satisfied but was completely matter-of-fact about the magnitude of the offer. She authorized the client check, agreed to be drug-tested the following day, and ironed out compensation terms for her two associates and her secretary.

Thirty-six hours later, Liz had passed her drug test, the institutional sales force had reported back that it had spoken to 23 institutional clients about Liz, that six had said very positive things about her, 10 had been mildly positive, five had been indifferent and two had been openly and unequivocally negative. Hardly an overwhelming endorsement, David thought, but good enough. And so, with great fanfare, David announced on April 4 that Liz Tytus had joined BCS as a managing director and the firm's new senior tobacco analyst.

And Liz, who in fact had never received an offer from *anyone* other than David, laughed all the way to the bank.

* * *

Around 7:30 the following evening, as David finished reading his backlog of e-mails, he heard a rustling sound by his office door and was surprised to find Samantha Smeralda, the librarian, looking his way and smiling.

"Hi, David, do you have a minute?" Samantha had a short, day-glow blue leather jacket and a black leather skirt on, and a shopping bag in each hand. The shopping bags were emblazoned with the word "Unique" on both sides. The logo seemed vaguely familiar to David but at first he couldn't place it. Then he remembered. Unique was a clothing store in Greenwich Village, on Broadway south of 8th Street, that had sold tie-dyed T-shirts, jeans and tank tops to real hippies, aspiring hippies and nerds who just wanted to look like hippies. Much of Unique's offerings were second-hand and thus cheap, which to real hippies was Unique's principal allure, and much of the clothing, if not truly unique, was highly unusual, apparel you'd never find at The Gap. David hadn't seen or heard about Unique in a long time and was surprised that it was still in business.

"Sure. What did you bring me?"

"Uh-oh." Samantha feigned horror at having shopped only for herself and then laughed. "Kathy told me once that you took unusual vacations, you know, to strange and exotic places like India and Africa and Bora Bora. Is that true?"

"Yes, I love to vacation far from home and to see things I've never seen before."

"Kathy said she thought you once went to Egypt?"

"Kathy never lies. Many years ago, I went to Cairo for a week and saw the pyramids and the sphinx, and then I spent a week cruising down the Nile. The temples were unbelievably beautiful, but the food on the barge wasn't always refrigerated properly so I got sick as a dog and lost 10 pounds in six days."

"And you didn't have 10 pounds to lose!" Samantha volunteered. "Did you see the King Tut exhibit when you were in Cairo?"

"I did. You were probably a baby then, but the year before I went to Cairo, many of the best pieces from that collection went on a world tour that included a stop at the Metropolitan Museum of Art in New York. I saw the show, which was pretty spectacular, and it pushed me to stop talking about going to Egypt and to go. The jewels and the gold that Howard Carter found were very beautiful, and that burial mask!"

"I've seen photos of it" Samantha said. "It was blue and gold and had that long, golden beard on it."

"That's the one."

"Well, since you've been there, I thought you'd get a kick out of something I found at Unique today that I just had to buy." Samantha rummaged through one of her shopping bags and pulled out something small wrapped in white tissue paper. She looked at it for a minute, then looked up at David and said, "I need to put it on. Let me run to the Ladies' Room. I'll be right back."

While she was gone, David checked more e-mails. Halfway through his third message, Samantha returned.

"Are you ready?" Samantha looked very much as she had when she'd first poked her head in. The black leather skirt was the same and the day-glow blue leather jacket was still on, but instead of holding her shopping bags, which she'd left in the office, Samantha held her blouse and bra in one hand. She threw them hurriedly into one of the shopping bags, then straightened up, moved to the center of David's office, faced him, and grabbed the large left collar of her jacket with one hand and the zipper on the front of the jacket with the other.

"Ready?"

"I think so," David answered, feigning trepidation, at which point Samantha slowly unzipped the day-glow blue leather jacket and opened it. She was laughing. "Well, what do you think?"

Under the jacket Samantha had donned a sheer white T-shirt. At first David was glued to the two large breasts that strained against a garment that was several sizes too small. David could see the outline of both nipples, high on her rib cage, pointing up and slightly away from each other. Then he focused on the artwork on the T-shirt itself. On the upper left and the upper right were two identical, blue and gold Tutankhamen burial masks, and below them, written horizontally across the upper belly, in dark gold glitter, was a warning: "Don't touch my Tuts!"

David couldn't help but laugh. Samantha was obviously pleased that he found her entertaining. She knew that he'd like how badly the T-shirt fit her and she arched her back a little as she laughed so he could see her bare belly below the bottom of the shirt.

As if she'd anticipated the awkward silence that was destined to follow, Samantha quickly picked up her shopping bags and her jacket, gave David one last look at her Tuts, and walked to his door.

"Of course, for you David I'd make an exception," she said with her biggest smile. Then she was gone.

* * *

Finally, after three false starts spanning five weeks,

Van Trudell turned up to interview. David greeted him at the reception desk on the 64th floor, set him up in one of the conference rooms and showed him his schedule. "This morning you've got four meetings: Matt Speiser, my Associate Director of Research, Laura Payden whom I'm sure you know…"

Van nodded. "Does Arthur know I'm here?"

"I doubt it. I don't think he and Laura are that close, so Laura may have just agreed to see you and assumed that I'd handle Arthur." David paused for a second and then added, "But I'd made clear to Arthur in February that this was going to happen. I never recruit my analysts' competitors behind their backs."

"That's pretty unusual, David."

"It's just the way I am, and it's served me well. Anyway, Matt and Laura, then Rebecca Suess, my environmental services analyst, and Alan Gildersleeve who's a young paper and forest products analyst whom I hired late last year. Lunch is with the bankers." David, anxious to avoid a rerun of the Louis Liddy debacle and remembering how upset Van had been over Prudential's firing of all of its investment bankers, had decided to give Van to the bankers between noon and 2:00. "In the afternoon we've got some institutional salespeople, John McLain who runs Institutional Sales, Paul Pitcher who's a big deal in Retail-land, and Carl Robern who runs Capital Markets."

"That's the waterfront," Van said, looking very satisfied.

"We try." Matt knocked on the open conference room door and walked in, extending his hand to Van and introducing himself.

"I'm going to leave you in Matt's good hands,"

David said. "I'll catch up with you at the end of the day, Van."

"If I'm still conscious, David."

* * *

"It's Michael Zisk," Lisa yelled. David picked him up. It was 2:05 P.M.

"So, what'd you think?"

"You've gotta hire this guy, David, and I mean today. Don't let him out of the building until he's signed a contract."

"Does that mean you liked him?"

"It means that this guy can help us do a lot of business. He loves banking. He did a little of it at Pru before they shut Investment Banking down and he was rip shit over losing his bankers just as the window seemed to be opening for deals in his space. He says he's just been waiting and waiting for a firm with a serious banking effort to call him. We did and he's ready to join us. He just needs a contract."

"Is he well connected?"

"Definitely. He's close to the managements of seven companies we can do business with. We're not going to be lead manager on any major chemical companies' equity deals any time soon, but we can land solid positions as co-lead manager based on his ties. We checked him out this morning before we met him for lunch with quite a few people in industry and he's the real McCoy."

"Did you tell him that you'd done that?"

"Yes."

"Was he upset?"

"Didn't seem to be. He said he'd prefer that we

didn't talk to clients about him yet but he didn't seem to mind that we'd talked to his managements."

David shook his head. Never an ounce of discretion and so utterly consistent.

"What did everyone else think of him?" Michael asked.

"I don't know. I haven't gotten the feedback forms back yet but I will by the end of the day so check with me then."

At 6:15 P.M. Michael called back. "So, did you hire him?"

David sighed. "I saw him before he left, Michael, and he seemed in very good spirits. He said he'd had good meetings, especially with your crew, and that he was eager to hear back from me regarding how things had gone from our end. I promised him that I'd call him tomorrow."

"What does that mean?"

"It means that he did surprisingly poorly with most of the research and sales types who saw him today. Matt was lukewarm, Laura thought he was better than Arthur but not much…"

"She wants the job, David. She's not going to bless Van or anyone else from outside. She wants everyone you bring in to flunk so you can let her broaden from specialties into commodities."

"That may be true. I'm just telling you what came back. Rebecca Suess was neutral, Alan Gildersleeve liked him, he got thumbs down from both institutional salesmen who saw him and from John McLain, Paul Pitcher was lukewarm, and Carl thought he was fine."

"This is bullshit, David. This guy's *II*-ranked and banker friendly. How often do you find that? Hardly ever if you ask me."

"I hear you, Michael, but I've got to tell you that

the analysts questioned his smarts and the sales types questioned his selling skills. He may be a good banker but that's not normally enough to justify a job offer from me." David felt caught. He wanted to hire Van. He needed his *II* vote but he also needed broader support for Van than the feedback sheets had evidenced. How could he justify hiring Van to all the people who had seen him today and nixed him?

"My suggestion?" he said to Michael. "Call Carl and tell him what you think."

"Done." David's phone went dead. It was 6:20. Seventeen seconds later it rang.

"Let me guess," he said to Michael Zisk.

"He's gone for the day. I'll leave him a voicemail and call you back in the morning after I reach him."

"Good luck," David said. To both of us, he thought.

* * *

Carl called David at 9:35 the next morning.

"Hire the guy."

"Why?"

"Because he can generate $10 million of banking fees during his first 12 months with us, that's why."

"John and his crew didn't like him."

"Not true. I spoke to John and the sentiment in Sales was that the guy was smart enough, orders of magnitude better than Arthur, and an okay marketer."

"Their feedback sheets are more negative than that."

"Fuck their feedback sheets. I'm telling you how they feel. Send the asshole to Communispond to improve his presentation skills. Those things can be fixed, you know."

David cringed. He'd been the one, several years earlier, who had told Carl about how Communispond worked with analysts on their verbal presentation skills. Now Carl was hurling it back in David's face.

"I'll have to talk to Dieter."

"No, you won't. I already talked to him and he said you should hire the guy."

"Okay, but you tell John and Paul Pitcher why."

"When I'm not so busy," Carl said and hung up.

David called Dieter anyway. "I just want to be sure you understand what's going on here," he said. "Research and Sales nixed the guy. Banking loves him, probably because he's willing to spend 50% of his time doing deals and because they're comparing him to Arthur Litt, our weakest analyst. Normally, we try to get a solid majority of the people who interview a candidate to give him a thumbs-up before extending an offer. We don't have one here."

"Carl said he can generate $10 million of banking fees."

"Carl got that number from Michael Zisk. He has no way of confirming it."

"David, he's a ranked analyst, which helps you, and perhaps he can generate $10 million of banking fees, which helps me, so just do it already."

"Okay, but if you hear some grumbling in the field about the quality of the hire I hope you'll remember this conversation."

"Just do it, David."

David hung up, smiled ever so slightly, and added a notch to his "newly hired All Stars" tally.

* * *

"Dave Hart."

"Dave, it's David Meadows. Got a minute to talk about Van Trudell?"

"Lisa sent me the feedback sheets. Not too good, it seems."

"Not too good, but apparently good enough to justify an offer."

"You're kidding."

"No, I'm not. The bankers love the guy and they've convinced Carl and Dieter that I should hire him."

"How do you like that?"

"What are his numbers?"

"He's making $2,350,000 now. Nothing from banking, obviously. He has $675,000 of handcuffs. I think you can do him for three."

"Okay, call him, please, and get him here ASAP for an offer."

"Will do."

At 1:00 P.M., Van collected his offer: Managing Director, base salary of $200,000, guaranteed bonuses from Research of $2,800,000 per year for two years plus $675,000 of restricted BC Holdings common stock. Van agreed to get drug tested and authorized the client check and, two days later, with the client check reading 10 positive, 16 okay-not-great and 4 negative, Van got the words "subject to a client check that is satisfactory to BCS" stricken from his offer and signed it.

* * *

David called Donna Thorenson in Human Resources. "It's Arthur Litt time."

"Right now?"

"Can you?"

"How about in 20 minutes?"

"Perfect. Where?"

"Not in your office, David. This will be upsetting

enough to Arthur as it is, and it'll be two on one no matter where we do it so a neutral location will limit the trauma. Also, we'll give Arthur a little time to protest but, if it looks as if he's going to be really argumentative, you can get up and return to your office and I'll stay behind with Arthur and try to talk him to a better place."

"A conference room?"

"Preferably one away from Research."

"How about Conference Room C on 64 in 20 minutes."

"Give us five minutes alone before you schedule Arthur to arrive."

"Bingo. See you then."

David and Donna had done this before so there was an air of familiarity surrounding their get-together. It had been a while, though, and David welcomed the chance to refresh himself on who'd say what to whom before Arthur arrived. It was agreed that David would do most of the talking initially and that Donna would take the baton after about five minutes.

Arthur looked very anxious as he entered the conference room. Sometimes, David had found, analysts who should have known this was coming never knew.

"Hello, Arthur," said David, rising, motioning him to a chair by the circular table and closing the conference room door behind him. "Arthur, I think you know Donna Thorenson from H.R.?"

"I do," he said, shaking her hand and sitting down next to her.

"Arthur, I'm afraid we have some bad news." Arthur looked directly at David, eyes widening slightly, silently. "We've decided to let you go."

"Oh David, no!"

Arthur's voice was loud in his ears but David kept to his script. "You know that we talked about how you were performing during your October review and that I warned you in February that we might seek to hire someone in your space with much stronger institutional client penetration and, as it turns out, we have."

"You're letting me go?"

"I'm afraid so."

"Who did you hire?"

"It doesn't matter, Arthur. Nothing's been announced yet, nor will it be until we give you a chance to spin the story in a way that will feel least uncomfortable to you."

"I'll bet you hired Van Trudell."

"I don't think that's appropriate for us to discuss yet, Arthur," Donna said gently.

"What we want to do," David continued, "is discuss your severance package with you and ask you how you want to describe your departure."

"You know how long I've been here?"

"Twenty-six years."

"That's right."

"Which is why your severance package will be materially better than average."

"And that means…"

"Twenty-six months of salary which I believe is $433,000."

"What about my bonus?"

"Your last bonus was $35,000 so we're going to add $35,000 to that $433,000 because you probably would've gotten that kind of bonus in April had we not hired anyone. So the total package is $468,000. You'll also receive outplacement assistance."

"That hardly seems enough for a lifetime's work."

"It's more than twice firm policy. Normally, the firm never pays more than 12 months of salary even to employees with more than 12 years of service. Under the old EFS guidelines, you'd only be entitled to $200,000. The extra 14 months of salary and the final bonus are over and above the norm."

"I'm overwhelmed," Arthur said sarcastically.

"You will, however, be required to sign a release before you get this money."

"A release meaning that I agree not to sue you for age discrimination?"

"Or for anything else."

"What a deal."

David let it slide. "Now, we can say when we announce this…"

"Why does it have to be announced?"

"Because your successor will be arriving soon and we'll need to explain where you went, and why, as part of his announcement. We can say that you decided to retire or that you resigned to pursue other opportunities or something else that would limit any embarrassment to you."

"I'm not retiring. I need to keep working and I'll no doubt find a position with one of your competitors so I don't want this described as a retirement. Say I resigned because 26 years in this Hell hole is more than enough for any man, and that I'm going to finish up my career at a professionally managed, highly profitable competitor of BCS's."

"I'm sure that Arthur and I can work out the wording, David, and show it to you for approval before we release it," Donna said helpfully.

"I can't believe you're doing this to me, David."

"This isn't personal, Arthur, at least not on my side.

I just think that a fresh start would be beneficial for both of us."

"My numbers aren't the worst in the department, you know. There are analysts with numbers that are much worse than mine. Why aren't you firing them?"

"David, I think you have a meeting that you're late for," Donna interrupted. "Why don't you head off to it and Arthur and I will finish up here?"

David checked his watch and nodded. As he rose he looked at Arthur and said, simply, "I'm sorry, Arthur. I hope this works out for the best for you."

"For me," Arthur answered, "yes. For you, no."

* * *

Van Trudell arrived two days later, and a press release went out announcing that he'd been hired to replace Arthur Litt, a 26-year veteran of BCS and its predecessors who had decided to pursue other business opportunities.

The following evening, when David returned home after a recruiting dinner at Bice, he found two messages on his answering machine from a Hugo Silaski, "S-I-L-A-S-K-I," of *The Wall Street Journal*, who said he was writing a story about Arthur Litt's departure and seeking a comment from management. He'd left his work and home phone numbers. David knew, instinctively, not to return the calls. Instead, the next morning, he passed them on to Jennifer Von Moos, and in the afternoon Jennifer called back with an update. Hugo Silaski was a *Wall Street Journal* reporter who covered chemicals and who was writing a story about Arthur. Silaski wanted to know why Arthur was fired, whether "failing to make *II* " was grounds for termination, and whether making *II* was now a departmental requirement for ongoing employment at BCS.

"For your ears only, Jenn, Arthur hasn't been *II*-ranked for many years. But I've got to tell you that, if eight analysts on The Street are named All Stars in the chemicals category, I'm entitled to aspire to employ one of them, and if Arthur can't be one of them, I'm entitled to seek a stronger replacement. Arthur has performed badly for many years, and all *II* has done is confirm what I already knew about his standing in the eyes of institutional clients. I've always said that *II* is the thermometer, not the temperature."

"What about *II* being a departmental requirement?"

"It isn't. We have plenty of analysts who didn't make *II* last year who didn't get fired."

"Let me call Katherine and see how she wants to handle it," Jennifer suggested.

Fifteen minutes later, Jennifer was back. "Katherine instructed me to call Silaski back and tell him that we don't elaborate on employee departures."

"Did you?"

"Five minutes ago."

"And?"

"I think he expected me to say what I said. You never know with these guys. Hopefully he'll lose interest."

The next morning, when David returned to his office after a recruiting breakfast at Adrienne, Matt was waiting for him, *Wall Street Journal* in hand.

"Did you see it?"

"I didn't see *The Journal* this morning. I got *The Times* delivered but no *Journal*."

"You're not going to believe it."

"Read it to me."

"Twenty-Six Year EFS Veteran Ousted For Young

Star by Hugo Silaski." Matt looked up at David for
reaction. David seemed genuinely puzzled and
motioned Matt to keep reading. "Arthur Litt, 55, one
of Wall Street's first chemical analysts and a 26-year
veteran of BCS predecessor Equitable Finance Securities, was forced out of BCS earlier this week and
replaced by Van Trudell, 31, an *II* runner-up who had
previously worked at Prudential Securities. Sources
close to BCS and Litt said that Litt had been termi-
nated for failing to make the *Institutional Investor* All
Star team in recent years. A spokeswoman for BCS
declined to comment on the circumstances surrounding Litt's departure as well as on whether making *II*
has become a requirement for ongoing employment
inside BCS's Research Department since BC Holdings
acquired EFS in February. Litt, reached in Anguilla
where he is vacationing, declined to comment."

"Jesus. Is Silaski a buddy of his?"

"It would seem so," Matt said. "What can we do
about this?"

"Probably nothing. Let me call Katherine."

David dialed Katherine, listened intently for a
minute and then hung up. "We're going to ignore it.
Katherine is convinced that we can't win with this
guy no matter how hard we try and that we're better
off letting it fade away than inflaming it. She also said
that Litt has refused to sign his release which means
he'll probably sue us for age discrimination, and that
I better get my files in order and build up our case
against him."

"What about the analysts?" Matt asked. "Should
we put out an e-mail that doesn't comment on Arthur
in anyway but states for there cord that making *II* is
not, in and of itself, a requirement for ongoing
employment here?"

"I don't think so," David said, eyes closing slightly. "Tell a few analysts and it'll get around. But I need every one of them to make *II* this year, and letting them think, even a little, that it *has* become a requirement can only help our ranking next October."

* * *

"The *Greenwich* books are in," Lisa yelled.

" *Greenwich* " is *II*'s kid sister. Like *II*, it is a poll of institutional investors that measures how each sell-side firm's research effort is regarded in the aggregate and how individual analysts rank in roughly 70 different industries.

At least in part because it hasn't been polling clients for 30 years, as *II* has, *Greenwich* has always been viewed as the less prestigious survey. When an analyst is referred to as "ranked," it always means that he's made the *II* All Star Team, not that he's highly ranked in *Greenwich*. When companies planning to sell stock to the public tell competing investment bankers that they want "ranked" analysts to support their deals, they always mean *II*-ranked, not *Greenwich*-ranked.

In *Greenwich*, firms are ranked based on the fraction of all clients who cite them as one of the 10 best research sources on The Street. In *II*, firms are ranked based on the number of All Stars they have and get just as much credit for a Runner-Up (typically the number four to number eight analyst in a particular industry) as for the number-one-ranked analyst. This fact was critically important to David, who held out little hope of growing or hiring any top-three analysts but much greater hope of employing analysts who ranked fourth through eighth in their fields and might thus be named Runner-Ups in their categories. The great perversity of *II* lay in the fact that, if one firm had 30 analysts and they were all Runner-Ups, and another firm had 29 analysts and they all ranked number one, the firm with the 30 Runner-Ups would rank higher in *II* than the firm with the 29 best-of-the-bests. What David valued most about *Greenwich* was its ability to predict how *II* might look six months hence. *Greenwich* queries clients during the first quarter of each year and publishes its results each April, while *II* polls clients between April and June and publishes the All Star Team each October. Thus, each new *Greenwich* reflects client views that are nine months fresher than those reflected in the prior October's All Star standings. David grabbed his *Greenwich* summary book. He needed to know how BCS had ranked overall and what *Greenwich* said about each of his analysts' likelihood of making *II* in October.

BCS, he discovered, had finished in a five-way tie for number eleven with Prudential, Deutsche Bank, Bank of America and SG Cowen. Each firm had been named one of the 10 best by 12% of all respondents. In contrast, Merrill, Morgan Stanley, Salomon Smith Barney, Goldman Sachs and CS First Boston were all in the 50%-55% neighborhood. UBS, thanks to its acquisition of PaineWebber in 2000, Bear Stearns, Lehman, J.P. Morgan and Sanford Bernstein rounded out the top 10, but each was cited only 20%–25% of the time. BCS was exactly where David had expected it to be and almost exactly where EFS had been since 1998.

Next, David tried to assess what *Greenwich* was predicting about BCS's prospects in the next *II* poll. Assuming that *II* might name the top seven or eight analysts in each industry to the All Star Team, he quickly made a list of all of his analysts who had finished eighth or better in *Greenwich*. Happily, all five of his prior-year All Stars were still safely within the top eight in their categories. Keith Jackman was sixth in leisure time/entertainment, Robin Lomax seventh in retailing/department stores, Nancy Natolio fifth in integrated oils, Tim Omori fifth in regional banks but eleventh in multinationals, and Will Rivas fifth in medical supplies and devices. Liz Tytus and Van Trudell both ranked sixth but were listed under Prudential because they'd changed firms after *Greenwich* had finished its polling.

Among all his other analysts, David found only 10 other top-eight finishers: Steven Kalagian was eighth in wireless services, Laura Payden seventh in specialty chemicals, Rebecca Suess eighth in environmental services, Phil Suprano eighth in supermarkets and drugstores, Matt Burlingame seventh in managed care, Alan Bellone eighth in REITs, Mark Noel eighth in server and enterprise hardware, James Hovanian sixth in semiconductor capital equipment, Bruce Soslow seventh in economics and Linda Logan sixth in strategy.

So where did this leave him? David could count seven All Stars almost for sure, and 10 more with varying degrees of likelihood. If they all made it, they would take BCS from five All Stars to 17, and from number fourteen to number ten, but never in David's experience had these top-eight-type analysts all made *II* on the next pass. In truth, if half made it, David would be pleasantly surprised. And 12 All Stars would only get BCS to number twelve.

To get to number eight this year, David would need 20 All Stars. To get to number seven he'd need 29 and to get to number six he'd need 36. His best guess was that he now had 10. At a minimum he'd need to double that but, to maximize his payday he'd need to do better.

Much, much better.

* * *

"Can I have an update, please, on review prep?" David was sitting with Lisa in his office, catching up. It was 9:15 A.M.

"Almost everything is back. We're tabulating the Client Vote and Sales Vote rankings this morning and I'll have them for you before lunchtime. About 90% of the feedback from the traders is in. Paul is bringing me the results of his poll of the brokers today. Matt is almost done amassing the data on reports, phone calls, Morning Meeting appearances and so forth. Everything should be done by the end of the week."

"The feedback from the bankers is in?"

"Only about half of it. I have calls in to Mennymore's office and I've also called 11 MDs directly. They're always last to get their stuff to me so I'm not worried about this. It just puts extra pressure on us that we don't need."

"Should I call Mennymore?"

"No, it's under control."

"I'm sitting down with Matt after lunch to review the Client Vote and Sales Vote numbers?"

"You have back-to-back meetings starting in 15 minutes and ending at 2:00, which is when you and Matt are supposed to meet."

"Good. Do you have an updated comp spreadsheet that includes Liz and Van?

"It's in my office. Let me get it for you."

Lisa ran back to her office and returned with one hard copy of four 8 x 14" sheets on which all of the senior analysts' salaries, recent bonuses and guaranteed future bonuses were arrayed. David ran through it quickly, focusing on the analysts who hadn't been offered contracts, circled seven current-year numbers that looked too high or too low based on how he guessed those analysts were performing, wrote comments about various analysts and their compensation levels in the margin for Matt to consider, folded the sheets so that the blank sides faced out, and walked quickly to the Xerox machines down the hall to make Matt a copy of the marked-up spreadsheet.

The room was empty, and David walked to the Xerox machine that was farthest from the door and placed the first sheet under the copier's lid, adjusted the page size to 8 x 14" and hit Copy. When the copy came out, he placed it on top of the machine, with the original, face down, slid the second sheet under the lid and hit Copy. As he did this for the fourth time, Lisa suddenly appeared in the doorway of the copy room, eyes wide.

"David, can you come, please? Shanna Pender just called. Nancy fainted."

Nancy Natolio had fainted once before, two years earlier, David recalled. "I'm coming," he yelled back. As quickly as he could, he gathered up all of the comp sheets and the copies that he'd made and raced down the hall towards Nancy's office. Three minutes later, as Nancy was reviving, Phil Suprano walked into the copy room, an issue of *Drug Store News* under his arm, and approached one of the Xerox machines. As he prepared to place page 48 of the magazine under the lid, he noticed a sheet of paper on top of the glass and picked it up. At first, all he saw were numbers, but then he saw his name. Above it he recognized several others: Schager, Schuler, Shatz, Soslow, Staub and Suess. And under it he recognized more: Trudell, Tytus and Vargo.

"Shit!" he said in a loud whisper.

Phil folded the sheet in half, stuck it into his *Drug Store News*, walked to the door of the copy room, saw no one nearby and raced, eyes down, back to his office.

When Matt arrived at David's office door at 1:55 P.M. he realized that something was wrong. David was in a panic. He had seven pages of compensation spreadsheets instead of eight.

As Matt stood there, David ran past him down the hall to the copy room but, as he'd feared, there was no sign of the missing sheet.

"What happened?" Matt asked when David returned to his office.

"I was making a copy of the marked-up comp spreadsheet for you this morning when Lisa ran in and told me that Nancy had fainted. In my rush to gather up all of the papers, I may have left the original fourth page under the cover of the machine."

"Who's on page four?"

"S to Z."

David and Matt both pondered the significance of that fact. "At least it doesn't have Natolio or Jackman or Lomax or Omori or Rivas on it!"

"That's true, but it does have something much, much worse … and that's the name Liz Tytus coupled with the number four million."

* * *

Julia Harris had wasted no time cranking up her

search for an airline analyst, and it was the most likely candidate, Bear Stearns's Marsha Yamamoto, with whom David now found himself breakfasting.

David liked Marsha. He liked the way she approached the airlines, which was more as trading vehicles than long-term investments, and the degree to which she seemed connected to her managements. She also appeared to have plenty of third-party sources in the travel industry on whom she relied for data confirming or challenging what her managements had told her, and she seemed more attuned than average to the need to make clients money and not merely provide them with information.

"I *am* a little worried about retail," she admitted late in their session.

"Bear Stearns has a little of it, but you have so much more, and my group is both very retail-friendly and pretty darn volatile. Why is Retail so important to BCS?"

"Because the demographics are so powerful, because you can charge a lot more than the nickel-a-share that most firms charge large institutional accounts, and because it can be very profitable if it's managed well. Prudential never made much money from retail, at least according to the press reports I read, but PaineWebber seemingly printed money in retail, in part because Joe Grano and Mark Sutton managed that business so well.

"I saw Grano speak at an SIA meeting a couple of years ago where he said, I think, that 70% of all the financial assets in the U.S. are held by people who are 50 or older, and that most Americans make the most money and accumulate the bulk of their wealth between their early-to mid-50s and age 65. So Baby

Boomers who were born in 1950, for instance, are just starting to move into their peak earning and wealth-building years, and they're going to stay in them for the next 10 to15 years."

"That's pretty amazing," Marsha agreed, "so how do you manage the brokers so the analysts feed them well but aren't driven crazy by them?"

"Well, first, we have a terrific Equity Research Marketing Group full of sharp, aggressive MBA-types who do nothing but act as middlemen between the analysts and most of the brokers. Next, the analysts earn points for visiting or calling branches or participating whenever we put 300 of our best brokers in a ballroom somewhere."

"I bet that 10% of your branches get 90% of the analysts' visits."

"Unfortunately that's true. The easiest-to-get-to branches get the bulk of the analysts' visits."

"What else do you do?"

"We poll The Desk and they poll a large sample of brokers who are very attuned to research about the analysts' accessibility, money-making skills and report writing, and those results are discussed with the analysts during semiannual reviews."

"How much do those polls impact compensation?"

"A fair amount but I limit that weight for three reasons. First, many brokers have misimpressions about the accuracy of some analysts' recommendations. Some analysts who've done well over the past two years still get nailed by Retail because of a blow-up they had three years ago, and that shouldn't be. Second, many brokers give the highest marks to the analysts with the hottest groups, who may not be our best analysts. Third, we may have in the department some analysts who rank high in *II* and are very valuable to Banking but who get low marks from Retail. I need to keep those analysts in the fold and, if I were to dock them a lot because of Retail, they'd pack up and move."

"So it's important but not very important."

"I'd say that analysts who do well by Retail are rewarded, but that many analysts who do badly by Retail aren't really punished."

Marsha looked at her watch. "David, I'm sorry, I've really got to run, but I'd like to come in and meet some of your people if you want me to. Should we pick a date?"

"Let me get your availability from Julia and then put a schedule together for you."

"Sounds great, David. I really enjoyed meeting you. I'd heard lots of good things about you from other analysts and now I know why."

David just smiled and shook Marsha's hand.

"It was my pleasure, Marsha. I hope we can convince you to join us."

* * *

"Lavery."

"Ken, it's Peter." Peter Paul Rushing was Ken's investment banker.

"I'm downstairs smoking. Come join me."

"I'll be right there."

Ken hung up, checked his watch and then took the elevator quickly to the lobby. He could see Peter standing outside. There were no signs of a cigarette. As Ken passed through the revolving door, Peter walked up to him to meet him. "Let's walk," he said. When they'd reached the corner and turned it, Peter said quietly, "I think Noo-Clone wants to sell a million shares."

"Why do you think that?"

"I just do, although you didn't hear it from me. What's your rating on the stock?"

"Hold."

"Why?"

"Because it was a good value when it was under 10, but in the 30s it looks pretty rich. It's still years away from getting its first FDA approval."

"We can't get in the deal with a Hold."

"Could we with an Accumulate?"

"Yes." The two walked for 15 seconds in silence. "Do you have an excuse to upgrade it?"

"No, I'd have to fabricate something."

"Can you?"

"How much time do I have?"

"I think they'll pick their underwriters next week."

"I'll do it before Friday," Ken promised. And he did.

* * *

It was lunchtime at Wendy's for the twenty something crowd. With spring in the air, Phil Suprano had grabbed Alan Gildersleeve, Ron Vargo and John Henriksen and the four had walked up Water Street, past Fulton, to their favorite fast feeder. They ordered a bunch of Doubles with cheese, the largest fries on the menu, some Frosties and one Diet Coke, and planted themselves at a table in the corner, in the sunlight. For 30 minutes they watched the girls go by, complained about work, worried about upcoming reviews, compared vacation plans and clogged their arteries. As back-to-work time neared, Phil suddenly sprung it on his guests.

"Guess how much Liz Tytus makes?"

"Who's Liz Tytus?" John asked.

"She's the new tobacco analyst from Pru. Short brown hair, real short skirts, bad-girl attitude?"

Alan, Ron and John looked at each other for help.

"She's *II*-ranked," said Ron.

"She covers, what, three stocks?" asked John.

"How do you know how much she makes?" Ron asked skeptically.

"Just shut up and answer the question."

"Two and a half," Alan guessed.

"Three," Ron said.

"No way," John disagreed. "Two two."

"Four," said Phil.

"Bullshit artist."

"Four."

"Like you would know."

"I *would* know. Do you want to bet?"

Alan, Ron and John all stopped jeering in unison and tried to read Phil's expression. To their amazement, he seemed unusually self-confident. The four young men just watched each other for a minute. Finally, Ron said, "A thousand dollars." He looked at John and Alan. "Split three ways?" John and Alan nodded.

"A thousand dollars…" Phil repeated.

"… says you can't prove she's making $4 million."

"Done," said Phil, hammering his fist on the table. "I've whited out other names to protect the innocent," he said, remembering that one of those names was Ron's, "but take a gander at what I found on the Xerox machine, thanks, I'm sure, to Lisa Palladino."

As he passed copies of the compensation spread-sheet page around, with only Liz's numbers still visible, he watched with glee as six eyes widened, six cheeks reddened and three jaws dropped.

* * *

II season brings out unusual behavior in many of Wall Street's most famous analysts. Once All Star ballots have been sighted on clients' desks, the campaigning-while-pretending-not-to-campaign intensifies. Sellsiders visit their clients at a frenzied pace and the volume of e-mails and voicemails quadruples or more. Few Sellsiders admit to what they're doing, but everyone on the Sell Side and Buy Side understands clearly what's going on, and the Buy-siders tolerate it, are amused by it or get really put off by it.

But as Matt Speiser passed Mark Noel's office late one Monday evening in the middle of April, he saw something he'd never seen before: outside of his office, Mark, his two associate analysts and his research assistant were stuffing hundreds of FedEx envelopes with as many of Mark's reports as they would hold. For the longest time, no one even looked up. Finally, Matt could resist no longer.

"What are you doing?"

"We're sending our reports to clients," Mark answered.

"But why such a sense of urgency?"

"Because they have to arrive in Menlo Park on Thursday."

"Why?"

"Because that's when these companies are presenting."

"Which companies?"

"Agilent, Brocade, EMC, Hewlett, Network Appliances and Sun."

"Presenting where?"

"At Goldman's Technology Conference."

"I don't understand."

Mark stopped stuffing for a second and looked up at Matt. "Today Goldman began a week-long technology conference in Menlo Park. Thursday is Enterprise Hardware Day, and Laura is hosting Agilent, Brocade, EMC, Hewlett, Network Appliances and Sun."

"So?"

"So we're FedExing all of our recent research on those six stocks to the clients who are attending the conference."

"How do you know where they're staying?"

"We called their offices and asked their secretaries."

"So you're FedExing them tomorrow so they'll arrive on Wednesday…"

"…and all of the clients will take our reports into their meetings at Goldman's conference on Thursday."

"So the clients will be carrying around BCS reports all day long…"

"… and seeing everyone else carrying around our reports too."

Matt wondered why he'd never heard of this before. "Is this legal?"

"Of course it's legal. I always send clients my reports. They're traveling this week so I'm sending them to the hotel where they're staying. That they happen to be attending a competitor's conference has nothing to do with me, and if they decide to bring my reports to the conference, I didn't ask them to, they decided to on their own."

"Laura isn't going to like this," Matt said, referring

to Laura Conigliaro, the number-two-ranked analyst
in Mark's space and a Goldman Sachs veteran.

"I'm not going to beat Laura," Mark said, "but I can
try to get my clients to associate my name with hers
and to write my name on their ballots after they've
voted for her. After a whole day of seeing and thinking
Goldman/Conigliaro/Noel, some will."

"We'll see," said Matt. "I think I'll just let David
know in case he or Koster or Vilhelm gets a call from
someone in Goldman's Legal Department on
Thursday morning."

"Whatever. Goldman doesn't have to like it, and
by then it'll be too late to stop me."

* * *

David was lunching, for a change, with a new and
especially irritating recruit, Daniel Roe, an Internet
analyst at UBS Warburg. Daniel had spent most of
his time watching David eat and explaining in greater
detail than David needed why he was destined to
"smoke" Holly Becker and Mary Meeker, two much
more famous competitors.

"I know my companies better, I'm more respected
by my managements, I write the most objective
reports and I'm by far the best stock picker. Holly's
my toughest competitor. Mary got to the top of the
heap when there were only a handful of analysts in
the space. If you only had three analysts doing Internet, all three could get ranked, but as soon as more
analysts started doing it, Mary slipped. Holly's better
than most, but I'm better than she is."

My my my, thought David. Aren't we smitten with
ourselves?

"I also can bring three deals to BCS."

"What deals?"

"I'm not going to say at this point. It's much too soon."

"Then how do I know you're serious?"

"Because the CEOs told me they'd do the deals with me regardless of where I was working."

"That's surprising," David said. "I understand managements that like particular analysts but *regardless* of where you're working?"

"That's right. What they want is me, my coverage. These guys get so much of their comp from stock options that their net worth can swing wildly based on how much their stock is up or down. So, they want to be followed by an influential analyst who will love their stock to death, and they'll give their banking business to whoever employs him. In their eyes, I'm that analyst. They know that I love them, that I have far more credibility with clients because I don't love everyone, and they've told me that I will get their next deal regardless of where I work."

"That must be nice to know," David mused.

"It's not only nice, David, it's very valuable, to me and potentially to you."

"We'd be able to confirm this with those managements prior to hiring you?"

"Absolutely."

"So… when would you like to come in and see some people?"

"For your sake, David, the sooner the better. I'm not exactly a well-kept secret, you know."

* * *

"David, your green sheets are counterproductive at

best and dangerous at worst," said Michael Zisk, the chemical industry banker.

"Why?"

"Why? Because you're going to give Laura a nervous breakdown and cost me a lot of money." David waited in silence for elaboration. "Are you there?"

"I'm here."

"Listen, I've gotten very close to the guys at Millipore and there's business for us to do with them if we treat them right, but Laura tells me that she's gotten one of those green sheets from you on Millipore for three straight weeks now, demanding that she downgrade her rating from Accumulate to Hold and, frankly, I don't even see how you'd know that it should be a Hold."

"Michael, I couldn't care less what Millipore's rating is. I'm not one iota happier, and I don't make one penny more, if it's Buy or Hold."

"Then why are you demanding that she downgrade to Hold?"

"I'm not demanding anything. Laura is being flagged because Millipore is selling at its target price, and her Accumulate rating and her target price are thus mutually exclusive."

"No one cares about target prices."

David ignored him. "Just so we're clear, Michael, Laura can do one of two things right now. She can raise her target price and keep the Accumulate, or she can keep her target price and cut the rating to Hold."

"She can't downgrade the stock, David, it'll kill me. We'll never get a shred of business out of them if she goes to Hold. You know better than I do that, in the real world, Buy is Buy, Accumulate is Hold and Hold is Sell. She's already at a Hold in the eyes of institutional clients and our retail brokers."

"Then she'll have to raise her target price."

"She says she can't, that she's stretching already."

"Then the stock is fairly valued, Michael, and that means that we shouldn't be recommending that people buy it."

"Why can't she suspend the rating?"

"You must be kidding. She's paid to have a rating, not to suspend it whenever you disagree with it."

"She can't downgrade it, David. I'll talk to Carl if I have to."

"It's a free country, Michael. Laura can raise or lower, it's all up to her, but she can't recommend purchase of a stock that she thinks will be selling at the same price a year from now that it's selling for today."

"You're forcing her to downgrade and you're going to cost the firm, and me, a lot of money," Michael said. "You just don't get it, I'm afraid."

"Nor do you."

* * *

On Wednesday evening, April 16, Ken Lavery took Continental Airlines' flight #1718 from Newark to Tampa/St. Pete, rented the closest thing to a Bentley he could find (a Lincoln Town Car) and checked into a suite at the Renaissance Vinoy Resort on Fifth Avenue in downtown St. Petersburg. What the Hell, Retail was paying for it, so why not?

After ordering dinner, he spread a pile of papers out on the king-sized bed. Some papers related to recent transactions in his brokerage account that Ken hadn't had time until now to review. Within 10 minutes, every confirm had been checked for accuracy and completeness. Everything looked good. Several of his stock holdings had changed little in recent months, including the $600,000 worth of Regeneron that Ken had purchased in September and October and the $900,000 of Amgen and Genentech that he'd held for several years, but two holdings had changed a lot, and they were The G-NOME Company (of which Ken now owned 140,000 shares at an average cost of slightly over $7) and Genomic Innovators (140,000 shares at an average cost of just over $7.50). With G-NOME at 9 and Innovators at 11, those 280,000 shares were worth a cool $2,800,000 and Ken's entire portfolio had ballooned to $4,300,000. Including the original $1,400,000 that he'd borrowed in October to double up in Regeneron and establish his initial penny-stock positions, and the $750,000 he'd borrowed in March to buy more "genomic junk," Ken's margin debt now totaled $2,150,000, or 50% of the value of his stock holdings.

Ken thought back to October, when his account had been worth $1,400,000, and realized that, by using margin and talking up "the G's" in Boston and elsewhere, he'd made himself $750,000 in six months without really doing anything. "If only I'd started using margin sooner," he said out loud, but he stopped bemoaning his tardiness when he realized that, from here on out, every point that either of "The G's" moved up would be worth $140,000 to him and that there were a lot of points between $10 and infinity.

To Ken's right were maps and itineraries relating to the next two days. Martin Gool had scheduled him well. Thursday would begin with a 7:00 breakfast in BCS's St. Petersburg office, after which Ken would drive about 40 miles south to Sarasota for a 9:00 pre-opening meeting with the FAs there. Then he'd have about two-and-a-half hours to drive 140 miles farther south to Naples, where he was scheduled to hold a 12:15 broker meeting over lunch. Assuming that meeting ended around 1:15, he'd then have three hours to drive 110 miles due east on Alligator Alley to a 4:15 post-market-close meeting with the FAs in Ft. Lauderdale.

Then he'd drive 50 miles north to the Breakers in Palm Beach where he'd crash and see where "The G's" had closed. Friday morning would start with a 7:00 breakfast in the Palm Beach branch, continue with a 9:00 pre-opening meeting 30 miles south in Boca Raton, and end 50 miles farther south in Miami, where he'd meet with one branch at noon and the other at 4:15.

"God, this is going to be boring!" he thought. "But God it's going to be nice summering in the Hamptons."

Room service startled him. Ken jumped up, opened the door and bellowed at the Cuban-looking man holding his shrimp cocktail and steak, "To shingle or not to shingle, that is the question."

The waiter, understanding not a word, simply smiled, nodded and said, "shingle."

"We'll see, Jose," Ken answered, giving the waiter the eye, "but you just might be right."

* * *

"Ask Matt what he thinks."

Mark Noel was making the suggestion, but James Hovanian, the semiconductor capital equipment analyst, wasn't buying it. "I'm sure he'd disapprove.

That's not to say that he wouldn't let me publish it, but he'd give me a long list of reasons why I shouldn't before he signed off on it."

"Maybe you don't want to ask Matt because you don't believe what you're saying."

James took back his copy of the report that he'd asked Mark to read. "I believe most of what I'm saying," he said defensively.

"What do you believe?"

"I believe that Electro Wafer Tools is a great company, that it has one of the best management teams in the industry, that it has one of the best records in the industry and that it will be among the fastest growers in the industry over the next five to 10 years."

"Do you believe your earnings estimates?"

"I might be $0.10 to $0.15 too high."

"Why is that?"

"Because I can't get to the target price I want to use unless I use that estimate."

"So use a lower target price."

"I can't."

"Why?"

"Because the whole purpose of this exercise is to find a stock I can recommend with a target price that's twice where the stock is now selling. I need to be able to say that I see the stock doubling over the next 12 months."

"What if its upside potential is only 75%?"

"No good. Do you remember Henry Blodget and Amazon?"

"Who doesn't?"

"That's my point. The stock was $200, he said it was going to $400, he was right, he got famous, he got hired by Merrill for a zillion dollars, and I can guarantee you that if he hadn't had such an outlandish target price in that Amazon report, history might have unfolded very differently."

"You're insane," Mark said seriously. "You don't need to do this."

"Yes I do. Jay Deahna is back on The Street at J.P. Morgan, and I've also got to contend with John Pitzer at CSFB, Mark FitzGerald at BofA, Glen Yeung at Salomon, Tim Arcuri at Deutsche Bank, James Covello at Goldman, Brett Hodess at Merrill, Robert Maire at Bear Stearns and Steven Pelayo at Morgan Stanley. That's not exactly an easy crowd to join."

"Where were you in *Greenwich* this year?"

"Sixth."

"Without doing something irresponsible like this."

"It's not irresponsible, it's just good marketing. If I put a lot of people in EWTI at $30 and a year from now it's $50 instead of $60, no one's going to call me up and complain that I promised 100% and I only delivered 70%. In the meantime, I'll get much, much more media attention with a report predicting that Electro Wafer Tools will double in price than that it will rise 70%."

"You don't need to do this, James."

"Let me think about it," he said, looking glum. "Thanks for the advice."

Two days later, at 7:35 A.M., James began his Morning Meeting presentation as succinctly as he could: "I'm raising my rating on Electro Wafer Tools, ticker EWTI, this morning from Accumulate to Buy. I now expect the stock to double in price over the next 12 months."

* * *

Suzanne Considine sat on the edge of her chair and

said "thank you" very graciously. She and her sidekick, Bill Musicke, were pitching Charles Otis, the CEO of family-owned Twelve Dollar Stores, on the merits of an initial public offering that BCS would lead, and Mr. Otis had just complimented Suzanne on the quality of her work.

"We've enjoyed every moment that we've spent here today with your people, Charles. You've built a truly exceptional team. And speaking of teams, we can't tell you how excited Robin Lomax is about the prospect of assisting us on your IPO."

"You've discussed our situation with Robin?"

"We have indeed." Suzanne measured her words very carefully.

"We all know about Robin," Charles mused, "but we didn't really expect that she'd know much about us!"

"Oh she does, and she's *very* excited about being associated with your offering."

"Really!" Charles couldn't contain his surprise.

"Absolutely. She asked us to make certain to tell you that she was prepared to market your stock very aggressively to all of those clients who made her the *Institutional Investor* All Star that she is today, that she'll also push it very hard to our retail brokers, and that she'll have an absolutely glowing report on you ready to go, subject to your approval of course, the moment the quiet period following the IPO is over."

"She's looked us over, has she?"

"In great detail, Charles."

"Did you mention to her the offering price range that we discussed this morning?"

"Yes we did, and she said she thought we were too low."

"Too low! Really!"

"We'll see what her clients say, Charles, when we bring them their prospectuses, but the good news is that Robin will not only have a Buy rating on you at the offering price but she guaranteed us that she'll be able to maintain and reiterate it even if your stock moves up significantly in the after-market, as we think it will."

"This is wonderful to hear," said Charles. "Of course, I still need approval from my Board before giving you the green light, but with Robin on the team, and her stature as an *II* All Star, and the enthusiasm that she'd bring to our offering, I don't see why BCS shouldn't be a finalist when the directors meet next week."

Suzanne and Bill stood and extended their hands to Charles. "We look forward to making your IPO a home run," Suzanne said.

"A grand slam!" Charles corrected. All three laughed, one sincerely.

As they reached their rental car in Twelve Dollar's parking lot, Bill turned to Suzanne and said, "That was really great... what you told Charles about Robin. I didn't realize that you'd spoken to her about the deal."

"I didn't," said Suzanne. "For all I know, she's never even heard of this piece of shit."

* * *

As Suzanne had been BS'ing Charles Otis and his kin, Ken Lavery had been BS'ing no fewer than 150 brokers in St. Pete, Sarasota, Naples and Ft. Lauderdale.

"Biotech is the single most exciting industry on the

planet," he'd told them. "...my target price is $40 so upside is 30%... $1.65 for 2003... at $35, it's down 100 points... cystic fibrosis... the cure for cancer... what do I own in my personal account?... these are $10 names... I've warned you, now I'll answer you... The G-NOME Company and Genomic Innovators... G-NOME and Genomic Innovators... G-NOME and Genomic Innovators."

How easy it was to run on auto pilot in front of the brokers. He could tell them anything and they'd believe it, not because they weren't smart but because biotech was so strange and unfamiliar... long words, lots of science, no way to check up on him, every chance to snow them. But in only one part of his presentation did Ken fabricate utter nonsense and, with GNOM now at 11 and GINV at 12, that nonsense had made Ken over $400,000 during the day. "Why that's $100,000 a branch and $100,000 an hour," he said to himself as he collapsed on the Breaker's king-sized bed.

"Four more branches tomorrow," he mumbled as sleep overtook him. "Should I buy or should I build?"

* * *

Friday was more of the same but better. Four branches, 200 brokers, same questions about Genentech and Amgen, Millennium and Regeneron. "What do you own in your personal account? What would you put your own money into? Why do you own stocks that you don't cover?" they asked.

"GNOM and GINV, GNOM and GINV, GNOM and GINV. Because they're too risky for the majority of our clients. Because I can't cut 5,000 of you loose on them."

"Did you tell the branches you visited yesterday about them?"

"Yes."

"That's why they were up yesterday?"

"I don't know."

"That's not really fair. You should've visited us first!"

"It doesn't matter."

"Why?"

"Because if they're going to $25, whether you get in at $10 or $12 won't matter to your clients."

"And you're sure they're going to $25?"

"I'm never sure of anything. There are no guarantees."

"I didn't mean that. I meant you believe strongly that they could."

"Yes."

As things turned out, it must have sounded pretty good to many of those 350 brokers because Ken flew home on Friday night almost $850,000 richer than he'd been when he'd flown down. G-NOM closed the week at 13, up 4, GINV at 13, up 2.

And that meant that Ken's portfolio had expanded while he'd been in Florida from $4,300,000 to almost $5,150,000, and that Ken could now borrow $850,000 more.

* * *

Ron Vargo surprised himself. He was much more nervous than he'd expected to be as he entered the St. Regis Hotel and walked towards Lespinasse. "He really wants to have dinner with you," Claire had told him. "He said he's spent very little time with you, one on one, and he wants that to change."

"I'd love to," Ron had said. "Where and when?"

"He adores Lespinasse. Do you know it?"

"Of course."

"How about Friday the 25th at 7:00?"

"That'd be perfect."

"Do you mind if I join you? I'm still learning about Milbanks, you know."

Ron tried hard to sound blasé. "Not at all," he'd said.

And so, here Ron was, at Lespinasse. When he identified himself at the reception desk he was escorted to a table for four against one wall, from the inside of which stood Tom Lukin, CEO of Milbanks, and Claire, hands extended. Ron took the chair on the outside that faced Tom.

"I'm so glad to see you again, Ron. I've enjoyed reading your most recent research and I must say that it's a cut above, if you know what I mean."

"You're very kind, Tom. I told Claire that the chance to sit down with you and talk about Milbanks informally was too good to pass up."

Lespinasse was widely considered to be one of the five best restaurants in Manhattan. Its Louis XIV gilt-wood chairs, lush carpets, rich upholstery and extraordinary food presentations put it in a league of its own. For two hours, amidst crispy sweetbreads and black truffles, muscovy duck with caramelized grapefruit, and veal loin and osso bucco with a flan of bone marrow, Ron and Tom talked in great detail about Milbanks's business. Ron asked many of the same questions he'd posed during his first meeting with Claire and noticed her smiling and winking at him when they heard things they both recognized. Ron took pages and pages of notes and Claire periodically wrote things down when Tom touched on areas with which she was less familiar.

Just before 9:00, everyone took a break for lemon parfaits and banana kumquats, and at 9:25, to Ron's surprise, Tom stood up, extended his hand, apologized for having to catch a 10:00 shuttle and thanked Ron for joining him. With a quick gesture to Claire, seemingly to make sure she knew to pick up the tab, he dashed for his limo to LaGuardia Airport.

Claire slid to her left, along the banquette, into the seat that Tom had vacated so she was directly across from Ron's chair. "He's a good guy," she said.

"I really hadn't had much direct exposure to him," Ron admitted. "I'd spoken with him briefly at some analysts' meetings, and for ten or fifteen minutes on my last two visits to your offices, but it was nothing like what we did tonight."

Claire was nodding.

"I really appreciate your setting it up." As Claire continued to nod, and smiled, Ron suddenly felt her toes between his legs. His look of surprise made her laugh.

"Something disagree with you?" she asked, moving her foot up inside his thighs.

"Actually, it agrees with me a lot, but I'm pretty sure we shouldn't be doing this."

Claire stretched her leg but her toes couldn't quite reach. "This table's too wide."

"Maybe I should slide in a little," Ron volunteered.

"Or maybe we should go upstairs."

Ron looked at her, puzzled.

"I took a room for tonight, just in case."

Ron still said nothing.

"It's big enough for two, you know." Her big brown eyes had him hypnotized.

"Are you sure?"

"Are you?"

"Yes," he whispered.

Her toes massaged his penis. "Can you stand up?"

"No, but I will."

Claire smiled, grabbed Ron by the hand and headed through the restaurant, down the long St. Regis corridor and into the elevator just before the front desk.

"Cat got your tongue?" she asked, noticing how quiet Ron had become.

"I guess so."

"Well, get it back, handsome, 'cause in five minutes, I'm really gonna need it."

* * *

The last two weeks of April were devoted exclusively to semiannual reviews, which were similar to October reviews with one exception. In October, the bonus pool had been down, bonuses for analysts without contracts had been down more and almost everyone had gotten 80% cash and 20% stock. This time, however, many more analysts had guarantees, the bonus pool had been increased slightly by BCS as a sign of good faith and almost everyone got 65% cash and 35% stock.

Late in the afternoon on the fourth day of reviews, David and Matt sat staring at an incredulous John Henriksen, their property/casualty insurance analyst.

"It's incomprehensible," John said.

"How often do you call your traders?"

"Quite frequently, perhaps thrice daily."

"How often do you visit the desks?"

"At least once a day, perhaps twice."

"Do you have good conversations with them?"

"If you're asking me, I'd say they're excellent, but the traders clearly disagree."

David squinted. "Would you say that you typically give them more information or that they give you more?"

"I'd say that I think through what the traders might find helpful and then give them, as concisely as possible, a summary of what's new or different in my group and what's likely to impact the price of particular shares."

"What about what they give you?"

"It's usually of limited value, frankly. I'd characterize it as a considerable amount of noise and a quite limited volume of truly helpful insights."

"Then why do you think that, if you call them a lot, visit them a lot and give them good information, they gave you such low scores?"

"I haven't the foggiest."

David looked at John and repeated I haven't the foggiest to himself.

"How many syllables do you use when you speak to the traders?"

"Sorry?"

"How many syllables?"

"I don't know what you mean?"

"Do you say 'quickly' or 'with considerable speed'? Do you say 'lower' or 'at a level below where it last traded'? Do you say 'I'm worried' or that 'I'm suffering from considerable consternation?'"

John smiled. "Oh, I'd say that I'm worried."

"Why don't you try taping yourself the next few times that you talk to trading and see what you sound like. Don't talk unnaturally. Try to be as typically John as you can."

"And then?"

"Count up the total number of words that you've used and the number of two-syllable words. Then divide the latter by the former. If it's less than 75%, you know what you need to do. If it's more than 75%, I'll poll the traders and get some words to go with the low numerical scores they gave you."

John looked unconvinced.

"It's going down now. Not, it appears likely to decline somewhat in the hours immediately ahead. Got it?"

"Crystal clearly."

* * *

Mark Noel had a good review with one exception. "So five bankers opined on me?" he asked.

"It would appear so."

"Do you know which ones?"

"No, although I'm sure I can find out."

"You know I have no one calling on any of the server companies."

"I assumed as much," David said.

"There's no one in The Bank with any expertise in my space."

"So who do you deal with?"

"The only banker I have any interaction with is Jim MacDuffin. He seems to know e-commerce pretty well but, since we don't have anyone doing those stocks, he's tried to move over to the Internet infrastructure space to work with Byron."

"And he knows how much about enterprise hardware?"

"Zippo."

"And you can't think of four other bankers who might've opined on you?"

"No, the only banker I ever talk to is Jim and, frankly, even he's not qualified to review me."

David shook his head. Five inputs from bankers who rarely if ever dealt with Mark, knew little or nothing about his space, yet gave him poor scores that glowed in the dark relative to his marks from Sales, Trading and Retail. *II* Next Generation last fall, number eight in *Greenwich* in April, potential All Star next October, and sounding hauntingly like Will Rivas before he came within an inch of leaving for Goldman.

"Let me find out who scored you how and why," David said, "and in the meantime, put a giant X through the whole Banking Poll section in the review. As far as I'm concerned, those scores never happened."

* * *

The last review that April was Alan Bellone's. Alan had come into David's office assuming he'd have to play defense owing to the toll he'd expected his porn surfing to have taken on his vital signs, but he'd been wrong. As David walked him through his Progress Report, everyone could see that Alan's rankings with Institutional Sales, Trading, Banking and Retail were all relatively stable. There were hints of trouble to come, principally in the Sales and Retail polls, where Alan's visibility had been scored poorly, and in the summary of Alan's written report output which was well below average. Still, his middle-of-the-department performance prompted Alan to put his rationales for poor performance away.

Having no clue what was going on in Alan's head,

David was not surprised when, late in the review, Alan said, "David, what are the chances of me getting a contract?"

"I don't know," he answered. "If truth be told, I had you on the original list, but your lack of an *II* ranking or a top-10 finish in *Greenwich* had been non-starters for Dieter and, at the eleventh hour, he scratched you."

"But now I'm number eight in *Greenwich*."

"That's true," David said, "and that gives you a shot at making Runner-Up in *II* in October," David thought to himself.

"Doesn't that justify revisiting the issue with Dieter?"

"Yes it does, and I will."

This guy had no handcuffs on him and he certainly appeared to be a legitimate All Star contender. Glue him to the floor, David said to himself. Glue him now.

* * *

Louis Liddy, the Goldman Sachs restaurant analyst, returned in late April to complete the interviewing cycle that Craig Lucie had so badly disrupted the month before. Paul Pitcher and Matt had both missed their interviews with Louis so they were first on his dance card this time around. David had added several institutional salespeople, a trader and an hour-long slot for himself at the very end.

The early feedback on Louis was positive but inconclusive. Craig had obviously liked Louis so much that he'd absconded with him for almost 90 minutes. Robin was upbeat, although she expressed some concern about how much time Louis was spending on McDonald's to the detriment of his other names. John McLain had said that Louis seemed to know the right people at many of BCS's most important institutional accounts.

Throughout the day, David called for real-time feedback from those Louis had just seen in order to prepare himself for his own session. Matt and Paul were of one mind about Louis: He was smart, articulate, personable, appeared to write well, but also seemed to devote 90% of his time to McDonald's, a potential problem for Retail which often cared much more about the small-cap fast feeders than stodgy, troubled McDonald's. Other than that, he seemed fine. The feedback from the trader was, "Yeah, he's pretty good, we could work together," and the three salespeople were all in the okay-not-great camp owing more to Louis's seeming inability to talk with specificity about Brinker, Outback and Starbucks than to any flaws in his analytical makeup.

At 6:00 P.M. Herb Hirschorn escorted Louis to David's office, and Louis and David sat down to summarize where things stood.

"Today went very well," Louis said when asked about his meetings. "I liked Matt very much. He has interesting ideas about ways to help analysts like me get to the top of the polls, and he's been an analyst himself, as have you David, so you both can relate well to everything we go through every day on the job. Paul did a very good job of explaining how Retail works which, of course, would be new to me. Because my group is very Retail- friendly, that was an important meeting for me. The sessions with the salesmen and traders were fine. We compared notes about whom we knew and how close our relationships were, and we talked about McDonald's mostly, plus a few smaller names. All in all, I was very pleased with the people I met and how the interview progressed. Did you hear anything from their side?"

"Yes, and it was all positive. I guess, though, that there was some concern about how much time you're spending on McDonald's versus all the other names in your category so I'd like to hear what the real story is."

"David, I spend more time on McDonald's than on any other name because it's so dominant in my space. In some ways it's to fast food what Microsoft is to software. My clients want to talk about McDonald's more than any of the other stocks in the group. I try to allocate my time based on my clients' wants and needs so, when lots of the smaller chains are struggling or failing, I may spend 50% of my time on McDonald's. On the other hand, during those rare periods when the group is hot, all the chains are doing better and smaller chains are coming public, I increase the time I devote to them and reduce the time I devote to McDonald's."

"And clients are happy with that?"

"I don't think I'd be *II*-ranked if they weren't."

"You'll probably need to spend more time on some of the smaller or mid-cap names here, though, because we have 5,000 retail brokers."

"Understood and not a problem, David."

"Any other areas of concern that we should talk about?"

"I still haven't spoken with the analysts you said you had in Europe and Tokyo that also cover my group."

"That's next on the docket. I wanted to see how your meetings here went first and, on the assumption that they'd go well, which they did, hook you up next in a conference call with two of our non-U.S. analysts, Karl Neumeier in Frankfurt and Fred Foy in Tokyo."

"Excellent. When can we do that?"

"Within the next 48 hours if you're available. I'll have Richard Lipstein work with you on times that are most convenient. It will probably have to be early one morning New York time so we can get Karl in his office and Fred after he's had dinner."

"Of course."

"Other than that?"

"Other than that, David, we're set. Perhaps we should talk again after the conference call." After five more minutes of pleasantries, Louis headed home and David called Richard Lipstein.

"He's making just under two," Richard said. "Assuming the conference call goes well, you should be ready to be all over him with as long a contract as you can swing. Can you do three years?"

"No, never done one and no one's going to let me start now."

"Okay then, two years."

"At…," David figured Richard would recommend twice what Louis was making.

"You're competing against Goldman for his services. Under normal circumstances I'd say your chances would be 25% at best but he's hot under the collar right now which gets you up to 35% to 40%. If you blow him away financially you'll move into the 50% to 60% neighborhood which is probably the highest BCS can go against Goldman. It won't happen very often but it could happen with Louis."

"Don't tell me I need to do $4 million."

"It would maximize your chances because Goldman would never match it, but if you offered him double what he thinks he's now making it would accomplish almost the same thing."

"So, $3.6 million?"

"I'd do $3.8 million if you can't do four."

"Okay. You line up times for the conference call and give them to Lisa, ask Lisa for bios on Neumeier and Foy, take Louis's temperature before and after the call, and then tell him we're ready to make him an offer ASAP. Then circle back to me?"

"Done."

* * *

Three days later, the conference call had gone well, David had given Louis his $3.8-million-a-year-for-two-years offer, Louis had authorized the client check, Lisa had conducted it, and David now sat reviewing it with Richard.

"It's really remarkable," David mused.

"What is? You didn't expect him to check out badly, did you?"

"No, but we spoke to 32 clients, and 26 of them said they only use him for McDonald's."

"So, you'd take that to mean that he knows McDonald's really well?"

"No, I'd take it to mean that he doesn't know any of his other names really well."

"True, but he'd have to be a pretty good source on McDonald's to make *II* if he's a bad source…"

"… no source…"

"… on everything else." Richard paused. "Would his being a one-stock analyst scare you off?"

"If I had a choice, yes. Do I have a choice?"

"No. I got a very clear no-thank-you from Joe Buckley, Janice Meyer, Peter Oakes and everyone else who ranked. He's the only All Star you can hire in the restaurant space."

"If I reworked our offer to make it subject to his ability to pick up a certain number of small-or mid-cap names during his first 12 to 24 months with us…?"

"You'd lose him."

David paused to think. "So you're saying that I can encourage him to pick up other names in order to enhance his value to the firm over the long term…"

"… but you can't force him to and it definitely can't be a qualifier in his offer."

"Four million a year for coverage of McDonald's."

"Three point eight."

"Sold," David sighed. "Tell him to call me so I can congratulate him on passing the client check and help line up his movers."

"I'll tell him he better stay ranked or else," Richard said lightly. "Not."

* * *

Two evenings later, Nick Denisovich took Elite to JFK, British Air to Geneva, and a cab to Pictet, where Monsieur de Rousseau confirmed receipt of a brand-new wire transfer and the crediting of $1,520,000 to his account.

As he'd done on all of his previous day trips to Geneva, Nick read and reread his written update from Pictet all the way home and then burned it so well in his livingroom fireplace that nary an ash darkened the Greenwich Street pavement outside his window.

MAY

Two months into his All Star recruiting drive, David reassembled his headhunting team so he could take stock of where everyone stood.

"Larry, can we begin with you?"

"Of course. In autos and parts, we've struck out with Steve Girsky at Morgan Stanley, Gary Lapidus at Goldman and John Casesa at Merrill. Tim Parish at Cowen acted at least somewhat interested at breakfast, I understand, but then never returned a single call of mine when I followed up."

"Very peculiar," David said, shaking his head.

"Agreed, but probably someone you don't want for that very reason. In cosmetics, household and personal care products, I've gotten definite no's from Carol Warner Wilke at Merrill, Amy Low Chasen at Goldman, Ann Gillin Lefever at Lehman, Wendy Nicholson at Salomon and William Steele at BofA..."

"How come Wendy Nicholson only has two names?" Les Carter asked.

"And I got a no from James Gingrich at Bernstein" David added.

"So the only legitimate candidate will probably be Christopher Chadwick at Morgan Stanley who'll meet with you, David, within the next few weeks.

"In gaming and lodging, Gregory Lent of CSFB

344

seems to want to interview. Michael Rietbrock at Salomon showed no interest, nor did Jason Ader at Bear Stearns, David Anders at Merrill, Steven Kent at Goldman or Harry Curtis at J.P. Morgan.

"In imaging, Ben Reitzes passed, as did Jonathan Rosenzweig at Salomon, Gibboney Huske at CSFB and Caroline Sabbagha at Lehman. Kurt Coviello at Bear Stearns had a great breakfast with you but is still happy enough to want to stay put for now.

"In leisure, we have one candidate but not the one you wanted. Robin Farley wasn't interested. Felicia Rae Kantor at Lehman, Dean Gianoukos at J.P. Morgan, Jill Krutick at Salomon and Brian McGough at Morgan Stanley also passed. The only person who'll interview is Katherine Lillard at Merrill Lynch, about whom I have reservations but, given that we're turning up, in most categories, only one semi-viable candidate if we're lucky..."

"... beggars can't be choosers," David said, smiling. He was a realist. "Thanks, Larry. Richard, why don't we stay in the consumer space and hear where you are."

"Well, we've landed Liz Tytus from Prudential to cover tobacco."

"How much did we pay her?" Les interrupted.

David hesitated for a moment and then concluded that, if he wanted them to all work as a team, he'd treat them all as members of that team.

"Four."

"Four? Isn't that a million a stock?" Julia asked.

"No, $800,000."

"Yikes."

"You do what you have to do," David said. "I'll get her coverage up over the next few years to the point where she'll wind up having robbed us, but not blind."

Richard was nodding. "In other searches, I don't want to jinx things, but I believe we've landed Louis Liddy of Goldman Sachs to do restaurants."

"Really!" Larry Fraser exclaimed.

"It ain't over 'til it's over," David mused, "but Louis has signed a contract and given Goldman two weeks' notice, and he plans to take a week of vacation between jobs so, if everything plays out as he says it will, he'll be here on May 8th."

"Congratulations, David!" Julia said. "That would be a real coup."

"Wait, Julia, at least until his cartons arrive. Richard?"

"In hardlines retailing, I eliminated Dana Telsey, who's also number one in apparel retailing and thus conflicts with Richard Geyer, I got nowhere with Gary Balter at CSFB and Alan Rifkin at Lehman, and Aram Rubinson recently left UBS for BofA, so we struck out.

"In food we have one candidate, Don Pinkel of UBS Warburg who says he isn't under contract. Two of the other four ranked analysts are at bulge-bracket firms: Andrew Lazar at Lehman and David Nelson at CSFB. Eric Katzman at Deutsche Bank declined, and John McMillin, whom you all know well and who'll retire from Prudential one of these days, was another definite no."

"What about Jaine Mehring?" David asked.

"She fell off of *II* in 2002 so I didn't call her. Should I?"

"No, I will. She was robbed. She was within an inch of Eric Katzman, I think, and I'm sure she'll be back on this year. I really want Jaine…I'm gonna call her."

"You should," Lipstein agreed. "Finally, in apparel, footwear and textiles we struck out with Robert Drbul at Lehman, Margaret Mager at Goldman, Dennis Rosenberg at CSFB and Jeff Edelman at UBS. Susan Silverstein at BofA seems to have moved into management."

"Thanks, Richard. Good work. Liz is here and Louis is coming." Richard nodded.

"Les? How about technology?"

"I'd be delighted. Let's start with contract manufacturing. Lou Miscioscia at Lehman is number one and Jerry Labowitz, who's been at Merrill forever, is number two. Lou wasn't interested, and Jerry you'll have to call yourself, David, because I can't touch Merrill. Christopher Whitmore at Deutsche Bank said no when I thought he'd say yes, and Tom Brinkley of CSFB said yes when I thought he'd say no, so we'll get Tom in the door this week or next and see how he stacks up. I found him, personally, to be a very, very sharp young man. The others, Tom Hopkins at Bear Stearns, Michael Morris at Salomon and Roger Norberg at J.P. Morgan, all passed.

"In the Internet space, two of the six ranked analysts just retired: Henry Blodget at Merrill and Jamie Kiggen at CSFB. Of the four newer names, Holly Becker at Lehman, Anthony Noto at Goldman and Lanny Baker at Salomon all declined. That left us with Daniel Roe at UBS, who *isn't* under contract, who seems to be shopping himself pretty aggressively and was willing to 'allow' us to interview him. He's a little smitten with himself, if you ask me, and he'll want, I'm sure, a considerable amount of money, but he's our only legitimate Internet candidate so we shouldn't rush to disqualify him. He also seems very banking-oriented."

"What does 'a considerable amount of money' mean, Les?"

"Well, I'm sure he was just posturing, but he told me that he'd consider offers...how did he put it... with seven zeros and no decimal points in them."

"So $10,000,000."

"Or $20,000,000," Les added, smiling.

"What an asshole."

"You don't have to marry him, David, you just need to rent his votes."

David was frustrated but he pushed on. "How about PCs and semis?"

"In PCs, I didn't call Steven Fortuna because he works at Merrill. You can call him, David, but he's not going to come. I had lovely conversations with Richard Gardner at Salomon, Don Young at UBS, Kim Alexy at Prudential and Andy Neff at Bear Stearns, but all of them opted to pass. And in semis, I only called Jonathan Joseph who's number two and who's at Salomon and Mark Edelstone who's number three and who's at Morgan Stanley, both of whom were happy and disinterested."

"I'll call Joe Osha at Merrill because you can't, but what about Dan Niles?"

"Dan is number one in semiconductors and also a Runner-Up in PCs. I thought we should talk about him first before I placed the call."

David knew what was coming. "Why?"

"Well, Dan would be the perfect hire in my view. He's an *II* double-teamer, he's seemingly very well regarded by your clients and he'd probably be a big hit with your brokers as well. I also understand that he's banker-friendly."

"But…"

"But technology analysts never come cheaply, David, even mediocre ones, and Dan is the antithesis of mediocrity, so you'd have to stretch to get him in my judgment."

"This is break-the-bank territory we're talking about?"

"I don't know for sure, but I've checked around and put together a best guess of what BCS would have to offer him to get him."

"How long a contract?" David asked.

"Five years."

"And how much for Mr. Double-Teamer?"

"A hundred million, David, give or take."

* * *

It was 12:30, and Keith Jackman was behind schedule. He'd mapped out the day, hour by hour, and he should have just completed a 30–minute visit with his traders so he raced up the internal staircase to the 64th floor, waved from afar to Billy Lynch, who headed all of trading, and made a dash for Steven Pryor's desk. Steven traded all of Keith's NYSE-listed names including Disney, Viacom and AOL Time Warner. He and Keith typically spoke several times a day by phone and Keith made a point of stopping by in person several times a week whenever he was in town.

"Keith, buddy," Steven said, smiling, "how's it hangin'?"

"What's doing?"

"I'm dyin' here. It's sunny and 78 degrees outside, it's six weeks 'til summer, and I'm sittin' inside callin' and callin' cause no one's callin' me."

"Did Jessica say something about Disney?" Keith asked, referring to his competitor at Merrill Lynch.

"Not that I heard. Why?"

"It's sloppy, and someone told me that they thought she did."

Steven nodded. "I'll check."

Keith looked around the trading floor. The phones were surprisingly quiet and many of the traders, who never leave their desks between 9:00 A.M.and 4:00 P.M. except for the men's room or the cafeteria, were eating their lunches at their stations. The only movement that caught Keith's eye was that of two traders standing near and looking out of the floor-length window that faced north. While Keith couldn't hear them, they were clearly talking with great agitation, and one of them was pointing down at something. As Steven asked him about his summer vacation plans, Keith noticed the two traders motioning others near them to look out and, within 15 seconds, 40 traders had lined up along the window and looked out and down with great interest.

"Steev-a-reeno," one yelled, waving for Steven to join them.

"What the fuck are those yokels up to? Wanna see?"

"Sure," Keith said, not wanting to but fearing insulting Steven by saying no, so Steven and Keith walked to the window and looked down.

Across the street, on the roof of the 60–story office building that ran for half a block, east to west and an entire block, north to south, a man in a blue shirt and dark blue pants and a woman in a knee-length fur coat were making out.

"Jesus," Steven said. "Look at 'em go. And what the

fuck does she have a fur coat on for? It's 80 fucking degrees outside."

Before anyone else could speculate on that heady subject, the woman pushed the man she'd been kissing away from her and opened her coat. Beneath it she was nude. The traders began hooting and waving for their peers who were still at their desks to come join them. "He's gonna fuck her," someone yelled.

"Holy shit!"

"Blow him!"

"Do you believe this chick?"

"Bet she gets it in the ass!"

Keith suddenly felt uncomfortable. Most of the desks that were closest to the windows were now empty, and the long wall of glass was blanketed with twenty-to fifty-something-year-old white men, often three or four deep. Many were yelling as if they were watching the Knicks at The Garden or Lennox Lewis in Memphis. Billy Lynch, Keith noticed, was nowhere in sight. Halfway down the floor, Keith saw a young woman, presumably a secretary, walk to the window and look out. She only stayed for a second, then returned to her desk and picked up a phone.

"That cunt is hot!" someone yelled in Keith's ear.

When he looked back across the street, he could see that the couple remained alone on the roof, that the guy had his pants down around his ankles, that the woman was now on her back, on top of an air vent of some kind, with the fur coat between her back and the vent's grating, and that the guy had a hand between her legs.

Keith could hear some phones now, ringing many times, all going unanswered. I should get out of here, he told himself, and he panned the room looking for the least obvious way to the internal staircase.

Everything looked unfamiliar to him. A hundred men were lined up at the window, yelling, several clusters of young women, looking nervous and whispering amongst themselves, were now scattered across the trading floor, more and more phones were going unanswered and, outside the window, on a beautiful, early spring day, a man was screwing a woman in a fur coat on an air conditioning vent.

Suddenly, a short, slim figure, moving quickly, caught Keith's eye. It was Carl. He was, it seemed, staring at all of the phones that were ringing away and growing more furious by the moment. "Get the fuck away from there," he bellowed as he raced towards the window. "Get back on your stools, you assholes. Get the fuck back to your desks and answer your fucking phones!"

At first, almost no one could hear Carl, but within a minute, the 100 traders at the window were scattering in whatever direction put the most distance between them and Carl. Carl grabbed several traders and pushed them away from the window, out of which he made certain to look as often as he could. "What are you morons thinking? Don't you hear your phones ringing? Don't you know we're losing money?"

Keith, walking as briskly as he could with his back to Carl, hoped not to be recognized. Carl's anger, he knew, related not to his moral indignation over the sexually inhospitable work environment that his traders had created for the women working next to them but to the business that was being lost as orders went untaken.

As he reached the corner of the trading floor that was closest to the staircase, Keith took one last peek over his shoulder at the bedlam behind him. Dozens of traders were still scrambling, dozens more were now sitting at their desks pretending to talk to clients, and Carl was yelling, shaking his head at them and looking out the window, yelling, shaking, looking, yelling, shaking, looking.

* * *

When David and his headhunters returned from lunch, Bob Taylor was up.

"I have the three financial services searches and specialty pharmaceuticals," he reminded everyone. "In brokers and asset managers, Henry McVey at Morgan Stanley passed, Guy Moszkowski at Solly wasn't interested, nor were Richard Strauss at Goldman, Mark Constant at Lehman, Brad Hintz at Bernstein or Joan Solotar at CSFB. The last runner-up, Anne Reiss at Deutsche Bank, *was* interested. Hopefully we'll get her in to see you next week, David."

"I've heard bad things about her," Larry piped in. "Maybe true, maybe not, but I interviewed Eva Zamora, who sits two doors down from her, during a different search and she mentioned that Anne had cut back her workweek a lot over the past two years, during which Anne had been out on maternity twice."

"I'm amazed she's working at all with two kids under two," David said.

"She's working enough to continue to rank," Bob said, slightly defensively.

"Let's give her the benefit of the doubt for now," David sighed. "Sometimes it just takes my breath away."

"What?" Larry asked.

"How nasty some women in the business world can be to other women."

"You think they're worse than how men treat other men?"

"Absolutely. Maybe it's because they have to compete harder with each other for fewer opportunities."

"You mean for promotions?" Bob asked.

"I mean opportunities to get hired *and* for promotion. I bend over backwards to try to hire qualified women but, no matter what I do, I still wind up with an analytical staff that's 80% male."

The room was quiet for a moment.

"Show me women," David said at last. "I need more women in the department."

Everyone nodded and Bob continued. "In life insurance, we also have one candidate, Vivian Zimm at Morgan Stanley. Six ranked analysts work at bulge-bracket firms and five of them were unwilling to interview: Colin Devine at Salomon, Ed Spehar at Merrill, Eric Berg at Lehman, Caitlin Long at CSFB and Joan Zief at Goldman. Andrew Kligerman at Bear Stearns wasn't interested, nor was Vanessa Wilson at Deutsche Bank.

"Why is Vivian willing to talk? Morgan's bulge-bracket."

"I'm not entirely sure, David. She just said that she was reassessing her whole job situation in light of Alice Schroeder's arrival and that she'd meet with us."

"When will I see her?"

"Hopefully within a week."

"Good. And on the property/casualty side?"

"Strike out. Speaking of Alice Schroeder, she said no, as did Jay Cohen at Merrill, Alain Karaoglan at Deutsche Bank, Tom Cholnoky at Goldman, Alice Cornish at Pru, Ron Frank at Salomon and Charles Gates at CSFB."

"Michael Smith?"

"Sorry. He's at Bear Stearns, also a no."

"And specialty pharmaceuticals?"

"Unless you replace Michael Mellman in the major pharmaceuticals area you're not going to hire anyone," Bob said matter-of-factly.

David was surprised. "Fire Michael?"

"Yup. Three of the four ranked analysts I spoke to said they wouldn't work with Michael. They said he was weak and would never rank. One said he was 'paralyzed by perfectionism.' He has a reputation for saying he'll do things but not doing them."

"Michael was really the reason why they said no?"

"He wasn't the only reason but he was an important one. And this came up without any prompting on my part."

"Who was the fourth analyst?"

"Angela Larson at Salomon, whom I liked a great deal, but she expressed gratitude to Salomon for having given her a big, stand-alone break when she was unranked and unknown and said she was too loyal to leave."

"She used to be Jeff Chaffkin's junior at PaineWebber?" David asked.

"Correct, and while Culp gave her a shot at her own group, it wasn't until she separated from Jeff that, at least in her mind, she succeeded as her own person. She's a great gal, but she's not interested."

David nodded. "How about you, Mr. Hart? How did we do in natural gas?"

"Not well. There are only five ranked analysts in this space. Three who are at bulge-bracket firms all passed on us: Curt Launer at CSFB, Richard Gross at Lehman and Ray Niles at Salomon. Ron Barone also declined, and Carol Coale, who finished first last year and is at Prudential, said she thought trading to BCS wouldn't be a step up for her."

"How about the cyclical searches? We're off to a great start there!"

"Well, that's right. We did succeed in prying Van Trudell loose from Prudential and he's already started, replacing Arthur Litt."

"I'd love to have been a fly on the wall during *that* meeting," Hart said, smiling.

"It was no fun but it had to be done. We got some embarrassing press out of it, but we also got a stronger department and that's all I care about, other than that we treated Arthur right financially." Many heads bobbed up and down.

"Electrical equipment, however, looks like it's going to be a strike-out. I've already gotten no's from Jeff Sprague at Salomon, Bob Cornell at Lehman, Martin Sankey at Goldman and Michael Regan at CSFB."

"What about Nick Heymann? Seeing his neighbor, Mr. Trudell, leave Prudential for BCS should help our case, shouldn't it?"

"Not necessarily, I'm afraid. He's not returning my calls, which tells me he's happy."

David winced. "Packaging?"

"This one's tough because only four analysts ranked and one of them, Scott Davis at Morgan Stanley, just changed groups. George Staphos is happy, and Daniel Khoshaba is probably well paid at Deutsche Bank, having been one of its first big-name hires, and probably won't be interested. But, fortunately, we got a yes out of Tom Batchelder at Merrill Lynch."

"Not hireable," said Les.

"Why?" David feared that Les might have had to say that to feel loyal to Merrill.

"I just don't see it."

"It's a tiny group that's easily lost in the sea of Merrill analysts and we could pay him some ridiculous amount of money, far above what Merrill could justify."

Les was silent.

"Don't underestimate the value of his *II* ranking to Merrill, David," Julia warned. "You know how important it's been for Merrill to be number one in *II* and how badly many people there felt when they lost the top spot two years ago. They changed Research Directors, which might have had nothing to do with it, or everything. Andy Melnick is a very well-regarded guy, and to see him 'retire' from Merrill and then turn up only weeks later at Goldman Sachs makes me suspicious. Just my opinion, but I know I'm not alone. Merrill's within *one vote* of regaining the number one spot in *II* so, while packaging may sound unimportant, as long as Tom is ranked, Merrill will probably fight very hard to keep him."

"I agree completely," said Larry.

David was shaking his head. "I'm not saying that hiring out of Merrill is ever easy, just that Tom seemed pretty frustrated when I met him."

Dave Hart agreed. "We'll give him the best shot we can." When no one else said anything, he moved on to the multi-industry search. "This last one looks bad. Jeff Sprague, who's number one in electrical equipment, is number one here, and Bob Cornell, who's number two in electrical equipment, is a Runner-Up here. Beyond them you're left with four candidates. The bulge-bracket guys, John Inch at Merrill, Jack Kelly at Goldman and Don MacDougall at J.P. Morgan, were all quick to say no. Nick Heymann also ranks here."

"Thanks, Dave. Good luck in packaging. Julia, can we finish up with you?"

"Of course. I now have airlines, airfreight and surface transportation, satellite, networking, wireline equipment and the macro searches which I'll save for last.

"In airlines, I suspect that there's nothing for us, which is also why Lehman hired James rather than a ranked analyst. The best guy in this space is Sam Buttrick at UBS, who's rather unconventional."

" *Wonderfully* unconventional."

"I don't know, David. It's as if he speaks a different language than everyone else and then gets mad at you when you don't understand it. In the middle of my first and *only* conversation with him, he began asking me about the value-added that I thought headhunters provided."

"To whom?"

"To anyone. He said, 'David needs an airline analyst. I'm an airline analyst. David does his homework and concludes that I'm good. David wants to hire me. So why wouldn't David pick up the phone and ask me if I'd like to be his airline analyst?'"

"In a perfect world, Julia, he's right."

"In a perfect world he's right but I tried to explain to him that, when you're trying to do 30 to 40 searches simultaneously, sometimes you need help."

"Did you convince him?"

"Not in the slightest."

"What else did he say?"

"He asked if we ever tried to bust contracts."

"And you said…?"

"No, that if he was under contract, we'd respect that, and perhaps we could talk in the future when his contract is up."

"Is he under contract?"

"He wouldn't say. Instead, he started giving me what could easily have been an hour-long dissertation on his problems with employment contracts. You know, they're used when there's no need for them, they aren't used when it makes the most sense to use them, they liberate those who should feel imprisoned and imprison those who should feel free, blah blah blah."

David was laughing. "You have to admit that he's one interesting guy. Beyond how smart he is, he's such an out-of-the-box thinker."

"Maybe that's how he's stayed sane following the same 10 airlines for all these years," Richard said.

"Could be," David agreed. "None of *us* could have done it. Anyway, if Sam said no, who else is there?"

"Brian Harris at Salomon, Glenn Engel at Goldman and James Higgins at CSFB. None was interested. I'm still working on Susan Donofrio at Deutsche Bank and James Parker at Raymond James but I'm not hopeful. The only nibble I've gotten is from Marsha Yamamoto at Bear Stearns who's due to come in within two weeks. My sources tell me that Marsha wasn't called for the Lehman job, although Marsha says she was and turned it down. I've heard very mixed things about her, but she's ranked so we're pursuing her. We'll see how she does."

"I liked her," David said with a shrug, "but what do I know?"

"In airfreight, four of the five ranked analysts also cover rails and truckers and thus conflict with Tim Laboy.

"You could fire Tim, David," Les probed.

"Not if I can help it. Tim's doing a decent job and

firing him wouldn't go over well with many of my best analysts."

"Nor," Julia added, "with most of the analysts who compete with Tim. They're not anxious to get a job that someone else was fired to create."

"Remember Letterman and Ted Koppel?" Bob asked.

"Exactly right," said Julia. "Even if we were to tell these guys that Tim is doing a bad job and is going to be replaced anyway, they probably wouldn't believe us. Barry Simonetti at Merrill, who *doesn't* do the rails and truckers, was interested in doing airfreight *and* airlines, and I'm continuing to see him through the interviewing process."

"Good. How about networking and wireline equipment?"

"Very, very tough. Nikos won't leave UBS, and Alex Henderson wants to stay at Salomon. Chris Stix just left Morgan Stanley, and I got polite turndowns from Tim Luke at Lehman, Alkesh Shah at Morgan Stanley, Paul Sagawa at Bernstein, Steven Levy at Lehman, George Notter at Deutsche Bank, James Parmelee at CSFB and Wojtek Uzdelewicz at Bear Stearns.

"The only other possibility is Grace Flagler at Pru who ranks in wireline equipment but said she'd only be interested if you offered her wireline *and* networking. I'm pursuing her."

David made some notes.

"In satellite, there are only five ranked analysts and four of them work for bulge-bracket firms: Marc Nabi at Merrill, Vijay Jayant at Morgan Stanley, Armand Musey at Salomon and Ty Carmichael Jr. at CSFB. All four said no, and the fifth analyst, Karim Zia at Deutsche Bank, isn't returning my calls."

"What about the macro searches?"

"The macro searches we have to talk about. We'd started to make our calls and we'd gotten you together with James Sephton, the small-cap analyst at CSFB…"

"…who started breakfast by telling me he'd only come if we granted him, on day one, half a million options on BC Holdings at a 10% discount to the market."

"Must've been a short breakfast."

"Not short enough. Anyway…"

"I was calling around and had begun setting up some breakfasts when, two days ago, I got this peculiar phone call from someone named Inga Breuer saying she was calling from Dieter Schmidt's office and asking me to stop all of the macro searches."

David was blindsided. He squinted. "Inga works for Dieter. *What* did she say?"

"She asked me to stop all of the macro searches. Accounting, convertibles, quantitative, derivatives, small caps, technical and Washington analysis."

"Why?"

"She said that, apparently, Dieter's been trying to sign Linda to a five- year contract as a strategist and Linda went ballistic when she heard that you'd interviewed a small-cap analyst."

"So…"

"… so she told Dieter that she wanted wording in her new contract guaranteeing that, during the five years in question, BCS would hire no one in any of those categories."

"And Dieter agreed to this?"

"Apparently."

"He never said a word to me about it."

"I can't explain that, but I got the message loudly and clearly from this woman that under no circumstances would you be allowed to hire anyone in any of those sectors."

"What will you do if Linda doesn't sign?" Larry asked.

"Have Julia recruit Ed Kerschner to replace her. He's one of the best in the business."

"I bet Linda placed the call herself," Larry guessed.

Julia shook her head. "She didn't. I was suspicious too so yesterday I called Dieter's office, where I got Inga, and Linda's office, where I got Linda. Both confirmed the original message. Linda's new contract, which apparently she's *still* refusing to sign, says that you can kiss hiring All Stars in any or all of those six categories goodbye."

* * *

Now I can answer this, David thought.

In his hand he held a letter from *II* soliciting suggestions regarding how the current year's All Star Poll should be conducted. As always, *II* was asking for input from each Research Director on The Street on which industries should be added to the poll, excluded from the poll, combined with others or spun out into their own categories.

Long ago David had discovered that his counterparts at other firms had made a habit of lobbying for changes for one reason and one reason only: They thought those changes would help them rank more highly in the next poll. If they had a strong analyst covering the coal industry, they'd argue that coal should be included in the All Star Poll. If they had a strong gaming analyst and a strong lodging analyst, they'd argue that gaming and lodging should be separated so they could get two of their analysts ranked instead of one. If they had a strong Internet analyst, they'd argue that Internet was too broad a category and should be split into portals and e-commerce and infrastructure. And if their ranked tobacco analyst had just quit and joined a competitor, they'd argue that tobacco, comprising only four or five publicly traded stocks, was no longer a full-time job and thus no longer worthy of inclusion in the poll.

So, holding his nose, David went to work crafting his letter. Combine electrical equipment and multi-industry, he suggested, pointing out that Jeff Sprague, Bob Cornell and Nick Heymann all ranked in both and that many analysts who did one of those groups also did the other. Keep tobacco, he argued, citing the large market capitalizations of Philip Morris and others in the group and making certain not to reference Liz Tytus's recent hiring. Kill apparel, footwear and textiles, he argued. No one cares about those stocks any more and most firms don't even have analysts covering them.

Specialty pharmaceuticals? Can you name one of those companies off the top of your head? It's not a real category and it clearly shouldn't be included. Combine data networking and wireline equipment, he wrote. They're really just subsets of the same industry. And satellite? Does any firm on The Street still *have* a satellite analyst? David suggested that satellite be eliminated now that he knew he couldn't hire anyone in that space.

Finally, David wrote, the single best thing that *II* could do would be to eliminate those crazy macro categories that have nothing to do with fundamental equity research: accounting, convertibles, quant, derivatives, small caps, technical analysis and Washington analysis. Many of these "arcane sciences" were held in low regard by serious investors, David alleged. Their inclusion merely distorted *II's* rankings each year. Keep strategy and economics, David wrote, but kill all the others.

Knowing full well that virtually none of these wishes, or rather, recommendations would actually be enacted, but recognizing that if he didn't venture he certainly wouldn't gain, David sealed up his letter, messengered it *and* e-mailed it, just to be safe.

In the last *II*, David remembered, the difference between ranking number eleven and number eight had been four votes. And in his contract, David recalled, the difference in his bonus between BCS ranking number eleven and number eight was $2,000,000. Every vote mattered.

* * *

After having given Goldman two weeks' notice and taken a week off in Hawaii, Louis Liddy finally turned up at BCS, which announced with great fanfare the hiring of its third *II-* ranked analyst on May 8.

Once his orientation sessions were out of the way, Louis settled into his new office next to beverage analyst Joe Altschuler's, which his secretary had set up during Louis's vacation, and began planning several days of calling to let clients know his new phone number and e-mail address, and why he'd left Goldman for BCS. Louis also knew that he'd have to tee up some short reports on each of his stocks and a short industry overview for the conference call to institutional and retail salespeople on which he'd launch restaurant coverage at BCS. But this wouldn't take long because he only planned to cover seven stocks initially: McDonald's of course, plus Brinker, Darden, Outback, Starbucks, Tricon and Wendy's.

Five minutes after he'd begun calling institutional clients, Louis's phone started ringing. Retail, it seems, had found him.

"Hi, Louis?"

"Yes."

"This is Bob O'Reilly in Santa Clara."

"How are you, Bob?"

"Great, great. Say, are you going to be covering Bob Evans Farms?"

"Not initially, Bob. Why?"

"Just wondering. I've got some clients who used to work there and who still have quite a bit of stock, and it would really be great if I could tell them what you thought about it."

"I understand. Perhaps after I've gotten settled in I can take a look at it."

"Great, great. Do you know when that would be?"

"I really don't yet, Bob."

"That's okay, but do you know if you'd rate it a Buy?"

"Oh it's much too soon to tell," Louis answered, "and I'm not sure I could tell you that anyway, even if I knew."

"Why's that?"

"Because Compliance requires that all salespeople hear about my ratings at the same time."

"Gotcha. Of course. Should've thought of that myself!"

"Not a problem," Louis said. "Anything else?"

"Nope, just wanted to check on Bob Evans. Listen, Louis, thanks very much for talking with me. It's great having you on board."

"My pleasure, Bob." Louis hung up, smiling.

Fifteen minutes later, just after he'd hung up with Hank Hermann at Waddell & Reed in Kansas City, Louis heard his phone ring and he picked it up.

"Louis?"

"Yes."

"Marlene Gettinger in Memphis. How are you doing today?"

"Fine, Marlene, and you?"

"Very well thank you. Say, will you be covering Ruby Tuesday?"

"I don't think so, Marlene."

"Really! I'm surprised. The stock's done awfully well lately, and without an analyst covering it, it's been hard for me to do anywhere near the business in Ruby that I want to. It's a big favorite down here, you know, headquartered in Tennessee and all."

"I'm sure it is."

"And it would be a huge help to our office if you'd follow it."

"I wish I could, but its market cap is only about $1 billion, you know."

"Oh I know that, but it's bigger than lots of other restaurant chains. It just seems logical to me that you'd pick it up when you were looking to add to your universe."

"It's possible, Marlene, I just wouldn't want to promise it."

"I understand. Say, would you mind if I checked back with you in a while?"

"Not at all," Louis said innocently.

"Well, that's mighty kind of you Louis. I'm glad we had this chance to visit, and we in Memphis welcome you. Hope you stop in and see us the next time you're in town."

"I'm sure I will, Marlene. Nice talking to you."

All morning and all afternoon Louis's phone never stopped ringing.

"It's Elizabeth in Boise…"

"Betty Sue in H3…"

"Are you going to rate McDonald's a Buy?"

"Ron in F11…"

"Myron in Baltimore…"

"Are you doing Applebee's?"

"Will you be covering Krispy Kreme?

"Do you have a Buy on Ryan's?"

"Do you think you might pick up Steak 'n Shake?"

"My father works for California Pizza Kitchen…"

"Will you have the same ratings at BCS that you had at Goldman?"

"The CEO of Luby's has all of his family money with me…"

"I think I can get the banking business from Papa John's…"

"I can get you into Landry's…"

"… Marty in Dallas…"

"… Rhonda in the S103 satellite…"

"Could you help me out here and do Jack in the Box?"

"Do you like Wendy's?"

"… J.P. in the JP branch. Ain't that a hoot?…"

"I need Sonic covered."

"You've gotta help me out here with Cheesecake Factory…"

"I can get Burger King to the merger table if you can get McDonald's there."

"My friend has these two drive-thru-only burger restaurants in Florida and wants to come public…"

"Could you do a conference call to some of the brokers in our office?"

"Could you come see us?"

"Could I come with you the next time you visit Wendy's and maybe get you to help me land some of their top guys as clients?"

"I need..."

"I need..."

"You've gotta help me..."

By 4:30 that afternoon, Louis's head was reeling. He'd called almost none of the institutional clients he'd planned to talk with, he'd written not a stitch of research for his "come public" launch to the sales force, and Craig Lucie was now pacing outside his office. Louis waved him in and asked his secretary to take messages.

"You look a little tired," Craig said. "Hard to come back from Hawaii?"

"I can't believe this! Retail is all over me! I can't be off the phone for 15 seconds before some broker from some PDQ branch has got me on the hook for coverage of some rinky-dink chain that's in his town or owned by his father-in-law or about to give its investment banking business to us if only we'd cover them."

"They're idiots," Craig said. "All retail brokers are idiots. You'll figure that out pretty quickly if you haven't already. Banking needs them because they can distribute product for us, and they help defray costs like the Research budget that Banking wouldn't be able to fund by itself. But the less you have to do with these morons, the better. They're dumb, they're selfish, they'll take all the credit when one of your ideas works out and they'll try to get you fired when their clients threaten to sue them because one of your ideas didn't. They have no loyalty except to themselves and they'll tell you how great you are to your face and then bad mouth you to everyone in their office and to all of their customers the minute you're gone. They're a necessary evil, Louis, and I underscore *evil*. So protect yourself."

Louis hadn't expected this from Craig, and it didn't exactly calm his nerves, but he tried to put his Retail hand-wringing aside, take some deep breaths and shift gears.

"So what would *you* like to talk about?" he asked Craig.

"I'd like to talk about this. You're going to launch with seven stocks, right?"

"Correct. They're the seven largest market caps in my space."

"Good, good. You need those names for credibility." Louis nodded. He was glad that Craig understood. "But they won't help me at all. We're not going to bank McDonald's at BCS, nor Wendy's nor Darden. What we *can* bank, is AFC Enterprises... you know them, right?"

Louis squinted. "Popeyes and Church's and Cinnabon?"

"Exactly. And we can bank Buford's Barbecue, CKE, which is Carl's Jr. and Hardee's, The International House of Pancakes, Maria's Casa Mexicana, O'Charleys, RARE Hospitality which has got the LongHorn Steakhouse chain, and Triarc, which is Arby's."

"I don't think we want to bank some of those."

"Don't say that, Louis. These are good companies, solid brands with good real estate and, in some cases, new and improved management. They need money, unlike McDonald's, and they haven't been in bed with Goldman and Morgan Stanley forever either. They're in our sweet spot and we can get them if we do one thing."

"And that is…"

"We need you to cover them as quickly as you can."

"All of them?"

"For starters. How quickly can I tell them you'll be covering them?"

"I don't know. This is my first day at BCS. I haven't been able to take a leak for seven hours. My clients haven't heard my voice in a month and David wants an industry overview and reports on seven names within five days so he can 'bring me public.'"

"I don't need my reports this week."

"When do you need them?"

"I don't know, four within 30 days and the rest within 90 days?"

"Let me take all this stuff home and sort it out, Craig. I've just got everyone clamoring for everything I never covered before and I haven't got a clue where to start."

"You've gotta help me out here, Louis," Craig said. "I did a lot to get you that offer of yours and the least you can do is get me the coverage that I need to do business."

At 5:20 that evening, Craig shook Louis's hand, welcomed him again to BCS and returned to the 66th floor.

At 5:25 Louis placed one phone call.

And at 5:30 he brought David a letter of resignation and returned to Goldman Sachs.

* * *

After the Morning Call the next day, Laura Payden, the specialty chemicals analyst, poked her head in the door and asked anxiously if David had a minute.

"Of course. Come in, Laura."

"I have Michael with me," she said, meaning Michael Zisk, the managing director in charge of chemical industry investment banking. Laura sat on the sofa and Michael in one of the side chairs. They didn't look at each other. Sensing a disagreement, David naturally let his analyst speak first.

"Michael wants me to give Ecolab to Van."

David was surprised. "Why?"

"He says they want to be followed by commodity chemicals analysts and not by specialty chemicals analysts, which makes no sense to me."

"Is this true?"

"This is what they're telling me. I've been calling on them now for two years, and Laura has been helpful to that calling effort, so it's nothing personal and it has nothing to do with her coverage of the company. It's just that, with a market cap of $6 billion, they feel that they're surrounded by other specialty chemical companies that are 10% their size or less and they want to be compared to the big boys, against which they think they'll stack up exceedingly well."

David didn't believe this. He didn't know a lot about chemical stocks but he was pretty sure that the larger-cap, commodity chemical companies were slower-growing and much more cyclical than the specialty chemical companies and thus sold at lower P/E ratios. Why would Ecolab want to jeopardize its P/E, which was now around 30?

"They told you this?"

"They're telling this to all the firms on The Street. They're looking to be covered by the chemical analyst, not the specialty chemical analyst."

"Who covers Ecolab at other firms?" David asked, looking at Laura.

"All of my competitors."

"Are there any ranked analysts in your space who *don't* do Ecolab?"

"None that I'm aware of, David. It's the fourth-largest market cap in my space so it's a must-cover stock if you're a specialty chemicals analyst."

David pondered in silence. "May I talk with Michael alone, please?"

"Of course." Laura, looking worried, stood up and walked out David's door.

"I'll call you in a minute," David said after her, closing the door when she'd gone.

"What's really going on here, Michael?"

"Look, David, I didn't want to say it in front of her, but she's a good-not-great analyst competing against great analysts at all the firms you just mentioned. I've got great ties to Allan Schuman and he told me..."

"Who's Allan Schuman?"

"Chairman and CEO. Allan told me," Michael lied, "that he wants to see us compete for their business, and that if I can't distinguish myself on the basis of the firm I work for, and its global capabilities, I should try to distinguish myself in some other way, perhaps on the research front, and that means I need the All Star, David...I need Van."

Now David understood.

"They'd rather have Van follow them than Laura?"

"I think they would. They have nothing against Laura, but Van is ranked and, if I can offer them the All Star, I believe I can get mandates. It's as simple as that."

David nodded, which prompted Michael to relax and smile. "So, let me be sure I understand what you'd like me to do as a matter of policy. Whenever we have a ranked analyst, Mr. Smith, in a group that looks something like another group in which we have an unranked analyst, Ms. Jones, whenever we think it will help The Bank, we'll take some of Ms. Jones's most important stocks away from her and require Mr. Smith to do them, even if no other firm is covering those stocks that way and despite any competitive disadvantage to which we subject Ms. Jones."

"Do you want to intellectualize about this, David, or do you want The Bank to turn a profit again during our lifetimes?"

"Both."

"We can't do both right now, I'm afraid. You want to maximize your *II* ranking, which is why you fired Arthur and replaced him with Van. For all I know, you've got plans to fire Laura anyway and replace her with a ranked analyst if you can get one."

"Absolutely untrue."

"So you say right now, but that could change. Laura's unranked. If she quits in a huff, you won't have lost any votes. As a matter of fact, that would give you a great chance to hire a ranked analyst in her space which would help you next October."

"And which of Laura's competitors would come here if Ecolab is given to Van?"

"None, but if you could hire any ranked specialty chemicals analyst I'd be okay with taking Ecolab away from Van and putting it back under the specialty chemicals umbrella."

"So the only thing we care about is coverage by a ranked analyst, is that right?"

"That's it."

It never failed to amaze him…the hoops through which bankers would jump for a mandate. "No," he told Michael. "And if you promised *anyone* at Ecolab that you'd deliver Van Trudell to him you'd better call and tell him that his package has been delayed. Permanently."

* * *

Lisa dropped David's mail in his in-box. She'd already discarded all of his junk mail and any correspondence on issues she was sure she could handle herself.

"Anything good?" David asked.

"New blueprints for 65," she said. "On top."

David found them. At first everything looked the same. Then, he realized that he saw many more inside offices than he'd remembered. "What's different about this?"

"The Market's gone!" Lisa said with great satisfaction.

"They killed it?"

"Killed it."

"Is it going somewhere else?"

"I'm not sure, but it's definitely not going on a Research floor."

"How do you know?"

"I called Katherine's office when I saw the plans and asked her secretary."

"And she said…"

"…that Katherine had decided it was a bad idea."

"Why?"

"Too much foot traffic in Research and Banking."

David picked up the phone and called Carl.

"Thanks," he told him.

"For what?"

"I just saw the new plans for 65, and The Market is gone."

Carl was quiet for a second, and then said, "So you're happy?"

"I'm happy, and it was the right thing to do."

"Swell," Carl said. "You're welcome." No cafeteria on 65? It was news to him.

* * *

Tom Batchelder was in, making the rounds. David had set him up with Rebecca Suess, and with Van Trudell and Alan Gildersleeve whom David had asked to stress the ease with which they'd made the transition from their old firms to BCS; as well as with Laura Payden who was still a little tender from her Ecolab skirmish with Michael Zisk. David had thrown in John McLain and several institutional salesmen, asking them to focus on how easy it was for analysts to set up marketing trips to see their institutional clients; Paul Pitcher; a banker; a trader; Matt Speiser; and Jennifer Von Moos from Public Relations.

"Tell him how you can help him find the right balance between being public and being private," David had told Jennifer. "He's underutilizing CNBC and he's wary about raising his profile. Show him how we can help him find the right level of exposure and what it can mean for his visibility with clients and with Retail.

"He's happy at Merrill," David had written in the cover memo, "but he sometimes feels like a little fish in a very big pond and he has trouble getting to see clients because the Merrill salesmen are busy selling analysts with more important groups, hot deals or both. Please focus on these issues when you see him."

They did and, by the end of the day when David and Tom reconvened, Tom seemed more open to the idea of coming to BCS than he had at breakfast. "They're an impressive lot," he said. "I liked the salesmen a great deal and I had a good session with Jennifer Von Moos. She was very helpful in sorting out what's good press and bad, what's a good use of my time and a bad one, how much CNBC I should do or not do."

"What did you conclude?"

"More than I'm doing right now, but not necessarily a lot more unless either I'm really bullish on my group or have really non-consensus opinions that we want to flag."

"Sounds right."

"We don't have any support like that at Merrill."

"Just one more reason to come here. How did the rest of your meetings go?"

"Very well. I liked Van and Laura a lot. Rebecca too. Really, everyone was quite nice and quite sharp."

"Can you see yourself as a bigger fish in a smaller but still good-sized pond?"

"I think so."

"Are you satisfied that we'll get you more client exposure than you have now?"

"Yes. The department is smaller so the in-house competition is less intense."

"And our Bank is good but it isn't churning out the deal calendar that Merrill is, against which you're also competing."

"That's definitely true."

"You're going to need more client exposure to topple George Staphos."

"That's right."

"So, are you ready for us to put an offer together for you?"

"I don't really know, David. I suppose so, but I still want you to understand that I'm pretty happy overall at Merrill and more inclined to stay put than to move."

"I understand, Tom, but my job is to give you our best shot. I've shown you good people, I've built a logical case, exclusive of money, why you'd be better off here and now it's time to add the economic incentives and convince you to move."

"Fair enough. I'll circle back to Dave Hart and fill him in, and you two can figure out what to do next."

That evening, David and Dave compared notes.

"It'll be hard," Dave said. "Merrill analysts will gripe and gripe and gripe but, at the end of the day, it's still Merrill and they stay put far more often than they move."

"What's he making?"

"High twos. He was a little evasive. Say two eight."

"Shit. So I need to go to four?"

"At least."

"I can't go above that, Dave, not for a packaging analyst."

"I understand. I just want *you* to understand what you're up against. The feedback on him was good, right?"

"Right. He's smart, he's articulate, his print is good and he's a nice guy."

"So there will be a lot of support for hiring him, right?"

"There's support, but there are also several comments along the lines of 'Do we really need someone to cover Pactiv and Ivex?'"

"I hear you."

"So, four?"

"If you can do four and a quarter it'll feel like up 50% to him, and that should be enough."

"You honestly believe I should offer him $4,250,000 to cover Pactiv and Ivex?"

"I'm not saying it makes complete economic sense,

David. I'm saying it's what you need to do if you want to get him."

"Okay," David sighed, "get him back here so I can make him his offer."

"Will do. And if you feel bad about this, remember... you paid Liz Tytus $4 million for five stocks but Tom covers 10 stocks so you're getting him for half price."

A week later, after Merrill had made the seemingly inconsequential decision to postpone a marketing trip of Tom's through the Southeast because signups for his meetings had been light and a very important IPO road show was conflicting with them, Tom Batchelder joined BCS.

And unlike Louis Liddy, he stayed.

* * *

Listless and bored, Carl wandered around the Research Department, poking his head into various analysts' offices and shooting the breeze. Several analysts picked up their phones when they saw him coming, knowing that he'd merely waste their time, and Nancy Natolio locked her door. But Robin Lomax, still relatively new to the firm, didn't know better and waved Carl in when he passed by.

"Robin, Robin, how's my Robin red breasts?"

"They weren't red the last time I looked," she joked, a touch uneasily.

"How's business in retail-land?"

"It's okay, Carl. I'm dialing for dollars, you know. Gotta stay visible until all the *II* ballots are back."

Carl nodded. "Say," he said, "wanna hear something funny?"

"Sure."

"This girl goes to tennis camp, and while she's hitting with one of the pros, the teacher notices that she isn't gripping the racquet the right way. He tries a couple of times to help her, but to no avail. So finally, he says to her, 'just grip it the same way you'd hold your boyfriend's cock.' After that, she starts hitting one winner after another, in the corner, down the line. The pro gets all winded so he stops running for a second and says to her, 'Much better, much better. Now try taking the racquet out of your mouth.'"

Robin's eyes widened and she could feel herself blushing. She looked away, pretending she was distracted by someone walking outside her door. Carl stared long and hard at her, then checked the door to be sure no one was there.

"How's Liz Tytus settling in?"

Surprised by the sudden change of subject, but also relieved, Robin hesitated momentarily and then blurted out, "Liz? She's fine. We're not really interacting much yet but when we start planning the next Consumer Conference I'm sure that'll change."

"That's some dress she's got."

"Dress?"

"Yeah, the blue one? With the white polka dots?"

"I don't recall it."

"Real short."

Robin continued to shake her head.

"*Real* short."

Robin just stared at Carl.

"Makes you just want to walk up behind her, bend her over and give her some back door action she'd never forget."

By now, Robin realized she was trapped.

"You have to admit, she has a great ass," Carl said,

"but you know, her tits are kind of small. I guess you can't have everything."

"I've really got to make some calls, Carl."

"Now Nancy Natolio, on the other hand, has got great tits. Every once in a while, she wears one of those silk blouses that you can see her nipples through? Not much of them, just a hint, but she knows exactly what she's doing. She's saying, 'You know you'd just kill to suck on them, but I'm not going to let you. I'm going to control you by teasing you and leaving you frustrated.' She's a bitch."

Robin was up out of her chair, walking slowly around the side of her desk, looking out her door for help.

"You know, I'd give just about anything for a blow job from Nancy," Carl said, looking directly at Robin. "You're not close to her, are you Robin?"

Robin was almost out the door.

"You couldn't put in a good word for me, could you?"

Robin was gone.

Carl sat alone for a moment in Robin's office and laughed. Bet I turned her on, he thought as he stood up, walked back into the hall, and headed for Laura Payden's office.

* * *

As Carl busied himself harassing the women in David's department, Marsha Yamamoto interviewed in one of the conference rooms on the 64th floor. By late afternoon, she'd seen Tim Laboy, the rail and trucking analyst, Matt Speiser, Paul Pitcher, John McLain, Paula Hainsworth, Barbara Malek and Maryanne Miles from Institutional Sales, a female trader, and Desmond Haverty, the head airline banker.

"So?" David asked as he picked her up and walked with her back to his office, "did Julia portray us accurately?"

"She did, David. I had very good meetings."

"The feedback on you has been very positive, Marsha." This was true. David had checked throughout the day. After they'd seated themselves in his office, David asked, "Are there yellow flashing lights or areas of concern we should talk about?"

"None that I could see, David. Paul Pitcher put my mind at ease about Retail, which you probably remember I asked you a lot of questions about." David nodded." And Tim Laboy was really great. He'd be fun to work with."

"So does this feel good to you?"

"It does, David. It's a great firm from what I've seen, better than I thought it would be, and I liked that you seem to have more women here than Bear Stearns does."

David smiled to himself. "But as I told you at breakfast, I'm not unhappy at Bear and I'm not sure I really need to make a change right now. Also, changing firms in the middle of *II* season makes me skittish."

"You'll get a lot of attention that can only help your visibility," David said. "You know, *The Wall Street Letter, Investment Dealers' Digest,* that sort of thing."

"But it's very disruptive at a time when you need to be working as efficiently as you can."

"I'm sure it would work out fine," said David, not completely honestly. "If the economics were attractive, would you have enough reasons to switch?"

"I don't know. The big difference between the firms, it seems to me, is Retail. The institutional platform may be a little stronger at Bear, banking is probably pretty even, and environmentally I'd say that you have the edge. If the money was better, Bear could match it and then I'd have trouble seeing compelling reasons to move."

She was a straight shooter, which David liked.

"There is one thing that might make a difference, and you might not want to do it, David, which I'd understand, but what if you gave me airfreight in addition to airlines?"

"You could do both?"

"With four associates, two for airlines and two for airfreight."

"I take it you've watched Ed Wolfe in action?"

"Ed's *awfully* good, but airfreight isn't all that competitive, and if *II* ever separates airfreight from rails-and-trucking again, I could be ranked in two categories instead of one."

David had assumed this might happen. Giving Marsha airfreight would kill his chances of hiring Barry Simonetti, the Merrill Lynch analyst who was a Runner-Up in airfreight but didn't conflict with Tim Laboy on ground transportation. If he was lucky, he'd get an airline analyst who wanted to add airfreight or an airfreight analyst who wanted to add airlines, and David knew his odds would be better with a candidate from Bear Stearns than with one from Merrill Lynch.

"You clearly can't do airfreight where you are as long as Ed's around."

"Clearly not."

"So, if we made the economics attractive, provided enough support and promised to lobby *II* to separate airfreight from ground transportation on its ballots, would you come?"

"I'd probably come."

"I'll do it," David told her. "I'd rather have you in the department than try to hire ranked analysts in both spaces."

"Could you wait until June 15th if it was really important to me?"

"Why? So *II* season is over?"

"Yes."

"Would you promise to come if I did?"

"If the money's right."

"Then I could."

David and Marsha laughed, shook hands and left the office 10 minutes apart. The following morning Julia Harris presented Marsha with her brand-spanking-new, two-year contract dated June 15.

* * *

Ron Vargo read and reread the e-mails that had gone back and forth between his desk and Claire O'Daniels' earlier in the day. As the volume of e-mails between Ron and Claire had increased, Ron had changed his password so his secretary could no longer access his mailbox, but he still worried that BCS might stumble upon his correspondence during one of its many random, firmwide checks of incoming and outgoing e-mails.

It wasn't as if he was spreading any inside information or writing anything pornographic. Was he spending too much time using e-mail for personal reasons? Yes. But was he guilty of anything worse? No, and that's what mattered.

Three weeks from now, Milbanks Media would

hold its annual offsite for analysts, this time in Atlanta where its most recent acquisition was headquartered. The meetings, including a dinner, would be held at the Ritz Carlton in Buckhead.

And in between management presentations, Ron and Claire had promised each other to do lots and lots of Bucking.

* * *

Alan Bellone was comparing older and newer photographs of Anna Nicole Smith on his PC when his secretary knocked loudly on his door and startled him. Instinctively, and instantly, he pulled up a page of text in Microsoft Word from a report he'd been writing for months and would never finish, and it covered Anna Nicole completely.

"David wants you as soon as you're free."

"Did he say what it was about?"

"Nope."

"How did he sound?"

"Fine."

"I'm on my way." As Alan walked towards David's office, he wondered if, somehow, he'd been discovered. Had he accidentally left his machine on one night with an incriminating photo up on the monitor? Had someone seen a reflection in a night-darkened window behind him? Had his secretary figured it out and told her friends? Was software residing secretly on his hard drive that automatically tracked his every move and reproduced, on David Meadows' computer, images of each web site he visited? Alan could feel his heart beating hard as he approached David's door but he tried to smile.

"Were you looking for me?"

"Alan, hi, come in for a second." David closed his door behind him, which heightened Alan's anxiety. "Sit" he said, pointing to the sofa.

As Alan tried to make himself comfortable, David walked to his desk, picked up some papers, returned to the sofa and handed Alan several sheets. But instead of seeing evidence of his porn-site surfing, as he'd expected, Alan saw two copies of an employment contract with his name on it.

He looked up at David, unable to conceal his surprise. "Dieter said yes?"

"Dieter said yes."

The contract was for $1,300,000 per year for two years, which was right where he'd been most recently, plus $1,300,000 of restricted BCS stock that would vest three years hence. "God, David, this is great!"

"I'm glad we were able to do it, Alan. Your *Greenwich* numbers tell me you're as close as you've ever been to making *II*, and Matt and I want to help you cross that finish line, this year or, at the latest, next year."

"Can I take this with me for a minute and read it?"

"Of course."

"I can't tell you how much I appreciate this, David."

"It was my pleasure. Take it, read it, sign it, keep a copy and give Lisa the other."

They shook hands. "Thanks again." Alan stepped out of David's office, walked briskly down the hall and returned to the waiting, online arms of Anna Nicole.

* * *

"I never wanted to do the deal!" Keith Jackman was screaming.

Barry Seels, his banker, who had been sitting in Keith's office, stood up and closed the door. "You're acting as if the company's going out of business," he said defensively.

The company was Primo Theaters, over which Keith and Barry had squabbled in February when the IPO price was being set by BCS's Commitment Committee. Initially, Keith had been satisfied with the outcome. The IPO had been priced at $10, the stock had moved quickly above $11 in after-market trading, and then it had settled down between $10.50 and $11.25. Keith had kept his Buy rating on Primo, even at $11.25, for fear of being accused of "flipping" his ratings too much, but found himself forced to talk about Primo's "long-term appeal" more and more as the stock neared his 12–month price target. Still, at least early on, everyone seemed satisfied including Primo's CEO.

But in early April, barely a month after the deal had been done, Primo preannounced that its March-quarter earnings would fall several cents short of analysts' expectations and the stock dropped from $11 to $9. Keith had cut his full-year estimate from $0.40 to $0.35 but, with the stock having fallen faster than his earnings estimate, he'd reiterated his Buy rating.

What was prompting Keith's bellowing at the moment was a sudden, further price break in Primo's shares, to $7.70, sparking fears of another earnings shortfall in June.

"It's not going to happen," Barry assured him.

"The market is telling us that it is."

"The market's wrong."

"I don't believe you."

"Look, Keith, just stick with it. They need our support right now. If you liked it at $10, assuming $0.40 of earnings, you have to love it at $7.70, assuming $0.35."

"They're not going to make the $0.35." Keith saw yellow lights flashing everywhere but he knew, based on the information he had in hand, that he had no basis for downgrading the stock.

"I have to do more digging."

"You're wasting your time," Barry replied, rolling his eyes. Fucking analysts.

* * *

Ken Lavery felt carefree as he bobbed and weaved between BMWs, Mercedes, Lexuses and Lincolns on the Long Island Expressway. It was a beautiful, warm, dry Saturday morning in May, he looked good, he smelled good, the top was down on the Bentley and it was house-hunting weekend in the Hamptons.

Ken didn't know the Hamptons well but he'd been e-mailed detailed driving directions and he followed them closely. He took Exit 70, Route 111 South, and Route 27 East past Westhampton and Quogue, Hampton Bays and Southampton, through Water Mill and Bridgehampton and finally into East Hampton. In mid-spring, only some of the huge trees that lined both sides of Main Street were fully in bloom, but the white, Colonial bed and breakfasts on both sides of the road, the pond and the swans, the small cemetery and the fancy shops in the heart of town made his heart leap.

"I belong here," he told himself.

At the corner of Newtown Lane, the traffic light turned red, giving Ken a chance to look around him at the stores, the East Hampton Cinema, the huge windmill up ahead and the fork in the road in front of him where he'd been told to bear left. Just past the fork he saw the sign reading The Lamb Agency, and he turned left into the driveway of what must have once been a private home that now housed one of East Hampton's most successful realtors.

As he turned off the engine and put the roof up, Ken reviewed one last time his economic situation and its implications for his house-hunting endeavors. His Regeneron shares were worth $650,000, his Genentech and Amgen $950,000, his 140,000 shares of G-NOME $2,240,000 and his 140,000 shares of Genomic Innovators $2,100,000. So his stock portfolio had mushroomed to almost $6,000,000 and, when you deducted his $2,150,000 of margin debt, his equity now approached $4,000,000.

"So," he said out loud, "should I buy a $4,000,000 house for cash or a $20,000,000 house with 20% down?" The answer was neither. What Ken really needed to do was to borrow another $2,000,000 and put another $1,000,000 each into GNOM and GINV, to keep talking those stocks up to anyone who'd listen, to sell his $1,600,000 of Regeneron, Genentech and Amgen, and then to buy whatever kind of house that $1,600,000 down payment would get him.

No, Kim, I think $20,000,000 is a little beyond me, he imagined himself saying, but $3,000,000? $5,000,000? $7,000,000? $8,000,000? Why sure, I'd love to look.

Inside the Lamb Agency, Ken asked for Kim Hovey, the president, who'd been recommended to him by David. David knows Hamptons real estate better than anyone else in the office, Ken had figured, and David had been quick to pull up Kim's number when asked.

Kim was young and quite tall and had very straight blond hair that flowed down past her waist. "I'm delighted to meet you," she told Ken, shaking his hand.

"Me too, Kim. David spoke very highly of you."

"David and I go back a long way together."

Ken looked around the office. "So, should we talk first or drive around first?"

"Talk first," Kim said, pointing to her small office in the back. "Then I'll give you a tour of the different areas, talk about who your neighbors might be, and show you properties in each that are on the market and ones that have recently sold so that you can get an idea about values. This way, when it's time to pull the trigger, you'll be ready because you'll have an understanding about the market here. I'll call and make appointments to see the interiors of the ones you like. Kim paused and checked her watch. It was 10:30. "You did say I could have you for the weekend, didn't you?"

"I did. I'm staying at the 1770 House."

"Good. We'll need two days." Kim pulled out a large map and placed it between her and Ken, facing Ken. "If you're planning to buy a property between five and ten million, you should confine your search to the estate areas, south of the highway, and try to get as close to the ocean as you can. I can show you listings in Amagansett but most of the houses there are less substantial except for the rare offerings on Further Lane, of which there are none at the moment. So let's skip Amagansett for now. In East Hampton, you should look in Georgica, which is our estate area, and along Further Lane near the Maidstone Club, which is the road at the eastern end of town that's closest to the ocean. Moving west, in Wainscott, which is mostly wooded, and Sagaponack, which is open farm fields, you can get more for your money than in the village. Just to their west are Bridgehampton, and Water Mill which surrounds Mecox Bay." Kim pointed the bay out on the map. "And finally there's Southampton Village, which also has an estate area and other properties close to the ocean."

"I heard that Southampton is old money and East Hampton is new money."

"Not necessarily. That may have been true 20 years ago but there's a lot of new money in Southampton now too. Southampton has more older houses, especially in the estate area, but that's not the same thing as old money. South is a little more conservative, East is a little more family-oriented, a little more relaxed and a little less formal, and has a little 'Hollywood' in it."

"Got it."

Kim put the map aside and pulled a file with Ken's name on it out of a drawer in her desk. "Let me show you some of the properties we're going to look at from the outside today. In East Hampton I'm going to drive you past two houses for starters. The first is a favorite of mine. It has 8,500 square feet plus a 3,000–square-foot finished basement, five bedrooms, a pool, poolhouse, Har-tru tennis, and it's very close to the ocean. It's $12 million, but it's negotiable and you should see it just so you know what's out there and have a basis for comparison with other properties. I'm also going to show you one of Jeffrey Colle's new houses. He's an excellent designer/builder who is very well known and respected in the area. This house is so well built and has 8,000 square feet, seven bedrooms, on two acres only 400 yards from the ocean, with pool, spa, Har-tru tennis and lovely landscaping. It's much less... $8,950,000.

"In Wainscott we'll go by Goose Creek, which may be a tad out of your budget. Goose Creek sits on five and a half acres overlooking Georgica Pond. It has eight bedrooms, 11 baths, a 110–seat state-of-the-art screening room, a spa, gym, sauna and steam room, indoor *and* outdoor pools, a tennis court, and landscaping that includes 100,000 daffodils and 50,000 tulips. The house is listed at $15 million. There was a separate guest house on two and a half acres that was asking $6 million and just recently sold for $5.2 million. I'd like to show you that as a comp."

"Maybe we should just look at the guest house."

"I feel we should look at both to compare values. The last house we'll drive by in Wainscott is a one-story traditional with cathedral ceilings, on 1.8 acres in the Georgica Association. Here you have to be approved by the membership in order to become a part of the association, which has tennis courts and its own private beach with pavilion. The ask is $5.5 million." Ken nodded.

"Then, in Bridgehampton, we'll see this new, 11,000–square-foot barn-style residence with six bedrooms, six baths, on 2.7 acres with a pond. It's $5.5 million. In that same price range are two houses in Sagaponack. The first is on Parsonage Lane, which is a good location. The style is English country and the house is on two and a half acres abutting a 30–acre farm. There are 7,000 square feet, six bedrooms, a 900–square-foot carriage house, bluestone terraces, a 55–foot heated gunite pool and a Har-tru tennis court. It's on for $5.5 million. The other house is a gambrel traditional with 7,500 square feet, seven bedrooms, a 55–foot heated gunite pool and… nope, no tennis on this one."

"How much is it?"

"Asking $5,250,000."

"And no tennis?"

"This house is only on an acre and a half so you wouldn't be able to get a pool *and* tennis." Ken was amazed.

"Water Mill is very exclusive and very expensive. I'm going to show you four properties there in different price ranges. The first is this Mecox Bay waterfront, which has six bedrooms and six baths, a sauna, a pool, a private dock and a separate building parcel that you could keep or sell off; it's listed at $9 million. Then there's this gorgeous 10,000–square-footer with 350 feet of frontage on Mill Pond, on five acres, with seven bedrooms, gunite pool, tennis and its own private dock. The ask here is $7.9 million.

"We'll also see this new 6–bedroom Tudor, which has six fireplaces, a gym, on two acres, tennis, gunite pool, poolhouse and three-car garage, for $6,950,000; and this traditional on Burnett Creek with a private dock and access to Mecox Bay, six bedrooms, five fireplaces, heated gunite, Har-tru tennis, on almost two acres, listed at only $6.5 million."

"Only," Ken laughed.

"Now Southampton has lots of listings. We could spend several days there alone but I'm going to show you four for starters. First, this property in Southampton Village has six bedrooms on two-plus acres, gunite pool, three-bedroom guesthouse and room for tennis. It's $8.9 million."

"*Room* for tennis?"

"You're paying for location here," Kim explained. "It's got room if you want to add a court, but this is in the village, and that's the A-plus address. Also in the village is this eight-bedroom traditional which comes with a two-bedroom guesthouse and a pool for $8.25 million. This one you can't get a tennis court on...the site is too small. But again, it's in the village.

"The third house we'll see is also in the village, on 2.3 acres with access to Shinnecock Bay, 6,500 square feet, five bedrooms, waterside heated gunite pool, no tennis, $6.75 million."

"Is there room for tennis?"

"Probably not. Finally, there's this Georgian, which is very beautiful, in Southampton village, in the estate area, six bedrooms, no pool, no tennis, $5.5 million."

"Yikes! Five million doesn't go very far in Southampton."

"Not in the village," Kim concurred.

Ken was getting itchy. "That's the list?"

"For today. Are you ready?"

"Ready. Who's driving?"

"As much as I'd love a spin in that Bentley of yours," Kim laughed, "I'll do the driving, you do the looking."

* * *

Phil Suprano checked his watch. It was 10:25 P.M., and he'd been dining with Brock Bosslevyn for almost two and a half hours. That's how long dinner at Jean Georges takes, if not longer, and Phil, having done his homework, had timed things perfectly.

Brock, Phil had discovered, worked at *II* in a sort of hush-hush area devoted exclusively at certain times of the year to the compilation of *II* All Star votes. His was one of three names that Phil's detective work had unearthed, and Phil had called all three editorial staff members seeking a meeting over lunch or dinner at which topics of mutual interest could be discussed. Only Brock had said yes.

And so, they had dined on expensive food and consumed large quantities of expensive wine and talked about life as a sell-side analyst, life as a journalist, the state of the business, life at EFS after it had become BCS, and the enormous impact of the *II* All Star Poll on analysts' job security and compensation. During the conversation, Phil had also probed Brock about the impact on *II* of competing polls conducted by *Greenwich, The Wall Street Journal, theStreet.com* or *Fortune*. "All Star only means one thing to 95% of the people who work on The Street," Brock had said, "and that's someone named to *II's* All-America Research Team. Period." Phil knew he was right.

Occasionally, Phil had tried to push for information regarding exactly what was done with the ballots once they were filled out and returned to *II*. Who collected them, tabulated the results and double-checked those tabulations? Who was the last person to sign off on the rankings in each category before they were typeset? Was it true that *II* "massaged" the results from time to time, helping one analyst and hurting another?

Brock had not been very forthcoming most of the time. When he and Phil were discussing other topics, and when he wasn't distracted by every young woman who walked past him to powder her nose, Brock was relaxed and funny and very outgoing, just as he'd seemed on the phone. But whenever Phil had broached All Star Poll topics he clammed up. Even on the topic of massaging the numbers, Brock wasn't helpful. "It would be impossible to do now," he'd said, "owing to the enormous amount of backup data we provide to each subscriber, and even before that database was made available publicly, I never heard of *any* massaging."

Phil had nodded, seemingly agreeing and understanding. But as he and Brock were finishing their after-dinner drinks, Phil broached the topic once more. This time, Brock seemed less patient.

"Who told you there had *ever* been any massaging?"

"I don't remember for sure," Phil lied, "but I think I heard it once from an analyst who said he'd once heard it from Michael Culp."

"Who?"

"He used to be the Director of Research at PaineWebber and Prudential."

"Oh yeah, I think I remember him. Retired, right?"

"Yup. But supposedly he told this analyst when he was recruiting him that he was convinced that, from time to time, *II* massaged the results a little, especially for the sake of consistency."

"What does that mean?"

"That, say, 20 years ago, when none of the backup data on who voted for whom were made available to The Street, *II* might rank analysts slightly differently than the way the votes turned out if it meant that they could avoid big year-to-year changes in who ranked where. Maybe *II* felt that, if the results changed too much from year to year, their accuracy might be questioned."

"Why did Culp think that?"

"It might have been personal. Supposedly, he told this analyst that, in 1982, which was Culp's first year as a sell-side analyst, he's convinced that he finished number one in his category, which was restaurants I think."

"But we didn't rank him number one?"

"No, supposedly you said he'd finished number two, and that Joe Doyle, who had been highly ranked in that category for many years, beat him by a hair."

"You mean it wouldn't have been believable if we'd said that a rookie had ranked number one so we said that Doyle beat him but just barely." Phil nodded. "How would Culp know that?"

"I don't know. I heard all of this third hand, but supposedly Culp finished number one by a wide margin in every year after that until he became a Research Director so it isn't completely far-fetched."

"Sounds like a real jerk," said Brock. "What's so bad about finishing number two your first shot at it? He sounds like a sore loser."

"Probably," Phil agreed, "but it made me wonder whether, at least in those days, the rankings were the rankings or there were times when someone could... you know, help someone out a little bit."

Brock was shaking his head. "I don't know about then, but I can tell you that, right now, to the extent I've been involved, the ballots are tabulated and the results are presented correctly."

"I suppose someone could always 'lose' a few ballots," Phil mused.

"Now that might be *theoretically* possible. If you had two analysts vying for a Runner-Up slot, and you 'lost' some ballots that named Joe but not John, you could conceivably get John ranked when he didn't deserve to be."

Phil just looked at Brock in silence and, after a long moment, nodded slowly. As he was nodding, the maitre d' approached their table, a woman in tow.

"Hi, Phil," she said, beaming and extending her hand. Phil stood quickly, returned the smile, kissed the hand he'd never seen before and looked down at Brock, who seemed both surprised and interested. The woman standing by his left shoulder was tall and very thin, had short blonde hair and long legs, and wore an elegant, black evening gown covering everything but her back. She turned immediately towards Brock and said, "Brock! You're even better looking than Phil said you were."

"Do I know you?" Brock asked, slightly flustered.

"You do now," she said. "And in five minutes, up on the 38th floor, you're going to know me much, much better."

Brock looked towards Phil, puzzled but excited.

"Brock, this is Danielle, and she's yours for as long as you want her."

"Mine?"

"All taken care of, my friend. Go have some fun."

Danielle grabbed Brock by the arm and started walking him towards the front of the restaurant. "It's so convenient having Trump's hotel right above us," she said.

"It sure is."

"Can you be late for work tomorrow?"

"Very late. Very, *very* late."

* * *

Memorial Day weekend was only seven days away, and David was thinking too much about it as he breakfasted with Christopher Chadwick. "He's not a strong candidate," Larry Fraser had warned, "but he's your only candidate, so see him."

Larry was right as usual. Christopher followed the cosmetics, household products and personal care products companies for Morgan Stanley. The mere fact that he now worked at Morgan Stanley made his candidacy suspect. What could BC Securities offer him that Morgan Stanley couldn't?

"A sales force that sells analysts instead of deals," he'd said. "A work environment that doesn't tolerate abusive bankers, a smaller pond in which to be a bigger fish, more money."

"At least he's honest about it," David thought. "How much are you making now?" he'd asked casually.

"I'd rather not discuss specifics," Christopher had answered. David knew from prior experience that analysts who asked you to make them an offer but provided no information about their current compensation range were usually earning far less than you'd have guessed, and often for good reasons.

"It's hard for me to put a financial package together for you, Christopher, if I don't know where you are."

"That can come later." David doubted that it would.

Christopher was surprisingly unimpressive, especially for a Morgan Stanley analyst. He was in his early 40s, David thought, he followed the same names as all of his competitors, wrote similar reports, didn't call that much and spent a fair amount of time on banking but had seemingly contentious relationships with his bankers. David couldn't recall ever having seen him on CNBC. Christopher claimed that all the time he'd spent on banking had hurt his credibility with clients and that he didn't consider Morgan Stanley a friendly place to work. Also, he resented the fact that he'd failed repeatedly to be made a managing director and said he'd expect to join BCS as an MD if it made an acceptable offer.

David did his standard song and dance for Christopher and demonstrated much more enthusiasm than he truly felt. At the end of breakfast, David pushed him to come in and meet other people, and Christopher agreed to do so within two weeks.

That night, David and Larry Fraser compared notes.

"He's not very impressive."

"I warned you. He's very unimpressive in fact. He distinguishes himself in no way that I can discern and I suspect that he's ranked merely because the competition in his space is so limited."

"He wouldn't talk to me about money, even generally," David said.

"Nor to me, which means he's been really cut back recently, probably deservedly so."

"*II* ranked seven analysts, and he finished seventh?"

"Correct. He's the lowest vote-getter among all ranked analysts in that category."

"And in *Greenwich* he was thirteenth, down from eighth last year."

"So he could fall off of *II* this year."

"Yup." David paused, deep in thought. "You think Morgan is pushing him out?"

"It definitely crossed my mind."

"I've gotten the feeling over the years that Morgan's more inclined to suggest to an analyst like Christopher that he should start fresh elsewhere than to actually fire him."

"Which would explain why he's interested in BCS."

"He's the weakest candidate I've seen so far, Larry. He's not the most arrogant or the most obnoxious but he's clearly the weakest intellectually and analytically."

"So pass on him."

"No."

"Why?"

"Because he's the only ranked analyst I have a chance to hire in this space."

"If you hire him, he could easily fall off of *II* in October."

"That's right, and if I don't I will *definitely* have no one ranked there in October."

"So he's better than nothing."

"Exactly right. He's better than nothing."

* * *

Daniel Roe had outdone himself again, and that wasn't easy. David had known, after having breakfasted with Daniel, that he might not play well inside BCS. Too egotistical, even for a sell-side analyst, too arrogant, too condescending and definitely not a team player.

"That's the way they all are," Les Carter had said. "Technology analysts think they're like no others. Truthfully, David, they're right, and when it comes to Internet analysts, they're the worst of the bunch."

"You know, Les, I could understand that if it was the spring of 2000," David had answered, "but not now. Before the bubble burst, everyone wanted to be an Internet analyst and those who already were and who ranked highly had their employers by the balls. But Jesus, they rode their favorite names from $100 to $1, they did every deal they could do while the window was open, and Holly Becker seemingly became number-one-ranked by being the least bullish of the lot. Now Mary's fallen off *II* entirely, Henry and Jamie have left The Street, and along comes Daniel Roe thinking he's the newest king of the universe."

"I know, David, I know. The kid's barely shaving

but I have to tell you, he's in demand and he's the only ranked analyst in the space that you can hire right now. Holly's not available, Anthony Noto's not available and Lanny Baker's not available. If you want an All Star in the Internet space, Daniel has to be your guy."

So, David had held his nose and scheduled Daniel to see 10 people: analysts Mark Noel, Byron Shatz and James Hovanian, Matt Speiser, John McLain, Paula Hainsworth, Herb Hirschorn, Paul Pitcher, Jim MacDuffin in Banking and Carl. Throughout the day, David had grabbed the feedback forms as soon as Daniel's interviewers had submitted them so he could tally up how things were going. The word "badly" came to mind.

"He's a prick," Carl had written, "but he can tell a good joke and it looks like he can bring three deals with him so I'm voting yes."

"Arrogant, superficial in his knowledge base and not nearly as good as he thinks he is," wrote Mark Noel.

"Obsessed with toppling Holly. Period. Not a good hire," wrote Byron Shatz.

"Not a team player, probably would disrupt the Tech Team or just not join it. Very self-absorbed, very immature and maybe even a head case. Good luck, David. You're going to need it," James Hovanian had opined.

"Very rough around the edges," Matt had begun. "Very competitive, very high energy level, very focused, all of which is good, but get the feeling he'd cut corners to achieve his ends more quickly. Seems to know his companies well, but we should do a thorough client check on him before we make any offer. Think Sales would like him. Banking too. I'd say okay not great overall."

"Liked him," wrote John McLain. "Very presentable, articulate, good selling skills, lots of energy, would play well in front of most clients. I vote yes."

"Needs work but has some potential," wrote Paula Hainsworth. "Pitched well and had answers when challenged. Don't know if they were the right answers but they sounded credible. If he's malleable I can turn him into something good. If not, he'll be a problem."

"Absolute mistake," wrote Herb Hirschorn. "Superficial, gave me incorrect answers to two questions I'd posed, smug, arrogant, still wet behind the ears but feels no moisture. The other tech analysts will hate him. Big mistake."

"Shit!" David said out loud.

"Hire him this afternoon!" Jim MacDuffin had written. "He has three deals in his pocket that will travel with him to BCS if we can land him. He's a pain in the ass and he likes being that way, but he can ring the cash register and that's what counts. We need more analysts who are less 'nice' and more 'commercial' around here and he'd be a big step in that direction. I'm telling Mennymore that Roe is a must hire. He is."

That left Paul Pitcher, who was in with Daniel at the moment. In truth, it didn't matter much what Paul thought. Chances were that Paul would be wary but positive because Daniel's group was very retail-oriented, the guy could sell well, and he was the only established gun for hire in the category at the moment. Paul would probably see the same yellow flashing lights as everyone else who was perceptive but still vote yes.

"So," David thought, "Research hates him, most of

Sales likes him or at least tolerates him and Banking loves him. Not a good profile."

When Paul finally brought Daniel around to David's office, it was 6:30 and everyone seemed tired. David thanked Paul, took a quick look at his vote, which was a conditional "Yes," pointed Daniel to a chair and closed the door.

"So, we didn't scare you away?"

"Not at all, David. Nothing scary about this place."

"What did you think about the people you met?"

"Mixed bag, if I can be honest with you. You have good salesmen and bankers and weak analysts. Mark Noel was adequate, but Byron and James were pretty average."

"I'm surprised."

"Why? None of them is ranked."

"Well, Mark was named a 'Next Generation' All Star by *II* last October and he finished eighth in *Greenwich* in a very competitive category. Byron can't rank because *II* killed his category in 2001 but he's still viewed very positively internally, and James finished sixth in *Greenwich* just now and will almost definitely rank in *II* this fall."

"Maybe, but they've got their work cut out for them."

"Could you work with them?"

"I can work with anyone, David. I'm a team player. I know when to shut up and not pick a fight. I don't let people walk all over me, but can I fit in? Of course I can."

"So you liked the salesmen and you liked Jim Mac-Duffin," David recapitulated.

"And I liked Carl. He's your boss, right?"

"One of two."

"I liked him a lot. He tells good jokes, you know. And it turns out we're almost neighbors!"

"You're in Cove Neck too?"

Daniel nodded. "He's a pretty smart guy. You'd have to be to get into the London School of Economics."

Did you two talk about BCS at all or just tell jokes?"

"Oh, we talked about BCS, and I told Carl about the three deals I can bring with me, which really got him excited."

"I've heard."

"MacDuffin too. He's been spending a lot of time with Byron, it seems, because he has no one doing my group, but mine are actually the companies he knows best, and I have no doubt that we could bring in a lot of banking business together."

"So you could see yourself working here."

"Oh without a doubt. It's a decent platform. It isn't Goldman or Morgan Stanley, but it could do for a while."

"What does 'for a while' mean?"

"Nothing, nothing. I didn't mean to sound like I'm planning to come here for a couple of years and then, when my contract expires, trade up or anything, but you're a realist, David. No one can guarantee anyone anything in our business. How do I know that *you'll* be here two or three years from now? I don't. All we can do is say that, today, we'd like to work together and that we hope it works out long term."

David nodded. That was closer to the truth than he wanted to admit.

"So where do we go from here?" Daniel asked.

"Well, we're done torturing you if that's what you

mean. Did you miss anyone today that you'd like to come back and see?"

"I don't think so."

"Anyone you saw today you'd like to spend more time with?"

"Not really."

"And tell me again why you're not under contract?"

"I refused to sign one."

"Why?"

"I just said to them, 'Look, right now, you want me to be here and I want to be here, so I'm here. I don't need a contract. I'm going to trust that you'll pay me fairly because you know I'll leave if you don't. You can trust that I'll stay and do a good job for you without locking me in with a contract, and I'm sure you'd rather have me than force me out because I won't sign, so let's just go forward together, contractless.' "

"And they agreed?"

"They agreed. I can't say everyone was enthusiastic. There was a point where I thought Joe Grano was going to punch me out. The chemistry between us isn't all that good. I don't know why but I seem to bring out the Green Beret in him. Eventually things cooled off, though, and that's where they stand."

"And if we made you an offer, you'd let them match it if they wanted to?"

"Yes. Frankly, the platforms aren't that different. If you were in a position to offer me something that UBS clearly couldn't, like a partnership in Goldman pre-IPO, I'd just sign and quit, but you can't so I'd be morally bound to at least tell them what I have and give them a chance to counter."

"But they'd definitely want you to sign a contract at that point."

"At the right price, I'll sign a contract with anybody. Obviously, if you hire me, it'll be with a contract, so I'm not completely against indentured servitude, but until I feel I'm being paid on the come for where I'll go over the next two years, and I don't feel that UBS is paying me that way yet, I won't take myself off the job market."

"I understand." David paused for a moment and then suggested that both he and Daniel touch base with Les Carter and that the three of them agree on what to do next.

"Sounds good to me," Daniel said. He shook David's hand, thanked him for setting up the meetings, and headed for Yankee Stadium, where, he said, his buddies and his girlfriend awaited him.

As the Yankees took the field that evening, David and Les talked from their respective apartments.

"Did anyone shoot or stab him?"

"No, luckily for him, but the analysts wanted to."

"Not Sales or Banking."

"No, they were okay with him."

"That's no surprise. I suspect that the analysts were threatened by him."

"Why?"

"Because he's so aggressive and he's ranked and they're probably worried that he'll be named Director of Technology Research as part of any deal he cuts to join BCS."

"And become their boss? I'd never do that."

"I don't think, fortunately, that you need to."

"How will he check out with clients?"

"You'll get some clients who hate his style or question his substance, but you'll find more who think he's a resource. All that energy of his goes into digging for material that isn't in the 10K or 10Q, and that's what clients like about him. He has good contacts, especially for someone so young, and they'll only get better over time. Also, for an Internet analyst, he's a pretty good stock picker."

"Meaning that his favorite stocks only go down 75% at a time?"

"No, meaning that clients have told me he's been less bullish and more selective in his recommendations than most of the other ranked analysts."

"Did you talk about money with him?"

"To the extent he'd allow."

"And?"

"Well, there's a lot of bluster on the surface that you have to cut through. You know. Mary Meeker makes $15 million a year, and I'm better than she is so I should make $20 million. Then you push him and he backpedals. You tell him that Mary may never have made $15 million but that, even if the press was right, she probably only made it in one extraordinary year, and you tell him he's still no Mary Meeker in most clients' eyes. So he says okay, but I'm an All Star and she's not, I'm on the come and her ranking has slipped, the Internet will come back as the economy improves, the deal potential in the space is there and the opportunities for any firm on The Street to hire a ranked Internet analyst are extremely limited."

"What a brat."

Les was patient. "Look, David, only you can decide how much you need this guy. Is he brash and immature? Yes. Is he going to be tough to manage at times? Probably. Could he be divisive inside your department? He could. But your mandate is to get your *II* ranking up, and that means you'll have to make, and you're *already* making, all sorts of compromises. You want to be a purist and reject every ranked analyst

407

whose personality doesn't suit you or whose skill set underwhelms you? It's a free country. But you know and I know this: if you want to be perceived as having done a good job this year, and if you want your bonus to reflect that, you need to hire All Stars when they're available, warts and all."

"You never told me how much he's going to cost me."

"Eight figures would get him without hesitation."

"I can't do that."

Les was quiet for a minute.

"Are you there?"

"David, I'm here. I frankly don't know how much lower than that you can go without losing him."

"We're talking about pure research comp here, right?"

"Banking would be over and above."

"He knows we won't guarantee any banking bonuses?"

"He understands that."

"So, do this, Les. Bounce $6 million the first year and $7.5 million in year two off him and see what he says."

"I'll do it at my club," Les suggested, "so I can see the body language."

"And Les, make sure he understands two things: first, he'd be the highest-paid analyst in the department, and second, if word ever got out, I'd have to kill him."

JUNE

As David deleted his 150th e-mail, two evenings after Memorial Day, the triple peaks came to visit. The giant mound of puffed and fluffed brunette curls came into view first and the two instantly recognizable pectoral peaks followed close behind.

"Samantha!" David said with genuine surprise. "Where have *you* been?"

"I've been here," Samantha pouted. "It's just that you never come to visit me and Kathy always sends one of the other girls up whenever she has stuff for you." She paused, and then added with a grin, "I think she knows about us!"

David laughed and played along. "I think it's for our own good."

Samantha had another of her sheer silk blouses on. This one was a very pale purple that matched a very short, purple leather skirt and a purple bow in Samantha's hair. Unlike the night she'd stopped by to show David her new "Don't Touch My Tuts" T-shirt, Samantha carried no jacket tonight and no shopping bags, just a brown paper bag large enough to hold a newspaper.

"I brought you a present!" she said, eyes widening and smile broadening.

"Really? And what's the special occasion?"

"I'm famous! And I thought you'd want to share my moment of stardom with me." David had no idea what Samantha was talking about. "Did I ever tell you that my boyfriend and I are nudists?"

"I don't think you ever mentioned a boyfriend before, not that I'd be surprised."

"Oh yeah. We've been together for more than a year. His name is Louie, and he works at a restaurant at the Jersey Shore called Baci. It's Italian."

"Really!"

"Yup. I met him on the boardwalk in Point Pleasant of all places. He lives down there, which is where I go most weekends when it's not cold."

"You two don't live together?"

"Not yet. I still live with my mother on Staten Island. She's very conservative, you know, and until I get engaged at least, she gets real uptight if I mention moving out of the house. It's okay. Louie works nights anyway, so he's never home when I'm home during the week, but on weekends we have lots of time to hang out together.

"Anyway, Louie and I like to go to Sandy Hook a lot during the summer. Do you know where that is?" David didn't. "It's on the Jersey shore, in the Gateway National Recreation Area. Most of the beach is for regular people and families but one part of the beach is a nudist beach, and that's the one we use. We've made lots of friends there."

"Is everyone naked?"

"Almost everyone. You get some guys with clothes and cameras every weekend but most of the time they don't bother you. They just strap on their telephoto lenses and keep a safe distance away. Once I actually went up to a guy and started talking to him and it really freaked him out."

"All of this has something to do with your becoming famous?"

"Yup. Last fall, there was a guy walking up and down the beach taking pictures. At first he seemed like lots of other guys I'd seen with cameras, but he stayed on the beach all day and he took a lot more pictures than usual. I saw him take about five or six of me, and he actually took more, I found out later. Anyway, late that afternoon he came up to me and said he was doing a shoot for a magazine."

"Right."

"That's what I thought, but then he pulled out this release form and asked if I'd be willing to sign it in return for having him use a photo of me in his story. I figured, 'What the Hell, I look better than most of the other girls on this beach and 99% of the girls who don't come to this beach, and it'd be pretty cool to be in his magazine.' Louie was off getting us something to drink, so I decided for myself. I signed it."

"And?"

"And... I'm famous!" Samantha took the brown paper bag and handed it to David. "Check it out. The story starts on page 113."

David, somewhat puzzled, took the brown paper bag and emptied it. The magazine inside was face down and there was an ad on the back cover that gave no clue as to its contents. *GQ?* Not likely. *Playboy?* Could be. *Maxim?* More likely. *Penthouse?* Hope not.

All wrong. As David turned the magazine over, he felt himself blush.

" *Hustler?*"

"Yeah, I know. I wish it had been *Penthouse* or something a little more, you know, classy? But it's not as if I had a bunch of magazines fighting over me or anything, and it's okay, actually. It's not what you're thinking."

David imagined the entire Board of Directors of BCS walking into his office and finding him talking to Samantha "climb my peaks" Smeralda and holding a copy of *Hustler* in his hand. Great.

"I'm not really sure I should be looking at this," he protested half-heartedly.

"Should I close the door?"

"Okay, but don't lock it. Just stand near it so you block their view if anyone starts to come in."

Samantha dutifully closed but didn't lock David's office door and planted herself a foot away from it. David, hands moist and hearing a voice telling him he was living too large at the moment, leafed through the magazine until he found page 113. *Hustler's* "Nude Beach Guide." How original. Well, maybe it won't be so bad, David thought. Maybe there'll just be some swimmers and volleyball players.

There were, at beaches in southern California, Florida and South Carolina. Nothing familiar to David, no one David knew, until he got to page 117. And there it was, Sandy Hook, New Jersey. A paragraph detailed driving instructions via the Garden State Parkway, which parking lots to use and how the crowd differed from those at the other beaches mentioned earlier in the story. Next to the squib were two photos. The first showed a guy with an amateur bodybuilder's physique and lots of body hair seemingly putting suntan lotion on his wife or girlfriend who was long and thin and blond and lying on her side. You could see one of her breasts well, and a hint of pubic hair, but that was it. Not the end of the world.

The second photo was of Samantha. David held

his breath as he absorbed it. Unlike the other photos he had seen, the subject in this photo, Samantha, seemed completely aware of the photographer. She seemed to be looking right at the camera. Samantha was lying on a large, pink beach blanket, on her back, resting on both arms, her head propped up by two large towels so you could see her entire face and look into her eyes. They stared back confidently. Her breasts were firm and large, although not as large as David had imagined, probably because she was lying down. She was very, very tan. And her legs were spread far apart so you couldn't miss how closely she'd shaved herself. Every detail of Samantha's genitalia was publicly displayed.

"Yikes. You knew he was there?"

"Not initially, but after I signed the release, he suggested taking a few more shots with me staring at the camera and with my legs spread. Once I knew it was *Hustler*, I figured my chances would be better if you could see my pussy than if you couldn't. Do you like my pussy, David?"

David could hear an inner voice telling him that living large no longer adequately described how he was acting. Finally, he heeded it. "You're very beautiful, Samantha," he answered.

"Make you hungry?"

David ignored her, folded up the magazine and held it out in Samantha's direction. "Louie is a lucky man."

Samantha made no move to take the magazine back. Instead she stared hard at David for what seemed to be a very long time. She smiled, genuinely and almost lovingly, opened David's office door and began walking through it. Then she turned back towards David for an instant and, before heading down the darkened corridor said, "It's for you, David. Keep it. I know you'll put it to good use."

* * *

Almost 800 miles away, in the Ballroom of the Ritz-Carlton Chicago, Linda Logan was winding up her pre-dinner presentation to 250 of BCS's most successful brokers in the Midwest Region who had gathered for two days of investment workshops. The brokers who were invited to these meetings were typically not the biggest producers in the firm, the "Chairman's Club" members, but they were still big producers who focused on selling stocks rather than bonds, very open to new ideas and very influential in their respective offices. Often, they would share what they'd learned at these meetings with the other FAs in their branch, so selling the 250 ballroom brokers on a particular idea meant selling hundreds or thousands of others on it as well.

To feed the brokers new ideas, senior management would typically ask Linda Logan and a small group of analysts to present at these meetings and to field questions once their canned spiels were done. Management usually drafted analysts who were articulate, enthusiastic and persuasive, and who followed groups that either were performing especially well at the moment or were of considerable interest to the FAs.

While most of the analysts usually spoke during morning or afternoon sessions at meetings like this and were allocated 45 minutes apiece, Linda was usually asked to be the dinner speaker and was given, as she'd begun insisting on long ago, "as much time as I damn well want." In fairness, Linda needed more than 45 minutes to cover her views on the economy, the stock and bond markets, sectors and industries that she found most attractive, and particular stocks that fit into this big-picture investment framework. Also, Linda had made a habit of confining her formal remarks to about 30 minutes and then letting the Q&A session run until it was out of steam. That could mean 30 minutes or 90 minutes. Linda knew well when to keep the questions coming and when to pack it in, and her reputation for calling things as she saw them served her well with most brokers.

One thing Linda also insisted on was speaking before dinner, never after it, which was unusual but also logical for several reasons. First, Linda eliminated the risk of needing to speak over clattering dessert dishes and coffee cups as the tail end of dinner was delivered or cleared. Second, the brokers' attention span and weariness were inversely related so the later she went on, the less well she played. Third, after one particularly rough post-dinner presentation many years earlier to an FA group that had had too much to drink with its surf and turf, Linda vowed never to talk to drunken FAs again. Finally, if Linda spoke at 6:00 P.M., she'd be done by 7:30, limo'd to her private jet by 8:00, on the tarmac at Westchester Airport by 11:15 and back in her mansion in Greenwich by 11:30 Eastern time. No waiting around at O'Hare to check in for the 9:00 United flight. No unnecessary overnight at the Ritz-Carlton. Not for Linda Logan.

"So let me leave you," she was telling the 500 eyes that she'd once again succeeded in glueing to her, "with these key points. First, get real. The years of 15% to 20% gains in the S&P and NASDAQ are gone and they aren't coming back any time soon. The market is only going to rise 5% to 7% a year for many years to come.

"Second, if you can outperform by 300 basis points a year using the Strategy Group's superior stock-picking skills, then you should be able to make your clients 8% to10% a year in equities. That's it. Will it look lame relative to what your clients made in 1999? Yes, it will. Will it look good relative to what they lost from 2000 through 2002? Yes, it will. Will it look good versus 3% on bonds? Yes, it will. And will it look good if inflation stays low? Yes it will.

"Third, stick with the sectors that I talked to you about tonight. Don't try to beat me because you can't. My Recommended List has served you well in the past and it will in the future. Use those names. You don't need to look beyond them. And stop trying to trade the market. You can't. You're too stupid. I'm too stupid. Only the *Wall Street Week* 'elves' are smart enough to trade it and we're not elves. So, buy and hold. Buy and hold and you'll do fine and so will your clients. Thanks for having me."

The room erupted in applause and several dozen hands started waving with eagerness to begin the Q&A session.

"Aren't you starving?" Linda asked. "Don't you wanna eat?"

"We can wait," several brokers yelled back. "How about some Q&A?"

"I'm here to serve," Linda quipped. "Who wants to start? Yes."

"Linda, are you and Bruce in complete agreement about the economy?"

"Bruce and I are never in complete agreement about anything. Bruce locates the consensus economic forecast on Wall Street and then tucks himself squarely

in its core. As for me, I will steer clear of the consensus whenever I can but the laws of math suggest
that, once in a blue moon, the consensus actually will
be correct and we're close to that point right now.
So, my views and Bruce's are as peaceful together as
they're likely to be. But when life isn't so simple, and
you have to choose between Bruce and me..."

"We'll choose you!" someone yelled from the
audience.

"Smart boy," Linda smirked. "Yes."

"Linda, I'll grant that your Recommended List has
done well over the long term, but I'm sure you'd agree
that you've had more disappointments this year,
meaning more stocks that you put on the list when
our analysts liked them and then took off the list at
much lower prices, than you'd had before."

"That's true."

"Can you comment on why that happened?"

"Why did it happen? It happened because the
quality of the Research Department's stock picking
has gone down recently. As you know, when it comes
to selecting specific stocks to own if you want to
capitalize on my investment strategy, I limit myself
whenever I can to stocks that our analysts are also
recommending. It's too confusing and too counterproductive for me to have one view on a stock and our
own analyst to have another.

"Unfortunately, our stock picking, as a department,
really sucks right now." Linda watched the heads jerk
up and the notetaking stop for a moment. "And it's
starting to take its toll on the performance of my
Recommended List, which is still quite good and
much better than any of our analysts' own recommendations, but obviously not quite as good as it was last
year and the years before."

417

"Why is that?"

"Why? Well, we've always had some really bad stock pickers in the department. Every department on The Street has its share of bad stock pickers, and we've certainly had ours. You know who I mean... the Nancy Natolios of the world, the Martin Hogues, the Keith Jackmans, the Arthur Litts, may Arthur rest in peace wherever he lands, the Tim Omoris. I'm not telling you anything you don't already know."

Linda paused, then looked around the room. "How many of you can honestly say that those analysts made your clients any money over the past few years?" Only a smattering of hands went up.

"Nancy made me a lot of money!" one FA near the front of the room yelled.

"Really! And how was that?"

"I just shorted everything she told me to buy."

The room erupted again, this time with laughter.

"Perfect contrary indicator, huh?" Linda nodded. "Look, these analysts must be valuable to the firm in some other way or like Arthur Litt they'd've gotten shot by now."

"Valuable to whom?"

"Valuable to investment banking, perhaps, or to institutional sales. I don't know." Linda shrugged her shoulders. "Investment bankers don't care about stock picking because there's only one rating that any 'good' analyst would use on their clients and you know what that is." Lots of nodding.

"And institutional salespeople don't care about stock picking because most of their clients do their own stock picking. That's not what they pay sell-side analysts for. They pay them for everything *but* stock picking... industry knowledge, company knowledge, management contacts, financial models, reports, blah

blah blah. So, if Tim Omori wants nothing more in life than to endear himself to every institutional client on the planet so he can become number-one-ranked in *II*, the institutional sales force is going to love him no matter how bad his stock picking is.

"But you're different. You don't care about investment banking because we've never had any so you've never really missed it, and you sure as shooting don't care about *II* rankings because they have nothing to do with money-making skills. All you care about is making your clients money, and most *II*-ranked analysts can't pick stocks to save their lives either because they don't know how or they aren't spending enough time on it to succeed, which brings me back to why our stock picking is deteriorating.

"Beyond already having our fair share of banking-oriented analysts who are bad at picking stocks, and our fair share of analysts who just care about making *II* and who know that stock picking isn't the key to getting there, you've got David Meadows telling *all* of our analysts that they'd better make *II* this year and, at the same time, literally moving his office into the Peninsula Hotel so he can try to hire every *II*-ranked analyst he can from other firms. Linda watched the creases form on 250 foreheads.

"That's right. David's mission is to get BCS's standing in next fall's *II* poll up as much as possible, in part by pressing our existing analysts to focus on *II* and in part by hiring as many All Stars as he can from competitors. That's what our new parent seems to want from him and that's what he's going to deliver to them. Just look at whom we've hired this year: a tobacco analyst from Prudential; a chemical analyst from Prudential who admittedly seems better than Arthur Litt was but that's definitional; and a packaging analyst from Merrill Lynch.

"Now let me ask you a question, and I want you to be completely honest with me because I could be dead wrong about this, okay?" Everyone nodded. "How many of you called David within the past six months and *demanded* that we fill the holes in tobacco and packaging before we did anything else?" The brokers were yelping.

"You know, it's laughable, but it's also pretty serious business because the more ranked analysts come into the department, the more bad stock pickers we're going to have. As the mix of the department swings away from analysts who are at least trying to make your clients money, albeit with mixed results, and towards analysts who live and breathe nothing but "making *II*," our stock picking as a department will only go south."

"Why doesn't David do something about this?" a broker yelled from the back of the room.

"You're not listening to me. I just told you that BCS has decided that it wants a good *II* ranking and it's pushing David hard in this direction. David knows that the Krauts determine his bonus so he wants to keep them happy, and keeping them happy means hiring ranked packaging analysts. Do you give a shit about packaging?"

"No!"

"Has Tom Batchelder, whom I've never met by the way, made a name for himself as an astute stock picker and money maker that any of you are aware of?"

"No!"

"I'm sure Tom's a lovely man, and this isn't really about Tom. It's about what happens to the Research

Department's focus on Retail, and on its ability to make your clients money, when the hiring priorities are skewed towards ranked analysts and ranked analysts alone."

"Don't *you* want to make *II*, Linda?" asked one broker standing along the side of the ballroom.

"Sure I'd like to, and one of these years I will, but I'm not sitting at home each evening mapping out what I will do the next day to enhance my *II* ranking. I do tons and tons of these meetings for Retail, and you know what that gets me in *II*? Nothing because there isn't one person in this whole ballroom who votes in *II*. Yet I do many more of them than any analyst in the department. Do I do them enthusiastically? You tell me. Do I spend all day thinking about getting votes or how to make your clients money? You tell me."

"Making clients money!"

"That's right. And I'm going to continue thinking about that, even if it costs me in *II*." Linda knew this was really resonating with the brokers.

"So what can we do?" asked an FA in the front row.

"What can you do?" Linda paused, panned the room slowly and then shook her head slowly from side to side. "Why, you tell those analysts who don't care about you, who don't want to know you, who've hurt you...you tell those analysts to go fuck themselves. And wherever I walk, you follow."

* * *

At his corner table at Adrienne, David breakfasted with Vivian Zimm, the life insurance analyst at Morgan Stanley. David had liked Vivian from the get-go. She was older than many of the young whipper snappers he'd been seeing of late, had a maturity and sophistication about her that David found refreshing, was razor sharp and articulate, and clearly understood the business.

David, always curious about the inner workings of firms whose analysts he rarely saw, pushed her gently for information about life inside Morgan Stanley. Vivian spoke glowingly about her firm, about how smart most of the people were who worked there, about its first-rate investment banking capabilities, its global push which didn't affect her as much as many other analysts, and about the quality of Research management. David listened intently, trying to determine why Vivian had consented to breakfast with him. So far, he'd come up dry.

"And how has life changed for you since Alice Schroeder was hired?"

Vivian stopped talking, looked down, took a sip of lukewarm coffee, and sighed perceptibly. "I've been thinking a lot about what I want to do over the next five to ten years on The Street," she said, "and Alice's arrival has pushed me to think longer and harder than I'd expected to."

David nodded quickly. "And…?"

"… what I've concluded is that what I most want to do is switch groups."

"To trade life insurance for something else?"

"Yes."

"For property/casualty insurance?"

"Yes."

David continued nodding. This wasn't the first time he'd heard this. P/C analysts often covered more important companies, companies of greater interest to institutional investors, companies with greater investment banking potential. Thus, they almost always earned significantly more than their life insurance analyst counterparts. "So you're exploring to see which firms on The Street would allow you to trade?"

"I wouldn't say *that* exactly. You're the first firm I've spoken to. As I'm sure you know, life insurance analysts don't get a lot of calls. Yours may not be the last one, but it's been the only one so far."

"Would Morgan have allowed you to switch had Alice not been hired?"

"It's possible. The firm is very good about that kind of thing. If an analyst is doing good work and can convince management that she or he could make a bigger contribution in a different area, it's not uncommon for that analyst to be permitted to move around a little bit."

"But now, with Alice on board, that possibility no longer exists."

"I think that's clear."

"So you want to give up life insurance and take on property/casualty."

"Correct. Now I know you have John Henriksen doing the group."

"Have you met him?"

"Not really. I've seen him at a couple of financial services conferences but I don't think we've ever spoken. He's a little stiff, if you know what I mean, but he's obviously smart and I have no idea how he's doing but it wouldn't surprise me if he was doing fine, so BCS could be the wrong place for me given my career plans."

"John is very nice," David concurred. "He's 28, I think, but 28 going on 50. He's very professorial in his demeanor, which is okay to a point, but he also gets pompous and pretentious too often and that really turns the sales force off. I also think it's turning clients off because he's not faring well with many of them."

Vivian nodded. "I wouldn't want to cost anyone his job, David."

"I understand, nor would I want to hire you to replace someone who was doing a good job, but John is struggling and everyone realizes it, even John. He's been told this in his most recent reviews. I don't believe in surprising analysts that way."

"But if you want me for my *II* vote in life insurance, there's no way I can stay ranked in life if I drop it to pick up P/C."

"That's true and not true. It all depends on the timing."

"You mean August?"

"Yes."

David and Vivian both paused and drank some water. Then David said, "if we were to hire you seemingly to do life insurance, with a private understanding that, once *II's* job-hoppers' deadline had passed in August, we'd let John go and ask you to switch from life to P/C, how would you feel?"

"I'd feel very badly for John but otherwise it's a good plan. Until the job-hoppers' deadline, say, in mid-August, I would appear to have joined BCS to do life insurance and, assuming I did well enough this year in the balloting to rank again, which I'm sure I did, *II* would credit you this October with my All Star ranking even though, as of mid-August, I'd have given up life and begun working on property/casualty."

"Correct."

"You realize, David, that I'm not going to rank in either category next year."

"I know that, Vivian. You'll lose your life insurance ranking and you won't be up and running in P/C long enough to rank there."

"So you'll get a vote for me this year, and you'll hopefully resume getting a vote for me two or three years out, but you're going to lose a vote next year."

All David could focus on right now was the short term. Next year he'd work on hiring more ranked analysts and offset Vivian's falling off of *II*.

"Is this the only basis on which you'd consider joining BCS?" he asked.

"I'm afraid so, David."

"Then let's do it."

* * *

"I know it's there!"

"You can't find it because it doesn't exist."

"Primo wouldn't be trading at $7 if they could clear $0.12 for the quarter."

"They'll do $0.12, Keith. The market's been sloppy. It's the market, not Primo."

"I know there's something wrong. I just can't find it."

"Stop torturing yourself over this," Barry Seels said.

"I should've downgraded it at $10 right after they preannounced the shitty March quarter. I knew it. I just didn't have the balls."

"How could you downgrade it 30 days after we did the deal? We would have looked like traitors."

"We would have looked like we'd figured out what was going on. The real question is, how could we do the deal for them in March and then let them preannounce a bad March quarter 30 days later?"

"The whole shortfall was in the last two weeks of

the quarter, Keith. You know that. We've been through this a thousand times. No one knew the quarter was going to be short when the deal was done."

"I don't believe it."

"Look, even if they do $0.10 or $0.11 instead of $0.12, they're still going to make $0.35 this year, and the stock is down to $7 from over $11. You thought the stock was attractive when it was $10–$11 based on your $0.40 estimate. Now you can buy the same stock for $7, with earnings of $0.35. The P/E is down to 20 from 28. You can't like it less at 20 times earnings than at 28 times."

"It smells bad, Barry, and you know it."

"I don't smell anything."

"The market is telling you they're going to miss the quarter, and when you call me two weeks from now and tell me the quarter is going to be $0.10 or $0.11, I'm not going to take the call. You understand me?"

"Grow up," Barry sneered, and walked out of Keith's office.

* * *

Denisovich was desolate.

Over and over again he ran through his entire universe of names looking for something to feed to Piotr. Stocks that seemed wildly overvalued or that could be misrepresented as such. Stocks that were selling for half of what they were worth or that could be lied about to that effect. Companies where Nick could raise his earnings estimate far above, or cut it far below, the current Wall Street consensus without looking completely irresponsible.

Nothing.

Nothing.

Nothing.

He read through old reports he'd written and reviewed all of the Morning Meeting Notes that he'd submitted on the stocks he'd fed Piotr before. He looked at all of his competitors' estimates on *First Call*.

But his monitor told him nothing.

Nick knew that Volkov would be calling soon but, for the first time since his business partnership with Piotr had begun, Nick felt empty-handed.

Maybe it was time to call it quits. He'd made his millions, albeit not as many as he'd hoped for. Maybe he should cut back the number of ideas he was required to feed Piotr each year. Maybe he should change the arrangement so he could signal Piotr when he really had something good for him, rather than prepare himself for contacts with Volkov that had been predetermined by mutual consent.

"No," Nick said out loud, "not yet. I've got to find something."

But deep in his belly, he knew he wouldn't.

And it frightened him.

* * *

Alan Bellone, emboldened by his newly signed employment contract guaranteeing him $2.6 million over two years plus an additional $1.3 million of restricted BCS shares vesting in year three, really buckled down, but to surf, not to analyze. He did a token amount of report writing but always in the form of two-page *First Call* notes, never anything more substantial. He returned important clients' calls, of which fewer and fewer came in, and he made token appearances at the Morning Meeting and on the Sales and Trading floors so people would say that they'd seen him around and spoken with him not that long ago. But most of the time Alan remained behind closed doors, seated at his PC where he revisited familiar porn sites and surfed for new ones.

For someone to whom porn sites are a novelty, it isn't hard to spend a few hours bouncing from one accidentally discovered site to another without getting bored, but for Alan, who'd devoted hundreds of hours to this endeavor, things were getting stale. Long ago he'd exhausted everything the Internet had to offer for free on Anna Nicole Smith and Danni Ashe and Ramona Drews and Jessica Hahn and Pamela Anderson. He'd seen all that *Playboy* and *Penthouse* and *Hustler* offered for free, and he'd clicked and clicked from one site offering "members" thousands of photos of nude Hollywood stars to another, fearing that, despite their assurances that they only wanted his credit card number to prove that he was an adult, he'd start getting charged for his aimless wanderings and that somehow this would hunt back to BCS where he'd get caught.

For many months, Alan had resisted following one hot-link path that had been offered up repeatedly, but today, restless and cranky, he dropped his defenses and followed it. Soon, the photos of long-haired blondes with artificial breasts began to abate, and very different, unfamiliar images replaced them... images of children in sexually compromising positions. Above these images, more often than not, were giant warnings in day-glo letters: "STOP! TURN BACK! If you find graphic images of children having sex with adults offensive, EXIT NOW!"

Alan didn't. He walked farther and farther down this new and dangerous path. At first, the images of children, seemingly happy but probably not, having sex with middle-aged and old men, was very unnerving to him. While the children didn't appear to be suffering, or abused, Alan knew in his gut that his surfing had turned in a very different direction. Viewing photos of Anna Nicole or Pamela Anderson, he thought, would be considered a very bad use of his workday in the eyes of BCS, should it ever find out, but it would also be viewed, perhaps only privately, as normal, healthy, heterosexual behavior. He'd be considered a jerk for having done it during work hours, but nothing more.

Child pornography, however, would be indefensible. No one, publicly or privately, would even attempt to understand, identify with or justify his behavior, and that, oddly enough, made it all the more irresistible to Alan. Most of the predators were old men. Half of the children were boys. And all of the images were fresh and new and, to Alan Bellone, addictive.

So, as summer arrived, Alan shifted gears, leaving his Hollywood starlets in the dust and openly, unhesitatingly embracing his darkest underbelly.

* * *

For two weeks David and Les Carter had gone back and forth with Daniel Roe.

"Does he want to come or not?" David had asked exasperatedly. .

"He wants to come, David. He's just very immature and he doesn't know how to handle himself like a professional."

For several days, Daniel had refused to budge from his initial demand… $10 million per year for three years. Only towards the end of the first week of "negotiating" did he accept the fact that BCS didn't do three-year deals. Daniel had reiterated his belief that he should outearn Mary Meeker who, he was sure, was making much more than $10 million yearly, and David again rejected it. Daniel had demanded to be named Director of Technology Research and to have all the other technology analysts report to him. David had rejected this too.

Daniel had reminded David of how strongly Carl Robern and Jim MacDuffin had wanted him to be hired, but David countered that Daniel had gotten a lukewarm response from the other tech analysts he'd met and would have to be an especially good team player to turn them into fans. Daniel reminded David that he'd be the only *II*-ranked analyst in the Technology Group and that he was the only *II*-ranked analyst in his space that David could hire. David acknowledged both facts but told Daniel that he'd hire no one sooner than hiring a mistake and tried to believe the words as he said them.

Late the second week, after dozens of phone calls and two more meetings between Les and Daniel at Les's club, the economics were ironed out and Daniel authorized the client check. To no one's surprise, the verdict was uninspiring. Of the 40 clients who opined, 16 were positive, 12 were indifferent and 12 were negative.

Hoping that Carl would change his mind, David showed him the client check results. Carl bellowed, "Just hire the fucker already, will you? What are you waiting for, David, the three deals in his pocket to get done by UBS?"

And so, during the last week of spring, David announced the hiring of his fourth *II* All Star, Daniel Roe of UBS Warburg.

"Congratulations," Les told David. "You really got him at a good price."

"Fourteen million over two years, plus a full-time chauffeur who's available seven days a week? That's a *good* price?"

"For Daniel Roe, it's a good price."

"I'd sort of wished that UBS had found it in their hearts to match it or beat it at the eleventh hour," David sighed.

"They were pretty sick and tired of him, from what I understand," Les said. "I called Grano, whom I've known for many years, as a courtesy, right after Daniel said he'd told UBS about our offer."

David stopped reading his e-mails and focused on what Les was saying. "And what did Joe tell you?"

"He was funny. Grano can be that way. He said at first he almost threw Daniel out the window, but then he calmed down and just told him to make sure the door didn't hit him in the ass on his way out."

* * *

The following day, on the Morning Call, David introduced Marsha Yamamoto, formerly of Bear Stearns, an *II* All Star in airlines who was joining BCS as its new senior airline and airfreight analyst.

"You aren't doing airfreight now," said Maryanne Miles, who had interviewed Marsha when David had been courting her.

"No," Marsha confessed, "but I've worked side-by-side with Ed Wolfe, who's the number-two-ranked airfreight and surface transportation analyst on The

Street, I've learned a fair amount about airfreight through osmosis, and I've figured out what it will take to become a top source on those stocks."

"Music to *my* ears," said Paula Hainsworth, who had also interviewed Marsha and given her an enthusiastic thumbs-up. "Marsha, welcome to the firm. We're very glad to have you." Barbara Malek, the young saleswoman whom David had also put on Marsha's dance card in an effort to trot out as many women as possible, gave her a big smile and a little wink. Marsha was clearly very happy with her decision.

So was David who, when he'd returned to his office after the Morning Call, opened up a notebook that he kept in his bottom drawer and reviewed his progress. Five All Stars to start with and five hired: Liz Tytus in tobacco, Van Trudell in chemicals, Tom Batchelder in packaging, Daniel Roe in Internet, and now Marsha in airlines. So that was 10 All Stars now, excluding any existing analysts who might rank for the first time this year.

Where did that leave him? It moved BCS past Sanford Bernstein, he thought, from fourteenth place to thirteenth place. Two more hires would get him to twelfth place, six more to eleventh, seven more to tenth, and ten more to eighth.

"If only Louis Liddy had stayed!" he groaned.

All those breakfasts, all those rounds of interviews, all that hemming and hawing with analysts who were hesitating, and what had it gotten him? A one-rung gain and a $500,000 raise to $3,000,000. Seven more hires would get him to $4,500,000, and 10 more to $6,000,000.

Vivian Zimm and Christopher Chadwick. I've got to get them both.

* * *

Ron Vargo and Claire O'Daniel pulled the luxurious Ritz-Carlton Buckhead's sheets over their heads and laughed. They were giddy. Down the hall, Tom Lukin, the CEO of Milbanks Media and Claire's boss, was holding court with several die-hard sell-side competitors of Ron's who just couldn't ask enough questions or spend enough time with MM management. Throughout the dinner presentation, Ron and Claire had looked at each other, poker-faced, and counted the minutes until they could be alone.

At 11:45 P.M., Claire had finally snuck into Ron's room, and for the next hour they'd made love almost silently for fear of being heard. Now, sleepy but excited, they rolled around and laughed some more and talked, at first about the day's events and about dinner, and then about something nearer and dearer to Claire's heart.

"Sit up," she commanded, "we have to talk."

"Can't it wait until tomorrow?"

"It *is* tomorrow, silly, and no, it can't."

"Okay, I'm listening."

"Good. Here's the deal. Remember when you told me how you wanted to raise your rating on Milbanks to Buy from Accumulate and I told you to wait?"

"After dinner at Lespinasse."

"Correct. You wanted to push the stock to Retail and help get it higher in order to make my stock options more valuable."

"Right."

"And that was very sweet of you. Options are a big part of senior management's comp at Milbanks so I'd have *lots* of people wanting to thank you for goosing the price of the shares."

"But…"

"But the timing wasn't right."

"Why?"

"Because doing it in April would have been a little helpful, but doing it in June could make a much bigger difference."

"Why?"

"Because we're on, as you know, a June fiscal year, and the Board of Directors approved changes in the stock option programs last year as a result of which new options will be granted based on how the stock did during the prior fiscal year."

"In English."

"The better the stock does between July 1st and June 30th, the more options management will receive when year-end bonuses are paid in early August."

"And what does that mean, specifically?"

Claire looked slightly embarrassed for a minute but quickly regained her composure. "It means this. The stock closed at $41 last June 30th. We had a good year, record profits, a successful acquisition and a lot of support from The Street. The stock, today, closed at $47.40, so we're up about 15%."

"That's not bad in the crappy market we've had this year."

"No it's not, but here's the thing. The stock option hurdles are: a) up 10%, b) up 20% and c) up 35% or more. MM is clearly going to be up 10% for the year and it's clearly *not* going to be up 35% or more with only two weeks left in the fiscal year, but it's $1.80 a share away from being up 20% and that's where you can be helpful."

"You need the stock to close on June 30th at or above $49.20."

"You're such a genius," Claire laughed. "That's the other reason why I love you so much."

"What do you mean, the other reason?"

Claire reached under the sheets, grabbed Ron's penis and began to stroke it. Ron looked down, laughed silently, and tried to concentrate on stock prices and stock options.

"You know I'd do anything for you," he said.

"Then get the stock to $49.20," she said, stroking him faster.

"We're talking serious money here, I presume."

"Serious money. I don't know about Tom and the other guys," Claire answered, "but the difference to me between $49.19 and $49.20 is 150,000 options."

* * *

"It's in," Lisa announced, holding the new issue of *Fortune* magazine.

"Did you see how we did?" David asked.

"I didn't have time. I just saw it in the mailroom and brought it up right away."

"Let's take a peek." David took the magazine from Lisa, noticed the reference to the new *Fortune* All Stars on the cover and found the article in the table of contents. As sure as it was June, it was time for another poll naming Wall Street's "best" analysts. Beyond *II* every October and *Greenwich* every April, there was *The Wall Street Journal's* All Star Team each July and *Fortune's* All Star team each June. In 2000, even *theStreet.com* had published an All Star team but that had been a one-shot affair.

Fortune's All-Stars had also premiered in 2000. Unlike *II* and *Greenwich*, which ask institutional investors whom they consider to be the best analysts in dozens of industries, or *The Wall Street Journal*, which tries to eliminate the "popularity contest" aspect of those polls by measuring, coldly and objectively, the accuracy of each analyst's stock recommendations, *Fortune* went searching for analysts who were consistently good stock pickers, in bull markets and bear, and named 10 of them.

David scanned the team, determined that none of the All Stars worked for BCS, decided that nothing else needed to be done, filed the article away and headed for a mandatory meeting for all seniors and associates that he'd called the night before.

Upstairs on 74, about 175 analysts and juniors awaited him. David smiled and waved as he entered the conference rooms, walked to the front, and began talking without a microphone. Behind him stood a tall stack of white papers.

"This is going to be very quick," he said. "For several months now we've talked periodically about how the firm might change ways in which we do business to minimize potential conflicts of interest. As we're all painfully aware, there's been a great media frenzy on this topic, including CNBC asking people every 35 seconds on the air if they own the shares or have investment banking relationships with the companies they're recommending. It's pretty tiresome to listen to but it's not going away any time soon.

"The trend on The Street is clearly towards prohibiting analysts from owning, personally, any of the stocks that they cover, and that's the policy that BCS will be adopting effective August 1st. Any stock that you have estimates and an investment rating on is a stock you will no longer be able to own personally, and "personally" will mean you, your spouse, your kids, your parents, your siblings, or anyone else living in your home whom you support.

"If you normally have a rating on a stock but that rating has been temporarily suspended for some reason, you still cannot own it. The same would be true if you temporarily suspended your earnings estimates. If you don't estimate earnings but you estimate cash flow or EBITDA or funds from operations or anything else in lieu of earnings, you cannot own the stock.

"What happens now if you currently own some of your stocks? You have until July 31st to sell them, and I suspect that most of you will because, if you opt not to sell them for some reason such as that you have huge gains in some of them and want to wait until those gains change from short-term to long-term in order to reduce your capital gains taxes, you will be subject to extremely onerous restrictions after July 31st on when you'll be able to sell those shares and how. I'm talking about long holding periods, an inability to sell any shares rated Buy or Accumulate, no investment banking involvement with the company during the prior 12 months and a long list of legal and compliance approvals that you'd need to secure prior to any such sale. So, unless your reasons are extraordinary, sell the shares between now and July 31st and simplify your lives greatly."

"What if you own stocks in your group that you don't cover?" asked Ken Lavery.

"The new policy doesn't apply to them. The rule is simple: if you rate it, you can't own it. If you can influence the price of the shares by moving from Hold to Buy or Buy to Attractive or Hold to Sell, then you can't have a personal position in those shares. Similarly, if you can influence the price of a stock by talking about it on CNBC... and we all know that you *only* discuss stocks that you cover on CNBC, don't we?... then you can't own the stock. If you own a stock in your sector that you don't cover, you can hold on to it, but if you decide later that you want to start covering it, you will be forced to sell all of your holdings *well* before you initiate coverage. Are we clear about this?"

"Is the firm going to allow us to sell all our shares without charging us commissions, given that it's forcing us to do this?" asked Keith Jackman.

"No, but the firm will discount all such mandated trades by 75% from whatever your normal commission schedule is. It varies, you know, from person to person, but if you normally pay one percent, you'll pay a quarter of one percent. Other questions?"

There were none.

"Okay, please take a memo from the stack behind me and extras for anyone in your group who didn't make it to this meeting. If you have questions later, please see me or Matt or Jim Molloy. Thanks."

Seven minutes later, the "other" Tom Hanks answered his phone.

"Tom it's Ken Lavery."

"What's doing?"

"I need you to sell the biotech names I cover. You know, to comply with the new firm policy?"

"Let's see what that means." Tom paused and pulled up Ken's account on his screen. "There's the Regeneron... about $650,000 worth...and you've got some Genentech and Amgen... that's about $950,000, and then you've got the two little ones... that's over $4,000,000."

"Don't touch the little ones."

"They stay?"

"I don't have to sell them because I don't cover them. Just the big boys."

"So I'm going to sell the million six and leave the four mil alone."

"Correct. And these trades are done at the 75% off rate, right?"

"Right. So, if I'd normally charge you a millionth of one percent, on these particular trades I'll only charge you one four-millionth of one percent.

"Very funny, Mr. Tahiti."

"Send the funds or hold them?"

"Hold them. I'll tell you where to wire that money as soon as I know."

* * *

David's phone wouldn't stop ringing, and Lisa was not around to pick it up. It rang four times and stopped, rang four times and stopped, over and over again. Someone, it seemed, didn't want to leave a message.

As things turned out, that someone was Madelynn Masters, the seniormost BCS banker in the Insurance Group, with whom Vivian Zimm had just interviewed.

"Out of the question," Madelynn told David.

"Why? She's gotten very good reviews from everyone else she's seen today."

"I don't care. She's the least commercial analyst I've ever interviewed. I'm amazed that she's at Morgan Stanley. Maybe they're pushing her out."

"I don't think so."

"You wouldn't know, David. You know how banking drives that firm. Do you know how many deals she's done over the past two years in her space?"

"No."

"Two."

"And why in your judgment didn't she do more?"

"Because her standards for what's a good deal are unrealistically high. She had something critical to say about every company I threw at her. She was quite critical of many of the managements we talked about. She thought valuations were too high on almost every stock I asked about."

"So you mean she has a backbone."

"It has nothing to do with having a backbone. I have a backbone and she's nothing like me. What this is about is not wanting to do deals."

"Any deals or bad deals?"

"Any deals. She claims that she'd support any deal in which everyone wins. You know how many of those we've done lately, David, don't you?"

David ignored her.

"She's going to hold these companies to such ridiculous standards, she's going to only bless flawless management teams, and she's going to be a real stickler about P/E's and stock prices. I can't imagine that more than 5% of everything we'd show her would cut her mustard."

"Maybe that's how it should be."

"David, get real. The Bank's unprofitable. The way to change that for the better is to do more deals, not less, to hire analysts who understand that they work for the firm, not just for Research, to hire analysts who understand that every deal has its blemishes but that deals can be good even if they aren't perfect."

"And you're convinced that Vivian understands none of this."

"She's clueless."

"She's got standards and they've seemingly served

her well, especially with clients. Otherwise she wouldn't be *II*-ranked."

"I don't care about her ranking, David."

"If you showed her high-quality deals, you think she'd balk?"

"The kinds of deals she'd support we don't do. We're BCS, not Goldman or Morgan Stanley. We get what we can get. If the fruit is bruised a little, that's life."

"I'll note your No vote, Madelynn, but I've got to tell you that everyone else thinks she's a high-quality analyst, a real pro, and someone they'd like to work with. If you'd voted No because you thought she was stupid or lazy I'd have to talk to Dieter about it. But all you're voting on is her potential unwillingness to bless your crappy deals and, for that reason alone, I'd hire her."

The next day, David did.

* * *

"Why does Liz Tytus make $4 million when I make so much less?"

The typeface was so standard that it could have come from any PC, anywhere in the world. The envelope containing it had been addressed to David Meadows, Personal and Highly Confidential, and passed on to David, unopened, along with the rest of the day's mail by Lisa Palladino.

David walked to Lisa's office, envelope in hand.

"Where did this come from?"

"No idea."

"Just in my mailbox along with everything else?"

"Yup. Why? You look upset."

David shook his head. "It's nothing."

As he returned to his office, he considered his options. To let it slide would be to let someone who seemingly had determined how much Liz was making walk around the department, bitter and therefore dangerous. To ask Security to fingerprint it might lead, ultimately, to a forced admission by David that he'd left very sensitive papers detailing not just Liz's compensation but everyone's from S to Z on the Xerox machine accidentally. And if his instincts were right, there'd be no fingerprints any way.

David sighed for a very long time. Then he shredded the note.

* * *

A week before its June quarter was to end, Primo Theaters issued a press release stating that June-quarter earnings would fall short of analysts' expectations and that management was now more comfortable with $0.08–$0.09 a share than with $0.12, the prior guidance. Full-year guidance was also cut to a range of $0.33–$0.35.

Not wanting to antagonize the management of an investment banking client, Keith Jackman cut his own estimates to $0.09 and $0.33 and, with the stock under $6, reiterated his Buy.

"At 18 times earnings," he told Sales, "it has more than discounted the shortfall."

"They're drowning," he told Barry Seels later, "and I'm going down with them."

* * *

Nick Denisovich also felt himself drowning, but in a dream, in a lake of clear, icy water that made his body shake violently and his eyes burn. He was dressed in a solid blue suit, white shirt and blue tie, and he could see that the laces on his black dress shoes had come undone.

His arms flailed wildly. His hands reached for his head, then fell back towards his shoulders, reached again, fell back. His head, under enormous pressure, was being pushed down below the water's surface and towards his chest. He could feel searing pain in his lungs but hear nothing but the water gurgling around him. Suddenly, his forehead hit something hard, the side of a rowboat he told himself, and he could feel himself losing consciousness.

"I'm dying," he thought.

And though he couldn't see, he knew that the hands that were pressing so hard on his skull were connected to arms, to shoulders, to a neck, to a head with a face on it, that the face was purple with rage, and that the face was Piotr's.

* * *

Christopher Chadwick was due momentarily. He'd spent the entire day interviewing at BCS and the feedback had been far from spectacular. Marsha Yamamoto, still glowing from her recent job change, was kindest towards Christopher. "He seems very experienced," she'd written. But the other consumer analysts were much tougher. "Not very impressive," said Robin Lomax. "Adequate at best," wrote Phil Suprano. "I'm surprised he's ranked," said Liz Tytus.

Matt had characterized him as "very average, not very impressive... suspicious why he'd leave Morgan for BCS, seems to have developed bad relationships with banking."

"Nicely done, Matt," David thought to himself.

Carl had called him "acceptable if there are no other choices." John McLain had written, "doubt the sales force would greet this hire enthusiastically." Herb Hirschorn wrote "Every time I vote No you hire him anyway, so I think Christopher is spectacular. Let's see if it makes a difference."

"Shit," David thought. "I hate being so transparent."

Ken Lannigan, the MD in banking who did Christopher's group, wrote "Could be helpful in getting us into deals as a co-lead manager. With no coverage, it's hopeless." And Paul Pitcher had written "hiring him would be a non-event for Retail… boring group, high-priced stocks, uninspiring analyst."

Every single person who had interviewed Christopher had expressed serious doubts about any good analyst's willingness to leave Morgan Stanley for BCS and several had asked if he'd been fired. When one of the traders brought Christopher around to David's office, close to 6:00 p.m., Christopher looked pooped. "I guess we've put you through the ringer" David laughed.

"This is worse than institutional marketing but it had to be done."

"And how did it go?"

"It was fine as far as I'm concerned. The analysts were okay. I'm glad I won't be the *only* ranked analyst in the department."

"What a schmuck," David thought.

"The sales guys were okay, trading was fine, the banker… what was his name? Lannigan? Ken Lannigan?…he seemed resigned to doing some co-lead managed deals in my space which, at BCS, is the only reasonable expectation. He wasn't anywhere near as sharp as my bankers are now, but then again, he was nicer to me than they are which, frankly, is more important. I'm sure we could work together."

"How'd you hit it off with Matt?"

"Fine. He seemed pretty solid."

"So, Christopher, does moving to BCS make sense to you?"

"It could, David, under the right circumstances."

"Meaning…"

"Well, I'd need to come in as a Managing Director, I'd need a commitment from you that you'd help marshal much more support from the institutional sales force than I've gotten at Morgan, I'd like mutual agreement that I won't spend more than 20% of my time on banking, and I'd like a three-year guarantee at my market value."

"We don't do three-year deals, Christopher."

"Well then, a two-year guarantee would have to be even higher."

"How much are you making currently?"

"David, I told you I'd confide that information in you at the right time. If you're prepared to put an offer together for me now, I'll tell you."

"Go."

"Well, to be honest, I was woefully underpaid last year. In the three years before last year I averaged about $2,000,000 per year but last year I was only paid $1,200,000."

"Why?"

"They said because the bonus pool was down and because I did less banking."

"But you believe…"

"…that my bankers want me out and that they're pressuring Research management to squeeze me out by cutting my comp in half."

"Did you ask if that was true?"

"Yes, and I was told that 'some people' felt I might be more appreciated at other firms but that no one was 'forcing me out.'"

"So you think your market value is closer to $2,000,000."

"At least."

"But your *Greenwich* ranking was thirteenth, down from eighth."

"It's because I spent too much time on banking and the sales force didn't support me adequately. In a better work environment my rankings would come right back up."

"I see." David's belly was screaming "Pass on him!" but David knew he couldn't. "Well, did you see everyone you needed to see?"

"Yes."

"Are you ready for us to put an offer on the table for you?"

"Yes."

"Good, then I'll talk with Larry Fraser tonight and Larry will circle back with you in the morning. Will you be around tomorrow?"

"Yes."

"Good. Maybe we can wrap this up quickly."

"I hope so, David."

After Christopher had left, David compared notes with Larry.

"He did exactly as we expected him to," David began.

"Meaning everyone thought he was mediocre or worse."

"Right."

"Then pass on him, David."

This is what David most liked about Larry. There were no other ranked analysts in the space for David to hire. If he passed on Christopher, Larry would lose six figures worth of income, yet Larry never hesitated to talk *down* a bad candidate's appeal.

"I can't."

"You can."

"Not if we're going to crack top-ten in *II*."

Larry was silent for a moment. "What do you want me to test him with?"

"He made $1,200,000 last year, down from $2,000,000, or so he says. I bet he made $1,000,000."

"He wants $2,000,000?"

"At least."

"Did you discuss his *Greenwich* ranking with him?"

"Yes. It's all Morgan Stanley's fault."

"We could try $1,500,000."

"We could, but I'm disinclined to."

"Why?"

"Because he's such a prissy little guy. He could get insulted, which he seems to do a lot, and decide he'll wait for some other firm to rescue him from Morgan Stanley. He wants out, clearly, but he doesn't seem to have a deadline that someone else has set for him."

"So, two for two?"

"Offer him $2,000,000 in year one and $2,500,000 in year two. Tell him we know that year one will have to be a rebuilding year for him and that we expect his numbers will look better in year two so his comp should be higher."

"You don't need to go that high."

"He's my only ranked candidate in the space. I've got a $250 million budget but I'm not going to be able to spend all of it at the rate I'm hiring so let's not nickel and dime him. He's ranked, I need the ranking, let's get him over here."

"When will you do the client check if he authorizes it?"

"Tomorrow."

"I'll be back to you." Larry hung up.

The following day, Christopher authorized the client check and got drug-tested. The drug test said he was clean. The client check came out 40% positive, 20% neutral and 40% negative. Several clients confided that they'd heard he'd been fired.

In a move that surprised both Larry and David, Christopher rejected $2 million in year one and $2.5 million in year two, but agreed to come after his first-year guarantee was rewritten up $500,000.

"He tried to guess which of us was more desperate," David said to Larry after the contract signing was done, "and he guessed right."

* * *

Ken waited nervously for the call, alternating between watching GINV and GNOM trade and worrying about his margin debt. If I take the $1,600,000 out, he thought, I'll still have about $4,300,000 worth of stock and $2,150,000 of margin borrowings, so I'll be 50% equity and 50% debt. Still pretty manageable...

No call.

...as long as the stocks don't go down.

Ken jumped. His phone had startled him.

"Lavery."

"Are you sitting down? It's a go! The owner has accepted our offer," Kim Hovey told him.

"You're kidding."

"Nope, and they said they'll close as soon as you can close."

Once again, Ken read through the listing on the house he'd been bidding on. Sagaponack South, English-style traditional, 8,000 square feet, double-height great room, 8 bedrooms, 8 baths, 2 powder rooms, Sub Zero, Thermador wine cooler, Bosch dishwashers, 60–foot gunite pool with jacuzzi, whole-house audio, media room, central air, all on two beautifully landscaped acres.

The asking price had been $5,400,000, but Ken had bid $4,500,000 initially and had balked at going above $5,000,000. Once the owner offered to sell the house furnished, however, Ken had instructed Kim to make his "final" offer of $5,200,000 and, according to Kim, the seller had just said yes.

"How quickly can you close, Ken?"

"I'm preapproved for up to $5,000,000 of mortgage money as long as loan-to-value doesn't exceed 80% so I'm going to put down $1,600,000 and finance $3,600,000 which would only be 69% of the purchase price. As soon as we can get the title search and the inspection done, I'm good to go."

"Excellent!" Kim said, clearly pleased that Ken had greased the skids.

"But tell them I want the house's purchase price listed as $5,175,000 and the furnishings listed at $25,000 so, if I ever want to use that last $540,000 of borrowing power, no one hassles me that my loan-to-value is over 80%."

"Of course."

"Should I tell people I'm in Sagaponack, Kim, or should I say Southampton?"

"You can say either. Sagaponack is in the town of Southampton but not in the village of Southampton. If you want to say you're in one of the Hamptons you can say you're in Southampton."

"Too bad I won't be in for July 4th," Ken bemoaned.

Kim was quiet for a minute. Then the lightbulb went on. "I have an idea. I know the sellers are going to be away for the 4th of July. What if I ask them if, assuming you've signed and sent the contracts, with your down payment of 10% or $520,000, to the seller's attorney, they might be willing to do a July 4th long weekend for $25,000, which could be applied towards the furniture purchase. If for any reason you don't close, the owner would keep the $25,000 as rent."

"That's a *great* idea, Kim."

"But first things first. Let's get contracts sent to your attorney, review them while doing the engineer's report, and then send them back with the down payment check ASAP."

"But you'll ask them about the rental now, won't you?"

"Of course, Ken."

"Great. Kim, I can't thank you enough."

"No need to thank me. Just get your attorney teed up to turn this around quickly."

"Will do." Ken hung up, rocked back in his chair, and imagined himself, surrounded by friends, loved ones and supermodels, sipping margaritas by his 60–foot gunite pool, waiting for the sun to set and then heading for the Grucci's fireworks show on Main Beach in East Hampton.

God... life was good.

* * *

BCS's Annual Research/Banking Summer Cruise was a ritual that had been established many years earlier by Ed Koster as a way of getting most of the senior people in Research and Investment Banking together for four hours of informal conversation and fun. The cruise boat that EFS had chartered could hold 350 people but fewer than 200 usually came because the cruise was limited to senior analysts, senior bankers and senior management and administrative types from both departments. The boat sailed from 23rd Street and the East River, went out into the harbor and around the Statue of Liberty, up the Hudson for a mile or so, back out into the harbor, and then up the East River under the Brooklyn and Manhattan bridges before returning four hours later to 23rd Street. Hors d'oeuvres and drinks, including beer and wine but nothing harder, were served all evening, and a limited number of entertainers, typically fortune-tellers, magicians and the like, provided distraction when the analysts and bankers got bored.

For the first couple of hours at least, most analysts and bankers truly enjoyed themselves. They took advantage of their captivity by sitting and sharing triumphs, frustrations, rumors and jokes. Sometimes they talked seriously about business, but often they just talked about summer plans, their kids and other personal-life matters. The casual attire, the wine and beer, and the salt spray from the harbor all lifted the analysts' and bankers' spirits. Beyond spending play time with their bankers, analysts also spent time with other analysts, and bankers with other bankers, something that happened all too rarely during normal business hours. Names were matched with faces, bonding occurred.

David swept up one side of the ship and down the

other, stopping to chat briefly with as many of his analysts as he could. He also made sure to pay attention to the members of his management and administrative teams who were on board, and he chatted with the bankers with whom he worked most closely, as well as a few whom he knew less well. He saw Tom Mennymore early on and talked business with him for five minutes. When he stumbled upon Dieter, he took him aside, did one piece of business with him and then asked about his kids. And when he saw Carl, he waved and made sure to get caught up in conversation with whoever was nearby, simply to avoid him.

The one wild card on R/B Cruise Night was the weather. Once or twice it had rained, forcing everyone down on to the lower decks which were still spacious but far less appealing than the top deck under the stars. Luckily, this year, the sky had been clear and the sunset, with help from all the chemicals in the air above New Jersey's horizon, had been spectacular. In the afterglow, the Manhattan skyline looked tranquil and dreamy. As David soaked it all in, Matt Speiser tapped his shoulder and said hi.

"So when are you off to Yellowstone?" David asked.

"Two weeks. School ends tomorrow. I want to get there in July. It'll still be jammed, I'm sure, but maybe not as badly as in August."

David nodded.

"And you're going to be in Southampton all summer?"

"Well, July and August anyway. I'm planning to do Botswana and the Seychelles in the fall."

"Sounds good!" Matt looked around, didn't see anyone he felt he needed to touch base with, and then added, "I think I'll go down a level and see who's around."

David thought that was a good idea and joined him. One deck below, several large groups had gathered, the most substantial of which was near the bar. There David found many of the analysts with whom he'd already spoken so he opted to go down another level, to the deck where the fortune-teller, the magician and other entertainers were working. The fortune-teller, he could see, was doing a reading for Laura Payden. The background music here was louder, forcing almost everyone to yell.

"You will make *II*," David shouted when Laura saw him.

Laura laughed. "She didn't say that, David."

"Just wait. Your reading isn't over yet."

"What's her batting average, by the way?"

"If she says you'll make it, it's very high. If not, I've never seen her before."

Farther down the deck, a magician was doing a trick with three soft, red balls. He juggled them, made various balls disappear and reappear, and was starting to incorporate them into a more elaborate trick including three much larger blue and yellow balls when David came near. In the crowd watching the magician were Phil Suprano, Ron Vargo, Alan Gildersleeve, Carl, John Henriksen and Liz Tytus. All the guys were dressed similarly... blue or red polo shirts and khakis. Carl had a blue, pinstriped dress shirt on and a lightweight blue blazer in addition to the khakis. Liz looked startlingly different. She wore a very short and sheer white dress that wrapped around her and tied on the side. She also looked very tan, much more so than the boys on both sides of her.

The magician juggled again, and then took one of the small red balls and handed it to Liz. "Take this," he told her, "and squeeze it gently in your right hand."

Liz grabbed the red ball with her right hand, looked down at it and then looked up at the five men surrounding her. "Why do people always assume I'd be good at this?" she asked them, squeezing the ball suggestively and winking.

"Now put the red ball in the palm of my hand," the magician instructed, extending his left arm.

Liz did as she'd been asked. The magician then wrapped his fingers around the red ball, waved his magic wand high in the air with his right hand, tapped his hand with the wand and unwrapped his·fingers to reveal two blue balls and a yellow one.

"Not bad," said Alan.

"Wow!" was all Phil could muster.

"That's amazing!" Liz seemed most impressed.

"I know how he did it" Carl yelled to her.

"Really? How?"

Carl whispered in her ear.

Liz shook her head. "Again?"

Carl spoke slightly louder, but Liz indicated that she still couldn't hear. He straightened up, waved a finger towards himself and then walked 10 steps farther down the deck into a narrow corridor connecting one side of the ship with the other. Carl took several steps down the corridor, which was empty but well lit and quieter, and turned back to face Liz, who had followed him.

"He obviously has the blues and yellows in his right hand," Carl told her, having no idea what he was talking about.

"I didn't see them. Are you sure?"

"Oh yeah, he had them, and when you put the red

one in his left hand, he got ready to make the switch. But he needed something to distract you with first, which is why he brought out the magic wand. Once he started waving the wand, everyone started watching the wand, and while we were watching it he made the trade."

"Doesn't sound right to me," Liz said. "I didn't see his two hands get close enough to let him move the red ball out and the blues and yellow in."

"But that's exactly what he did. I used to do magic, you know. I didn't do that exact trick but I did one that was very similar to it and that's just how it worked. It's all about distracting you, getting you to look away from his hands."

"But when did he put the blues and yellows in his right…?"

Before she could finish asking, Carl was all over her. He pushed her hard up against one wall of the corridor, clamped his lips on her mouth and stuck his tongue down her throat. Liz fought back instantly, much faster, Carl realized, than Maryanne Miles had, but Liz was smaller than Maryanne, and not as strong. With his right hand, Carl started trying to loosen the tie that secured Liz's dress on the side, but Liz squirmed and made it hard for him to maintain a grip on it so he reached, instead, for her left breast. Still, Liz squirmed and frustrated him.

While his hands kept missing, his tongue remained firmly planted inside Liz's mouth, and his lips moved up and down, side to side, exerting great pressure. What had lasted only seconds seemed endless to Liz. And then, just as quickly as he'd been on top of her, Carl was off her, looking with great concern down the corridor.

No one.

Carl looked back at Liz, who appeared shaken but was still fully clothed, quickly mouthed the words "Never happened," and walked to the end of the corridor, out the door and up two flights of stairs to the top deck.

* * *

The following morning, as all the analysts except Liz Tytus were recounting what a great time they'd had on the cruise, Joan Atwell called David. "Mr. Mennymore asked if you could come see him for a moment."

Mr. Mennymore, David thought. Just imagine Lisa calling people up and saying "Mr. Meadows would like to see you." It was so ridiculous, so pompous, so "Banking."

"I'll be right there."

The drill was always the same. David was asked to come right away, he was asked on arrival to wait in "Mr. Mennymore's conference room" adjoining Mr. Mennymore's office, and then, once David had cooled his jets for 10 or 15 minutes, the great one would appear.

Twelve minutes after David had settled in, Tom walked briskly into his conference room.

"Nice cruise last night."

David nodded.

"Good stuff. We should do more of that, but on a *real* ship."

David nodded again.

"So, here's the deal, David. There's an auto analyst at SG Cowen named Tim Parish and you're going to hire him."

David squinted.

"I need you to meet the guy, size him up, stroke him a lot, make him a big offer and get him the Hell over here pronto. I know someone who can introduce you to him."

"I don't need to be introduced to him, Tom. I've already met him."

"Great, so we can skip the getting-to-know-you bullshit."

"He's not interested. I tried to recruit him and he never returned any of my calls, or the headhunter's, after we'd had breakfast together."

"None of this matters. This isn't rocket science, David, it's all prostitution. You agree on the act and then on the price. The act is this: Tim Parish joins us to do autos and Mitch Potvan goes bye-bye. And the price is whatever it takes to make that happen."

"He doesn't seem to want that to happen."

"David, David, David… everyone has a number at which he changes from not wanting to wanting. How much do you think Tim is making?"

"I have no idea. Say he's making two and a half."

"So four or five might or might not do it, but six would."

"Six million for an auto analyst?"

"If that's his number."

"He's a Runner-Up. He isn't even top three!"

"He's what we need, David."

"Why?"

"Why? Because, and you breathe not a word of this to anyone, DaimlerChrysler is going to spin out Mercedes-Benz. I swear the guys running Daimler are geniuses. It's going to be a humongous deal, it's going to be oversubscribed a hundred to one, and right now, we're not going to get one cent of it because Mitch Potvan sucks."

"But…"

"Ahhhhhhhhh… you knew there'd be a but."

David smiled.

"But DaimlerChrylser loves Tim Parish. I mean they *love* the guy. And what they've told us, loud and clear, is that if we have Tim Parish on our payroll, we can be a co-lead manager on the offering."

"Cowen has Tim but Cowen won't be a co-lead manager?"

"Correct."

"And why do you think we're the only firm that has been told about this?"

"I didn't say that we are, David, which is exactly why you have to work fast."

"How much would we make if we co-lead managed the Mercedes IPO?"

"Conservatively? Twenty."

"As in million."

"No, as in $20."

"So we can afford to pay Tim a lot if we're sure we'll get the mandate."

"Duh."

"Did you run this past Carl and Dieter?"

"No, but I ran it past Vilhelm, who, as you might have guessed, wet himself."

"Do Carl and Dieter know?"

"I'll tell them. But they worked for Vilhelm the last time I checked."

"So as far as you're concerned, we're approved to do this."

"You're approved."

"Okay, let's give Mr. I-Won't-Call-You-Back another shot."

When he returned to his office, David checked with Carl and Dieter. Neither was aware of the proposed transaction, and both said they'd check and call David back. Dieter did. "Approved, David. Good luck."

* * *

From outside the Barnes & Noble on Broadway and 66th Street, Alexander Volkov placed the call that Nick had been dreading. "Is Nick there?" he asked.

Linda, in the middle of finalizing her plans for the July 4 weekend, mumbled instinctively, "May I say who's calling?"

"Gary from the JZ office."

"Please hold."

A long minute later, Nick picked him up. "Denisovich."

"Hi Nick, this is Gary from the JZ office. How yuh doing?"

"Fine Gary, fine. Yourself?"

"I'm good. Listen, I know you're busy, but my client wants to buy something in your group. Could you tell me what you're recommending?"

"Sure, sure, but I'll have to be quick." Nick knew that Volkov wouldn't say anything but he paused anyway.

"We're still pretty unenthusiastic about most of the gold stocks. We think bullion prices will average around $325 an ounce this year and $335 next year. Demand will be pretty stable, although weakness in some overseas economies may hurt demand from the jewelry industry for several more quarters. Supplies are plentiful, inflation on a global basis is low and interest rates are low, so fundamentals overall are not the kind that would push gold prices, and therefore gold stocks, sharply higher.

"The wild card in all of this, obviously, is an exogenous event like September 11th. Anything that would make the world unusually nervous such as a major terrorist attack on the United States or one of its allies could push gold prices higher near term and, as gold prices move, so will the gold stocks but, since you can't predict those events, I can't make recommendations on that basis so I'm still focusing on the fundamentals and they're still pretty lame.

"Everyone is going to watch Barrick, obviously, now that it's acquired Homestake, but I still have a Hold on it because I don't see much earnings growth this year, and Newmont is somewhat of a question mark following its acquisition of Franco-Nevada. I've got a Hold on it as well. I guess what I'm saying is that, unless gold prices move up sharply or some new Nevada mines come on stream, I wouldn't put any new money to work in this group right now."

"Okay, Nick. I'll look for something else. Thanks."

"My pleasure."

After hanging up, Nick took out his Palm Pilot and wrote "Holiday Weekend" in his calendar exactly six weeks later.

That evening, at 6:00 p.m. New York time, Volkov dialed Moscow.

After several long pauses, a lot of clicking and more static than usual, Piotr picked up.

"Is Stanislav there?"

"No Stanislav," Piotr told him.

Volkov hung up.

Piotr sighed, long and slowly. This well is getting dry, he thought. He got up slowly, walked next door to Anna's office and asked her to guess what Nick had fed them.

"Short Stillwater."

Piotr shook his head.

"Short Teck Cominco."

More head-shaking.

Anna looked befuddled. "Buy Newmont. I don't know. What?"

"Buy *New* Nevada."

"Jesus, darling, it's so thin. Is that all he could come up with?"

"So it seems."

"Well, we've got six weeks," said Anna. "Let's get to work."

* * *

On the morning of June 29, Ron Vargo went to the Morning Meeting. When Paula called on him, he made a short, sweet, 120–second presentation on Milbanks Media in which he raised his earnings estimate for the year by $0.05, raised his long-term growth forecast for the company from 11% to 13% and raised his target price on the shares from $55 to $62. "With the stock having closed last night at $48.50," he told the sales force, "my new target price changes the upside potential in MM over the next year from about 15% to more than 25%, and that's why I'm raising my rating from Accumulate to Buy."

Throughout the day, Ron worked Retail as hard as he could, starting with Paul Pitcher and the Equity Desk people and continuing with phone calls to individual brokers and two conference calls requested by branch managers.

That afternoon, Milbanks closed up $0.90, at $49.40.

And the following afternoon, on June 30, it closed up $0.70 more, at $50.10.

JULY

With *II's* job-hoppers' deadline only six weeks away, David met once more with his six headhunters, this time telephonically.

"Thanks for shuffling things everybody so I don't have to do this six times," he began. "When we last met as a group, we identified six searches that looked promising and I need to know where each of them now stands. Larry, two were yours, I think."

"Correct. In gaming and lodging, I'd indicated that Gregory Lent of CSFB was our only ranked candidate. Since then he's professed not to be interested, but I'll give him one more chance today and, if he hesitates at all, I'll scratch him and say we struck out. In leisure, I've kept Katherine Lillard at Merrill Lynch warm but, as I indicated before, she's a well-below-average analyst and would almost certainly be viewed as a questionable hire. I can turn the heat up on her if you feel we have to, but not enthusiastically."

"I do, Larry. I know you've got your standards, and I have mine, but we should at least look her over closely before eliminating her. Richard, how about food?"

"Don Pinkel at UBS Warburg has been a real pain in the ass to deal with. He told me when I first called him that he was not under contract but, when I asked him to say that in writing before we went any further with him, he balked. I'm convinced that he's lying, and I've back-burnered him for now." Richard paused. "What about Jaine?"

David pursed his lips. "I put my best selling hat on for her, and she listened, but I just couldn't get her in the door. Smith Barney gave her the chance to trade specialty chemicals for food, which was a longstanding dream of hers, and she's loyal because of that. Frankly, while I'd love to have her, I'm also strongly inclined to respect analysts who are loyal. She should only come if she sees good reasons, and she doesn't."

"Agreed. So I'll give Don Pinkel one last try."

"Good. Bob?"

"David, in brokers and asset managers, Anne Reiss at Deutsche Bank said she could be interested but only after *II* season was over."

"She's the one who had the two babies in two years?"

"Correct."

"So, now that *II* season is over, have we reapproached her?"

"Not yet, David. She said to call her in July so I'll call her today."

"Good. Les? Contract manufacturing?"

"David, the candidate I'd mentioned at our last meeting was Tom Brinkley at CSFB. He still could be a candidate but he's slowed things way down with me recently because he's going through a fairly messy divorce and child custody battle, and it's just kept him from finding the time to interview."

"Scratch him."

"Scratch him?"

"Scratch him. Analysts who are about to start, are in the middle of, or are just done with messy divorces

463

have been bad bets for me in the past. They may be well-intentioned and they may give it their all, but they're so emotionally spent from all that stuff that they just don't have what it takes to compete. I'd be exactly the same way if it happened to me so I'm not being callous about it. All I'm saying is that this job is tough enough when you aren't getting yelled at and threatened by hostile spouses and their lawyers all day long. Purely from a business standpoint, these have almost always been bad hires for me. I won't make any more of them."

"Understood. I'll take care of it."

"Thanks, Les. Who did I miss... Julia? Your wire-line equipment search?"

"David, the candidate we've been focusing on is Grace Flagler at Pru, who's a Runner-Up in wireline equipment and who wasn't interested in talking until we also put networking on the table. We set her up three times to meet with you but she postponed all three times."

"I remember that."

"First she had to go out of town to see institutional clients. Then she had a relative in the hospital and couldn't take time off to interview."

"And the third time?"

"The third time she actually came out and said that Pru was contemplating giving her networking and that she didn't want to risk getting caught interviewing just before it gave in to her wishes."

"That may explain the first two cancellations too."

"I'm sure it did. It would've been nice if she could have been straight with us but she wasn't."

"So what happened?"

"I don't know. As of a week ago, Pru was still did-dling around with her and she was getting pretty impatient so my guess is that she'll push them to make a decision soon and, depending on what it is, we'll either have a candidate or we won't."

"I doubt she's a candidate, Julia."

"Why?"

"Because they're going to give her the group. They're not going to be able to hire a ranked networking analyst, they don't have all that many All Stars to begin with, and they're not going to piss her off by putting a no- name in the networking slot."

"You may be right. I'll keep checking and let you know when I hear something."

"Okay, so, just to review. Larry, you've placed Christopher Chadwick and you're working on Gregory Lent and Katherine Lillard. Richard, you've placed Liz Tytus and you're working on Don Pinkel. Les, you've placed Daniel Roe and you'll scratch Tom Brinkley. Bob, you've placed Vivian Zimm and you're working on Anne Reiss. Julia, you've placed Marsha Yamamoto and you're working on Grace Flagler. And you, Dave Hart, having placed Van Trudell and Tom Batchelder, can take the summer off. Correct?

"Correct."

"Dave and Les, don't get too mellow because, obviously, we're all going to tee up to do this all over again starting in the fall, so be ready for Round 2 in September."

"Will do," Dave Hart said.

"Thanks for your business, David," said Les Carter.

"Good job so far, everybody. But, I want the four of you who're still working on searches to remember one thing...we hire them before the job-hoppers' deadline or we don't hire them at all."

* * *

As soon as he'd ended his conference call, David called Larry Fraser. "I have to tell you something but I didn't want to do it on the conference call."

"Yes?"

"I'm going to try to hire Tim Parish again."

"Did he ever return anyone's calls?"

"No."

"So why are you trying again?"

"Because the bankers want me to," said David, careful to provide no specifics.

"Do you want my help?"

"No. Thanks. I'm going to go straight at him, hard, and either get him or be able to demonstrate that we pulled out all the stops and failed."

"Understood."

"But I want you to know that, if he starts to nibble, I'm going to get you back into the fray in some way so I can get you paid."

"That's not necessary, David."

"Yes it is. You do a lot of work that you never get paid for. In this case, you did work, you'll do more work and, if we're lucky enough to get him, you'll get paid for it."

"Entirely up to you."

"I know, and that's how we'll do it."

"Fingers and toes crossed," Larry said.

"And eyes."

* * *

As David hung his phone up, James Hovanian heard his phone ring. He checked Caller ID, recognized the number and picked up.

"Hovanian."

"James, it's John Gantt." John was CEO, chief investment officer and chief portfolio manager at Gantt Capital Management, a firm he'd founded four years earlier following successful stints as an analyst and portfolio manager at Strong Capital Management in Wisconsin and Rocker Partners in New York.

"Hi, how are you?"

"I'm fucking rip shit, how are you?"

James knew why.

"Tell me you didn't do it."

"Do what?"

"Didn't downgrade CWCC this morning." CWCC was the ticker symbol for California Wapher Corp., a small manufacturer of semiconductor capital equipment.

"I'm guilty as charged."

"What are you, James, brain dead? The stock's down 25% in two hours!"

"I know, John, I know. I never intended for that to happen, but the stock got to 37, my target price had been 35 for a long time, I just couldn't justify raising it, I dragged my feet last week because I know how clients hate it when you downgrade just before the quarter ends and hurt their performance, and did it today instead."

"Thirty-five, thirty-seven, who gives a shit? Do you know what the beta on CWCC is?"

"It's very high."

"Bet your ass it is, so do you know what that means when you cut your rating?"

"That I'm probably going to push the stock down a lot."

"Sure as shit. And guess what, Mr. Know-It-All? The stock's now trading... God I could puke...at 28, down 9, so that target price of yours is now 25% away."

James said nothing.

"I think you should get back on the horn and tell the sales force that you're going back to a Buy on CWCC because it's now got 25% upside potential to your target price."

"I can't do that, John."

"Why not?"

"Technically, you're right. If it was a Hold at 37, it's a Buy at 28, but I can't flip ratings back and forth the same day. It would look really bad. So I'm going to have to keep the Hold on it for a while and, if the stock stays down in the high twenties, go back to a Buy, or at least go to an Accumulate, after the smoke clears."

"You're killing me, James, and I don't even think you've done your homework."

Again, James was silent.

"Well, kill me, kill you. You know that *II* ballot that's sitting on my desk here? The one that was due back two weeks ago and that I was going to FedEx today? Well, let me tell you something about that ballot, James. It's going FedEx today all right, but it's going with your name whited out, and I hope to Hell you finish one vote short of making the team this year because, let me tell you…you're the *last* sell-sider who deserves to be an All Star."

* * *

"He's still not interested," Larry Fraser told David. "He won't even agree to have breakfast with you."

"What can you do? He's happy where he is so we should leave him alone."

"Sorry."

"Me too. Any word on Katherine?"

"I'm having breakfast with her tomorrow. I'll call you right after."

"Thanks, Larry."

David hung up slowly, pulled the notebook out of his bottom drawer, opened it, and crossed off Gregory Lent's name. Gaming and lodging would remain uncovered. More importantly, this cut the maximum number of new All Stars that David could hire this year before the job-hoppers' deadline to 12 from 13.

I had five to start with, he recalled, I've hired seven and I've got five more that are still in the works: Katherine Lillard who stinks, Don Pinkel who says he doesn't have a contract but probably does, Anne Reiss who's now researching for five hours a day and breast feeding for 10, Grace Flagler who's going to play me off against Prudential for the networking stocks, and Tim Parish who doesn't return calls.

If I hire all five of them, that would get me to 17 All Stars, to a ranking of number ten, and to a pay day of $4,500,000, and if three of my existing analysts who got close last year but didn't make it actually made it this year, I'd have 20 All Stars, up from 5 last year, finish in a tie with Deutsche Bank and UBS for number eight and qualify for $6,000,000 in comp.

That would be great! David thought. But it was also unlikely. He wasn't going to get all five analysts who were still in contention, there was no guarantee that all 12 analysts who were now on the payroll and who had made *II* last year would make it this year, and it wasn't even safe to assume that three exiting analysts would make *II* for the first time. Just as important, Bernstein, Prudential, J.P. Morgan, Deutsche Bank and UBS weren't going to just sit around knitting while he was out recruiting so aggressively. They could hire and/or grow ranked analysts of their own and make themselves even tougher to pass.

I took Liz Tytus and Van Trudell from Prudential, he figured, and Daniel Roe from UBS. That's good. But if I can snatch Don Pinkel from UBS, Anne Reiss from Deutsche Bank, and Grace Flagler from Pru, I'll not only have gained six All Stars but they'll have *lost* six, and that would be even better.

* * *

It took David four phone calls to reach Tim Parish.

"I'm so embarrassed, David," Tim said.

"Why, because you dropped us like a hot potato?"

"I handled the situation very badly."

"As you can tell, there aren't any hard feelings on our end."

"You're very kind, David. I should've had the maturity and the decency to just tell you or Larry that I simply didn't want to pursue the opportunity, and that speaking with you had made me feel sneaky and disloyal, but I didn't."

"Testing the marketplace from time to time is something most analysts do to reassure themselves that they're being paid fairly or to find out that they're not."

"You know David, on paper, I understand all of this. It's rational and logical, but it also left me feeling dirty afterwards and, even though it may have all been in my head, it made me want to forget it had happened which is why I didn't return the calls. You and Larry are very good salesmen and I didn't want to be pressured into meeting with you again or seeing your people. I'm happy at Cowen and I want to stay put."

David's mind raced. "I didn't scare you off by mentioning auto parts, did I?"

"Not at all. That actually intrigued me, as did the idea of doing more investment banking. But despite that, I just came away from breakfast feeling bad, wanting to stay put and not wanting to subject myself to a hard sell from BCS."

"All right, how about this. I'd like to have one final conversation with you. Just the two of us, some place quiet, no Powerpoint presentation, no handouts and no pressure. Just 15 quiet minutes. I'll tell you my idea and then go away. You can reject it on the spot or simply agree to chew it over. I'll respect your decision, whatever it is."

There was a very long pause at the other end of the phone. Then, David heard Tim Parish sigh. "If I didn't like your style so much, David, this would be a lot easier."

David was silent.

"Are you going away for the weekend?" Tim asked, referring to July 4.

"Hopefully after we meet."

"How about a 15–minute drink tonight at Atlas."

"On Central Park South?"

"That's the one."

"What time?"

"Before it gets crowded. Six?"

"Perfect. I'll see you there." David measured each word, keeping his voice very low and soothing.

"Ciao, David."

"Ciao, Tim."

* * *

Tim was already seated at the bar when David arrived at 5:50 p.m. He greeted David warmly and waved for him to grab an empty stool.

"Are *you* going away for the weekend?" David asked.

"No, with so many people away, I'm going to stay in the city and do a little museum-hopping."

"Are there going to be any fireworks in the city?"

"Probably, but I have no idea where. I'm not big on fireworks...or crowds."

David nodded.

"And you'll be in Southampton?"

"Yup. I can't wait." David ordered red wine, as Tim had. As soon as it arrived, he leaned in towards Tim a little bit, dropped his voice slightly and began pitching.

"Tim, here's why I wanted to speak with you again. I've been updating senior management over the past few months about all the recruiting I've been doing." Tim nodded. "I told them, of course, that you'd passed on us."

"I hope senior management isn't 50 people, David."

"It's five, and they keep secrets well." Tim seemed relieved. "Anyway, initially, they accepted the news, with disappointment, and didn't talk any more about it. But a week ago, I was asked to repeat your situation for them and, when I was done, I was asked to move whatever mountains were necessary to change your mind."

"Why?"

"Because we've gotten very close to DaimlerChrysler and they've told us that they'd like to give us banking business but they can't if Mitch Potvan covers them.

They don't see Mitch as a first-tier analyst and I hate to say it but they're right."

"Did they say what kind of banking business?"

David knew he couldn't tip his hand to Tim and that, if Tim knew about the Mercedes-Benz IPO, he shouldn't either. "No, they simply said that they're so big and so global that there's always something to do and that, if we want some of those mandates we need you on board. They spoke glowingly about you, not surprisingly."

"They're very good guys. They told me once that my research was as good as Girsky's and that the two of us were head and shoulders above everyone else."

"That's a terrific compliment."

"It is."

"So, here's the bottom line," David said, looking at his watch and pretending he was panicking because his 15 minutes were almost up. "I don't know how much you're making now, but you would be much more valuable to BCS than you can be to Cowen because of the differences in our business models. We do much more business institutionally, we have 5,000 retail brokers who can do millions of shares of business in your stocks, and we have bankers who are working closely with some of your companies, including one in particular, and are convinced that there are substantial transactions we can do with them in the years ahead if you're part of the team."

"This is a little embarrassing, David."

"No it's not, it's just the way it is. If you were the nicest guy in the world but you couldn't help us do more business I'd tell you that. You happen to be a very nice guy *and* our ticket to some serious incremental revenues and earnings. If I told you anything else I'd be lying and I won't do that. So where does that bring us? I want you to come join us. You can do autos or you can do autos and parts. We'll provide you with as many associates and research assistants as you need, and with a two-year contract totaling $12 million…"

Tim stopped sipping.

"…that's structured however you'd like. If you want $8 million this year and $4 million next, fine. If you want $3 million as a signing bonus and $4.5 million at each year-end, fine. All you'll have to do is commit to stay for the full two years."

Tim was shaking his head slowly from side to side. "I don't understand this, David. I'm making $2.4 million now and I think I'm fairly paid, but you want to between double and triple my compensation after having had one breakfast with me…"

"…and after hearing from senior managers in the industry you cover that you're as good as they come."

"Analysts should cost less than the earnings they generate for their firms."

"I agree."

"Not less than the revenues they generate… less than the earnings."

"That's right. You should be a profitable investment for the firm."

"I'm pretty sure that I am, at Cowen, at $2.4 million, but I'm just as sure that I'd be a big money loser at $6 million a year at BCS."

"You might be but you probably wouldn't be. Here's why. If you're worth $2.4 million to Cowen, which has a solid institutional business and a small banking effort, principally in health care and technology, but no retail at all, you're worth $3 million to BCS plus your value to us on DaimlerChrysler. Our bet is that DaimlerChrysler could be worth at least

474

$3 million to us, annually, which is how we got to $12 million."

"I think that's a risky assumption."

"Look, Tim, we want to take the chance. If we're wrong, maybe we break even on you. If we're very wrong, we might lose some money. But we're no fools. We think our worst case is breakeven, our expected case is that you're profitable and the best case is that you make the firm oodles of money."

"What happens in year three?"

"In year three we take stock of what happened in the first two years. If $6 million turned out to be the right number we extend the contract at the same rate. If it was too high we agree to some lower number that's fair to everyone. And if we've done lots of deals because of you we extend at a higher number "

Tim still seemed unconvinced.

"Keep something in mind, Tim. We're taking a chance on you but you're also taking a chance on us. We're guaranteeing you $6 million a year including banking. If we do no deals you get paid too much, but if we do a ton of deals and you'd normally qualify for more than $6 million we're only obligated to pay you that much. The guarantee could be too high but it could also be too low." Tim nodded.

David looked at his watch again, "Okay, my time's up. You've gotten all the selling you're going to get. I'm asking nothing of you but to think about it, talk with your family about it, talk to some clients whom you're close to, and talk with the managements of some of your companies about it, especially the guys at DaimlerChrysler. I hope, and I believe, that they'll encourage you to do this, and I hope you'll respect their opinions enough to weigh them heavily as you decide what to do."

"How quickly do you need an answer, David?"

"We both need closure on this soon, Tim, but I'm not going to pressure you with a deadline. Think it through, talk to others and call me when you're done. You won't hear from me again. The next call will be the one you place to me with your answer."

* * *

Driving down Daniels Lane in Sagaponack you could hear the boom of rock music. It grew louder as you approached Peters Pond and softer as you passed it. Down Peters Pond, a block and a half from the ocean, 27 people sat around Ken Lavery's 50–foot gunite pool, behind his 8,000–square-foot, English-style traditional, listening to Linkin Park and P.O.D., eating hors d'oeuvres from Citarella, drinking St. Emilion and martinis, and congratulating Ken on his newest acquisition. From time to time, some of them would return to the house to use one of Ken's 10 bathrooms and powder rooms.

As the sun ambled towards the western horizon, Ken closed his eyes, listened to bits of conversations around him, and smelled the salt in the air. He dangled his bare feet over the side of the pool and looked around at his guests. Nearest to him were Paula Hainsworth, Barbara Malek from institutional sales, Ken's investment banker Peter Paul Rushing who had a house of his own in Southampton, Paul Pitcher, and two young traders who handled some of Ken's OTC stocks. At the other end of the pool, somewhat unto themselves, sat Matt Burlingame, Will Rivas, and drug analyst Michael Mellman. The rest of the crowd comprised spouses, significant others, friends, friends of friends, and Heydi Laing, a model-material girlfriend whom Ken had picked up at Rowdy Hall in East Hampton the weekend he'd been out house-hunting with Kim Hovey.

Heydi leaned down towards Ken ear. "We should go soon."

"Are you sure? The fireworks won't start until an hour after sunset, according to the *East Hampton Star*."

"I know, but driving to Main Beach will get very hard as we get closer to sunset. The police block off most of the roads to the beach and it gets very bottle-necked."

"You're the boss," Ken sighed. "What do I know about East Hampton fireworks?"

"Then tell them."

Ken stood up and waved for a minute to get his guests' attention. "Crawling in my skin, these wounds they will not heal…," Linkin Park blared around him.

"Everybody? Everybody? If you want to see the fireworks on Main Beach we have to leave soon."

"How many cars are we taking?" Matt Burlingame asked.

"I don't know. I'll take Heydi in the Bentley. The rest of you should partner up."

"I can take eight in the Explorer," Paula volunteered.

"Good. Six cars should do it. Heydi will guide me since I have no idea how to get to Main Beach. The rest of you should follow me. I've got blankets in the trunk."

All of Ken's guests were on their feet, rolling down pants legs or slipping on shoes.

"If you get lost, Heydi says you have to turn right when you get to the pond in East Hampton. You'll have to go left or right there. Go right."

"What are we doing after the fireworks?" Paul Pitcher asked.

"Nick and Toni's?"

"Couldn't get in," Ken sighed.

"Della Femina?"

"Couldn't get in."

"The Laundry?"

"Couldn't get in."

"McDonald's?"

"Don't be an ass."

"Lobsters at Gosman's," Heydi answered, "and then a skinny dip, if you're game."

* * *

Over breakfast, David asked Katherine Lillard to tell him about herself.

"Well, I've been at Merrill Lynch for three years and it's been a pretty good experience for me. It's a very competitive place, you know, and sometimes it's a little difficult getting the sales force's attention or getting on the Morning Call or getting to go out and see clients."

"What does your universe look like?"

"It's very varied... cruise ship companies like Carnival and Royal Caribbean, outdoor venues like Six Flags, International Speedway and Speedway Motorsports, Callaway Golf, Harley-Davidson, winter sports companies like K2 and Polaris, toy companies like Hasbro and Mattel, plus Bally Total Fitness, Huffy and Brunswick."

"How do you follow companies with such different products and customers?"

"It's not easy, but to some extent, these companies are all impacted by the strength of the economy, consumer confidence and consumer spending. Sometimes, consumers will cut back on the larger, more discretionary items like a cruise in favor of smaller-ticket items like toys and, if you can anticipate that shift, you can make money in Hasbro and Mattel. Sometimes, it snows very hard early in the season and, if you're quick, you can catch K2 and Polaris before they move. And then there are companies like Harley-Davidson that always seem to do well."

"She's not so terrible," David thought to himself. "What's your favorite stock?"

"Harley-Davidson."

"Why?"

"Because demand for its motorcycles is strong, shipments are continuing to rise rapidly even in a tough economy, and more and more of its bikes are higher-margined custom bikes which is pushing earnings up even faster than sales. We're estimating $2.10 share for 2003."

David thought she was fine. "Where's the *First Call* consensus on Harley?"

"I'm not sure. I think it's around $2.10.

"You don't know?"

"I don't really look at that."

"Wouldn't you want to know where you stand relative to other analysts so, if you were far above or below them you could ask yourself why, and if you wound up being right and the consensus wrong you could anticipate which way the stock might move?"

"I don't really pay much attention to what my competitors are saying. I just do my own research."

Not so good, but David let it slide. "What do you have Harley rated?"

"It's a Buy."

"Where is it selling and what's your target price?"

"It's around 45 and my target price is 52."

"Is that enough to justify a Buy?"

"It's 15% which is enough at Merrill."

"How did you get to 52?"

"Well, the stock is selling at 45, and they earned $1.80 last year, so it's selling at 25 times last year's earnings. If it continues to trade at 25 times, and they earn $2.10 this year, the stock would move to 52."

"What's the right P/E for the stock?"

"What do you mean?"

"What's the P/E at which the stock *should* sell?"

"I don't do it that way. I just assume that the P/E will remain constant and that the stock will increase in line with earnings growth."

David was amazed. "How fast did earnings grow in 2002?"

"Let's see... they earned $1.80, up from $1.43, so about 25%."

"And over the past three years?"

"The same, between 25% and 30% per year."

"And this year you're estimating 17% growth."

"That's right."

"And over the next three to five years?"

"I'd say... 15%."

"So growth is slowing from 25% to 30% a year to barely 15% but you're assuming that, simply because the stock is now trading at 25 times earnings, it will continue to?"

"I don't think the P/E can expand any more because earnings growth is slowing."

"But you aren't factoring in the possibility that the P/E might decline."

"No, I have no evidence suggesting that will happen."

"What if your forecast was for earnings to *decline* 15% this year?"

"Then I'd assume the stock would go down 15% too."

"So the P/E would stay the same, whether earnings were up 15% or down 15%."

"That's right."

"What if you thought the long-term growth rate was 2% instead of 15%?"

"Then I might estimate earnings growth of 2% for this year instead of 15%."

"And your target price and rating?"

"My target price would become 47, and the stock would be a Hold."

"So Harley, now a 2% grower, would still sell at 25 times earnings."

"David, if you're asking me if I'd pick a different P/E out of thin air, I wouldn't."

David measured his words and lowered his voice. "I guess what I'm trying to understand, Katherine, is why you wouldn't try to analyze what 2% growth stocks *deserve* to sell for and use whatever your analysis concluded, rather than using the multiple of last year's earnings at which Harley was selling."

"I can't tell you, David. It's just not the way I do things."

David nodded, indicating that he understood, although he didn't.

"It's a system that has served me well, you know. I'm sure I wouldn't be *II*-ranked if it wasn't a good system."

David shifted gears, asking her about how she allocated her time between researching, writing, talking to and visiting clients, and working on investment banking. He also encouraged her to ask him questions about life inside of BCS.

Twenty minutes later, weary and disappointed, he said, "Tell me what you wish Merrill Lynch did differently."

"I wish I could see more clients, I wish it was easier to get on the Morning Call, I wish the sales force paid more attention to me, I wish I wasn't pressured sometimes to pick up tiny little leisure companies with bad records, and I wish I was paid fairly."

"How much are you making now?"

"I made $2,500,000 last year."

"And you think that's below the market?"

"Yes. I know leisure isn't technology but I hear that there are other analysts in the department who are making twice what I'm making and I know they're no better than I am."

"You've discussed this with your bosses?"

"Yes and they told me they thought that, given my age, my group, my ranking in *II*, my standing in the department and the amount of banking I do, I'm fairly paid."

"Well, we've got a travel schedule that will get you in front of all of your clients at least once a year, we have a Morning Call that's easy to book time on, we let the analysts veto proposed banking transactions that they don't like, we don't force analysts to pick up small companies with bad records just to please the bankers, and I'm sure we could put something together for you, financially, that you'd find attractive."

"That sounds pretty good."

"Would you like to come in and meet some people?"

"I guess so."

"Good. I'll ask Larry to get some dates from you and we'll get you in ASAP."

Katherine nodded. "David, I'm assuming I'd come in as a managing director"

"That's a safe assumption."

"And managing directors fly first class?"

"Not everywhere, just on long domestic flights."

"What about overseas?"

David sighed silently. "Business class, which no one complains about."

"I'd like to fly first class everywhere."

"Then we'll have to pay you enough so you can afford to buy upgrade stickers because firm policy is firm policy."

"Do managing directors have their own dining room?"

"No."

"Do they get to buy or lease cars at the firm's expense?"

"No."

Katherine was silent for a moment. "I'd like to have someone drive me to and from work each day."

"Where do you live?"

"In Greenwich."

David looked at her and made his tongue bleed. "Everyone in the department who works in Greenwich takes the train or drives herself."

"I don't like to drive."

"Maybe we can deal with this after you've come in and seen some people?"

"That would be fine. I just wanted to mention it."

David shook Katherine's hand, said how much he'd enjoyed meeting her and promised to continue the process with her as quickly as possible.

When she was gone, he sat down again, finished

his coffee, and bemoaned his fate. "I've hired good analysts in crappy industries and crappy analysts in good industries," he thought. "Now I can add crappy in crappy." The trend, he had to admit, was disheartening.

* * *

"Are you happy?" Lisa asked when David returned from breakfast.

"What do you mean?"

"With how we did in *The Journal* ?"

"It's out today?" David had found the *New York Times* outside his door that morning but no *Journal*.

"Let me show you." Lisa pulled her copy from the window ledge in her office and handed it to David, who returned to his office, plopped down on the sofa and opened it up. Inside was a special section entitled the "Best on the Street Analysts Survey" which was published each June or July by *The Wall Street Journal*. David remembered the good old days when there had been only two polls to reckon with, *II* and *Greenwich*. Then came *The Journal*, *Fortune*, *Reuters/Tempest* and albeit briefly, *theStreet.com* all with "new and better" ways of assessing who the best analysts on Wall Street were.

The slant that *The Journal* had taken was straightforward enough. Whereas *II* and *Greenwich* sought the opinions of leading institutional investors about the quality of each sell-side analyst's work, *The Journal* opted for pure objectivity. It sought no opinions, just facts about how accurate each analyst's stock recommendations had been during the prior calendar year. *First Call* provided the data and *The Journal* published the scores. For several years, *The Journal* had also measured the accuracy of each analyst's earnings estimates but it scrapped that half of the survey in 2002.

David had major reservations about this poll, principally because it only measured the analysts' accuracy over one calendar year. Just as stopped clocks are right twice each day, a consistently bad stock picker could suddenly have one good year and score well in this poll, while an analyst with a great long-term track record could have an off year and rank not at all. Also, in general, the largest firms had the most All Stars and the smallest firms far fewer; the top-five firms in this survey employed an average of 50 analysts each while the bottom five averaged only 13.

So what did it prove? Absolutely nothing. It was just another visible poll that he needed to review and send out a memo about.

Not surprisingly, *The Journal* said that BCS had six All Stars and ranked fifteenth. David eyeballed the article and identified the BCS analysts who had been named: Steve Kalagian, Rebecca Suess, Donald Ferber, Laura Payden, Matt Burlingame and Will Rivas.

Keith Jackman, Nancy Natolio and Tim Omori, all of whom were *II*-ranked, had failed to make *The Journal's* All Star team and, of the eight analysts, including Robin Lomax, whom David had hired most recently, only Van Trudell had ranked in *The Journal* and he was listed under Prudential where he'd worked during the year being measured. David would make certain to include him in his memo and claim that, in truth, BCS had seven All Stars and had ranked fourteenth.

Every year, and each time a poll like this came out, David resisted at first and then gave in to a daydream in which he managed Research at Merrill or Morgan Stanley, at a firm that never had to spin its number fifteen ranking to make it look like number fourteen.

* * *

When David returned from a Commitment Committee meeting at 11:50 he found a phone message waiting for him from Richard Lipstein.

"So, how did things go with Don Pinkel?" he asked.

"You were right. He has a contract."

"Then why did he say he didn't?"

"He says it's not binding and that it can be easily broken."

"Not by me."

"Should I tell him you want to speak with his lawyer?"

"No because I don't. I'm not in the contract-busting business, Richard."

"So what would you like me to say?"

"Ask him if he expects UBS to honor every promise it ever made to him."

"And when he says yes?"

"Tell him he should do the same."

* * *

"Lame-O, I'm such a Lame-O," the voice on CNBC whined.

"Jesus" David whispered, "let it not be me."

On the Mitsubishi screen, David saw David Faber's face and heard him tell Mark Haines that, yes, he did indeed have another Lame-O award to present. "And this one, Mark, is different, potentially unique in the annals of CNBC."

For a moment, David Meadows' curiosity eclipsed his dread.

"And why would that be?" Mark asked.

"Mark, the story goes like this. The recipient of today's award, and let's allow him to remain nameless for a moment longer, recently changed firms. At his old firm, he'd covered VacationValueLink.com which, as you know, is a young, small knockoff of... what...Travelocity? Priceline? Expedia? You get the idea. It's 'a web-based provider of discount air fares, hotel rooms and the like for value-conscious vacationers.'

"At his old firm, our mystery analyst had rated VacationValueLink a Buy, with a target price of 125."

"What's its 12–month high?" Joe Kernen asked.

"It got as high as 96."

Joe nodded.

"Now if you watched us yesterday," David said to the camera, "and I'm sure you did, you know that VacationValueLink announced its June-quarter results late in the morning... I think it was around 11:30... and that the stock got hammered because they failed to meet expectations. In fact, VVLL finished the day at 11, down 10."

"Did you say 11, down 10?" Joe asked for effect.

"That's right, 11, down 10."

"That's a long way from 125."

"Yes it is," David agreed, "and that may well explain what happened yesterday afternoon at 4:15."

"What was that?" Joe prompted.

"Well, Joe, at 4:15, our mystery analyst resumed coverage of VacationValueLink at his new firm, along with coverage of all the other stocks he covers, and he once again rated the stock a Buy. But what he also did, which earned him this Lame-O, was to write in his report, and I quote, 'Our 12–month price target for VVLL is 15, implying almost 40% upside potential from current levels and fully justifying our Buy rating.'"

"Fifty?" Joe asked.

"Fif-*teen.* No mention, of course, that only weeks earlier, he'd been using 125."

"At least he didn't downgrade it to Hold at $11," Mark said.

"No he didn't, Mark, but any analyst who *adjusts* his target price from 125 to 15 and doesn't say so is lame enough in my book to deserve this award, and so today we honor Daniel Roe, formerly of UBS Warburg and now the newly hired Internet analyst at BC Securities."

Lame-O, I'm such a Lame-O.

"More in store," Mark Haines smirked "after these commercial messages."

* * *

David measured each word carefully. Breakfast with Anne Reiss at Adrienne had been scheduled for 8:30 at Anne's request, at least an hour later than normal, but David had said nothing about it. He'd made sure to do most of the talking early on, running through his canned remarks about how wonderful it was to work at BCS. When it came time to ask Anne questions, he'd made certain to ask none initially of a personal nature.

Anne described the universe of brokers and asset management firms that she covered, the pluses and minuses of being at Deutsche Bank, the way she allocated her time between researching, writing, marketing and banking, and the strengths and weaknesses she saw in Henry McVey of Morgan Stanley, Guy Moszkowski of Salomon, Richard Strauss of Goldman and Joan Solotar of CSFB.

"Henry will be tough to beat, but I'm rid of Amy Butte," she said, referring to one of her strongest former competitors who had left the Sell Side for an inside job at CSFB, "and the others I think are fair game."

"How important is *II* to you?" David asked.

"It's important. If you work hard 365 days a year, it's nice to be able to stop for a second on one of them and enjoy the news that you've made the team. It's an acknowledgment of the effort you've expended and the quality of your work."

David nodded. "Bob Taylor said you kept him at bay until *II* season was over."

"I told Bob that because I really needed to spend eight or ten straight weeks marketing very intensively to my clients. I'd felt that I'd lost some momentum because of the babies, and I really wanted to raise my profile as much as I could."

An opening at last. "The babies?"

"I have two of them. Molly is 20 months old and Shannah is 10 months."

"Wow. Ten months apart?"

"That wasn't the plan, David, it's just how things turned out."

"How are you managing?"

"Better than I'd expected. I have a terrific nanny who lives with us and puts in long Mondays and Fridays and very long Tuesdays through Thursdays."

David was puzzled.

"I work at home every Monday and Friday so I can help her on those days, although I'm unavailable to her a lot of the time because I'm talking to clients or to salespeople or writing reports. I take the babies all weekend so she has those days off."

"So you're in the office only on Tuesdays through Thursdays?"

"That's right, and I'm not typically in until 8:00 or 8:30 and I leave as often as I can between 4:30 and 5:00."

"What about travel? Are you still going out to see clients?"

"I've cut it back a lot and I'm trying not to do any overnights if I can help it. I'll go to Boston for the day, even to Chicago for the day, and then come right back. If I absolutely have to go farther, then I'll do a two-day trip with one overnight but no more. Alan would go nuts if I went away for a week and left him with the babies and the nanny."

"So you've seen your clients less over the past two years than you did before."

"Less, but I don't think it has hurt me all that much. I make a point of talking to them on the phone more because I'm seeing them less, and the important accounts in New York and Boston and Chicago are still seeing me as often as they did before."

"What if you have to travel for banking-related reasons?"

"The bankers know to try not to use me that way if they can avoid it." David wasn't crazy about this setup. "You know, David, after Molly was born, two Novembers ago, I worried about falling off of *II*, but 10 months later, Shannah was born, 11 months later I was still on *II*, and 20 months later I'm sitting here talking to you about how I plan to move *up* in *II* so I'm not worrying about this. A good analyst can do her job anywhere, David, but if this set-up bugs you, don't hire me."

David paused, then back-pedaled a little. "I want to hire you, Anne, but I also want to be sure that, if my sales force doesn't see you 40% of the time, they understand why and they work around it in ways that not only don't hurt you but help you."

"As long as their clients tell them I'm servicing them well, and picking stocks well, I'm sure they'll be as fine about it as Deutsche Bank's sales force is."

"Good. Then let's get you in to meet some people," David suggested.

"I'm all yours, David, any Tuesday, Wednesday or Thursday."

* * *

"Tom, Ken Lavery."

"Ken! How was your 4th?"

"Man, it was smoking. A bunch of people from work were out at the house and they all had a blast."

"You've moved in?"

"I haven't closed yet, but I'm in and I can't tell you how great it is. I should've done it years ago."

"So you're hobnobbing?"

"I'm not going out of my way to see people but I'm seeing people."

"Really! Anyone I'd know?"

"Spielberg and kids, Christie Brinkley, Billy Joel, Howard Stern, Alec Baldwin, Sarah Jessica Parker, Ralph Lauren at Gosman's, even... listen to this... Paul McCartney. They're everywhere."

"Do they all recognize you?"

"They do but they're very cool about it. They look stunned for a second, then they debate about whether to say anything or just pretend they don't know me, and then they always opt to be discreet and respect my privacy."

"Spielberg didn't ask for your autograph?"

"No, and I'm grateful to him for it."

"So, what can I do for you?"

"Look at my account, will you, and tell me what my margin situation is."

Tom had pulled up Ken's account while they'd talked. "It's right in front of me. You've got $4,340,000 of stocks, $2,150,000 of borrowings and equity of $2,190,000."

"Do I have any margin power left now that I used the $1,600,000 on the house?"

"Yes, you could certainly borrow another million if you wanted to. That would put you up around 60% debt and 40% equity. You shouldn't go beyond that because your stocks are volatile and you don't want them to drop one day, pushing your debt over 70% and triggering a margin call."

"So I could borrow $1,000,000 and that would get the portfolio back over $5,300,000 including $3,150,000 of margin debt."

"Correct."

Ken punched up GNOM and GINV. "Okay. I've got 140,000 GNOM. I paid about $7 a share for them and they're now worth $16 each. And I've got 140,000 GINV. I paid about $7.50 a share for those, and they're worth about $15 each."

"Correct."

"So I could buy another 30,000 shares of each with that $1,000,000 margin loan."

"That would run you about $930,000 plus commissions."

"And what would it do to my cost basis?"

"It'd pull you up to $8.60 on the GNOM and $8.80 on the GINV."

"Sounds good. Let's do it."

"Are you approved?" Tom asked.

"No, but I will be in 60 seconds, so wait 120 seconds and, if I don't call you back, you'll know we're good to go."

"Buy 30,000 GINV and 30,000 GNOM as close to the market as possible."

"Bingo."

Sixty seconds later, after having indicated that he had no intention of picking up coverage of either stock any time soon and that he was uninvolved in any investment banking business relating to either company, Ken was approved by Jim Molloy.

And 15 minutes after that he'd lined up a six-branch-office swing through America's heartland.

* * *

On the morning of July 12, barely three weeks after having preannounced $0.08–$0.09 for the June quarter and having revised its full-year guidance downward to $0.33–$0.35, Primo Theaters issued its second-quarter earnings report. The good news was that it had actually earned $0.08 for the quarter. The bad news was that, according to the press release, theater attendance during late June and early July, and especially over the July 4 weekend, had been far below plan "owing to a lack of product with major box office appeal." This had prompted management to scale back new-theater expansion plans by 12% and to cut once again its full-year earnings guidance to $0.28–$0.30.

The stock fell $0.80 to $5.12 a share and Retail began screaming.

"You couldn't cut your rating now even if you wanted to," Barry Seels said.

"If I cut it now the stock would go to 4, maybe lower. Retail would just dump it and we'd get sued for sure."

"They're spooked," Barry said. "They don't like being a public company. Before, if they had a crappy 30 days, they'd worry and try to fix it but they wouldn't see their shares plunge or get calls from brokers screaming to stop fucking up."

"Whose brokers are calling them?"

"Are you kidding? Ours. Dozens of them call Investor Relations every day now. They all say the same thing. They bought the stock at 10, they don't understand how earnings could be disappointing so soon after the IPO, their clients want to kill them and they need some encouraging words to pass on to them. If they don't like what IR tells them they get rude, abusive, even worse."

"Jesus."

"I knew these were marginal guys when I first met them," Barry sighed, but they're handling their first six months as a public company really badly. "They're their own worst enemies."

"When are they going to hit their numbers?"

"I don't know, hopefully this quarter."

"Can we sell them to someone for $10 a share?" Keith asked.

"You mean hostile?"

"No. A friendly deal. Get them private again, get investors their $10 back and limit the risk of lawsuits."

"They don't want to be sold."

"At the rate they're fucking up, they may change their mind."

"We'd never get the mandate if you cut your rating on them, you know."

"Well that's reason number two not to cut it, and two's all I need." Keith looked at Barry. "Let's have dinner tonight and figure out who we can sell this pig to."

* * *

"No word?" Larry Fraser asked.

"None." David had hoped to have heard from Tim Parish by now.

"What are you going to do?"

"Nothing. I told him I wouldn't badger him. I said that the next phone call would have to come from him."

"How long will you wait?"

"Until he decides."

* * *

The fourth time Julia Harris set Grace Flagler up to meet with David, Grace actually showed. David found her disarming. She was young, very self-confident, no-nonsense, tough, competitive, combative and obviously impatient.

"You know, David, it's going to happen. Maybe Pru will come through at the eleventh hour or maybe you'll do it. If not, someone else will. I got ranked in wireline equipment in 24 months. I don't know any-one who's done it faster. My job is my life. I do it 24/7. I do it in my dreams. Isn't that pathetic?

"But I don't need to spend 168 hours a week on wireline equipment. If I do, I'll certainly become

495

number one some time soon, and that would be fine in most people's books. But it would be overkill. When I'm number one, I won't be that much more valuable to my employer, whoever it is, than I am now as number five. I can land deals right now. I'd land more of them at a firm with bankers than I can at Pru, which has none, but I'm being paid as if I'm landing deals there because Pru knows that's the only way it can hold on to me.

"At a bulge-bracket firm I'd be just as valuable right now as I'd be two years from now after I'd toppled Nikos and been crowned Queen of Wireline Equipment. The same, I'm sure, would be true at BCS.

"However, and here's the big "but," I'd be more valuable to almost any firm if I was ranked highly in both wireline equipment *and* networking than simply number one in wireline. More companies to follow, more reasons to go on the Morning Call, more stocks in which to have large market shares on the trading desks, more ways to get votes from institutional clients, more ways to make clients money and, of course, more deals to do.

"Am I thinking only in my employer's best interests? Of course not. But, as you know well, the more valuable you are to your employer, the more your employer pays you if it knows what it's doing. I happen to work right now for people who can't seem to figure this out. They nod as if they understand but then they do nothing about it. They tell me that they're "working on it," whatever the Hell that means, but then months go by and nothing changes.

"So, David, am I interested in joining BCS if I can do wireline and networking? Yes I am. As you seem to realize already, I don't mince words or waste people's time. I'm a product and you're a provider.

The questions are simply, do you want me in your catalog and, if so, do you want the original version or the one with the add-ons that has higher margins. You'll get paid better for the latter, your cost-of-goods-sold will obviously be higher as well, but your bottom line from Product Grace will rise faster than your revenues will.

"I'm available. I've offered Pru its shot and it's failed to take it so it's time to move on. Now it's your chance to shoot. If you're game, get me in, show me the people who need to evaluate me and let them look me over. From my end, I want to see your best institutional salespeople, the head of Institutional Sales and the person who runs your Morning Call, the bankers who cover wireline equipment and networking and I hope to God they're different people, someone senior in Retail, the block trader and a couple of OTC traders who cover those stocks, whoever *your* boss is, and someone senior at BC Holdings so I can ask him about BC's intentions towards BCS. Don't do anything with Kalagian and Ferber. I know both of them. I will set up my own dinners with them and get the unvarnished version of whatever everyone else will tell me. Then I'll decide.

"Let me tell you up front what I'll cost you so that, if this is going to scare you away, it'll scare you right now. I have two associates and a secretary. They make $300,000 among them and I'd want them to make $400,000. I'd need two more associates to do networking. They'd cost $400,000 for two, so that's $800,000. As for me, I'm making $3,000,000 now. You'd pay me $4,500,000 per year for two years, plus a bonus if I make *II* in networking next year and/or the year after."

"How much of a bonus?"

"Three next year and two the year after."

"Why?"

"Because it's going to be much tougher for me to make *II* in networking in nine months than in 21 months so, if I make it faster, I get paid better for having done it."

"So if you double-team in both years you make $14,000,000."

Grace nodded. "That's motivational to me and it's a very good deal for you. It's like hiring me for 17% more than I'm making right now, which you know you'd never get me for, plus hiring a ranked networking analyst right now for $3,500,000. You'd pay *more* than $7,000,000 a year for ranked analysts in both spaces but, since all the money would be going to me, your price gets discounted."

David smiled. She was pretty nervy but she was also right. By either guessing well or having done her homework on David first, Grace had determined what was most important to him and then placed before him the business plan that would help her help him the most.

"When can you come in?"

"Whenever you want me to."

David activated his cell phone, called Lisa from the corner table and set the wheels in motion.

* * *

No sooner had David returned from breakfast, settled into his high-backed, leather armchair and looked towards his e-mailbox than Matt and Jim Molloy walked in, silently, and closed the door behind them.

"We have a problem," Matt said, as he and Jim took seats around the coffee table.

David remained in his chair. "What?"

"I think Jim should tell you."

David looked at his head of Compliance.

"David, we've discovered that Alan Bellone has been spending increasing amounts of time at work surfing the Internet instead of doing his usual work."

"Shit. How much time?"

"Well, as far as we can trace our records back, it may have been an hour or two at first, and most of that was after 5:00 p.m., but over the past six months or so the number of hours per day has increased to seven or eight and the hour at which it's begun has become earlier so he's now surfing by 10:00 each morning."

"I'm surprised that his vital signs haven't suffered more."

"They probably have," Matt said, "but when we did his review in April, he'd only been doing it, we think, for a few months, and the number of hours per day was about half of what it is now."

David nodded. "There's also a lag between when someone stops working or starts doing really bad work and when it turns up in the Client Vote or Sales Vote." Matt nodded. "Did this change after he got his contract?"

"Not as much as you might guess. He's doing a little more of it but it's more of an extension of a well-established trend than a big change in style."

"So it's not as if he wrangled a contract out of me and then shut down his workday completely."

"No."

David's mind was racing.

"But there's more to the story than that," Jim said, prompting David to look up at him. "What he's been surfing is pretty bad stuff."

"Meaning..."

"...that we're not talking Amazon and eBay here. He started out with soft porn, moved to harder porn and is now focused on kiddie porn including some man/boy sex sites."

"Jesus Christ!" David's voiced echoed inside his office. He could feel his face getting flushed and his heart pounding. "How did we find this out?"

"Random checks of where all the computers in Research are logged on if they're accessing the Internet."

"Is anyone else doing this?"

"No."

"Who else knows about this?"

"You, Matt, me, Charles Godfrey who works for me and, of course, Alan."

"Carl doesn't know?"

"No."

David looked down at the top of his desk and then at his watch, which displayed the date inside a little square by the number three. "We're going to have to fire him."

Matt and Jim nodded in agreement.

"But not yet." The heads stopped moving and the faces became perplexed. "He's got a shot at making *II*, " David explained, "not a good one, but a shot. The balloting was done in April and May. His numbers in the spring were still pretty good. If we fire him right now and he makes it he'll be listed as Affiliation Unknown unless someone else hires him quickly, in which case they'll get the credit for his ranking."

"You want to wait until October, when *II* comes out, to fire him?" Jim asked.

"No, I want to confront him 48 hours after the *II* job-hoppers' deadline has passed and fire him then.

Between now and then, we'll do nothing and tell no one."

"What would you like me to say to Charles?"

"Tell him he did good work, that you'll handle the matter from here, and that he must say nothing to anyone about it. Ever."

* * *

"David Meadows."

"David, it's Tim Parish."

"Should I sit down?"

"No, no, don't get excited. I'm calling but I haven't decided."

David breathed easier but also felt disappointed. "What's the news?"

"The news is this, David. I've spent more hours thinking about this than you can imagine. I'd really never expected to be put in a position like this, and it's forced me to shift gears completely. I've spent quite a bit of time talking with a short list of clients and with my managements about it, and the sentiment among them has been uniformly positive. The Daimler gang has been especially encouraging.

"But one thing has really bothered me from the outset about this and, frankly, it's been troubling me more and more with the passage of time, and that's Mitch Potvan."

David wasn't surprised. It would've bothered him too.

"You see, I've known Mitch for many years, and he's really a good guy. I suspect he's better than you think he is. He's certainly better than the polls say he is. He may not be the most dynamic personality in your department, but his gray matter works and the questions he asks at meetings are excellent. He also may not be visible enough to your salesmen and clients at times, but that doesn't mean he isn't working."

"What does DaimlerChrysler think about him?"

"They like him. They like me more, but they like him."

"So you feel badly that we'd have to fire Mitch to make room for you."

"Exactly. I've never taken a job in my life where someone else had to get shot right in front of me in order to make room for me."

David was stumped. "We could set him up with a really good headhunter and pay the cost of placing him somewhere else."

"I don't know, David. I haven't figured out what the best solution to this is. Maybe it's that I don't come, maybe it's something else. All I wanted to communicate to you is that I'm serious about this, that I'm doing my homework, that I'm weighing the feedback I'm getting and that I feel very badly about Mitch."

"Fair enough," David said. "Keep doing what you're doing and give me a little time to figure out what to do with Mitch. Are you okay with that?"

"I'm definitely okay. Thanks, David."

Isn't *that* refreshing, David mused after Tim hung up. But this was virgin territory for David. He didn't know, like the back of his hand, what his next step should be. And for many reasons, he could afford no missteps when it came to Tim Parish.

* * *

"Do you want to guess how Katherine did?" David asked of Larry Fraser.

"On a scale of 1 to 10?"

"Okay."

"Three."

"That's about right."

"Who actually liked her?"

David reviewed the feedback forms. "Banking liked her because she's a warm body. Carl liked her because, I'm guessing, she isn't pretty but her tits are nice."

"Who else?"

"Maryanne Miles in Sales liked her."

"Everyone else was unimpressed?"

"All the analysts who saw her plus Matt, McLain, Hirschorn, Pitcher, trading... everyone else gave her lukewarm reviews."

"Did anyone say flat-out no?"

"Nope. Almost everyone who saw her thought she was very, very average."

"So you still want to hire her?"

"Is she a ranked analyst?"

"I understand. How much do you want to offer her?"

"What's she making again? Two and a half?"

"Plus about a million dollars of restricted Merrill stock as handcuffs."

"Jesus. Tell her $3.5 million per year for two years, plus $1 million of BC Holdings shares that will vest whenever her Merrill shares would have."

"Subject to a client check of course."

"Naturally."

"I'll be right back to you."

A half hour later, Larry called back. "She wants a couple of additional things."

"Such as..."

"Managing Director."

"Done."

"Authorization to fly first class everywhere."

"No go. She can fly whatever class MD's can fly."

"And that means…"

"…business class or first class if business isn't available on domestic flights of more than three hours and business on all overseas flights."

"Got it."

"What else?"

"She wants a car and a driver."

"No go."

"Can you do anything instead?"

David thought for a second. "Tell her that, if she'll provide her own car and hire her own chauffeur, we'll gross up whatever he costs her up to $75,000 a year."

"So, if she hires a chauffeur for $75,000, you'll pay her an extra $150,000 a year, let's say, so that after taxes she'll clear enough to pay him?"

"Correct."

"This is crazy."

"You're right. One day it will all come crashing down around us, but not, I hope, before October. Does Her Majesty want anything else?"

"That's it."

"Okay then. If she's game, we'll do the client check tomorrow, she can get drug tested tomorrow and we'll move her over the day after."

"I'll tell her."

The next day, Katherine's client check surprised no one except Katherine. Three Yes votes, 27 Okay-not-greats and two No votes.

Worthy of a chauffeur if *ever* an analyst deserved one.

* * *

With a heavy heart, Ken Lavery watched his new beach house disappear behind him as Sagaponack Taxi whisked him to LaGuardia Airport for his Retail-only swing through America's heartland. He had 170,000 shares of GINV to goose, and 170,000 GNOM, and the stocks had softened right after he'd added his last 30,000 shares of each which made this marketing swing all the more important.

Over the next three days, Ken did his standard presentation in six cities and five states. A breakfast meeting in Columbus followed by a 4:15 in Cincinnati, breakfast in Indianapolis followed by 3:15 in Kansas City, breakfast in Milwaukee and then a 3:15 in Chicago. The turnouts had ranged from 22 brokers in Kansas City to 80 in Chicago and each meeting had been almost identical to the last and the next.

Ken worked harder on that trip than he'd worked in Florida and much harder than in Boston. Yet, the level of enthusiasm he was able to muster for his two favorite names was subdued and Ken didn't know why. While the stocks had been listless of late, and while no one felt the need to rush out and buy them, the stories still sounded irresistible to Ken and he'd expected more of the brokers to feel the same way.

But they didn't.

On his flight home, Ken reviewed his meetings and concluded that he'd seen 300 brokers and been just as good a salesman on this swing as on the others and that, if these stocks were going to $100, it shouldn't have mattered that they'd already moved from $6 to $16. Still, the numbers were the numbers. Trading volume in both stocks had barely budged while he'd been away and, to Ken's amazement, both stocks were about $0.50 *lower* in price when Ken flew east than they'd been when Ken had flown west.

* * *

Anne Reiss got mixed reviews which, at least, were better than Katherine's. Most of her interviewers had said she seemed smart and articulate and reasonably knowledgeable about her companies. They also noted how competitive she was and how *II*-focused she seemed. "Anyone who makes 100 calls a week for 10 straight weeks can't be all bad," John McLain had written.

Almost everyone also expressed concerns about her "four-day weekends." Tim Omori had asked if he could do the bank stocks from home twice a week, and Alan Bellone had asked whether hiring Anne would set a new departmental policy or guideline regarding when analysts needed to be in the office and when they didn't.

That's the least of your concerns, buddy, David thought. You're gonna be able to surf from home *seven* days a week before you know it.

The sales and trading types who saw Anne were more uncomfortable with, than envious of, her 60/40 workweek. The salespeople acknowledged her apparent success servicing clients remotely, as reflected in her current *II* ranking, but they remained edgy about the long-term impact on Anne's effectiveness as well as the precedent she might set inside the Research Department. The traders, who liked to see their analysts in person, were also uneasy about Anne's vocational lifestyle.

Anne's biggest No vote came from Bill Pressmen, the MD-level banker who specialized in Anne's groups. "She's useless to me," he wrote. David put Bill's feedback form on the top of the pile, opting not to address it unless he had to. At the end of the day, Anne stopped by briefly and told David that she'd had good interviews and that everyone except Bill Pressmen seemed perfectly fine with her in-the-office/out-of-the-office setup. David thanked her for spending the time and promised to circle back to her the following morning.

When she'd gone, he called Carl to compare notes.

"I'm not crazy about this," Carl warned. "It'll make other analysts jealous."

"That's clear, but if she can get the job done, I care about that more."

"You don't know if she can or she can't because it's July now, and the polling that got her Runner-Up in *II* last year was done 15 months ago."

"That's true, but she was down only one rung in *Greenwich* and, if she just spent 10 straight weeks calling 100 clients a week, she's clearly *trying* to get the job done."

Carl was quiet for a minute and then asked, "Who voted No on her?"

"Just Pressmen."

"Mennymore will make a big stink if you hire another analyst The Bank nixed."

David loved it. "If *you* hire…"

"I don't give a shit one way or the other. It's your call, David. Do whatever you think is right, but do it understanding that, if you're wrong, *you're* wrong."

David hung up and then dialed Bob Taylor.

"She did okay with everyone except on the work-at-home front, where she did badly with everyone. Bill Pressmen in Banking nixed her totally."

"Does that mean that you won't make her an offer?"

"No, it just means that this is going to be a pain in the ass for me, as usual, because Banking nixed her and all the other analysts in the department will start pushing me for similar arrangements as soon as they get wind of Anne's, which they probably have already." David sighed. "How much is she making?"

"She's not expensive. She's making one eight."

"Now that's a pleasant surprise."

"I thought so too," said Bob.

"So can we get her for two and a half?"

"You might be able to, David, but then again, it's Deutsche Bank and they'll be pretty aggressive in matching whatever you offer her."

"So your recommendation is what?"

"I'd offer her a million dollar raise and play up the fact that Deutsche Bank was seriously underpaying her and if they match it will only be with your gun to their head."

"So, two million eight for a woman with two babies who'll only be in the office three days a week, who won't go marketing for more than one day at a time and who won't travel for banking under any circumstances?"

"I know."

"What if we make it subject to her remaining on *II*?"

"We could try but I doubt she'd do it."

"Why don't you feel her out about it but make clear that you haven't broached this with me and you don't know how I'd feel about it."

"Sounds good, David. I'll come back to you in the morning."

The next day, before lunch, Bob reported back. Anne had responded well to the $2,800,000 but had gone ballistic over making it subject to her remaining on *II*. At 2:15, David called her directly, said he wanted to offer her $2,800,000 per year for two years with the understanding that she'd work at home on Mondays and Fridays.

"Is this subject to me making *II* ?"

"No, Anne, of course not. Bob told me he took it upon himself to feel you out about that and that you hadn't liked the idea. If he'd asked me first I would've stopped him dead in his tracks."

"Well that's a relief."

"I have no doubt that you're going to do well in *II*," David lied. "In fact, moving from Deutsche Bank to BCS will only help you in the rankings because our institutional sales force is so much stronger."

"Does the $2,800,000 presume that I'm going to move up in the polls?"

"No, Anne, it's our effort to pay you fairly for what you've already accomplished, which Deutsche Bank has clearly tried not to do."

"So you think $2,800,000 is my current market value?"

"Yes."

"And that DBAB has intentionally underpaid me by $1,000,000?

"Yes."

"You know they'll match it."

"Probably, at which point the question you'll face is, do you want to work for someone who recognized your value and volunteered to pay you fairly or for someone who tried to take as much financial advantage of you as they could until someone else came along and forced them to the right number?"

"You know what I'd say, David."

"That's right, I do. So authorize the client check and tell me when I can send you your cartons."

Anne did, and 48 hours later, she became David's "hire number nine."

* * *

"Three more issues," David thought when he noticed the July issue of *II* in his in box. He fished it out, opened it, found the article he was looking for which was entitled "II 300: America's Top 300 Money Managers," and tore the pages from the magazine.

The article comprised a few pages of text and a 13–page table that listed the 300 institutions that had the most money under management and included a breakdown of their assets between U.S. stocks, foreign stocks, bonds, real estate and cash.

David swung around to face his PC and dashed off a brief memo to all of his analysts and associates calling attention to the *II* 300, which he attached, and describing its importance. "While *II* makes a point of keeping the names of the firms that vote in the All Star Poll each year a closely guarded secret," he wrote, "it has said publicly that every *II* 300 firm receives a ballot. (Whether it fills it out or not is another question.) So, if you're interested in maximizing your standing in *II*, please make sure you're servicing as many of the *II* 300 accounts as you can."

Then David added, "By the way, every Top Tier and Extra-Efforts account is in the *II* 300 which is just one more reason why you should focus on them."

David buzzed for Lisa. "Make 200 copies, please, and hand deliver one to each analyst and associate."

"The tickets to stardom," Lisa suggested.

The tickets indeed.

* * *

"We're almost out of time," David told Matt and Lisa as they sat in his office.

"Did they say when the deadline is?" Matt asked.

"Friday, August 8th." David was referring to *II's* job-hoppers' deadline. Any analysts who changed firms after August 8 would be listed in the October issue under their old employer, so any All Stars whom David hired after the deadline had passed would do him no good, at least as far as the magazine was concerned. Sure, he could adjust BCS's published numbers and ranking to reflect any post-deadline hires in any memo he sent around, but what he really wanted was to be credited in the magazine, not to have to massage the published data to make himself look better.

David understood the need for a job-hoppers' deadline. Without one, *II* would have to recalculate its rankings, update its tables and rewrite the supporting text for its October issue each time a ranked analyst changed firms, which would become nightmarish as that issue's publication deadline neared. It would also increase the risk of making mistakes. But the existence of the deadline tended to create a feeding frenzy among Research Directors each July as they battled to hire All Stars before deadline day.

"What time did she arrive?"

"11:00," Lisa answered. It was now 11:35. "She's in with Paula and Matt is having lunch with her at noon."

"She had dinner with Kalagian last night," David said. "He gave her thumbs up."

"And she's having dinner with Donald Ferber tonight," Lisa added.

"So she'll be all done by this evening…"

"…unless someone who's scheduled to see her today doesn't show."

"Good. We'll get the offer to her tomorrow. Even if she ditzes around with Prudential for a few days, she'll still be able to say yes by August 1st, or a couple of days later, and get here under the wire."

"Who else is she seeing today?" Matt asked.

"You at lunch, me at the end, Carl, John McLain, Paula whom she's in with now, Herb, two guys from banking… probably Meineke Wiseman and Peter Marcone… three traders, Paul Pitcher and Dieter."

"Dieter?"

"Surprised?"

Matt was.

"She's the only analyst we've ever interviewed who insisted on seeing him. She said she wanted to know how the Germans really feel about their American subsidiary and what their plans for us are."

"I hope she tells us when she finds out."

"I'll ask her when I see her and let you know."

"You like her, David."

"I'm not going to bias you, Matt. Check her out. All I'll say is she's different."

Lisa laughed, having dealt with Grace and knowing what David meant. Matt and Lisa left David alone, and Matt didn't return until 3:30.

"So?" David asked when Matt had taken a chair.

"Holy cow!"

"What does that mean?"

"It means she was great. A little too aggressive perhaps but, other than that, I'd give her high marks."

"She's smart, isn't she?"

"Very, and practical about the business we're in, what she can bring to the party and what she wants in return."

"Did she mention money to you?"

"Do you think she did?"

"No."

"You're right, at least regarding specifics. But she did make clear that she'll want a lot of it to do both wireline equipment and networking, and you know what? She'll probably earn it."

David nodded.

"How's the rest of the feedback coming in?"

David reached for the stack of feedback forms on his desk and started reading from them in the order in which he'd placed them.

"Smartest recruit you've shown me."

"Excellent verbal skills, a natural marketer."

"Either knows her numbers cold or can snow me better than anyone else on the planet. Suspect the former."

"Razor sharp."

"Understands the business. A real potential money maker for the firm."

"Ferocious competitor, very high energy level, accomplished a lot in a little and has sights set on double-teaming within 12 months. Given her resume, she just might."

"So we might actually hire someone we respect?" Matt asked.

David laughed. "It's possible. Pru will probably fight hard to hold on to her. I'm sure they'll pony up networking once it's clear they have to but, if we're lucky, they'll have yanked her around for a little too long and it won't be enough to get the bad taste out of her mouth."

"Does she want to do banking?"

"Yes, and obviously she can't do any at Prudential."

"What's she going to cost us?" Matt asked.

MICHAEL CULP

"Up to seven a year but more likely six."

"Why?"

"Because I don't believe she can rank in networking next year. The year after? Sure. But not next year."

"So how do you get to six?"

"Four million five for two years, plus a $2 million bonus in year two for double-teaming, and a $1 million bonus that she wouldn't contractually be entitled to for year one but that we'd pay her for having tried hard to double-team next year but failed."

"You know something?"

"What."

"Everything we pay the analysts is insane, but this is actually much less insane than average."

David nodded. "She's going to deliver a lot of goods and she'll come closer to justifying what she makes than any other analyst in the department."

"I hope we get her," Matt said.

"Me too."

An hour later, Grace had finished her meetings and had been walked back to David's office by Meineke Wiseman. David always found it interesting how some analysts never wanted to be seen on a Research floor while they were interviewing and others didn't give a damn. It came down to whether they were really ready to move or not. Grace was, so if Prudential found out it wouldn't be a problem.

"So what did you think?" David asked, motioning Grace to a chair and closing the door behind him.

"Everything works. Good people, better than I thought, hopefully not the only good people in the firm, solid institutional platform that will grow as you hire more good analysts, interesting opportunities with a better retail sales force, and two adequate bankers with whom I can do business and who

514

hopefully will be upgraded later with some of the cash that will start flowing in from the initial mandates we get. I liked the traders a lot. They're a lot like me in some ways. They're focused on generating revenues, not bullshitting, not wasting people's time, just finding the most direct path to a ticket and running down the cobblestones. We'll have very high market shares in my groups, David, that's one thing I can promise you right now."

"Anything you didn't like?"

"I didn't like Carl. He told me a joke that I found offensive, not because I'm a prude but because it was derogatory more than sexual. He's a pretty vulgar guy in a business that's full of vulgarians." Grace paused. "He's not married, is he?"

David shook his head.

"Never?"

"Confirmed bachelor, or so he says."

Grace nodded. "I also thought he was, by far, the... how shall I put it?... the least smart person who interviewed me today. London School of Economics? Hard to believe. And what's with that fake British accent? Halfway through the interview I'm suddenly talking to Prince Charles! What's *with* this guy? And how did he get where he got?"

David shrugged. "I didn't make that call."

"I hear you, but he definitely has pictures of somebody."

"And Dieter?" David said, trying to change the subject.

"You work well with Carl?"

"We're fine."

Grace understood and said nothing.

"Dieter?" David asked again.

"Very cool guy."

David laughed. "I never really thought of Dieter as cool."

"And I'm sure he doesn't think of himself that way either."

"But he is?"

"He is. He's cool because he knows what he wants and he's working hard on getting it. He wants to be a true, big-league, global player in equities, to a lesser extent in fixed income, and in banking. He knows he can pump a lot of money into you and still wind up having spent a fraction of what he would have for an established global bank, and he's prepared to do it as long as he starts seeing some returns reasonably soon.

"He's not going to let you become a money pit, that's for sure, but he really seems convinced that your platform was solid to start with and that, with the right people bringing in other good people from outside, it will get stronger, it will become self-funding pretty quickly and it will surprise the nay-sayers."

"What did he say about Research?"

"He thinks you're doing a pretty good job on the recruiting side, although I definitely got the feeling he would've liked seeing more new hires this year."

"Me too."

"He said you'll be top 10 in *II* this year for sure and top 5 next year, which is impossible for me to believe, and that as Research builds it will help Banking build because strong analysts attract strong bankers."

"That's true. Anything else?"

"He's tickled that BC Holdings is going to look good and that Deutsche and Dresdner are going to look bad. A lot of stuff going on under the surface I think when it comes to BC's standing in the European global banking community. Some people are definitely trying to make names for themselves based on the Equitable Finance acquisition and, if I read him right, Dieter is one of them."

Yikes, David thought.

"So, David, assuming I don't have to deal with Carl on a daily basis, we're good to go. I'm having dinner with Donald Ferber tonight…"

"Where?"

"At Vong, and that will go fine, so if you want to messenger me a contract tomorrow, feel free."

David nodded. "The same numbers we talked about at breakfast?"

"Nine plus three plus two plus support."

"The offer will say that it's subject to drug-testing and to a client check."

"I'll authorize the client check when I see the contract. Same with the drug test."

"Perfect," David said. No wasted motions with Grace.

That night, David got the sign-off on Grace's numbers from Dieter, who had also liked her a lot, and prepared the contract. Then he called Julia Harris and mapped out their strategy. Julia would talk to Grace that evening and to David first thing in the morning, and David would messenger the contract to Grace as soon as Julia had confirmed she was ready.

* * *

At 11:00 p.m. that evening, as David reread Grace's offer letter for the last time and tried to calm himself before turning out the lights, Phil Suprano walked quietly from his office to the mailroom and randomly slipped Xerox copies of the final page of the Analysts' Compensation spreadsheet, on which he'd whited out every name but Liz Tytus's, into senior analysts' mailboxes.

He didn't care which analysts found it the next day because, once a few of them knew what Liz was making, everyone would. The only people he made sure to exclude from this distribution were David, Matt and Liz herself.

As he slipped the pages into the slots, he counted quietly to 30 and, when he got there, he stopped, walked to the mailroom door, checked to be sure he'd not been observed and then returned to his office. Quickly he grabbed his keys and locked his door, went into the men's room where he doused and slicked back his hair, and then donned his Yankee jacket and, despite the hour, a pair of sunglasses.

Downstairs in the lobby, he stopped at Security and signed out: Liz Tytus, 65 th floor, 11:15 p.m.

The guard never checked.

And while the video camera showed someone who looked a little like Phil Suprano leaving the building at 11:15, Ron Vargo stood ready to attest that he'd been at the movies with Phil that evening, until almost midnight, should anyone ever ask.

* * *

Early the following morning, Grace Flagler called David, told him to do the client check and agreed to get drug-tested by noon.

As usual, David had Lisa run the client check. At first it went slowly. Too many clients, it seemed, were on summer vacations or had taken long summer lunch hours when the sales force had called to ask about

Grace. But by late afternoon, feedback had begun trickling in and by lunchtime the next day David had what he needed. The drug test was fine, and the client check read 22 positive, one okay-not-great and no negatives.

"Jesus."

David called Grace and told her the good news. I can have a modified contract that eliminates the 'subject to...'stuff messengered to you within the hour," he told her.

"Good. Do it, please, David. I'm going in to resign right now."

To David's surprise, Grace called back less than an hour later.

"How did it go?"

"Just the way I assumed it would, unfortunately. Couldn't commit to give me networking, couldn't commit to match the money, couldn't commit, in fact, to anything. Lots of begging for more time, which at first I was prepared to give them but, when it became clear they were talking about days or maybe a week or more, I just told them to forget it. If they were good managers they'd have seen this coming and prepared themselves. Of course, they didn't. So, as I said to you before, they were given their shots and they didn't take 'em, so life goes on.

"Send me cartons. I'll see you in the morning."

* * *

Tom Mennymore was agitated. "Why don't you call *him* ?" he asked.

"Because Tim promised to call today, because it's only 2:30 and because he asked me not to call him at work and I said I wouldn't."

519

"I'm going to call him," Tom threatened.

"He doesn't even know who you are, Tom."

"Everyone knows who I am and, besides, that never stopped me before."

"Tom look, if I don't hear from him by 4:00, I'll call him. Okay?"

"3:00."

"3:30."

"3:15."

"3:23."

"3:19."

"3:21."

"3:20."

"Sold."

But at 2:45, Tim called.

"So where are you?" David asked.

"I'm in my office," Tim joked. "Why?"

"Very funny. You know what I mean."

"I'm almost there, David. The Daimler guys are very encouraging about this and so are many of my clients. As I said before, the only real holdup for me is Mitch."

"Good, Tim. Let me tell you what I've talked about with Carl and Dieter."

"Please."

"What we'd propose is to go to Mitch and tell him we're bringing you on board, that we all, and that includes you, want Mitch to land on his feet despite what he'll obviously view as a setback, and that we'll keep him on the payroll and help retrain him to do one of the uncovered groups that he's interested in learning."

"Any group?"

David hesitated. "Any group we both feel would be good for him to pick up."

"What if you can't agree on one?"

"I'm sure we can."

"But if you can't…"

"Then…we'd ask him to submit three choices and we'd guarantee him one of the three." David was winging it but it sounded good.

"That seems fair."

"Good, so are we set on this?"

"Almost. How long would you give him to learn the new group, where would you expect him to rank in it, and by when?"

This is ridiculous, David thought. "We'd expect nothing from him in year one and we'd hope for Runner-Up in year two."

"But you wouldn't require it."

"As a basis for ongoing employment?"

"Yes."

David hesitated again. "No."

"And what would happen to his compensation during those two years?"

"We'd pay him fairly."

Tim was silent for a moment. "Fairly can mean different things to different people."

"The only alternative to paying fairly is paying unfairly."

"David, I guess what I'm hoping is that, while I don't know what he's making, you'll agree to pay him the same amount over the next two years, even though he'll obviously be in a start-up mode and of less value to the firm."

David had feared it might come to this and had prepared himself in case it did.

"Is that what it would take to get you here, Tim?"

"I think that would do it, David."

"Then I'd commit to it."

"Wow. That's very decent of you, David." For a minute, no one said anything. "So when would you tell him?" Tim finally asked.

"As soon as you sign your contract."

Tim nodded and then realized that David couldn't see him. "Okay, let me sleep on it one more time. I promise to give you my answer within the week."

"Can we agree on Thursday, the 7th, as a deadline?"

"That's perfectly fair, David."

David thanked Tim and hung up. Then he looked at his calendar. Seven days to the job-hoppers' deadline. David could feel how wet his shirt had become, and he knew it wouldn't dry until the 8th.

* * *

"Can I talk to you?" asked Jennifer Ratliff, Liz Tytus's research assistant, who was standing in Liz's doorway.

"I've only got a minute but come in." Liz offered her a chair in front of her desk.

Jennifer closed the door behind her and sat down, pulling the chair towards Liz as much as the desk would allow.

"Is something wrong?"

Jennifer nodded.

"What?"

"Can I tell you something and ask you to promise that you'll never say I told you?"

"Yes."

"Okay. I was having lunch just now with Shanna Pender." Liz showed no sign of recognition. "She works for Nancy Natolio, the oil analyst. We've gotten to be friends since you and I came here and I have lunch with her two or three times a week."

Liz nodded. "And…"

"… and she said that Nancy told her that you make $4 million a year."

Liz could feel her heartbeat increasing but kept a poker face. "Four million? How would she know that?"

"That's what I said, and she said that Nancy had told her that someone had put a Xerox copy of your contract in her mailbox and that that's what it said."

Liz was confused. "Nancy told Shanna that someone put a copy of *my* employmentcontractinNancy'smailboxandthatitsaidImade$4million?"

"That's what Shanna said."

"That's outrageous!"

"I know it is but I was so shocked when she told me. I didn't know whether I should say anything to you about it or not, but then I started wondering if, in case it *was* true, you'd want to know that someone had given someone else a copy of your contract, and I realized that if it were me, I'd want to know."

"Did Shanna show you the contract?"

"No."

"Did she show you anything?"

"No."

"Did she say that she'd seen the Xerox copy of my contract?"

"No, all she said was that Nancy had told her that she'd received it, and that it had said you made $4 million."

"Can you ask Shanna to show you the copy?"

"You mean to get it from her?"

"Yes."

Jennifer looked scared but answered, "I can try."

"Would you, please?"

Jennifer nodded.

"Don't say it's for me."

"I won't. I'll just tell her I don't believe a word of it and that I dare her to prove it."

"She will," Liz said.

"I know."

AUGUST

"David, do you have a minute?" Jim Molloy was standing in David's doorway.

"Happy August, Jim. What have you got?"

"Do you remember me talking to you at the beginning of the year about George Schuler and Saruman Software?"

"It was a privately owned software company that George wanted to invest in?"

"That's right. It was co-founded by a friend of his, it makes add-on software for Palms and Blackberries, and it was doing a private placement in which George was invited to participate."

"We told him he could do it but that he had to update us quarterly."

"Correct."

"And did he?"

"He put the money in and he sent me March- and June-quarter statements."

"Everything was kosher?"

"Yup."

"So why are you here?"

"Because Saruman is doing much better than expected and, even though they'd said in the offering materials in January that they had, at the time, no plans to go public during the next 12 months, they've changed their minds."

"And we want to pitch for the IPO?"

"Oh absolutely. George thinks we have a very strong shot at the lead and that we're a no-brainer to be a co-lead manager because of his personal ties to management."

"And he'd cover it, of course, if we did the deal."

"Naturally."

David's eyes squinted. "George should be precluded from selling any of the shares he purchased in January until long after the deal is done."

Jim was nodding. "The normal lock-up period for insiders is 180 days but I'd recommend that, if we let George pitch for the business and he gets it, he be required to maintain his shares for a year."

"Even after a year he shouldn't be able to sell them unless he rated Saruman Hold or Sell."

"Which means never."

"It could."

Jim agreed and said he'd tell George what the conditions were. As he was leaving, David remembered what he'd forgotten to ask.

"How much money does he have tied up in Saruman?"

"He bought 100,000 shares at $1 each."

"Is anyone talking about a price range on the IPO yet?"

"George says it's very preliminary, but that the underwriters that have been pushing them to go public have been telling them $15 to $20."

"I wish I had friends who could make me 15 to 20 times my money in eight months," David mused. "Watch him closely, Jim."

"Will do."

* * *

High atop the New York Marriott Marquis in Times Square, in a booth in The View, New York's only revolving rooftop restaurant, Ron Vargo waited for Claire. After the waitress had brought him his Diet Coke, he unfolded two sheets of e-mails that the two had exchanged earlier in the day and reread them. In one, Ron had complained about how long it had been since he'd seen Claire. In another, Claire had offered to buy him dinner at The View at 6:15.

"You better not be e-mailing sweet nothings to another woman!" Claire plopped down on the booth cushion across from Ron, looked around, saw no one, and kissed him long and deeply and very tenderly. Her hand stroked the back of his neck, making Ron want to close his eyes. Finally, she pulled herself away and straightened her suit jacket.

"I couldn't wait to see you," Ron said. "It feels like forever."

"Me too. But we're here, so let's enjoy the moment."

The waitress returned with two menus. Claire ordered an iced tea. As soon as the waitress had left, Ron kissed her again.

"We should be careful," Claire warned. "I picked this place because it's 'Tourists R Us,' but you never know. All it takes is one wrong person seeing us and the jig is up."

"I hope I'm more than a jig."

"You're the most precious thing in my life, silly. You're not the jig, our relationship is the jig."

Ron nodded "So did you get your options?"

"Not yet, but they're coming... 50,000 that I would've gotten no matter what, and 150,000 that I'm getting because somehow, a miracle occurred and

527

Milbanks Media moved from $48.50 to $50.10 during the last 48 hours of the fiscal year."

"Really! And that was good for you?" Ron asked innocently.

"Oh, better than good! We were all praying for $49.20, and on June 29th our prayers were answered. You probably didn't notice, but the stock jumped $0.90 that day, to $49.40. Then we had to pray again for the stock not to drop more than $0.20 on June 30th."

"And it didn't?"

"Heavens no! It went up another $0.70 instead!"

"So those two good days in the market were worth 150,000 options to you?" Ron asked, playing the fool.

"Incredible but true. I feel like I should thank someone, but I just don't know who," Claire said, slipping a foot between Ron's legs.

"I thought you said we should be careful."

"Can you see my toes?"

"No, you're under the tablecloth."

"So do you think anyone else can see them?"

"Theoretically no, but they'll see me squirm if you don't stop."

Claire slipped her foot back into her shoe and acted insulted. She'd barely begun to pout when the waitress returned and asked for their orders. Claire picked the salmon and Ron ordered steak. As soon as the waitress was out of ear shot, Claire turned towards Ron and surprised him.

"I've got a proposition for you," she whispered. "I need your help."

Ron knew that there was nothing legal or slightly illegal that he wouldn't do for Claire. He wouldn't murder someone for her, or steal large sums of money, but if it was legal or questionable but not brazenly bad, he'd do it unhesitatingly.

"What?"

"What I'm going to tell you now you can never tell another soul."

"I understand."

"It could cost me my job if you did."

"You know I'd never do anything to hurt you."

"I could go to jail."

"You can tell me."

"Only one person who isn't on Milbanks's board knows about it, and that's me."

"And I'm going to be the second."

"Yes. Are you ready?" Ron nodded. "There's a little agency called Four Dimensions Media that Tom wants to buy. Do you know it?"

"I know a little bit about it but I don't cover it "

"Almost no one on The Street does. We checked pretty carefully."

Ron looked puzzled so Claire kept talking. "Our problem is this. Tom has had countless conversations with the top guns at FDM about taking the firm over and they've resisted. He's offered them long-term contracts and other lucrative financial incentives but they've been really ornery. And the worst part is that they don't even own much stock… maybe 20% of the company, tops."

"So why don't you do a hostile?"

"That's exactly what we've started planning, but as we've mapped out how to do this, we've run up against one serious problem and that's the price. We think these yo-yo's have let the word get out that we're trying to buy them, and the stock has gone from 14 to 17 over the past 30 days. The economics work for us if we offer 17 but we'd never get enough stock tendered to gain control if the stock was already selling at 17."

"Won't the stock settle back if nothing happens over the next few weeks?"

"Maybe FDM will drop back to 16 or 15 but I'd be shocked if it went all the way back to 14 because there'll be lingering suspicions about a takeover and some people will stick with it just in case."

"So, if it drops to 15, offering 17 wouldn't look all that compelling."

"That's right, and that's where you come in."

"Me? What can I do?" Ron laughed. "Initiate coverage on the stock with a Sell and see if I can push it down to 12?"

"Eleven would be better," Claire said, and kissed him again.

* * *

As Jennifer Ratliff stood in front of the vending machine in the mail-room, pretending that she was contemplating a purchase, Shanna Pender walked up beside her, said hello, looked around, saw no one, and then left a white envelope on top of the Xerox machine to their left. In silence, Shanna then left the mailroom. Ten seconds later, Jennifer followed.

Inside Liz's office, with the door closed behind her, Jenn handed the still-sealed envelope to Liz, who opened it, saw what she'd hoped not to see and then looked up. "Shanna Pender gave this to you?"

"Yes."

"You're sure."

"Positive."

"And she got it how?"

"She made a copy of the original Nancy got in the mail. Nancy doesn't know."

"You're positive."

"Yes, but you have to protect her, Liz. I promised her that no one would say she was the source."

"And no one will." Liz rose suddenly and stormed past Jennifer down the hall to David's office, envelope in hand. As she approached the corner of the floor, Lisa Palladino planted herself in Liz's way, even though she was physically smaller.

"I have to see him!" she screamed.

"He's interviewing."

"I don't care what he's doing, Lisa, I need to see him and I mean right now!"

"Can he call you as soon as he's free?"

"No, now, in person."

Lisa parked Liz in an empty office three doors down from David's. "I'll be back in a second." Lisa closed the door behind her. Liz was pacing and seemed wildly angry.

Lisa tapped on David's door and told him she needed him for a moment regarding something very important. David excused himself and came out in the hall, closing his door behind him.

"Liz Tytus is in there," she pointed, "and she's furious about something."

"Do you know what?"

"She didn't say. She just said that she needed to talk to you right now."

David nodded. "Tell him please that I'll be right back," he said, looking towards his office door. Then David went to see Liz.

"What happened?" he asked, closing the door to the office she'd been pacing in.

"You tell me, David! Look at this and tell me what it is."

David took the white sheet of paper from the envelope and scanned it. "It's a page from a compensation spreadsheet, I think. There are other names above and below yours that seem to be whited out. The numbers look correct. Where did you get this?"

"It doesn't matter where I got it, David. What matters is that someone distributed it to other analysts in the department and now everyone knows how much I make."

"How do you know that other analysts received it?"

"Because I got it from one of them and there's no reason to think that it only went to one person."

"It might have."

"It didn't! Someone got hold of this, whited out every name but mine, made copies of it, put those copies in other people's mailboxes, and now, because someone either got a Xerox or spoke to someone who got a Xerox, the entire department knows something that's none of their fucking business."

"I understand that this is very upsetting to you."

"Very upsetting? That's putting it mildly! This fucking firm is one nightmare after another."

"What do you mean?"

"I mean, David, that if someone from BCS isn't trying to fuck me in the office by telling the whole world how much I make, someone's trying to fuck me, literally, on the department's Summer Cruise."

"What do you mean? Did someone do something to you?"

"Does attempted rape qualify as something?"

David was horrified, speechless.

"That's right, David. Your fucking boss."

"Carl?"

"That's right. Tongue in my mouth, hands untying my dress, crashing me up against a wall so hard that my head almost split open, fondling me and then telling me it never happened."

"No one saw it?"

"Just Carl, and he's not going to testify against himself. He'll find 10 guys who report to him who'll swear he was up on the top deck all night and I'll just wind up all the more humiliated. If I file a complaint with no eyewitnesses, I won't be able to prove it and the entire firm will know what happened. I don't need that."

"I'm so sorry this happened to you, Liz. Let's go see Dieter right now."

"Fuck Dieter, David. We're not reporting this to anyone. First I'm sexually assaulted and then my most sensitive and confidential personal finances are publicly displayed for every analyst and secretary in this God-forsaken department to see. Do you know what the words 'hostile work environment' mean, David?"

David just looked down, gravely, almost hopelessly.

"Liz, let's report it to Dieter."

"No, David, for the last time. I'm putting you on notice. I'm going to consult with lawyers about this and determine the best course of action for me. I'm sure it will involve leaving the firm and suing you to smithereens. I'm not sure when and how but I'll let you know. How Carl remains employed, and in a position of great responsibility, I have no idea, and how the keeper of the analysts' compensation spreadsheets could let this page get away from him I have no idea either. But it's clear that I'm dealing with criminals and incompetents inside this firm and I'm going to put an end to it as soon as I can. You'll hear, I'm sure, from my lawyers." Liz opened the office door, walked through it and slammed it behind her so hard that David couldn't believe it when the glass didn't shatter.

"Jesus Christ," he yelled at no one. "How fucked up can things get?"

Of course, all of this had to unfold 96 hours before the *II* job-hoppers' deadline. Liz *should* go, David said to himself, and she *should* sue us. But I need to talk so slowly when her lawyer calls that it takes until August 9th to finalize the terms of her departure.

* * *

"Not in the slightest," Ken Lavery said into his hands-free-telephone headset. He paused and listened. "I agree with you. It would be nice if these stocks went straight to $100 and never looked back but that's not how the market works. They had a great run from $5 or $6 to the mid-teens, but you get to a point where you have to digest your gains before you can move higher and that's all that's going on right now."

Another pause and more listening.

"No, the fundamentals are entirely intact. There's nothing wrong at the companies. There's just some profit-taking going on. Once we're through this choppy phase, the next move should be to the $20 to $25 area, probably in September."

Ken was interrupted again, he listened patiently and then responded. "I'm not a technician so I can't tell you with pinpoint accuracy, but if these stocks are up 10 points each, a normal pullback would be, probably, three or four points. I don't see them dropping more than that. GNOM peaked at $16 and it's $13.40 now so it's down 16% which is very acceptable. GINV peaked at $15 and it's $13.05 so it's pulled back 13%."

The angry broker complained some more and Ken let him vent.

"I understand that not everyone got into these stocks at $5 or $6. You got in much more recently so you're under water now, versus other holders who still have big gains. But Kevin, if these stocks are going to $100, and I honestly believe they are, you're going to look back next year from wherever the Hell we are, hopefully $40 or $50 or more, and remember us agonizing on the phone about the wiggle between $16 and $13 and have a good laugh about it."

Ken listened one last time and then said, "Listen to what I'm telling you. Chill man. These stocks are small-caps, they're high-beta, they're definitely not for widows and orphans and they're going to fluctuate. If you can't live with the gyrations, wait until they come back up and get out of them. But I'm asking you... I'm begging you... learn to live with the ups and downs. You want safety? Buy bonds. You want to make 500% on your money? Don't just watch these two honeys and wait. Buy more."

After he'd rid himself of the broker, Ken picked up his calculator and did the numbers for the tenth time that day. At $13.40, his 170,000 GNOM were worth $2,278,000. At $13.05, his 170,000 GINV were worth $2,218,500. Together they were worth $4,496,500. After he deducted his $3,150,000 margin loan, his equity was down to $1,346,500, or 29.9% of the value of his holdings.

Ken's phone rang and it made him jump, but when he looked at his Caller ID, he sighed in relief that it wasn't Tom Hanks warning that he was inches away from a margin call.

It was just another angry broker.

* * *

The following day, ten minutes into the Morning Call, Paula Hainsworth said, "Next is Nick who's initiating coverage on a new name." Nick took the chair next to Paula's, smiled at her and nodded, and then turned to face the salespeople around the table.

"Good morning, everybody. This morning I'm initiating coverage on New Nevada Mining, ticker symbol NEWN, over the counter, with a Buy recommendation. The company lost $0.03 a share last year, and I'm estimating earnings of $0.10 for this year and $0.60 to $0.70 for next year.

"New Nevada is a very small gold-mining company, headquartered in Las Vegas, with properties in Nevada and, to a much lesser extent, Canada and Peru. Gold output, principally from the company's mine in Nye County, Nevada, totaled 295,000 ounces last year. By way of contrast, Newmont produces about 7,500,000 ounces of gold annually so you can see how small New Nevada is."

Nick could see the institutional sales force losing interest. This was not an institutional-caliber investment idea.

"Normally I wouldn't cover a company this small. New Nevada has about 15 million shares outstanding, and it closed at $11.10 yesterday, so the market cap is only about $165 million, but what's different about this stock is this: New Nevada purchased, about six months ago, exploratory rights to properties near Elko, Nevada, where Barrick has its Goldstrike mine, that I believe may be much more lucrative than the market is now discounting. Goldstrike, you may recall, is the largest gold mine in North America, with annual production of 2,000,000 ounces. Now it's true that these adjoining tracts have not produced, so far, commercially viable quantities of gold, but I believe, based on geological studies that I've reviewed and conversations with management, that as New Nevada expands its Elko mine north and east, it may well encounter substantial, new gold deposits.

"Predicting the size of these deposits is always extremely difficult, but my own research as well as maps that New Nevada's management has shared with me lead me to conclude that, conservatively, Elko could double New Nevada's gold output next year, which would push earnings up to the $0.60–$0.70 a share level, and that's what I'm using in my model. Could it be less? Of course. Could it be more? Just as likely, perhaps more likely.

"Why hasn't the market discounted this already? I think for two reasons. First, these properties aren't new and they've been disappointing to date so there's considerable skepticism surrounding their richness. Second, New Nevada, owing to its market cap and the thinness with which the shares trade, is not followed by any other major-bracket firms on The Street. It is followed by a couple of regional brokers and that's it. It's done no investment banking with The Street for many years so there are no bankers around pressuring their analysts to cover it. As a result, the story is not well known and the market, I believe, is pricing the shares inefficiently."

"Do you know what those other firms are estimating?" Herb Hirschorn asked.

"Neither is in *First Call*, Herb, but I understand from management that one is at $0.40 for next year and the other is at $0.50, which says to me that whoever the analysts are at those firms, they too are buying into the idea that gold output is going to rise as a result of New Nevada's expansion of Elko.

"If I'm wrong about Elko, I think the stock is dead money. I don't see a lot of downside from $11 because of NEWN's proven gold reserves, which are adequate, and its book value, which is $7 a share. But if I'm right and the company can make $0.60 to $0.70 a share next year, it might well be able to clear $1 a share the year after so I've put a target price on the stock of $15 which implies upside potential of about 40%."

"This isn't really suitable for most of our accounts," Maryanne Miles complained.

"You're right, Maryanne, and I'm not recommending it on that basis but, for small institutions and for individual investors, I consider NEWN an interesting speculation."

"Other questions for Nick?" There were none. Paula thanked Nick and moved on to Tim Omori. Nick returned to his office, closed his door, and turned on CNBC. For two hours and 20 minutes, he heard no mention at all of his initiation of coverage. During the first few minutes of trading the stock moved up a point on relatively modest volume. Shortly before 10:00, however, the volume picked up considerably and NEWN jumped another $1.75, and that's when CNBC got interested.

Shortly after 10:00, Leslie Laroche, reporting from the NASDAQ, told viewers that, among the morning's big movers, New Nevada Mining, ticker NEWN, had risen $2.95 a share, or 27%, to $14.05 on news that BC Securities had initiated coverage with a Buy and suggested that a new mine that the company was developing in Elko, Nevada could add $1 a share to earnings within 24 months. Badly pressed for time, Leslie made no mention of Nick's target price.

Throughout the morning and into the early afternoon, trading in the shares was unusually heavy and the stock rose as high as $19.15, up $8.05. A number of BCS's retail brokers, confused as to why the stock would rise so far above Nick's target price, began calling both Nick and the company. Nick told them that he wouldn't pay more than $15 for the shares but that he wasn't going to downgrade to Hold or Sell simply because the stock had spiked for a few hours. "I'm sure it will settle back," he told them, "and I don't want to look like a ratings 'flipper' or someone who's encouraging you brokers to 'churn.'"

The head of Investor Relations at New Nevada told the brokers who called, and later CNBC, that, while management was gratified that Nick had begun covering them, and while they too were highly optimistic about Elko's gold ore potential, they considered $0.60 to $0.70 "materially above internal projections" for next year, and $1.00 a share for the year after "an everything-must-go-right scenario" that they could not bless.

CNBC began running the story around 2:35 p.m. and continued updating it as the afternoon wore on, especially once it began influencing the price of New Nevada's shares. At 2:35, NEWN had been trading at $18.90. By 3:00, it was down to $16.70, by 3:30 to $14.45 and by 3:45 to $12.80.

As the market closed at 4:00, New Nevada traded one last time at $10.80 and finished down $0.30 on the day.

* * *

On Wednesday afternoon, August 6, Liz Tytus walked calmly into David's office and resigned. David offered her a chair and read the letter carefully. It was very low key, unemotional but powerful, and it made clear that her decision to resign had been forced upon her following an attempted rape during the Research/Investment Banking Summer Cruise in June and the public disclosure of confidential compensation information during July, a blatant violation of the terms of her employment contract which demanded secrecy on both parties' parts. Both of these events had created a hostile working environment in which Liz could no longer perform her duties. The letter said nothing about legal actions that might be taken against the firm or any of its employees, but did state that her resignation would be effective immediately.

David stood up, as did Liz, and he extended his hand. "I'm sorry, Liz," he said. Reluctantly, and unenthusiastically, Liz took it, keeping her eyes on the carpet. She shook it limply once and then left. David, deeply saddened, took the notebook from his bottom draw and scratched Liz's name off his " *I.I.* Hopefuls" list. He'd try to delay any announcement until Monday, but he knew that, one way or another, probably by a Research Director at a firm where one of Liz's friends worked, *Institutional Investor* would be informed that Liz Tytus had ceased working at BCS on August 6, two full days before its job-hoppers' deadline.

Wearily, David called Dieter and told him that Liz had resigned, and that he feared she might file some sort of harassment complaint. At the same time he made sure not to mention comp sheets and Xerox machines.

"When does she claim something occurred?"

"In June."

"Why is she only airing this now?"

"She has no witnesses and said that Carl has denied anything happened."

"Then we'll worry about it if and when her lawyer calls. My guess, David, is that he won't."

* * *

As promised, Tim Parish called on Thursday morning, August 7.

"So, are you calling to make my day?"

"Not yet, David," Tim said, "but hopefully this afternoon. I've told Cowen that I want to go and they've asked me to give them a few hours which I've agreed to do."

"Did they say anything else?"

"Just that they didn't want me to go and that they'd see what they could do to keep me."

"How long are you going to wait?"

"David, you've been very patient with me and I'm grateful for that. I know you want an answer today and I'm going to give you one. Right now, I'd say the odds are very strong that I'll be joining you. I just don't want to burn bridges if I don't have to."

"So when will I hear back from you?"

"By 3:00?"

"By 3:00. Do the right thing, Tim."

"I'm trying."

* * *

As things turned out, Tim Parish met David's August 7 deadline, but not until 10:20 p.m., after an eleventh-hour dinner that David had to arrange when Tim had called at 5:00 to say that he simply wasn't ready to commit.

Tom Mennymore had pressed hard to be included in the dinner, but David held his own and kept the meeting to a quiet one-on-one and, by the time the check arrived, David had convinced Tim to come directly to BCS on Friday morning, to resign telephonically, and to stay with David until his cartons had been picked up and delivered to BCS's office. At 8:30 a.m. on Friday, August 8, David e-mailed *II*, with Tim sitting at his side, that BCS had landed one last All Star before it imposed its job-hoppers' deadline.

* * *

All that day David focused on getting Tim through the resignation process, the contract-signing process, the drug-testing process and the carton packing-and-shipping process. There had been no client check this time. Tom Mennymore was the only client who mattered and he'd voted thumbs up long ago. David walked Tim around and introduced him to his new neighbors, and met at length with Mitch Potvan, challenging him to find a new industry that David promised to help him master and offering him a two-year contract at the same compensation rate at which he'd been paid most recently. Mitch, while disappointed, also seemed relieved.

David was elated that he'd been able to reel Tim in over dinner the night before. It helped soothe the wound that Liz Tytus's departure had inflicted 48 hours earlier, and it left him feeling as if, in the bottom of the ninth, trailing by two runs, he'd doubled with the bases loaded and knocked in three. It also left him completely unprepared when he returned to his office and found Nancy Natolio sitting in it.

"Nancy!"

"Congratulations, David. Tim seems very nice, very capable."

"Thanks," David said uneasily. "What's doing with you?"

"This is for you, David," Nancy said, extending a sheet of white paper to him but no envelope. David could feel his throat tighten and his pulse begin to race.

"What is it?"

"I'm leaving, David. I'm joining Deutsche Bank. It's being announced right now in their department and they're notifying *II* so they get credit for me in October."

David was crestfallen. "You're not even giving me a chance to compete?"

"You can't compete, David, and I don't want you to. I've thought long and hard about this for months. They've been hounding me since April. It's not as if I've made this decision rashly."

"But I thought you and I worked well together."

"We did, David. This isn't about you, although I'm sure that doesn't make you feel any better. It's about the kind of place that BCS has become, a place full of people I don't like and don't respect. It's a place where you're ripped off by The Bank just because it gets bankers high ripping analysts off, and where you're propositioned by senior management just because someone's bored and wants to play with himself."

"Did Carl touch you?"

"No, thank God, although he clearly wanted to. No, he just dangled a banking bonus that I had earned over my head and told me it was mine for a blow job."

"Dammit!" David looked long at Nancy. "Why didn't you tell me before?" he asked.

"Because it happens all the time, David. Open your eyes. It's all around you. It's not just me, it's in every corner of this department, on every floor, and it happens every day. I'm a big girl, I can take care of myself, but that doesn't mean I have to like it. Who knows? Maybe it'll be just as bad at Deutsche Bank. I hope not. The only thing I'm convinced of is that none of the women there whom I've met or called over the past five months has had to deal with anyone like Carl, and that's good enough for me."

"You're under contract, you know."

"I know, and I was very concerned about the non-compete, but you know what? This is just something I have to do. I'm going to hope and trust that you and BCS will understand and not try to beach me for a year or anything. Maybe there will be some financial penalty that Deutsche Bank will have to pay. They've told me they'll pay it if it comes to that. But maybe it's just better if I go away quietly because, if you come after me and antagonize me, you'll give me no choice but to fight back, and when the guns come out, and they're pointed at Carl's groin, it'll get ugly for everyone. You can keep that from happening, David. I'm counting on you."

"How much are they paying you?"

"Six and a half for three."

David whistled. "That more than covers the restricted stock you'll leave behind."

"It's a very generous offer. I'm not worth it, but no one in this business is worth what they're paid so you get while the getting is good and then you leave it all behind and try to make a life for yourself."

"Are you gone from the business when your contract is up?"

"Is that the way I sound?"

"Sort of."

"Who knows, David? Who can see three years ahead on the Sell Side? Not me. I go day to day, season to season, if I'm lucky year to year. We'll see what life is like working for the other Germans. It's so pathetic, you know."

"What is?"

"How ballistic they went when you hired Anne Reiss away from them."

David was surprised.

"If she'd gone to Merrill or Morgan or Goldman they wouldn't have cared, but she went to BCS, another German investment bank, and they took it very personally."

"That must have made them want you even more."

"That's exactly what happened, and in the end they got me."

Nancy stood up and extended her hand. "You've had a pretty tough week, David, between Liz and Tim and me. I hope you have someone you can confide in, or vent at. I hope you find a little peace and quiet this weekend."

"Me too," David said, shaking her hand. "Take care of your self, Nancy."

"And you, David."

* * *

David sat slumped in his red leather chair, weary, introspective and totally relaxed. His breathing was shallow and his body felt light, capable of floating right out of the building, over the Brooklyn Bridge, east along the Long Island Expressway, down over Southampton Village and into the great room of his house by the sea. For a moment, he closed his eyes and imagined he was there. Almost everyone else in the department was long gone, and the air was still. Hell, it was a Friday evening in August. What was *he* doing sitting behind his desk, pretending to read e-mails?

Suddenly the silence surrounding him was broken by the muffled sound of shoes on new carpet. Who'd be here at 7:00? A security guard? An analyst who had forgotten something important? The cleaning people? The answer surprised him.

"Why aren't you home?" asked Samantha Smeralda as she reached David's door and looked in.

"I could ask you the same thing."

"I'm going to see Aerosmith at The Garden tonight. Wanna come?"

"Oh, no thanks. I haven't been to a rock concert in a long time. I used to go all the time, you know, when I was young and cool. But not in a while."

"Who did you see?"

"I used to go some place that closed before you were born, I fear… The Fillmore East." David waited for signs of recognition. There were none.

"In the 1960s and 1970s, a rock promoter named Bill Graham operated sister concert halls in New York and San Francisco, The Fillmore East and The Fillmore West. The Fillmore East was on Second Avenue, around 6th Street. It had 3,000 seats and an amazing sound system. If you were nimble, you could get seats in the first five to ten rows of the orchestra to see almost every famous band on the planet."

Samantha was intrigued.

"I remember seeing Mountain one New Year's Eve at The Fillmore. Did you ever hear of them?"

"I think so."

"Leslie West?"

"I think I saw him on a Howard Stern video once playing Mississippi Queen?"

"That's him. But Leslie was 25 years old when I saw him. He's 55 now. He was huge when he was 25, tall and heavy, and he had this enormous Afro even though he was white. He played guitar, and he played loud, which made Mountain sound really good. It sounds very dated today, but Mountain was a very-hard-rock band 30 years ago. The bass player was Felix Pappalardi, and he was 5'9", maybe, and thin. He and Leslie looked ridiculous standing next to each other on stage.

"Anyway, that night Mountain came on stage in total darkness. We heard them tuning up, and it was very loud, and you knew you were about to be blown ten rows back the minute they started their first song. It was very exciting. The audience was screaming Leslie's name. And then, we heard Bill Graham's voice. Bill didn't emcee every concert at The Fillmore but he always did the important ones. At a minute to midnight, we heard Bill say, 'Ladies and gentlemen, Mountain,' and the stage lights went up, and there they were. Corky Laing in the middle, high up on his drum platform, Steve Knight on bass, all the way to the left, Felix between Steve and Corky, and Leslie all the way to the right, where I was sitting. Behind Steve were four speakers, two on top of two. The same behind Felix. The same behind Leslie. Four musicians dwarfed by three 12–by–20–foot banks of speakers. I had never seen Mountain before in concert and I never did again because they broke up after only a few years, but it was one of the best concerts I ever saw. Sometimes I think I can still hear my ears ringing from it."

"God," said Samantha. "I wish I could've been there. Sometimes when I go to The Garden or Giants Stadium, I feel like I'm a mile from the stage."

"You probably are. So, you like Aerosmith."

"Oh I love 'em. I know they're old, but Steven Tyler still looks good, and I love how he dances around the stage when he sings. Do *you* like Aerosmith, David?"

"I do. They can rock and they're also melodic. You know, as opposed to Pantera or Godsmack or Korn." David paused. He wondered if he'd surprised Samantha with what he knew about those groups. "And they've been together for so long that they actually can put together Greatest Hits CDs that are almost all hits."

"I love 'em," Samantha agreed. "Look what I'm wearing tonight." Samantha unzipped a lightweight, white leather jacket that she'd paired with white jeans. Underneath was a thin white T-shirt with a rainbow-like arch spelling Aerosmith in multi-colored glitter. Samantha arched her back to make sure David could tell she was braless. "Cool shirt, isn't it?"

"Where'd you get it?"

"Off the Net. It's a little too big, but it'll shrink when I wash it."

The little voice was back, telling David it was time for Samantha to go. It was now almost 7:45. "Aren't you going to be late?"

"No, silly. Trust Company is opening for them, and

even they won't go on until 8:30. It'll be 10:30 before Aerosmith goes on. I've got *lots* of time."

The silence was deafening. Samantha had her stare on again and David wore his ambivalence on his sleeve. Samantha looked out David's door. No one, no sound, little light.

She smiled and turned back to David. "Did I ever tell you about my favorite Aerosmith song, David?"

"I don't think so." David saw the words "set up" flash before his eyes. "What is it, Samantha?"

"It's 'Falling in Love Is So Hard on the Knees,'" she answered, flashing her biggest smile and kicking the door to David's office closed behind her.

* * *

On Monday morning, August 11, after confirming that the job-hoppers' deadline had come and gone, acknowledging reports that *II* had received on Friday afternoon that Nancy Natolio and Liz Tytus had both left the firm, and reminding *II* of Tim Parish's pre-deadline hiring, David focused on two items that had been scheduled weeks before.

The first required the summoning of Alan Bellone to one of the conference rooms on the 65th floor, where he found David, Matt, Jim Molloy, Donna Thorenson from Human Resources and another woman whom he didn't recognize. After David had offered him the chair next to Donna's and closed the conference door, he proceeded to tell Alan that, as he was sure Alan knew, BCS conducted routine and random spot checks of employees' Internet usage to ensure that all employees used the Net in keeping with firm policies and procedures, and that it had made discoveries involving Alan that were grave and deeply disturbing. Alan grew pale and his eyes widened slightly.

David then produced a list of "web sites that were visited by someone sitting at your desk and using your computer during normal business hours" that was hundreds of entries long and included dates stretching back many months.

"firstgradelove.com, barelyoutofdiapers.com, love-withyourdaughter.com, mangirlsleezysex.com. I'm not going to go on," David said, looking up at Alan from the list in his hand and shaking his head. "The woman to your left, Alan, is Janet Granowski from Legal, and she's going to explain to you what we're going to claim that you've done, which firm policies and procedures you've violated and why we believe that our only recourse is to terminate you for cause at this time. Janet will also explain your legal rights and your options concerning how we proceed from here."

As Alan looked at Janet, who nodded but didn't smile, David stood up, looked at Alan with disgust, left the conference room and returned to his office.

The other agenda item for that day was to let John Henriksen go and to announce that Vivian Zimm had been asked, and had agreed, to relinquish her coverage of life insurance and to pick up John's property/casualty insurers as quickly as she could. David did the former at 4:30 Monday afternoon and the latter on Tuesday's Morning Call.

At the end of The Call, long after David had returned to his office, Maryanne Miles opened her handbag, found $100 and handed it to Herb Hirschorn.

"Is that all you charged her?" Barbara Malek teased,

looking at Herb. "I'd heard that studs like you got $250 to $500, sometimes more."

"I do," Herb said confidently, "but this isn't for that."

"It's for Vivian Zimm," Maryanne explained. "Herb told me the day David announced Vivian's hiring that, a week after the *II* job-hoppers' deadline had passed, David would can John and give Vivian his group. I didn't believe a word of it and bet Herb a hundred bucks he was wrong."

"Pretty gutsy," Barbara mused. "Herb's been around so long he can see this stuff coming a mile away."

"Sometimes you suspect," Herb said, "but sometimes you know."

* * *

The firestorm over New Nevada raged uncontrollably. Unlike any of his other "big calls," New Nevada had infuriated a large number of BCS's retail brokers, several dozen of whom had called Nick daily to complain about how far under water their clients were in the stock. They asked for or demanded relief and, in some cases, threatened to "do something" if no help was forthcoming.

"My target price was only $15," Nick said defensively. "I never recommended that any of your clients pay $18 or $19 for the stock."

"Did you see how fast it moved? If you put in limit orders you got nothing. If you put in market orders you wound up paying more than $15 for it. That's just the way it happened."

"I don't know what I can do at this point," Nick sighed. The stock was back around $11, so the vast majority of BCS's retail clients had losses in their positions.

"We should bust the trades and give them back their money" said one broker.

"Why?"

"Because they lost so much money so fast."

"And if they had *made* that much money, would we also bust the trade and strip them of their profits?"

The broker was silent.

"Why this double standard?" Nick asked. "If we make a call and clients lose money, we're supposed to bust the trades and wipe away their losses, but if we make a call and the clients make money, we never seem to call them up and say that we want them to share part of their profits with us."

"We're paid to make the clients money," the broker answered.

"But we're not dealing in riskless investments. Clients have to assume risks to make money in stocks. It's absolutely absurd to think that they can keep all their winnings when we're right and demand that we bust their trades when we're wrong."

"Not every time we're wrong, Nick, just when we're very wrong."

"New Nevada isn't one of those."

"I think it is."

"I went to a Buy at $11, with a target price of $15. The stock went briefly above $15, largely because of CNBC which failed to mention my target price, and then it dropped back to $15 and ultimately to $11. I'm a buyer at $11 but I'm a holder at $15. No one can fault me on the recommendation. If your clients bought it above $15, they failed to follow my advice. I don't see that BCS owes them anything."

"I'm going to get sued over this, Nick."

"No you're not."

"Yes I am, unless I can get my manager to get approval to bust the trades."

"Do what you have to do," Nick sneered. "but don't expect the firm to pay your clients back. It's just not going to happen."

Day after day it continued.

"My clients are furious."

"I'm going to talk to my manager."

"My client says he'll complain to NASDAQ about us."

"The firm really owes my clients a refund."

"My client says he'll sue us."

"They'll do what they have to," Nick said, repeating his mantra. But just as he'd surmised, no help for the brokers or their clients was forthcoming.

* * *

"Can I come see you for a minute?" Paul Pitcher asked telephonically.

David looked at his watch. "In ten?"

"Perfect."

David hated when Paul asked to see him in person because Paul was exceptionally discreet and whenever he couldn't do something by phone it almost always spelled trouble. Today was no exception.

"Did I do something bad?" David asked as Paul settled in on the sofa and dropped a stack of papers on David's coffee table.

"No."

"Closed door?"

Paul nodded, so David closed the door and sat down directly across from him.

"Did you hear anything about Boston?"

David shook his head.

"We just finished up a regional FA gathering there. Big event, very successful, 300 brokers, all very equity-oriented."

"Analysts presented?"

"Four, and they all did a great job. Nothing wrong at that end."

"Then what?"

"Linda."

"Again?"

"Again, David, and worse than I've ever seen her."

"What did she say?"

"Wait," Paul said, reaching for a tiny tape recorder. "Thank God I didn't have to memorize everything."

He pressed Play and said, "Here we go, in the order she said things."

"My Recommended List's performance directly mirrors our own analysts' stock-picking abilities. Lately, both have sucked." Linda's voice was very recognizable.

"The worst thing that could've happened just did, and that's losing Nancy Natolio because if there ever was an analyst on whom you could make money, even if it was by doing exactly the opposite of whatever she said, it was Nancy."

David winced.

"You can't make *II* if you're a good stock picker. They're mutually exclusive. So, the more ranked analysts we hire, the worse this already-bad situation is going to get."

David nodded.

"The worst of the new hires is clearly Daniel Roe, Mr. Vacation Value Link, who shaded his price target, you may recall, from $125 to $15 when he joined us. Rumor has it that David paid Daniel $10 million a year to get him, which is a lot more than I make, so you can guess what I'm planning with respect to my own career development."

David could hear a great deal of laughter in the background.

"I'm also thinking about doing an Anne Reiss," Linda went on.

"Did the brokers know what that meant?"

"No," Paul said, shaking his head, "so she explained that it meant getting five days of pay for three days of work and having four-day weekends 52 times a year."

David sighed slowly. "What else?"

Paul pressed Play again. "Katherine Lillard is the single dumbest analyst I've ever met. I'd have nixed her in a heartbeat but, as you know, David has bent over backwards to exclude me from the interviewing process in recent years so I wasn't given the chance."

"What else?"

"In our quest for *II* legitimacy, we are sacrificing an ever-growing number of you at the FA altar, and I expect to see an exodus among our best producers over the next two years."

"Jesus."

"And in my quest to revive the performance of my Recommended List, I intend to begin using research from Salomon, Goldman, Merrill Lynch and Morgan Stanley."

"That makes no sense at all. They're more *II* -driven than we are!"

"I know, but no one challenged her about it. All they wanted to know was if it violated firm policy to send clients reports written by analysts at other firms."

"So Linda's position is that our analysts are no longer worth following."

"Many of them, I'm afraid."

"Great!" David rolled his eyes.

"She said one other thing that I think you should hear, David."

"Press that button."

"David? David you're asking about? Here's my two cents about David. Twelve months from now, he'll be gone, either because he found the job too frustrating or because of mounting pressure from many of you to replace him, or possibly both."

David was incredulous.

"This is simply my opinion. I have no firsthand knowledge to support this theory, but I'm sticking to it anyway. And in answer to the question about my interest in David's job, no interest…as in none." Paul pressed Stop.

David's body felt leaden. He could barely move. He thanked Paul for the feedback and shook his hand, but he couldn't even muster the energy to stand up and show him out. So Paul opened David's door himself and closed it behind him.

* * *

That evening, David made his way to 111 East 71st Street, to the office of Dr. Stephen Brill Kurtin, dermatologist. David had begun seeing Dr. Kurtin seven years earlier after his G.P. had spotted something on David's back that had looked suspicious. The "something" turned out to be malignant melanoma which, upon further testing and the removal of some surrounding tissue, was determined to have been caught early and deemed unlikely to have spread. David had insisted on going for quarterly checkups thereafter, even though Dr. Kurtin had suggested semiannuals, and three years later, Dr. Kurtin had found another small patch of malignant melanoma, this time on David's side. This too was very superficial, caught early and deemed unlikely to cause further trouble, but still David went like clockwork for his 90–day updates.

He had just finished stripping down to his shorts when Dr. Kurtin tapped once on the examination room door and walked in. "How are you?" he asked, smiling at David and looking quickly through David's file.

"Very well, Dr. Kurtin, and you?"

"Do you know the only time men brag about having the *smallest* one?"

"No, when?"

"When they're talking about their cell phones. Lie on your stomach."

David liked his dermatologist very much. Beyond respecting his abilities and his reputation (he was frequently listed in *New York* magazine's annual compilation of the city's best doctors), David found him funny, smart, interesting and easy to talk to. He'd learned over time a little bit about the doctor's wife (a successful Manhattan realtor), his three children (including a son in the hedge fund business in Boston), and where the name Brill had come from (his mother's maiden name).

"So how's business?" he asked as he examined part of David's back more closely.

"I need a vacation."

"Business is slow?"

"No, it's the job I think. It's walking on eggshells with mediocre analysts for fear of pissing them off and encouraging them to quit. It's dealing with investment bankers who have no respect for anyone else's time, no qualms about doing crappy deals and no prayer of landing better ones. It's having to cover up the ineptitude of a sales manager who can't figure out which accounts the analysts should be focusing on and why. It's having a gun to my head to recruit All Star analysts when we have nothing to offer them that their bulge-bracket employers aren't already providing. It's dealing with an egomaniacal strategist who can't stand competition and who constantly works to undermine me."

"Other than that, you love your job," Dr. Kurtin joked. "Turn over."

"It's analysts with Buy ratings and $30 target prices on stocks selling at $35. It's nightmares about getting Lame-O Awards on CNBC. It's retail brokers who say they'll lose $50 million accounts because we can't provide coverage on their clients' biggest holdings. It's needing to be more visible to the analysts, the institutional salespeople, the traders, the bankers, the marketing people in retail, the senior managers elsewhere in the firm and 300 of our best institutional clients yet being one human being. It's analysts surfing porn sites. It's analysts who want chauffeurs. It's analysts explaining to me why being in the bottom third of the department isn't underperforming. It's having no time to think about investment issues because I'm in the personnel business all day long."

"Can't someone help you?"

"Oh, I forgot. And it's having a boss who molests the women in my own department all day long.

"You're kidding."

"I'm not."

"Sit up. Everything looks fine."

David got up and started to get dressed. "You know, one day I'm going to write a book about this."

"Well if you do, make sure you write a scene with me in it."

"You mean one in which I say how smart and witty and wise you are?"

"That's a good start," Dr. Kurtin said, smiling, "and how I ooze with raw, masculine sexuality."

"It's a deal," David said.

"See you in six months."

"See you in three."

* * *

When his phone rang the following morning, David saw that Paul Pitcher was calling him so he picked it up.

"What's up?"

"Actually, the better question is what's down?" Paul said. David just listened. "And what's down, I'm afraid, is EWTI."

"EWTI," David repeated. He tried to recognize the ticker symbol but couldn't.

"Electro Wafer Tools." David punched it up on his computer and found it trading at $19.30, down $2.10.

"Is this a Hovanian stock?"

"Correct."

"That's interesting. I figured for sure that, if you were going to flag a problem in Hovanian's universe it was going to be California Wapher."

"That's a problem too. When he downgraded it in July, he really cleaned its clock. I think the stock went from $37 to $27 on the downgrade, but then it came right back to $33 so he never went back to the Buy on it. All he really accomplished was to blow a lot of our clients out in the $27 to $30 area which, with the stock now at $33, looks like it was unnecessary."

"I took a lot of angry calls on that one," David recalled, "but I can guarantee you that, if he'd continued to keep a Buy on it in the high 30s, with a target price of $35, I would have gotten a lot of 'How could it still be a Buy?' calls instead."

"That may be true. In any event, it isn't CWCC that's getting the brokers all agitated right now, it's EWTI."

"Why?"

"I don't know how up you are on James's original call on the stock, but some time in the spring he raised his rating from Accumulate to Buy and dangled in front of the brokers a $60 target price."

"I think I remember that."

"Most of the field liked the call and the guys ran with it. We bought a ton of stock in the low 30s and more in the high 20s when it dipped in June. All of those positions are well under water now."

"I'm surprised I haven't gotten calls on it."

"You're going to. I think what's happening right now is that the slow, steady erosion in the price of the stock during the summer is accelerating and it's getting some of the FAs very agitated. I've gotten a bunch of calls over the past few days with comments like 'He just did it because it was *II* season and he wanted to call attention to himself' or 'This smells just like Henry Blodget recommending Amazon except Henry was right and Amazon went up.'"

"So they're questioning his motives and the sincerity of his views."

"Exactly… and that's not a good thing."

"Let me do some homework so I'm prepared when the calls start to come in."

"I would, David, because they're coming."

David hung up and dialed Herb Hirschorn.

"Herb, do you remember Hovanian's call on Electro Wafer in the spring?"

"You mean the 'I'm-raising-my-rating-to-Buy-and-I-expect-it-to- double' call?"

"Yes."

"Of course."

"What did the sales force do with it?"

"Well, I can't speak for everyone, but New York Sales made it unenthusiastically and then pretended· that we hadn't."

"Why?"

"Because we're paid to make calls whether we agree with them or not."

"No, I mean why you didn't like it."

"You know why, David. If you can spell *II* season, or you can spell Henry Blodget, you can find what you're looking for."

* * *

"Meet me in front of the building," Barry Seels said into his phone. Ten minutes later, Keith Jackman did. Barry motioned for Keith to take a walk with him.

"Don't touch your rating on Primo," he said when they were alone.

"Remember when I told you that, if I pulled the plug on it, it would go to $4?"

"Yup."

"Well, it went to $4 any way so what did I accomplish by keeping the Buy on it?"

"You enabled us to get the mandate to sell them."

"You're kidding. They're willing to be sold?"

"If I can get them $10 to $12. I'll have to start at $15, and it won't be easy, but they're sick of being a public company with an ever-declining stock price and they're sick of dealing with angry brokers and institutional clients all day long."

"Have you started shopping them?"

"Tomorrow. And I have to work fast because they're going to miss their numbers again in the September quarter which isn't going to help the stock price."

"You shouldn't have told me this."

"I didn't. Just don't touch your rating."

Keith nodded.

"With the stock at $4, paying $10 to $12 will look extremely generous," Barry said.

"But with the stock at $2…," Keith said.

"… you're talking Magic Kingdom."

* * *

On Friday, August 29, the dog days of summer turned rabid. The Dow Jones Industrials fell almost 4% and NASDAQ plunged more than 6%, and over half of the decline occurred during the final hour of trading.

Ken Lavery had taken a long walk around the block at 3:30 because he just couldn't bear to watch his screen any longer. When he returned at 3:55 he found three messages marked Urgent from Tom Hanks which he opted not to return.

At 4:15, with GNOM at $11.90 and GINV at $11.60, he called Tomback.

"Jesus, what a day!" Tom said.

"Lots of margin calls?"

"Lots of margin calls, not that having company will make you feel any better."

"Where do I stand?"

"Let's see. You've got 170,000 GNOM at $11.90, so that's $2,023,000, and you've got 170,000 GINV at $11.60 so that's $1,972,000. So your portfolio is down to $3,995,000, your loan's still $3,150,000 so your equity is down to $845,000."

"And that is…"

"… 21% of the value of your holdings. We've got to get you back to 30%."

"How can I do that?"

"You can send me $600,000."

Ken swallowed hard. "And if I don't have that kind of liquidity?"

"Then we'd need to sell some of your stocks."

"How much?"

"About $1,200,000."

"God, Tom, that's 30% of my portfolio."

"I know, I feel awful, but that's the underbelly of margin. It's intoxicating on the way up and it's scary as Hell on the way down."

"Can't I sell less?"

"Afraid not. If you sold $1,000,000 of your stocks and took your margin loan back to $2,150,000, the loan would still be 72% of the value of your remaining portfolio. It can't be above 70%."

Ken was silent for a long time.

"Do you have $600,000 you can send me?"

"Not right now."

"Can you get it?"

"I don't know where to go."

"Can you get an advance on your next bonus?"

"I could ask."

"Any unused credit lines elsewhere that you could tap?"

"Maybe a bigger mortgage on my house."

"That'll take too long. We need to do this over the next 24 hours."

Ken was quiet again.

"Do you want me to sell the stock?" Tom asked.

"Can you give me until Monday morning?"

"Yes, but let's agree that, if I don't hear from you by 11:00, I'll go ahead and sell enough stock to get your equity back to 30%."

"And you think that's $1,200,000."

"It's about 50,000 shares of each, assuming they're flat on Monday morning."

"Okay," Ken said, "I'll call you by 11:00."

SEPTEMBER

Five minutes after David had returned to his office on Monday morning from a breakfast meeting with newly hired Investment Banking associates, he heard a knock on his door and saw Ken Lavery's face in his doorway.

"David, do you have a minute?"

"Ken! Sure, come in."

"Do you mind?" Ken asked as he closed the door behind him and sat down on the sofa.

"You look tired."

"I have a little problem that I need your help on."

"Shoot."

"Well, I'm sure I'm not alone but I got really nailed in a couple of stocks on Friday."

"Jesus, what a market!"

Ken nodded. "And I really don't want to have to dump them at the bottom, but I got a margin call and I have to decide what to do about it this morning."

David nodded but said nothing.

"I told my broker I wanted to send him the cash he'd need to restore sufficient equity to my account. My problem is that I need to increase my mortgage in order to do that and I can't in 24 hours. My banker has assured me that I have $540,000 of additional borrowing capacity because I put down a larger down payment than I needed to so there's no doubt that I can get the funds. It's just a question of how quickly."

"So you need a loan."

"Or an advance against my next bonus."

"What if the market takes another beating today?"

"Then I would throw in the towel. I just can't throw more good money after bad. But my hunch is that my stocks are so washed out at this point that I'll get at least a technical bounce out of them and that bounce will give me some breathing room."

"How long would it take you to get the additional mortgage money?"

"Two or three weeks."

"So if we advanced you $540,000 against your next bonus with the written understanding that you'd repay that advance in full with $540,000 from your mortgage refinancing, you'd be okay?"

"I'd be great, David."

"How about this. Let's not do anything until we see how the market opens today. If it opens sharply lower and you decide to sell stocks rather than send in more cash, I won't need to do anything. But if it's flat or higher, and if your stocks are too, then I'll ask Carl to approve it."

"That would be great, David. I can't tell you how much I appreciate this."

David nodded and waved his right hand back and forth in a "don't mention it" kind of way. "I'll call you at 10:30 and see what you've decided to do."

* * *

"It's Katherine, Carl," his secretary Heather Weeks yelled.

"Fuck!" Carl hated Katherine. She was smart, self-confident, capable, no-nonsense and powerful, everything he despised in a woman, and whenever she called it was always to give him work to do which was one more reason for profanity.

"Katherine?"

"Good morning, Carl. How are you?"

"Oh, swell."

"Good. Carl, I'm just calling to give you a heads-up that you'll be getting a memo from me this morning requesting, for budget-planning purposes, a complete headcount for all of your divisions, including hires this year, resignations and terminations, and open searches. I'll need it by the 30th."

"Not a problem."

"Good. Thanks." Katherine wasted no words, especially on Carl.

"Cunt," Carl sneered, slamming down his phone. No waste at his end either.

At his desk in the National Association of Securities Dealers' or NASD Market Surveillance Department in lower Manhattan, James Klenger read a letter that sounded very familiar.

"I am writing to you in utter disgust over the manner in which the shares of New Nevada Mining were manipulated last month," it began. "I'm sure I'm not the first person to complain about this. As your trading records will show, New Nevada went from \$11 to \$19 to \$11, all the same day, on very heavy volume. I believe that the recommendation to buy those shares that was put out by BC Securities that morning was responsible for the very sharp spike in their price during the morning and early afternoon. Further, I believe that management's disavowal of the earnings estimates used in that recommendation was responsible for the sharp sell off in the shares beginning around 2:30 P.M.

"I watch CNBC regularly and they carried stories about BC Securities' recommendation of NEWN in the morning as well as management's disavowal in the afternoon. Certainly, they contributed to the wild gyrations in the price of these shares, but I cannot help but believe that something else was at work here, something far more sinister, something that enabled individuals and/or BC Securities' trading desk to get into NEWN at $11 before the spike and to get out at $18 or $19 just before management made its comments. I personally bought 45,000 shares of NEWN after hearing the first story on CNBC, and I paid an average price of $16.85 a share. While I was somewhat concerned when I heard CNBC's second story, I never imagined that the stock would plunge eight points during the last 90 minutes of trading and finish back at $11, but it did and I lost more than $350,000 as a result.

"This smacks of market manipulation at its very worst. Clearly, someone or some organization, perhaps BCS's own trading desk, dumped vast quantities of NEWN on the market late that afternoon, and those shares, I suspect, were purchased at much lower prices before the BCS recommendation was made. Someone made a killing while others, like myself, got killed. I find this very disheartening, and I urge you in the strongest terms to investigate New Nevada and take action against those who profited illegally from a 16–point, one-day move in an 11-dollar stock." The letter was signed Paul Huntzinger, Palm Beach Florida.

Klenger made some notes indicating the date and

time that he'd reviewed the letter and added it to the New Nevada file on his desk which he'd created two weeks earlier and which had grown fat, quickly, with almost identical letters from impoverished and very angry investors in 16 states.

* * *

At 10:15, Ken heard his phone ring and Caller ID said it was David Meadows.

"Looks good," David said, and it did. The market had bounced and so had Ken's babies. GNOM was up $0.60 to $12.50, and GINV was up $0.80 to $12.40. Ken's equity had increased $238,000, to $1,083,000, and to 26% from 21% of the value of his portfolio.

"Do you still want the advance?"

"Please, David." By adding $540,000 of cash to his account, Ken would increase his equity to $1,623,000 or 34% of his holdings.

"Let's see what I can do."

Fifteen minutes later, David called back to say that Carl had approved the loan. Actually, what Carl had said was, "If he doesn't pay it back, David, I'll take it out of *your* bonus," but David didn't mention that to Ken.

At 11:00, Ken called Tom Hanks and told him to expect a wire transfer of $540,000 by the end of the day. At 4:00, when the market closed, with both stocks trading at $12.60 and with the wire transfer done, Ken's equity had almost doubled to $1,674,000 and his margin debt had been reduced to 65% from 79%.

For the first time in more than 24 hours, Ken felt his body unwind. "Please please please," he whispered, imagining himself on his knees before his mortgagee. "I'll pay it down with my bonus. I promise."

* * *

"Carl wants to see you," Lisa told David.

"Now?"

"Now."

"Okay, tell him I'm on my way," David said, heading for the elevators. When he got to Carl's office, he found his boss flirting with Heather Weeks again. Carl didn't wave David in but chose, instead, to keep him standing outside his office while he finished conversing with Heather.

"This real-good-looking, 25-year-old trailer-trash chick decides to try to get rich quick by marrying this 80-year-old billionaire and fucking him to death on their wedding night..."

Heather rolled her eyes and shook her head.

"...so she gets him to the altar, they get hitched, and they head off on their honeymoon. The first night, she gets undressed and hops into bed, waiting for the old fart to come out of the bathroom. She thinks he's going to have his jammies on or something. Anyway, when he comes out, he's stark naked, he's got this ten-inch hard-on, he's put on a condom, and he's got earplugs in one hand and nose plugs in the other.

"The chick doesn't know what he's up to, so she says, 'What the Hell are those things for?' and he says 'Darlin' there are two things in life that I just can't stand... the sound of a young girl screaming and the smell of burning rubber'"

"Go do your meeting," Heather said, nodding towards David.

Carl chuckled to himself and walked into his office.

David followed, and took a chair in front of Carl's desk.

"You know, you should be careful what you say to her," David said quietly.

"Why?"

"Because she's been a good sport so far, but one of these days she's going to wake up and decide she's tired of being a good sport and tell someone you're harassing her."

"That's bullshit."

"I don't think so, Carl."

For a minute, Carl just looked down at his desktop and said nothing. Then, he smiled and looked back at David. "Did I ever tell you what my take on sexual harassment is?"

"I can guess."

"No. Really."

David shook his head.

"It's short and sweet. It goes something like this. If you come to work one day, and on your way up in the elevator, you notice some really hot babe who works in your department, and she's got this really short, really tight dress on, and it's cut really low in the front, and she looks at you, and you're wondering what to say to her, don't say 'Gee I'd love to fuck you' or 'What would it take for you to blow me?' or 'You have an amazing body' or 'You've got such great legs' or 'You look really good today' or even 'How nice to see you.'

"You don't say any of things because, even though she's trying to turn you on by uncovering 90% of her thighs or flashing the top of her tits at you, you don't want to harass her so you just pretend that you don't care about what the rest of her tits look like, or whether she's got panties on or not, and you say to her, 'Good morning.'"

David rolled his eyes.

"That's it. Now if, after you've said 'Good morning,' she asks you if you'd like her to give you a blow job in the elevator, you're 100% free to say yes, because you didn't ask, she offered. But if she doesn't, you just say 'Good morning' and then watch the floors light up or something until you arrive wherever you're going."

"And that's Sexual Harassment 101."

"Sexual harassment is *bullshit*, David. Case closed."

David nodded. This was not worth debating with Carl. "So what did you want to talk to me about?"

"I got this love note from Linda Logan today," Carl said, picking a two-page memo up from the top of his empty desk "Have you seen it?"

"Was I copied on it?"

"No, just Dieter and Vilhelm."

"Well then you can assume I haven't."

"It's about stock picking," Carl said. "It details seven stocks that Linda had on her Recommended List that cratered this year. All seven were buy-rated by your analysts."

David loved how the analysts became "his" whenever they did something wrong.

"Which analysts?"

Carl scanned the memo. "Daniel Roe, Katherine Lillard, Keith Jackman, Robin Lomax, Tim Omori, Van Trudell and Vivian Zimm."

"What a coincidence?"

"What?"

"All *II* -rated."

"Who gives a shit!" Carl bellowed. "What matters, David, is that these seven analysts have all had blow-ups this year that have killed the performance of Linda's Recommended List."

"Can I see the list?"

Carl handed him the memo and David perused it. Sure enough, seven blow-ups covered by seven ranked analysts, all stocks that Linda had put on her Recommended List because the analysts had liked them.

"We've got a lot of company here," David protested.

"What do you mean?"

"I mean that we weren't the only ones who missed these stories."

"How do you know?"

"Because, Carl, stocks don't go from $40 to $25 in one trade because BCS had earnings estimates that were too high. When you hit bubbles like that it means The Street en masse got it wrong."

"You'll have to prove it to me. I don't buy it."

David shook his head. "What do you want, Carl, a memo detailing how each of our competitors rated each of these stocks before it blew up?"

"That would be good for starters. Besides, we're supposed to be better than our competitors. We're supposed to sniff these problems out *before* they do. Being as wrong as everyone else is nothing to be proud of."

David sighed. How easy it was to say these things when you were neither the analysts doing the research nor the manager supervising them.

"I need it right away," Carl said sternly. "Linda's gone to Vilhelm on this."

"Really! Dieter wasn't good enough?"

"It seems not."

"Why stop at Vilhelm? He's only the CEO. What about Gerhard Schroeder? Whatabout God himself?"

"That'll be her next memo… when Vilhelm doesn't punish you enough."

"This is such bullshit, such a complete waste of my time."

"Whatever it is, David, get me the answers ASAP." Carl gave David his "get out of here" look and David got out.

When he returned to his office he sent the seven analysts an e-mail asking them to document what each of their competitors had been saying about the blow-up stock in question prior to its implosion. Four of the seven analysts called to complain that this was a waste of their time, but David didn't give an inch. "Carl wants it and he wants it now so please don't debate with me about it. Just do it."

When the results were all in, David sent them on to Carl. "They're all the same," he told his boss. "Merrill missed them, Goldman missed them, Morgan Stanley missed them, CSFB missed them, Lehman missed them, Salomon missed them, everybody missed them."

David assumed that this would be the end of the story but, a week later, Carl called with word that he and David had been asked to meet with Vilhelm and Dieter about Linda's memo and that David should arm himself well because it wasn't going to be pretty.

* * *

Ken Lavery's phone rang incessantly.

"How can this be happening?"

"Don't you know what's wrong?"

"I'm getting killed here."

"I thought you said they were going to 100!"

GNOM and GINV were under pressure again and so was Ken. No sooner had he deposited his advance in his brokerage account, restoring sufficient equity and precluding, he'd thought, additional margin calls, then the baby biotechs had begun to falter again. GNOM had peaked at $12.70 but then dropped back to $11, and GINV, after having reached $12.85, fell harder, to $10.40.

"Dammit!" Ken yelled at no one in particular. His 340,000 shares had declined in value to $3,638,000 which, when added to his $540,000 advance, generated a total portfolio value of $4,178,000. But the $3,150,000 margin loan now represented 75% of that value and Ken's equity was once again down to 25%. "I'm waiting!" he bellowed at his telephone. "You know you want me."

But Tom Hanks was silent. Instead, more and more frantic brokers who were up to their eyeballs in GNOM and GINV called and shrieked.

"Why are people dumping them?"

"Did *you* sell your shares?"

"Can't you *do* something?"

"Can't you get management to *say* something?"

Over and over again Ken tried to keep his cool and to provide words of reassurance. No, there was no fundamental reason for the sell off. Yes, he still held every share he'd ever bought and was planning to buy more if he could. No, he had checked with management and they had no plans to issue any press releases just because the stocks were down. No, he didn't know when and where the stocks would bottom although he thought they were close.

Each time a broker called, Ken spoke, almost without thinking, keeping his eyes glued to his PC

screen…$11… $10.97… $10.93… $10.90… $10.85.
As the prices declined, Ken's heartbeat quickened. He
felt drenched and nauseous. His head spun. Sometimes, everything got dark, but only for a few seconds.

Finally the call came.

"Ken, it's Tom Hanks."

"I know, you need more equity."

"What do you want to do?"

"There's nothing I *can* do, Tom. I've got nothing
else to send you."

"So you want me to sell shares and pay down your
margin debt?"

"Yes." Ken swallowed hard and he could feel tears
welling up in his eyes. "How much will you have to
sell?"

"About $1,000,000. That would bring your portfo-
lio down to about $3 million, and your loan down
to about $2 million, leaving you equity of about $1
million or a third of your portfolio value."

"I'm going to lose a third of my stock?"

"I'm sorry."

"Wait while I get clearance." Ken put Tom on hold
and returned in less than a minute. "Do it," he
snapped. He hung up and sat, dazed and confused,
in front of the PC screen with all the red arrows on
it. For many minutes, no phones rang. All Ken could
hear, it seemed, was blood pumping in his ears…
thump, thump, thump… exactly when his heart beat.

When the phone rang again, Ken looked at Caller
ID and saw the words Unknown Number/Unknown
Name. A broker, he thought. With eyes unfocused
and head bowed, he drew the receiver slowly to his
ear.

"Lavery."

"Ken. You've done me a great disservice," the deep,

melodious, almost hypnotic voice said. "I trusted you and you've bankrupted me. Hardly fair, I'm sure you'd agree. I've suffered so much, you see, but you've suffered not at all, and that's something that I must change. *Must* change. You see, I know about 333 East 79th Street…"

Ken visualized his apartment.

"…and Peters Pond…"

Ken saw his Sagaponack home.

"…and 315 Ocean Drive…"

Ken saw his widowed mother's condominium in Florida, and her standing on her terrace, coffee cup in hand, watching the waves break.

"Wherever you are, Ken, I'm going to find you. And when I do…I'm going to kill you."

* * *

"Ron Vargo is next," Paula Hainsworth told the salesmen, "with an initiation of coverage. Ron?"

"Thanks, Paula, and good morning. We're initiating coverage today on Four Dimensions Media, which trades over the counter under the ticker symbol FDME. The stock closed last night at $14.90. My earnings estimates are $0.72 for 2003, versus $0.75 last year, and $0.80 for 2004. The *First Call* consensus is $0.74 for this year and $0.84 for next. We're initiating coverage with a Sell rating and a target price of $12.

"Four Dimensions is one of the smallest, publicly traded advertising agencies. It has a solid management team, several members of which are Omnicom and Interpublic veterans, a respectable and reasonably stable client list and a good long-term earnings growth record that will probably be broken this year but resume next year. There are four reasons why we're initiating with a Sell.

"First, the company is small and the industry is growing increasingly concentrated, with more and more clients choosing to consolidate their accounts with the largest and most global advertising and marketing services companies. This will prove disadvantageous to Four Dimensions longer term.

"Second, the company's product and service offerings are more narrow than those of their larger competitors. The company has less exposure to direct marketing, public relations, market research and other, similar services, making it more reliant on traditional advertising revenues, and thus more cyclical. We don't expect a material pickup in the advertising business for three to four quarters and we expect advertising to lag the economy as it emerges from the recession.

"Third, FDME's client base is skewed more substantially towards companies in the technology and telecommunications sectors, and many of those companies may not be able to materially boost their ad spending any time soon.

"Finally, the stock looks ahead of itself in the face of down earnings this year and only 10% growth next year. Part of the problem, in my view, has been speculation in some quarters about FDME's takeover appeal. We don't view FDME as especially likely to be acquired any time soon, management professes to be disinterested in combining with any larger organization, and we think the company should be valued on earnings and nothing more. Our target price represents 16–17 times this year's earnings and 15 times next year's, versus the P/E of 20 or more up to which the stock recently ran, seemingly on takeover rumors that turned out not to be true.

"Let me fill in a few holes by elaborating on these points and providing a little bit of additional background on the company…"

From a pay phone two miles away, Claire O'Daniel listened in to The Call using a dial-in number that Ron had given her, and smiled.

* * *

Later that morning, Keith Jackman found Barry Seels standing in his doorway. Keith didn't like Barry's expression.

"May I come in?"

"What do you think?"

Barry closed the door and took a chair next to Keith's desk.

"I suspect you're here to tell me why Primo isn't returning any of my calls."

Barry nodded but didn't say anything for a long time. Finally, he sighed and said, "They're going to issue a press release this afternoon pre-announcing a small loss for the September quarter."

"Jesus!" Keith yelled, standing up, picking a clock up off his desk and hurling it at his office door. "How could this fucking happen?"

"I don't know. Admissions are down, they hired too many people just before the IPO, the cost of opening new theaters got away from them, who can tell?"

"How much of a loss?"

"A small one. Maybe $0.02 to $0.03 a share."

"They're still going to get killed." Keith checked his PC screen. Primo was trading at $3.85.

Keith looked back at Barry and waited. After a moment, Barry shook his head slowly. "No buyers."

"At any price?"

"At anything with two digits in it."

"They'll have to take less," Keith sneered.

"Maybe, but they won't do a deal like that with us."

"You mean they'll give it to Goldman or Morgan?"

"Or Merrill or Salomon."

Keith just stared blankly at his PC for a long time. He remembered all of the times he should have downgraded from Buy to Hold but didn't. He could feel it eating holes in the lining of his belly.

"What are you going to do?"

"Drop coverage. I don't want to be associated with it any longer than I have to."

"Who needs to approve that?"

"David."

"When are you going to see him? I'd like to let Primo know before it happens."

"When's the press release coming out?"

"About 2:00."

Keith looked at his watch, saw that it was 11:45 and got to his feet.

"Right now. I want to drop it as soon as they announce."

*　*　*

"Okay, one more time," David was saying as he wrapped up a meeting on *II* that he'd been holding with Matt in his office.

"We started with five All Stars from last year's poll," Matt said. David nodded.

"We hired 12, but one of them, Louis Liddy, didn't stick, so we wound up only adding 11." David continued nodding.

"Liz Tytus quit…"

"…and Nancy Natolio quit."

"Correct," Matt said, "so we started with five, our net addition was nine, and that would give us 14 All Stars plus however many of the analysts who were with us last year and didn't make it last year *do* make it this year."

"And the best case there is 10."

Matt looked at his notes. The analysts who finished top-8 in *Greenwich* and who didn't make *II* last year were: Kalagian, Payden, Suess, Suprano, Burlingame, Bellone but he's gone, Noel, Hovanian, Soslow and Lerner."

"That's nine."

"So, 14 plus 9 would get us 23 All Stars, up from five, and our ranking would jump to eighth from fourteenth."

"But that's not going to happen," Matt said.

"Not even close. If half of them made it we'd wind up with 19 All Stars and we'd finish tenth. If a third of them made it we'd have 17 and also finish tenth."

"Either way we'd crack the top 10," Matt observed.

It was David's turn to nod. "It would be nice." Then he shrugged. "We'll know in three weeks."

Suddenly, Keith Jackman loomed large in David's doorway.

"Got a minute?"

David looked at Matt. "We're done?"

"We're done." Matt looked at Keith and then at David.

"Me or both of us?" David asked.

"Doesn't matter," Keith said.

David asked Matt to stay and Keith to take a chair. Keith closed the door behind him and, without waiting for an invitation, launched into his tale of woe.

"The issue at hand is Primo Theaters. I'm sure you

remember it, David. It was the IPO that we hotly debated at a Commitment Committee meeting in February that Matt had to leave. You relieved him."

David and Matt both nodded.

"We had filed with an offering range of $10 to $13. I had said that the stock was worth $12, and that I'd only be able to have a Buy on it if we did the deal at $10. Barry wanted to do it at $12, if not $13. I thought they could do $0.40 a share this year and $0.47 to $0.48 next year, and that 25 times earnings was a fair P/E for Primo."

"I think we worried that, even if we did the deal at $10, it would jump to $12 in the aftermarket and that you'd feel pressure to downgrade to Hold immediately, which would have looked pretty silly."

"That's right, and that's exactly what happened. We did the deal in early March, the stock got as high as $11.25, but I kept the Buy on it anyway because I didn't want to flip my rating so soon after the deal had been done. A month later, Primo pre-announced that it would miss the March quarter and I had to cut my full-year estimate from $0.40 to $0.35. The stock fell from $11 to $9. I kept the Buy on it."

"Why?" David asked.

"Because the stock fell faster than my estimate did, so it looked more under valued, even on the lower estimate, than it had before the press release was issued."

David said nothing.

"In May, the stock dropped below $8 for the first time but I stayed with it. In June, it got down to $7. I told Barry I was sure they were going to miss the June quarter but he told me I was wrong. He said the full-year number of $0.35 would be safe even if they only did $0.10–$0.11 versus my June-quarter estimate of $0.12."

"What *did* they do?" Matt asked.

"Within days after my meeting with Barry, they preannounced $0.08 to $0.09 for the quarter and cut their full year guidance to $0 33 to $0 35 The stock dropped to $6. It was 18 times earnings, versus 25 times when we did the IPO, so I kept the Buy on it."

"I know where this is going," David said.

"When they actually announced June-quarter results in July they reported $0.08 but they cut their guidance again, this time to $0.28 to $0.30. The stock fell to $5. Every cell in my body was screaming to downgrade, but Barry and I agreed that, if I went to Hold, I'd knock the stock down to $4 or less because Retail would dump it and we'd set ourselves up for a host of shareholder suits."

"That's why you kept the Buy on it?" David asked.

"Yes." Keith made certain to reference neither his conversations with Barry about trying to sell Primo nor their agreement that downgrading would kill any chances Barry had of landing that mandate.

"Then what happened?" Matt asked.

"The stock just drifted lower and lower. It dropped below $4 for the first time two weeks ago. It's $3.85 today."

"And...?"

"And they're not returning my calls. I'm sure they're going to miss the September quarter. They've missed every quarter since coming public. If they miss this one, the stock will go to $3, maybe even less. I just think it was a mistake, that it has no investment appeal, even at $3 or $4, and what I'd like to do is drop coverage."

"What would Barry say? It's still a banking client."

"I don't know. I haven't discussed this with him but the odds are that Primo isn't going to be doing any financing any time soon, so I'd hardly call it an ongoing client."

"Barry could be trying to sell the firm," David said.

"I wouldn't know, but I'd doubt that dropping coverage would have any effect on that, even if he was."

"You know, Keith, my feeling on situations like these is that you should've rated Primo exactly the way you'd have rated any stock that wasn't a banking client."

"I did, David."

"You've been wrong on the earnings and the stock has gotten hammered."

"Correct."

"And you now think, even at $3, that it's no longer a Buy."

"Their earnings are a moving target. I started out thinking they could make $0.40. Maybe they can only make $0.20 or $0.10. Even at $3 it's rich."

"You can't drop it," David said firmly.

"Why?"

"Because you've been telling Retail for eight months to buy it all the way down. You can't go from Buy to Drop Coverage. They'll scream bloody murder if you do and they'll be right."

"So when *can* I drop it?"

"First you'll have to downgrade it to Hold or Sell. You'll knock the stock down even farther but that can't be helped. Then wait 30 days, after which I'll let you drop it. It still will stink, but at least you'll have given the FAs 30 days of negative advice on the stock before you start pretending it never existed."

That afternoon, immediately after the preannouncement, Keith cut his estimates on Primo to $0.10 for the current year and $0.15 for next year and downgraded the shares from Buy to Hold.

Retail raged. And Primo lost more than half of its already shrunken value, plunging $2.10 in the afternoon and closing at $1.75.

* * *

As David scanned his e-mails, CNBC caught his eye. The market was up sharply, and Leslie Laroche was standing in front of "The Wall," pointing to various ticker symbols of over-the-counter stocks that were active and up or down sharply and explaining how and why they were among the day's market leaders.

"… and Microsoft is up 4.4% following an upgrade by Merrill Lynch," Leslie reported. "Just about the hottest NASDAQ name today, though, is a funny one… Saruman Software, as in Saruman from the Lord of the Rings, ticker symbol SARU. This was an IPO priced last night by Morgan Stanley and BC Securities that we'd been saying looked to be a hot deal, and hot it is! You may recall we'd been telling you that the original filing range was $15 to $18 and that the deal was increased in size and the filing range was raised to $20 to $22 last week. Well, even at $22, Saruman turned out to be a bargain because, as you can see behind me, the stock is currently trading at $57.50, up $35.50 or 161.4% from its offering price. Almost as good, Michelle, as The Two Towers' opening weekend box office, you'd have to admit."

"If Tolkien only knew what he's spawned here," said Michelle Caruso-Cabrera who was anchoring "Power Lunch." "Thanks, Leslie. Now to Bob Pisani at the Big Board. Bob?" David got up and walked down the hall to Jim Molloy's office.

Jim, who had been watching CNBC, looked up as David came in. "Hello, I'm George Schuler…," Jim said, reaching for and holding up a book on NYSE rules and regulations that had been sitting on top of his desk, "and you too can turn $100,000 into $5,750,000 in seven short months if you read my new book, "Private Placements and IPO's."

David burst out laughing. Jim sounded just like George and his numbers were right on the money.

"It's unbelievable, isn't it?"

"And legal even though it shouldn't be," Jim said.

"I just wonder how the hell he'll be able to put a Buy on this stock at $57.50 when the quiet period ends 40 days from now, knowing that he bought shares in it for $1 at the beginning of the year."

"He won't."

"He won't?" David was puzzled.

"He can't. If his target price is $65, he'll only be able to use Accumulate."

* * *

When David saw Jim Molloy standing in his doorway the following morning, he assumed that Jim was there following up on Saruman. The stock was up four more points, pushing the value of George's $100,000 investment over the $6,000,000 mark. But once he saw Jim's downturned lips he knew he'd been wrong.

"Do you have a minute?"

"Of course."

"Pat Erdenberger is about to call you," Jim said. Pat headed all of Legal and Compliance at the firm. Before he could say another word, David saw his phone light up and Pat's name and extension on his Caller ID. He looked up quickly at Jim.

"New Nevada," Jim said.

"Shit!" David picked up his phone. "Meadows."

"David, it's Pat Erdenberger."

"How are you, Pat?"

"I'm fine. Could you come see me please if you have a moment?"

"Sure, Pat, now?"

"That would be good."

"Should I bring Jim with me?"

"Your call."

"I'll be there in two minutes."

As David motioned for Jim to follow him to the elevators he asked, "Do you know what this is about?"

"I could guess, but no I don't."

"And your guess would be…?"

"…that Pat got a love note from the NASD."

Jim had guessed well, as he and David discovered soon after entering Pat's dark, wood-paneled office on the 75th floor.

"Tell me what you know," Pat said, skipping the pleasantries, "about New Nevada Mining."

David sighed. He'd been in six meetings recently on New Nevada, mostly at the request of Paul Pitcher who had been consumed by a maelstrom of broker fury over the huge losses that BCS's retail clients had taken in the stock. In each of the meetings, Nick's recommendation had been dissected, hour by hour, the magnitude of the losses in Retail land had been re-examined, and the debate over what to do next, including whether or not to bust the clients' trades and return their money, had raged.

"I know that Nick initiated coverage at $11 with a Buy and a target price of $15, that CNBC ran with the story but never mentioned Nick's target price, that the stock jumped to $19 after CNBC started talking about it, that management came out on CNBC in the afternoon and said that Nick's earnings estimates were too high, and that the stock plunged eight points in the last 90 minutes of trading, finishing the day at $11, just where it had started..."

"...and that Nick never changed his recommendation," Jim added.

David nodded.

From the top of his desk, Pat picked up a wad of white papers that were clipped at the top and looked down at them.

This must be the love note, David thought.

"David, this is a letter from the Market Surveillance Division at the NASD informing us that it has begun an informal inquiry into all trading activity in New Nevada shares prior to, on the day of, and subsequent to Nick's initiation of coverage. It wants names, addresses, phone numbers, account numbers, and life stories on everyone who bought or sold New Nevada shares through us. It also wants six months of back statements for all of those accounts, regardless of when the New Nevada trades took place."

"What are they looking for?"

"They never say, but it must be 10b-5 violations." Rule 10b-5 is the anti-fraud provision of the Securities Exchange Act of 1934 which addresses front-running, insider trading and similar abuses involving trading on information that someone shouldn't have.

"Do they want to talk to Nick?"

"They haven't indicated exactly who they'll want to interview but for sure they'll want to talk to some of our brokers who handled large trades in New

Nevada, they'll want Nick and they'll probably want you as his supervisor."

David sighed.

"What do I need to do to prepare for this?"

"Talk to Nick as soon as you leave here. Find out what aspects of this story you weren't told. Every little detail matters. Find out what paperwork exists relating to New Nevada, and I mean *everything* ...Nick's notes from his meetings with management, phone conversations he had with New Nevada especially immediately prior to his launching of coverage, notes he might have from conversations with brokers, institutional salesmen or clients about New Nevada prior to his launch, drafts of reports that were never published, everything.

"Also, check all trading activity in Nick's accounts for any traces of New Nevada."

"We already did."

"And...?"

"Nothing."

"Good. Anyway, tell Nick to destroy nothing, lose nothing, misplace nothing, shred nothing, flame broil nothing. Gather all of it as quickly as you can and bring it to me so we can review it."

David nodded. "And if we find that all he did was recommend a crappy stock with estimates that were too high and that CNBC never mentioned his target price...?"

"... we'll have dodged a very, very, very large bullet."

* * *

The downward spiral in GNOM and GINV accelerated. Ken felt paralyzed, unable to concentrate, to eat, to work, to sleep. His phone rang from morning 'til night. He never answered it. His secretary took messages, hundreds of them, all the same. Never a call from a bank trust department or mutual fund or insurance company or hedge fund. Not one call from an institutional salesperson. G-NOME and Genomic Innovators were not institutional names. They were retail names and Ken had singlehandedly built enormous positions in both stocks inside the BCS branch system. As the stocks had risen, happy brokers had averaged up but, now that the stocks were plunging, those brokers had turned vicious, frightened by their clients, by the prospect of suits and arbitrations and by the suddenly obvious lack of fundamental earnings power at either company. So they called and yelled, threatened and begged.

Ken ignored them all, focusing instead on his own account, on the way in which it had been decimated and the manner in which his margin borrowing was destroying him.

As promised, Tom Hanks had sold 50,000 shares of each name to satisfy Ken's last margin call. He'd gotten just over $10 a share for them and, after commissions, Tom had been able to pay down Ken's margin loan from $3,150,000 to $2,150,000. That had left Ken with 240,000 shares of stocks that had recovered to about $10.50 each once Ken's own selling had stopped depressing them. That $2,520,000 of equities plus his $540,000 advance from David Meadows had yielded a total portfolio value of $3,060,000 and equity in the account of $910,000. The margin loan had once again been brought back down to 70% of Ken's portfolio value. It would not be allowed to go higher.

But today, Ken felt his last hopes of ever seeing an end to the bear market in those two stocks fade away. At 1:55 p.m., Genomic Innovators pre-announced a surprisingly large September quarter loss of $1.60 a share. In prior quarters, the losses had been typically in the $0.15–$0.25 range, but this time the company had decided to write off costs associated with two products that no longer looked commercially viable, and the announcement was greeted with scorn by its already battered shareholders. Within half an hour, GINV had dropped $3 to $7.50 a share, and GNOM, in sympathy, had given up a point of its own and fallen to $9.50. By 3:00 the stocks were down to $7.20 and $8.80, and at the 4:00 close they were trading for $7.10 and $8.60, respectively.

"I've never seen anything this bad," Tom Hanks said when he'd called at 4:15.

"I feel so powerless, Tom. I just don't know what to do. All I do is stare at my screen, like I've been hit by a truck, and watch the prices fall."

"I know how upsetting this must be to you."

"It's not upsetting, really, I'm just numb. It's like I'm outside my body, floating high up in my office, looking down and watching me staring, doing nothing, waiting for your next call. I don't feel anything any more. It's so surrealistic... like it isn't real."

"But it is, Ken, and we have to do something, probably sell more stock."

"How much?"

Tom sighed for what felt like two minutes. Ken could feel tears again.

"Your 240,000 shares were worth $1,884,000 at the close. If we add your cash balance of $540,000, we get $2,424,000. But your loan is $2,150,000, so your equity is down to $274,000."

"You mean it's almost gone."

"It's $274,000, Ken, and your loan is up to 89% of your portfolio's value."

"So how much do you have to sell, Tom? Just tell me."

"A million and a half."

"Out of a million eight?"

"I'm sorry, Ken."

"How many shares are we talking about?"

"About 190,000."

"Out of 240,000."

"Yes."

"So I'm going to be left with 50,000 shares plus my advance from David."

"I'm afraid so."

"Hold while I get permission."

Thirty seconds later, Ken returned. "Sell it all," he told Tom Hanks.

"All 240,000 shares?"

"Every fucking share, Tom. Don't make me say it again."

* * *

Empty-handed, Nick went through the revolving door of Barnes & Noble on the northeast corner of 66th Street and Broadway and began walking slowly northward towards the Loews IMAX movie theater two blocks away. It was 6:15 and it was starting to get dark. He was high strung, he knew, from his recent exchanges with David over New Nevada and he desperately needed some distraction.

At the corner of 67th Street, as Nick waited for the traffic light to change, a slightly built man in a Burberry raincoat and dark glasses stopped just behind

Nick's right shoulder and said, quietly, "I'm a friend of Piotr. Look straight ahead and walk in front of me. I have a message for you."

Nick's upper body jumped involuntarily when he heard the name Piotr but he did as he was told and started walking slowly across the street after the crosstown traffic had stopped. For half a block his companion followed silently. Then, in front of The Gap, he said in a smooth, even cadence and at a volume that only Nick could hear, "Piotr asked that I tell you this. He has been contacted in recent days by two of his brokers in Europe, Morgan Stanley and Goldman Sachs. They informed him that one of your governmental agencies has requested records of his trading activity in New Nevada Mining and that both firms had turned those records over to this agency as requested. He is very concerned that two other brokers with which he does business, Merrill Lynch and Salomon, will also be asked for these records. He requests that, if you are doing anything that would call attention to New Nevada, you stop it at once." For a minute, Nick walked on in silence, looking straight ahead.

"And he asks," the voice resumed, "that you have no further contact with him, directly or through any of his associates, until this matter blows over."

Nick nodded and continued walking. At the corner of 69th Street, he stopped for another red light. When someone bumped into his right elbow, he instinctively turned to his right but all he saw was a baby carriage and a young mother who apologized for her clumsiness. And when he looked behind him, all he could see, half a block away, were two teenage girls with shopping bags full of jeans and tops from The Gap.

OCTOBER

In one of the rarest occurrences in the annals of BC Securities, Carl Robern burned the midnight oil. He'd procrastinated on getting Katherine the headcount numbers she'd called looking for at the beginning of September, and now it was October 1 and he'd missed her deadline. Needless to say, she'd called him that morning to ask where his numbers were, which had humiliated Carl no end, and he'd promised them within 24 hours, necessitating this late-night session with which Heather Weeks was helping.

In his office, as the clock struck eleven, Carl and Heather scanned all of the print outs and memos on the staffing history, status and plans for Capital Markets that they'd spread on top of tables and chairs.

Carl sighed out of fatigue. "So what's done? Banking, Sales and Trading?"

"Check. And Research is almost done."

"Fucking David. Why does everything have to be so convoluted with him? All this headhunter bullshit, all these contracts, all this *II* deadline crap. Why can't he just be like John and Billy?"

"Research is different, Carl," Heather said.

"Only in the minds of the analysts… and their boss."

For the tenth time, Carl eyed the thick stack of

papers that David had given him detailing all of the searches that had been done during the year, all the to-ing and fro-ing that had taken place in Research, the eleventh-hour resignations as *II's* job-hoppers' deadline had neared, the one-day employment of Louis Liddy, the almost-as-limited tenure of Liz Tytus, and the searches that had turned up no one and were slated to resume in January.

Carl recalled when David had told him why Liz had quit, how he'd told David that she was a liar, and how he'd characterized Liz when Dieter later inquired about any hanky panky between Carl and Liz in June.

"She's emotionally unstable and she's got a vivid imagination, Dieter, which is something she made sure no one who worked near her ever needed."

"What does that mean?"

"That she wore dresses that stopped just below her navel, and thongs, and she flashed all day long. Just ask any of the young Turks in Research about her."

Dieter had seemed satisfied and never broached the issue of Liz again.

Carl refocused on his staffing project and arched his back. "Let's break for five minutes," he suggested.

Heather smiled understandingly and sat back on the sofa. "We did good."

"You're pretty amazing," Carl said, shaking his head and looking at the mounds of paperwork surrounding them.

"You did most of it, Carl."

"No way." Carl sat quietly in a chair in front of his coffee table, almost directly opposite Heather. "Anyway, my mind's spinning. Tell me a joke or something."

Heather laughed, squinted as if she was trying to

remember one, and then began. "Okay. A guy walks into a bar and sees a man who's only 12 inches tall playing a piano that's next to some cocktail tables. He sits down at the bar, orders a drink and asks the bartender what the deal is with the midget. The bartender says, 'Before I answer your question you have to rub this magic lantern,' and he pulls a lantern from under the counter and places it on top. The customer rubs the lantern and out pops a genie who tells him he can have one wish, so, the guy silently wishes for a million bucks and rubs the lantern again. All of a sudden, there's a flash of light and the bar is full of ducks…in fact, there are a million of 'em. The guy gets hopping mad and screams at the bartender, 'I didn't want a million *ducks!*' and the bartender screams back 'Yeah, and I didn't want a 12-inch *pianist!*'"

Carl laughed. He'd known that joke for ages but he always got turned on when women told penis jokes.

"Do you know any Disney jokes?" he asked.

"Disney? Not many."

Carl didn't hesitate. "Mickey and Minnie Mouse are in divorce court. The judge says to Mickey, 'I see here that you want a divorce because your wife is crazy' and Mickey says, 'No, your honor, I want it 'cause she's fucking Goofy.'"

Heather giggled. "Okay. Snow White sees Pinocchio sitting on a table in Geppetto's workshop. She asks Geppetto to fetch her a glass of water and, as soon as he's gone, she picks Pinocchio up, throws him down on the ground and sits on top of his face. 'What are you doing?' Pinocchio yells in fright, to which Snow White replies, 'Stop your complaining and tell me some lies.'"

Two cock jokes in a row, Carl thought. He could start to feel an erection coming on so he got up quickly and closed his door. "I don't want anyone thinking you're harassing me," he said to Heather with a grin.

"God forbid, Carl."

"Know any blonde jokes?"

"Do I know any *blonde* jokes? What does this look like?" she asked, running her fingers through her short, platinum locks.

"Looks blonde to me."

"I know millions of 'em. What happens to blondes with Alzheimer's?"

"Their IQ's go up. How can you put a twinkle in a blonde's eye?"

"Shine a flashlight in her ear. What did the blonde decide to call her new pet zebra?"

"Spot."

"What did the blonde ask her doctor when he told her she was pregnant?"

Heather shook her head.

"Are you sure it's mine?"

"How do you keep a blonde busy?" Heather asked.

Carl was stumped.

"Give her a bag of M&Ms and ask her to put them in alphabetical order."

"Never heard that one before."

"Probably for a good reason. How can you tell that your landscaper is blonde?"

"The bushes are darker than everything else. What's the difference between a blonde and a parking meter?"

"You have to pay a quarter to use the meter. What did the blonde do when she was driving on the freeway and saw a sign that said Hollywood Left?"

Carl shook his head.

"She sighed with disappointment, turned around and went home."

"What should you do if a blonde hurls a hand grenade at you?" Carl asked.

Heather didn't know.

"Pull the pin and throw it back."

Heather was belly-laughing. This was clearly her favorite joke. As she rocked up and down, coughing and wiping a tear from one eye, Carl stood up, walked to his left around the side of the coffee table and sat down on the sofa to Heather's right. He looked quickly at his door and then back at Heather, who had reached out her right hand and grabbed Carl's left wrist in an effort to catch her breath.

Carl reached across and took hold of Heather's left forearm with his right hand, seemingly in an effort to help her regain her composure. Within seconds, Heather had quieted down but she continued to grin broadly.

"You okay?"

"I'm okay... but that last joke... pull the pin and throw it back..." Heather was laughing again. Carl leaned back and whispered something in her right ear.

"What?"

Carl waited for Heather to stop laughing and then whispered again, "Are you a real blonde?"

"Of course I'm a real blonde, Carl. What are you talking about?"

"I mean, a *real* blonde."

Heather suddenly felt uncomfortable and freed her left arm from Carl's grip.

"You know what I'm talking about." Carl extended his left arm behind Heather's neck and rested it on her left shoulder.

"Carl, you're making me nervous. What's *with* you?"

In less than a second, Carl's right hand darted under Heather's dress, up between her thighs and on to her panties. "I mean blonde down here," he said as he rubbed the top of her panties with two fingers.

"Jesus!" Heather screamed, squirming, trying to grab Carl's right hand with her own. "What are you *doing* ?"

Carl pushed Heather down on the sofa, held her down with his left arm and grabbed the top of her panties with his right hand. Heather was wild-eyed, more frightened than angry. "Carl, stop!" she yelled, over and over again.

But Carl didn't want to stop. He'd gotten Heather's panties down to her calves and now he was pushing her shoes off so he could get them past her ankles and over her toes. Heather looked towards the door to Carl's office but knew that even the cleaning people were long gone and that her screams would go unnoticed, unheeded. As hard as she tried, she couldn't get Carl off her, so she writhed and lurched, hoping Carl's left hand would slip from her breasts.

Suddenly, Carl's right hand went back between her legs, and Heather's fear turned to fury. "Get the fuck off of me, Carl," she yelled as loudly as she could. "Get off me, you pig!"

Carl's expression changed from one of total self-absorption to one of disgust. For the first time, his eyes met Heather's. "Sit on *my* face," he said.

"In your dreams, you asshole." Heather looked right at Carl, inhaled as deeply as she could and spit in his eyes.

Carl, enraged, grabbed her blouse and ripped it open. The violence with which he tore it snapped the buckle on Heather's bra, which slid from her breasts, leaving them exposed and Carl all the more determined. When he reached down to unbuckle his belt, Heather spit at him again, pulled her knees in towards her chest and then kicked with both legs as hard as she could. Carl, who, while strong, didn't weigh that much more than Heather, lost his balance on the sofa, lurched backwards and slid off at the end that was farthest from the door. Recognizing what might be her only opportunity, Heather leapt from the sofa at the opposite end and turned to run.

Carl lunged between the sofa and the coffee table and grabbed one of Heather's ankles. "Get over here, you cunt," he bellowed, but Heather shook him off, grabbed the doorknob, opened the door and ran down the darkened hallway. She pulled her skirt down and folded her blouse over her breasts. The carpeting felt rough on her bare feet.

As she ran, she looked back and saw Carl running out of his office after her. He'll follow me into the ladies' room, Heather thought. I've got to find the stairs.

The entire floor was dark, and there was no one in sight, but letting the dim night lights guide her, Heather raced around the inner core of the 75th floor and finally found the orange Exit sign above one of the internal staircases. Quickly she looked back. There was no sign of Carl so just as quickly she opened the door, raced down the stairs and didn't stop until she'd reached the offices of a law firm on the 54th floor.

There she found a conference room that she could lock, inside of which she straightened her clothing as best she could, called the building's Security Office and asked for guards to meet her on 54 and escort her to the taxi stand on Water Street.

* * *

The following morning, at 9:54, Ron Vargo got a five-second phone call from a woman who didn't identify herself. "CNBC," she said. Then she hung up.

When he turned on the TV in his office, which was always left tuned to CNBC, he found Leslie Laroche standing in front of The Wall, and Ron could see giant FDME letters and a stock price of $12.13 beside him. He listened.

"... details are pretty sketchy at the moment," Leslie told viewers, "and I've just been handed a press release so forgive me for reading, but here's what we know so far. At management's request, trading in the shares of Four Dimensions Media, a small advertising agency, ticker FDME, was halted about ten minutes ago and, as we speak, the company is distributing this press release which says 'Four Dimensions Media Receives Takeover Offer' and goes on to describe the offer as coming from another media company called Milbanks Media, ticker symbol MM on the Big Board, last traded at $52.40 but now also halted.

"The offer, as I read through this, is this: one third of a Milbanks Media share for each share of FDME outstanding, subject to the approval of shareholders of both firms. Four Dimensions, as you can see behind me, last traded at $12.13, so this is about a 40% premium to the current market price.

"The press release goes on to say that, while the management of FDME neither solicited this offer nor desires to merge with or be acquired by any other company, it will present the offer to its Board of Directors for evaluation and consideration. So..." Leslie said, looking up from the press release, "we should see FDME up smartly later today, when it reopens, based upon this news."

Ron pressed the MUTE button. He knew three things for sure. First, he'd better call Milbanks and Four Dimensions right away and get their official takes on what had transpired and why. Second, his phone was likely to start ringing soon with calls from angry brokers who had sold FDME, or sold it short, on Ron's recommendation which had been based in part on his stated belief that no takeover of FDME was likely. And finally, Claire O'Daniel owed him big time, and he'd start collecting that night.

* * *

As Ron watched CNBC, two men walked slowly up to the security guard sitting at the reception desk on the 75th floor and one of them asked to see Ed Koster without delay. When the guard encountered resistance from Barbara Summerville, he handed the receiver to one of the two visitors, a tall, grey-haired man who talked briefly with Barbara, nodded twice and returned the phone to the guard. A minute later, Barbara emerged from the executive suite and escorted both men to Ed's office. Ed, on a conference call with Vilhelm Drews, held up one finger and worked as quickly as he could to wrap up his call. It took over two minutes but, finally, Ed emerged from his office and looked at the tall, grey-haired man.

"Mr. Koster," he said, extending his hand, "I'm Stephen MacAllen. This is Officer Gula from the 1st Precinct."

Ed also shook hands with him. "Come in, please." The two men followed Ed into his office and Officer

Gula closed the door behind him. MacAllen and Gula took chairs in front of Ed's desk and Ed parked himself behind it.

"So what's this all about?"

"Mr. Koster, I'm the attorney for Heather Weeks, one of your employees, and for the Weeks family. Ms. Weeks called me late last night, in a state of enormous emotional distress and informed me that she'd just been the object of an attempted rape on BCS premises."

Ed looked alarmed.

"The perpetrator of this crime was her immediate superior, Mr. Carl Robern who, I understand, reports to you."

Ed hesitated, nodded, and then asked, "Do you mind if I invite Patrick Erdenberger, who heads our Legal Department, to join us?"

"Not at all," Stephen said, sitting back in his chair. A minute later, Patrick had joined the group, been introduced to everyone and assumed a chair next to Ed's.

"Pat, Mr. MacAllen is the attorney for Heather Weeks, who works for Carl Robern, and he says that Heather called him last night and told him that Carl had attempted to rape her in his office."

Patrick nodded, showed no emotions whatsoever, and looked only at Ed.

"Mr. MacAllen, I interrupted you," Koster apologized.

"I was saying that Ms. Weeks called me shortly before midnight, informed me that Carl Robern had attempted to rape her in his office on this floor, told me that she was bruised and in a state of shock from the trauma associated with this assault and asked for my help. I met with Ms. Weeks beginning just after

1:00 A.M., we were up most of the night reliving this nightmare and chronicling exactly what transpired, and this morning, at about 8:00, we filed a formal complaint against Carl Robern at the 1st Precinct, with Officer Gula."

Ed bent over backwards to show no sympathy. Carl was innocent until proven guilty as far as he was concerned, and so was the firm.

"The purpose of my visit this morning, Mr. Koster, is to inform you of this crime, to demand the immediate termination of Carl Robern, and to secure your commitment to cooperate fully with Officer Gula and other members of the N.Y.P.D. in the investigation and trial emanating from this tragic event."

Ed looked at Patrick, who said, "I'm afraid we can't do that, Mr. MacAllen."

"And why is that?"

"Because, as I'm sure you know well, Mr. Robern is entitled to the same presumption of innocence on which you or I would insist at a moment like this, should charges as serious as the ones you've just made be leveled at us. This is the first we're hearing of this and, obviously, and we've had no opportunity either to speak with Mr. Robern, who may have a completely different story concerning where he was last night and what he did, or to investigate this matter in any other way."

"Mr. Erdenberger, I understand that this news is new to you, but I'm sure you can appreciate the gravity of this crime and the desirability of addressing it in a confined, confidential manner that punishes the guilty but protects innocent people and the reputation and assets of your firm."

Ed looked at Officer Gula. "Officer, have you spoken with Mr. Robern about these allegations?"

"Not yet, sir. I'd like to ask Mr. Robern to come down to the station house and discuss where he was and what he did last night with me and one or two of my associates."

"When?"

"Now."

Ed looked again at Patrick.

"We'd prefer to speak with him first," Patrick asked. "Mr. MacAllen has told us what Heather says occurred last night. I think we're entitled to know what Mr. Robern's side of the story is."

"If you want to talk with him for a few minutes right now, that would be fine," Gula said, "but I'd like to talk to him as soon as you're done and, hopefully, have him return to the station with me."

"So your intention is to take no action against Carl," Stephen said.

"Our intention," Ed answered, "is to learn what happened or didn't happen last night and to take no action until we've investigated the matter completely, no matter how long that takes. We certainly aren't going to fire a valued member of senior management simply because a secretary has charged him with a crime that we've never even discussed with him and that he may never have committed."

"We will, of course, cooperate fully with you, Officer Gula," Patrick added. "If you're willing to give us a few minutes to talk with Mr. Robern, we'd be grateful. Then, if you want him to come with you and talk with you, we'll encourage him to do so."

"That'd be fine."

Ed and Patrick rose from their chairs but extended no hands. "Barbara," Ed called out, "ask Mr. Robern to come over and see me please."

MacAllen and Gula also rose. "I'll call you later,"

MacAllen said to the policeman, shaking his hand, at which point Barbara Summerville showed Gula back to the reception area and walked MacAllen to the elevator bank.

A minute later, Carl strolled into Ed's office, oblivious to all that had preceded him including the uniformed policeman awaiting him in reception. Heather hadn't shown up for work. Probably upset, probably wanted a day off. That was fine with him and that was all he knew. And that's why he was surprised to see Patrick Erdenberger.

"Closed or open?"

"Close it, please, Carl," Ed said.

Carl closed the door and took one of the chairs by Ed's desk. "How are you Patrick?" he asked.

Erdenberger just nodded and looked towards Ed.

"Carl, where were you last night?"

"When?"

"Last night."

"I was here working on headcounts for Katherine."

"How late?"

"I don't know, maybe 10:00."

"Who saw you?"

"I don't think anyone... some of the cleaning people, maybe. Everyone else was gone."

"Were you alone?"

Carl grew wary. "Yes."

"No one helping you?"

"No."

"No one?" Patrick repeated.

"Not at night."

"What does that mean?" Ed asked.

"It means that Heather helped me during the afternoon but she went home around 7:00. After that I was on my own."

"So Heather left the premises around 7:00," Ed repeated.

"Something like that, maybe 7:30, not later."

For a minute, Ed and Patrick looked at each other and then down.

"What's this about, Ed?" Carl finally asked.

"Heather says you tried to rape her last night. She's got a lawyer, and there's a cop waiting in reception to question you."

"Bullshit!"

"No bullshit, Carl," Patrick said. "She apparently has filed a formal charge of attempted rape against you and she's got a lawyer."

"This is bullshit, Ed! Heather went home at 7:00. I was here all by myself. I never touched her. I never even saw her after 7:00."

"Are you prepared to tell that to the police?" Ed asked.

"That fucking cunt."

"Carl!"

"Yes, I'm prepared to tell it to the police."

"Do you have any idea why Heather would say this about you?" Patrick asked.

"Fucking cunt. How the fuck should I know? I never did anything to her."

"Well, she's got a very different story, Carl, one that could cause you, and us, a load of trouble if it's true."

"It's not true."

"One last time. You were alone, Heather went home at 7:00 and you never touched her."

"That's right."

"Go tell the police," Ed said.

Carl nodded. "I'm sorry, Ed. You should never have been bothered with this."

"You're right."

"You're not going to say anything to anyone about it, are you?"

"If nothing happened, Carl, there's nothing to talk about, is there?"

Carl looked long at Ed, then at Patrick, and then at Barbara Summerville whom Ed had buzzed.

"Introduce Carl to Officer Gula, will you, Barbara?"

"And Carl, when you're done with the police, come back and tell me what you told them, will you?"

* * *

When Patrick Erdenberger returned to his office, he found one of his seniormost lawyers, Jerome Joh, awaiting him.

"Robern?"

Joh shook his head. "Ken Lavery."

Patrick squinted. "The biotech guy."

Joh nodded. "It's starting."

"How many?"

"Six."

"How much?"

"Five want compensatory damages of $11 million and punitive of a hundred."

"And the sixth?"

"Compensatory of $7.7 million and punitive of five hundred."

"Does Meadows know?"

"He does as of five minutes ago."

"What'd you tell him?"

"To gather everything he can on these two recommendations…The G-NOME Company and Genomic Innovators."

"Did he know them?"

"Not really. He said that Lavery owned some in his own account but that he'd sold most of it recently and that he doubted we'd have positioned much of either stock with our retail clients."

"And did we?"

"It depends how you define *much*."

"Very funny. How would *you* define it?"

"There are 14 million shares of G-NOME outstanding. Our retail clients now own 5 million, or 36% of them."

"Jesus!"

"And there are 11 million shares of Genomic Innovators outstanding."

"And...?"

"Retail's tucked away 4.7 million, or 43%."

"Why weren't they put on the Restricted List?"

"They were. We marked them 'Unsolicited Orders Only' when our ownership position went over 20%, but every order that came in after that was marked 'Unsolicited' so it was allowed to go through.

"So we've bought for individual investors almost 10 million shares of these two names."

"Yup."

"And they're down... what...10 points each?"

"Something like that."

"So our clients are out $100 million?"

"Yup," Joh confirmed. "And most amazing of all? We *never* covered them!"

* * *

That afternoon, Carl Robern returned to Ed's office and recounted his visit with the N.Y.P.D.

"I told them just what I told you, Ed."

"Which was..."

"...that Heather went home around 7:00, and that I worked alone in my office all evening. Never saw her, never spoke to her, never touched her, nothing."

"Did they ask you why you thought she'd say these things about you?"

"Yes, and I told them I had no idea. I've always been great to her."

"Did they ask you if you had any witnesses who could confirm your story?"

"Yes. I don't. The cleaning people came by around 6:30, I think, so they saw us together then, but I have no idea who went down in the elevator bank with her at 7:00 or who saw her come back into the building later."

Ed stopped reading the memo on his desktop.

"Come back into the building?"

"Yeah, it sounds like she came back into the building, maybe with her boyfriend or maybe some Mr. Goodbar that she picked up, and took him to some empty law offices on the 54th floor where she could fuck him in private. Whatever happened to her, it must've happened on 54 because she called Security from there last night and asked someone to walk her out of the building."

"Did she sign in or out in the lobby?"

"Seems not."

"But she left and came back."

"Yup, with someone who roughed her up on 54 that she didn't want anyone to know about."

"And that's why she's blaming this on you."

"That's how it looks to me, Ed."

Koster was pensive. When he didn't say anything for a long time, Carl got nervous. "Ed, you're not going to pursue this, are you?"

"Seems no point to it," Ed said. "You say you didn't

do anything, she has no witnesses and she calls from 54 to say something's happened and she needs an escort out of the building. It sounds to me as if we should put it aside and get back to work."

"So we're forgetting about it."

"No, Carl, we're not forgetting about it. There's a lawyer. He's been retained. You've been accused. The police are going to investigate. When they come to me and tell me there's no basis for continuing the investigation, or for charging you with any crime, we'll forget about it."

"And in the meantime?"

"Go back to work."

* * *

"Please, God, please."

Ken Lavery prayed, then answered his phone.

"Mr. Lavery, hi, it's John Politano at Citibank."

"Hi John, how are you doing?"

"Very well, Mr. Lavery, but I've got, I'm afraid, some disappointing news."

John went on for five minutes or so trying to explain why Citibank had decided that it couldn't increase the mortgage it had provided on Ken's new house from $3,600,000 to $4,140,000. There was nothing wrong with the house, Ken would be relieved to know. Rather, it was the recent, substantial reduction in the value of Ken's stock portfolio, and thus, his net worth, that had necessitated Citibank's move to rein Ken in. "Hopefully," John was saying, "those stocks will bounce right back, enabling us to augment your current borrowing facility at a later date."

On and on John went.

Ken heard none of it, lost in thought about how he'd explain this to David Meadows.

* * *

Stephen MacAllen phoned Ed Koster the following day.

"So, Mr. Koster, have you reached a decision regarding the termination of Carl Robern?" he asked.

"We have, Mr. MacAllen, and it's to do nothing at this time."

"So you're going to put your firm's reputation and its financial resources at risk to help the rapist in your midst?"

"There *is* no rapist, Mr. MacAllen. There are unsubstantiated charges, no witnesses and the presumption of innocence."

"You realize, I'm sure, that you will personally suffer, reputationally and possibly financially, should it be determined that you failed to act appropriately in addressing so serious a crime committed on your premises and on your watch."

"I realize, Mr. MacAllen, that your client called for help from the offices of a law firm on the 54th floor in this building, and that Mr. Robern was working alone some 21 stories away at the time. That's what I realize."

"After running down 21 flights of stairs, stripped half naked by Mr. Robern and fearing for her life."

Ed was quiet for a moment. "I know nothing about that."

"You will, Mr. Koster, but you may know it too late."

Again, Ed fell silent.

"If you opt not to terminate Mr. Robern, you'll force me to confront Mr. Drews with this sordid tale."

Ed didn't want Vilhelm involved in this. It was too embarrassing, and it reflected too badly on Ed. "Mr. MacAllen, please. It has been, from the start, my intention to seek the counsel of Herr Drews at the appropriate time. As things turn out, he'll be in New York a week from Monday. I'd like to discuss this with him, to see if he feels Mr. Robern should be suspended or not, and to come back to you with his inputs. I think that's a reasonable approach. I hope you agree."

"A week from Monday."

"That's right."

"You'll call me after you confer with him."

"We're lunching together at noon. I'm sure that, by 2:00, I'll be able to tell you what he said."

"I'll await your call," Stephen said. "If I don't hear from you, I'll assume you've changed your mind and decided to let me break the news to Herr Drews myself."

* * *

"Ken, I need $1,500."

Ken Lavery was surprised. "I thought I told you to sell everything."

"You did, and I did, but you're still short."

"That's impossible."

"You got an average of $6.47 a share for the Genomic Innovators and $7.07 for the G-NOME. All told, you got $1,624,800 for all 240,000 shares. After commissions of $16,248, you netted $1,608,552. I used that money, and the $540,000 from your advance, to repay $2,148,552 of your margin loan, but that still left a debit balance of just under $1,500."

"Citibank reneged on upping my mortgage."

"Why?"

Because all my equity has gone up in smoke. Can you blame them?"

"So you have no way to repay David's advance."

"Not until I get my bonus."

"That shouldn't be a problem."

"It'll only be a problem if the non-stock portion of my bonus is less than $1,000,000 and my take-home after taxes is less than $540,000."

"That's not gonna happen."

"It won't unless we get sued by unhappy GINV or GNOM shareholders."

"Have you heard anything?"

"Just general rumblings about edginess in client-land. We might have gotten named in a couple of suits, I'm not really sure," he lied. Ken knew of six so far and there were bound to be more.

"Sorry, kiddo, you've had one tough year."

Ken stopped and thought back on his Brioni suits, his Bentley and his mansion in the Hamptons. None of this made any sense to him any more. How could he have acquired so much in "one tough year?"

"You'll send me the fifteen hundred?"

"I'll send it," Ken said. He had no idea how.

* * *

Over cappuccino and chocolate ice cream, Ed Koster and Vilhelm Drews concluded their lunch in a private dining room on the 75th floor.

"I have two more things to update you on," Ed told

his boss. "The first is *II*, which will be out the day after tomorrow."

Vilhelm nodded.

"David tells me that it's very hard to call, but his best guess is that we'll have close to 20 All Stars this year versus 5 last year and despite the loss of one of those five two months ago to Deutsche Bank." Vilhelm winced at the mention of his arch rival.

"That sounds low."

"Well, to be honest, I'd hoped we might have done a little better, but if we can be up 15 All Stars this year and 15 to 20 next year, we'll certainly get into the number four to number six ranking range which wouldn't be bad for 24 months of work."

"BC Holdings... number five in *II*," Vilhelm said, closing his eyes and smiling.

"Well, we'll know where we stand in 48 hours. I'll call you as soon as we hear."

"No need, Ed. I'll still be in New York, and I'll make it my business to come here in the afternoon so I can congratulate everyone personally."

"Wonderful, Vilhelm. I know how much the analysts will appreciate that."

"Just tell me what time."

Ed nodded.

"And your last item?"

Ed shifted slightly uneasily in his chair. "There's nothing you need to concern yourself about or do anything about here. This is just so you know."

Vilhelm nodded.

"Recently, we had a peculiar episode involving one of the secretaries in Capital Markets who accused one of our senior managers of attempting to molest her in his office."

Vilhelm's look of concern was unmistakable.

"The manager is Carl Robern and the girl is his secretary."

"Was the girl hurt?"

"Not really. She claims that Carl tried to molest her in his office one night. Carl denies it, says she went home early and that he never saw her again, and that she may have brought a man back into the building with her and had sex with him on the 54th floor, which isn't one of our floors, because that's where she called for help from."

"And why does she say she was on the 54th floor?"

"Because she supposedly ran down 21 flights of stairs, half naked, after escaping from Carl's office."

Vilhelm sighed deeply and took a sip of his cappuccino. "There are no witnesses?"

"None."

"The police are investigating?"

"They were, and no one's told me they've stopped."

"Has she pressed charges?"

"Yes, and hired a lawyer."

"Does anyone know why she'd do this if it isn't true?"

"No. Some people think she's trying to hide her involvement with whatever guy she brought back into the building that night by blaming it on Carl."

Vilhelm shuddered. "I'd hate to think that some woman could come out of the blue and make such charges against me, and that with no evidence to support her, she could cause me trouble."

"I agree," Ed said.

Vilhelm ate some more ice cream. "You're satisfied that Carl didn't do anything?"

"No. There's no video in the lobby showing Heather leaving or returning, which casts doubts on Carl's story. On the other hand, he's never wavered in denying that he did anything to her, he told the police he was innocent, and no one can verify the girl's version of what happened."

"Well then, there's nothing more to discuss. He's innocent until proven guilty, he can't be proven guilty, so he's innocent. Is she a tramp?"

"Who? Heather?"

"Is that her name?"

"Heather Weeks. I don't know. I have no idea."

Vilhelm waved his right hand dismissively. "She has no case. Imagine that some tramp of a secretary accused you or me of such a thing but had no evidence to prove it. Should *we* be punished? I think not."

"I just wanted you to know."

"Shall we?" Vilhelm asked, standing up and gathering his notes and memos.

"Of course." Ed signed the voucher, walked to the dining room door and opened it. "Where are you going from here?"

"I have a 3:00 with Sandy Weill," Vilhelm said, stepping out into the hallway and walking slowly with Ed towards the reception area and the elevator banks.

"You're not planning to buy Citigroup, are you?" Ed joked.

"Not yet," Vilhelm laughed. "Just want to stay current on what he's up to."

As the two men approached reception, they noticed first the security guard with a perplexed look on his face, and then six people standing near him.

"They wanted to see you," the guard said to Ed Koster, "but I told them they couldn't go beyond this point."

"Who *are* these people?" Vilhelm asked, looking first at the security guard and then at Koster.

"I'm Heather Weeks," said a young woman, stepping forward. "Carl Robern attempted to rape me in his office on October 1st."

"I'm Liz Tytus," said the second, moving next to Heather. "Carl Robern sexually assaulted me during a BCS summer cruise in June.

"I'm Maryanne Miles," said the third, stepping up next to Liz. "Carl Robern sexually assaulted me at a restaurant he took me to last December."

"And I'm Nancy Natolio," said the fourth, stepping up on the other side of Heather. "Carl Robern demanded that I perform oral sex on him in return for an investment banking bonus that I'd already earned."

Finally, two men stepped forward. "Hello Ed," said the first, looking at Koster. "Herr Drews, I'm Stephen MacAllen and I'm representing Heather Weeks. This is Michael Kerwin, and he's representing Liz Tytus. We've all just spent four hours telling Officer Gula and his associates in the Sex Crimes Unit everything we know about Carl Robern. It's quite compelling stuff if you ask me. Maybe you should hear some of it."

"Your office, Ed?" Vilhelm asked, suddenly looking pale.

"Please," Ed said, motioning them towards his office. "Come with me."

* * *

Around the small, circular table in Patrick Erdenberger's office sat Patrick, Jerome Joh, David Meadows and Ken Lavery.

"Let me be sure I understand this," Patrick said. "You never covered either stock."

"Officially," Ken said.

"Officially. You bought them in your own personal account, but you never picked up coverage, you never wrote any reports on them or had ratings on them or had earnings estimates on them."

"That's correct."

"Yet, somehow, our retail system managed to buy almost 10,000,000 shares of these babies this year, mostly at prices in the low to mid-teens."

"That's what I've been told," Ken said.

"Well, you must have told someone something about them because I doubt that these brokers just decided on their own to put over $100 million of their clients' money into two tiny biotech names that BC Securities didn't cover!"

"Honestly, Pat, I have no idea how this happened. I never went out of my way to promote these names, I never called attention to the fact that I owned them in my personal account, I never wrote any reports, I never included them in my formal remarks at any branches I visited…nothing."

"Let me ask you again. How did we wind up buying 10,000,000 shares?"

"If you told me it was 1,000,000, I'd tell you I might know how, but not 10,000,000."

"And how might *that* have happened?"

"Look, you've been in retail branches. You know what brokers are like. You know how they work. You tell them what you like, you answer their questions, you encourage them to buy and hold, to focus on names you're covering closely, on names you're recommending, you do everything you can to steer them away from names that aren't appropriate, like GINV and GNOM but, no matter how hard you try, they still invariably ask the magic question."

"And that is…?"

"Ken, what do you own in your own account?"

"They actually ask you that?"

"Not all the time, but sometimes."

"And you say…"

"What am I going to do? Lie? I tell them the truth, but with all sorts of caveats about how inappropriate these names are for them and for their clients, that I won't be following them, that I won't be writing on them, and that they shouldn't buy them."

"But they buy them any way."

"Exactly."

"Why?"

"Because they've got sex appeal."

"In English, please."

"Because the last thing retail brokers want to hear about are sixty-dollar stocks with seventy-dollar target prices. They want ten-dollar stocks that are going to twenty or, even better, five-dollar stocks that are going to twenty. They like buying 1,000 shares at a time, and you can do it much more easily with five- and ten-dollar stocks than with sixty-dollar stocks."

"Did you tell them, when these stocks were trading in single digits, that they were going to 20?"

"Never."

"But you clearly told them something that prompted them to buy 10,000,000 shares."

"The fact that I owned them was good enough for some of those brokers."

"Maybe you shouldn't have owned them."

Ken looked impatient. "Look, Patrick, the firm adopted a policy recently that prohibited analysts from owning stocks that they covered. I obeyed it. I sold every share I owned of Amgen, Genentech and Regeneron. But the firm never outlawed analysts owning other stocks in their group that they *didn't* cover so I kept my GINV and GNOM because I never intended to cover them."

"Why? They were good enough for you but not good enough for our clients?"

"Don't be absurd, Patrick."

"Ken, let me explain," David finally chimed in. Lavery nodded. "Patrick, the market caps on these stocks when Ken first started buying them were somewhere, if I remember correctly, in the neighborhood of $75 million each."

"Correct," Ken said.

"No matter how much you might want to, you can't cut 5,000 retail brokers loose on $75 million market cap names without running the risk that you open *The Wall Street Journal* one morning and see the headline 'BCS acquires Genomic Innovators.'

"We have 5,000 brokers. If each broker bought only $15,000 worth of GINV we'd own the entire company. And $15,000 is peanuts so we never allow our analysts to cover companies with market caps that small. You buy and buy and buy and then, when it's time to sell, there's no one to sell to."

"And that's exactly where we are right now, David. Even though Ken didn't cover these names, we wound up owning 40% of them anyway and now there's no one to sell to."

"They should've been restricted," David said.

"They were."

"You should've banned *all* trades, not just solicited trades."

"It wouldn't have made any difference."

David rolled his eyes. "Patrick, I'm a broker and you're my client. I call you up and tell you you're doing great in GINV, you bought 10,000 shares at $10 and now it's $15 so you're up a cool $50,000.

You tell me what a great broker I am. I tell you I think you should buy another 10,000 shares and you say you think that's a great idea. Then I tell you that, because of big-firm bureaucratic bullshit, I can only place your order if it's marked 'Unsolicited.' You ask what that means and I say it just means that *you* thought of the idea, not me. You say fine, whatever, just buy it, and I do. Was it solicited? You bet. Was it marked 'Unsolicited' so we could end-run you? Darn tootin'. So, if you restrict only Solicited trades, you're restricting nothing at all, and that's exactly what you did on these two stocks."

Patrick shook his head. "All I can say is, if you can get these guys to buy 10,000,000 shares even though you're trying to talk them out of it, I can't wait to see how much they'll buy when you try to talk them *into* it."

For a moment, no one said anything. Then David asked, "Where do we stand regarding lawsuits?"

Patrick looked at Jerome Joh, who answered, "As of an hour ago, we've been named as defendants in 28 suits seeking compensatory damages of $31 million and punitive damages of $1.15 billion."

"Jesus." David's eyes were wide. "The last number I'd heard was six."

"It's accelerating," Patrick said. "It started with a couple of big investors who lost a couple of million each, but now it's spreading to the smaller fry."

"And it's not just the losses on these two stocks that are worrying us," Jerome explained.

"Why?"

"Because these suits are going to make headlines, and when retail clients who've gotten buried in other names that we recommended see those headlines, they're going to ask themselves why they shouldn't sue us too. And they will."

David sighed long and deeply.

"Of course, the firm will provide you with legal representation'" Patrick said softly to Ken, "but you might want to also consider hiring outside counsel of your own."

"Why?" Ken looked startled.

"Because, Ken, of the 28 suits that have been filed so far, you're a defendant in all 28."

* * *

The night before *II* was scheduled to be announced, at 7:50 P.M., Nick Denisovich arrived home to find two unpleasant surprises.

The first had been dictated into his answering machine: "Mr. Denisovich, my name is James Klenger. I work in the NASD's Market Surveillance Division. I'd like to speak with you, informally, about your recent New Nevada Mining recommendation. Please call me at your earliest convenience at 858–4000. Thank you."

The second had been slipped in an envelope under his door: It read, "Sapore, 55 Greenwich St. at Perry, 9:00."

It was signed "Anna."

* * *

Alone at his desk, at 10:00 P.M. the same night, David counted and recounted. He decided to assign each analyst a grade of "probable" or "possible" and to come up with his "best guess" as to how BCS would fare by counting *all* of the "probables" but only *half* of the "possibles."

First he considered the analysts he'd had on *II* the year before. Keith Jackman had made it last year and was sixth in *Greenwich* so he was a probable repeater. Robin Lomax had made it last year and was seventh in *Greenwich* so she was probable too. Nancy Natolio had made it last year but she was gone. Tim Omori had finished fifth in *Greenwich* in regionals but only eleventh in multinationals so he looked probable in mid-cap banks but highly unlikely in large-cap banks so David listed him as possible. Will Rivas had made it last year and was fifth in *Greenwich* so he was another probable repeater

Best case: 4 All Stars. Best guess: 3.5.

Next, David turned to his newly hired All Stars. Liz Tytus had gotten molested by Carl and had quit two days before the job-hoppers' deadline so she was a zero. Van Trudell had finished sixth in *Greenwich* so he was a probable. Tom Batchelder was fifth in *Greenwich* so he was possible but not probable because *II* didn't typically rank more than four analysts in this category.

Daniel Roe, hire number four, looked like a probable repeater, especially with Henry Blodget gone from Merrill Lynch and Jamie Kiggen gone from Credit Suisse First Boston. Marsha Yamamoto was possible. She'd finished seventh in *Greenwich*, but *II* had only ranked seven analysts in her space, so the risk of her falling off was palpable. Then there was Vivian Zimm who had finished eighth in *Greenwich* and could certainly repeat in *II* even though the magazine had only ranked seven analysts the year before. David listed her as possible.

Hire number seven was Christopher Chadwick from Morgan Stanley, whose plunge to thirteenth in *Greenwich* suggested that he was possible at best. Hire number eight was Katherine Lillard from Merrill Lynch. She'd finished sixth in *Greenwich*, but *II* had only ranked five analysts in her space, and she was so lame... David jotted her down under possible but didn't really believe it. Anne Reiss from Deutsche Bank had finished fifth in *Greenwich*, and *II* had ranked six analysts the year before, so Anne looked probable. Grace Flagler had finished fifth in *Greenwich* and *II* had ranked seven analysts so she looked safe. Finally, Tim Parish had finished fifth in *Greenwich* but *II* had only ranked four analysts so he looked possible.

Best case: 10. Best guess: 7.

Finally, there were all the analysts who hadn't made *II* last year but who had a chance to make it this year. David combed and combed his staff, looking for possible new stars. No matter how hard he tried, he couldn't find more than 10: Steven Kalagian, Laura Payden, Rebecca Suess, Phil Suprano, Matt Burlingame, Alan Bellone, Mark Noel, James Hovanian, Bruce Soslow and Linda Logan.

David imagined Alan Bellone looking up from his porn surfing at home upon hearing that he'd made *II*. Stranger things had happened. After one more pass through all the names, David settled upon the list of potential first-timers that he'd first drawn up hours earlier.

Best case: 10. Best guess: 3.

When David added all three subsets together, he found that his best case for the entire department was 24 but his best guess was only 13.5.

Thirteen and a half? How was that possible? Losing

Nancy Natolio and Liz Tytus had definitely hurt him. So had Louis Liddy's decision to come for one day and then return to Goldman Sachs. But what had hurt him even more was the fact that, despite his best efforts, and those of his six head-hunters, he'd succeeded in bringing only 11 ranked analysts through the doors of BCS all year, and some of them were so marginal that he couldn't even count on them to repeat.

"So what's the bottom line?" David asked out loud.

"With 24 All Stars, I'm eighth overall. I jump past Bank of America, Bernstein, Prudential, J.P. Morgan, Deutsche Bank and UBS, and Dieter pays me $6 million.

"And with 13.5 All Stars?"

"I'm twelfth. I only pass Bernstein and BofA and I fail to crack the top 10 but I still make $3.5 million. That's better than $2.5 million plus options, but it ain't $6 million."

As he stared one last time at all these "what ifs" under the harsh glare of his desk lamp, David felt empty, lonely and profoundly sad. There was no one at home to share his fears with, no analysts he could both supervise and open up to, and no boss whom he respected and in whom he could confide. He'd chased every analyst with a reputation in every industry his department didn't cover and even in a few that it did. He'd struck out with the best of them and been forced to hire good analysts in industries no one cared about or mediocre analysts in industries that mattered. If he was really lucky, their stock recommendations would prove to be right 50%–55% of the time. If not, several of them would bury clients with disastrous calls over the next 12 months.

Would they stay? Not for long. Would his non-competes hold up? Probably not. Could he build a culture? Probably not, because cultures took decades to build but only months to unravel, and BC Holdings seemed to have no culture of its own.

Was it possible to keep Research, Retail and Institutional Sales, Investment Banking and Trading all happy simultaneously? No. Was it possible to keep his analysts and his bosses happy simultaneously? No. Would anyone really remember anything that he'd done this year five years from now? Only if it was very, very bad.

David turned off his desk lamp and sat silently in the dark. "God" he whispered, "if you're out there, split the difference with me. Give me 19 All Stars. Rank me tenth. Buy me one more year to get them what they want."

When no one answered, David packed up, turned out the lights, locked up and went home. He knew he wouldn't sleep but he had to change his clothes.

* * *

The jetblack hair was longer than Nick had remembered but its luster was unmistakable. So were those huge brown eyes bouncing off the mirror behind the bar and watching his every step as Nick entered Sapore at 9:05 and approached Anna from behind. As he knelt to kiss each cheek, Anna raised her chin but made certain not to look at him. Rather, her eyes dropped to her lap and her face became stern.

"How long since I've seen you, Anna?"

"Many years, Nick, but you're none the worse for wear."

"Neither are you."

"Let's go for a walk." Anna rose from the bar,

627

turned and walked to the front door. Nick held it for her, followed her out on to Greenwich Street and then followed her lead again as she began slowly walking north.

"Piotr sends his regards," she said unconvincingly.

"I hope he's well."

"He's as well as old men can be."

Nick didn't know what she meant but opted not to pursue it. Anna seemed detached and distracted and Nick was more interested in learning why than in critiquing Piotr's state of physical well-being.

For two full blocks Anna said nothing. Then she stopped walking, turned around and asked, "What went wrong on New Nevada, Nick?"

"Almost everything, I'm afraid. It was a bigger stretch than usual to begin with. I spent weeks looking for something better but I always came up dry. It was small and thin and I knew it would be harder than usual getting you in and out, but I assumed that your lead time would be sufficient."

"It was."

"Good. Anyway, the call was a straightforward one. Buy at $11 with a target price of $15. It moved a little right after the market opened, then stalled, then started moving again. Nothing unusual at all until CNBC picked it up, which we wanted them to do. But Leslie Laroche looked pressed for time and never mentioned the $15 target price so lots of day traders and others who were probably not BCS clients rushed in around $14 or $15 and, before you knew it, New Nevada was $19."

"We liked that."

"I'm sure."

"We watched all of this as it was happening and it felt fine. Our cost basis was $11.50 so, once it cleared

$15, we were ready to start selling, but it went from $15 to $19 so fast. We'd gotten almost nothing done at $15 but were making great strides selling above $18 when management came out and said you were an idiot."

"That's not exactly what they said."

"They said you'd made your numbers up and that there was no way they could hit them."

"That's closer."

"Luckily for us we were mostly out by then. The rest we just dumped because we knew the stock was going to plunge. We probably got $14 to $15 for it on the way back to $11."

"So you did fine," Nick said.

"We made money if that's what you mean, but I'd hardly say we did fine."

Nick asked why without saying a word.

"How the Hell could New Nevada go from $11 to $19 to $11 in one day?"

"CNBC."

"No. An idiotic recommendation using numbers you knew management would never bless."

"I knew they'd think I was high. I never dreamt that they'd make a big deal about it."

"CNBC just fanned the flame, Nick. You'd already struck the match."

Anna started walking again. For three blocks she said nothing more. Finally, Nick could keep quiet no longer.

"You know about the investigation."

"Oh, we know all right. Goldman called me right away. Morgan Stanley was less than an hour behind them. And right behind those two were Salomon and Merrill."

"What did they tell you?"

"They all had the same story. The NASD had
launched an informal investigation into that day's
trading in New Nevada and they wanted all the
information they could get on everyone who had
bought or sold the stock that day."

"So they all sent the NASD your trading activity in
New Nevada."

"Yes, instantly. They're very afraid of the NASD,
it seems."

"So what will it show? That you had bought it
right, over a period of weeks, and that you suddenly
had the opportunity to take a quick profit when BC
Securities initiated coverage with a Buy."

"Yes. That's what it will show."

"So it would have been better had there been no
investigation but you're going to look lucky or smart
or both, but not crooked, when the NASD reviews
your trades.

Again Anna stopped in her tracks, but this time, as
she turned towards Nick, he could see fire in her eyes.
"Nick, it's not that simple."

"Why?"

"Because yesterday Piotr got calls from Goldman
and Morgan Stanley. I guarantee you that today, while
I was in the air, he got the same calls from Salomon
and Merrill."

"What kinds of calls?"

"Calls that said, 'The NASD wants more, Piotr. It
wants all your trading records for the past six months,
and we've agreed to honor its request.' Calls that said,
'The NASD may want to speak with you about your
New Nevada involvement'."

"The NASD wants to speak with *me*, Anna. They
left a message for me at home tonight after I didn't
return their calls in the office."

"What a surprise." Anna looked down at the sidewalk and then up into Nick's eyes. You know what this means, Nick."

"They're going to find Billings."

"For sure."

"But maybe not Yellow Gorge. That was more than six months ago."

"Don't be a fool. When they find Billings, they'll want to go farther. Maybe they'll turn it over to the New York Stock Exchange or to the SEC. Either way, someone will go the next step and look back six more months and six more months and six more months. They will find the connection between us, Nick. The patterns are easy to see if you know where to look. Each time they go back six more months they'll see us buying only weeks before you said Buy and selling the day you did, or shorting only weeks before you said Sell and buying the day you did. Buy it early, then sell into the strength. Short it early, then buy it back from those who are dumping."

Nick looked ashen under Greenwich's street lamps.

"So what are you telling me, Anna?"

"You know, Nick. Our business relationship is over. Thank you for all the money you made us, much of which we returned to you as you know. No thank you, though, for screwing up so badly on New Nevada. We will have to move swiftly if we're to pull our money from those brokers and vanish into the Wild West of mother Russia. But I promise you...we will."

"And as for me?"

"You, Nick, are a wanted man, but they have no idea yet how much they want you. Tonight they think you made a questionable call on New Nevada. A month from now, they'll determine that you did things far, far worse."

Nick looked to Anna for understanding but found none.

"I'm going to walk East now, Nick, so this is goodbye. Don't follow me. And for sure don't ever contact Piotr or me again. Do we understand each other?"

Nick nodded.

"You know what you have to do, Nick, so do it. And do it now."

* * *

Finally, the sun rose on *II* Day, Wednesday, October 15.

David arrived at work earlier than usual, just after 6:00 a.m., having slept for less than three hours and having dreamt of analysts knife-fighting each other over a handful of still unclaimed All Star Team positions. He e-mailed his department about what to expect during the day. As usual, *II* had provided a complete list of the number-one-ranked analysts to CNBC the night before, and CNBC was about to spend most of the day interviewing many of those analysts and mentioning the *"II* All-America Research Team," ad nauseam, presumably without charge to the magazine or its publisher.

At 4:15, *II* would release the standings to one representative from each Wall Street firm, in its Park Avenue South offices and, at 6:00, it would post the results on its web site for subscribers to, see. That would give David his usual one-hour window between 5:00 and 6:00 in which to review BCS's rankings with his own analysts before everything became public information.

"I will pick up our results at 4:15, meet with you and review them up on 74 at 5:00 and then party with you outside my office at 5:30," he wrote. "Lisa has arranged for hors d'oeuvres and champagne, so please make sure to come and share what I'm sure will be one of our happiest and proudest moments."

All morning David watched CNBC. He reveled in many of the familiar faces it featured, even if none of them was from BCS. He saw Janice Meyer and John McMillin, Ben Reitzes and Robin Farley, Mark Edelstone and Ron Barone, Ruchi Madan and Alex Henderson, Laura Conigliaro and Maury Harris.

And just before lunch, the long wait for Sam Buttrick finally ended.

"Why do you think you finished first in your category again, Sam?" Martha MacCallum asked.

"Probably because more clients voted for me than for the other airline analysts," Sam answered without even blinking. David couldn't contain himself. He felt a tiny teardrop form in the far corner of each eye and a sense of well-being that contrasted so sharply with the desolation he'd felt the night before. Despite all their nonsense, their whining, their temper tantrums, their refusal to play ball, their stubbornness, their selfishness and their insecurity, it was the analysts who gave meaning to his job. It was the genuine respect and affection that he'd developed, not for every analyst in his department but for the good ones, the ones who could never compete with Henry Blodget or Jack Grubman in a headline-grabbing contest but who just did their job each day, quietly and effectively, professionally and profitably. For Will

Rivas and Marsha Yamamoto, for Matt Burlingame and Mark Noel, for Grace Flagler and Tim Parish.

"If only I could spend all day with those analysts," David thought, "in- stead of dealing with all the garbage and nonsense and lunacy." But he couldn't. He never had and he expected he never would.

"I'd never want *your* job," people would always tell him.

"You have the toughest job in the whole firm," others would say.

At first, David took issue with all of them but, with the passage of time, he sometimes thought it was true.

As Sam ignored Martha's last question and opted instead of answering it to simply thank his clients and to express the hope that he'd do better by them next year, "assuming of course that there's an airline industry for me to cover," David's phone rang. He didn't recognize the Caller ID but he picked it up any way.

"David?"

"Yes."

"David, it's Nathalie Mertz in Palm Springs."

"How are you, Nathalie."

"Not well, David, not well at all."

"Why?"

"Why? Because I'm holding in my hand a report...well, it's not actually a report, it just looks like one of our reports because it's got the BCS logo on it, and the same colors and the same boilerplate. All it says on it is Primo Theaters, plus one sentence indicating that we're dropping coverage of the stock, which was most recently rated Hold and which closed last night at $1.48."

"And...?"

"And what I'd like to know, David, is how you

could allow Keith Jackman to recommend Primo from $11.50 all the way down to $2, to then downgrade it to Hold, and then, 30 days later, to drop coverage at a buck and a half. Do you have any idea what it's like out here in the trenches? In the real world? What am I supposed to do with this? I have clients in the stock, a stock we underwrote at $10 a share, who've lost 85% of their investment because our analyst is totally incompetent, and now I'm supposed to go back to them and tell them that we're dropping coverage? I can't do that, David. I simply can't do it."

David just listened.

"You know, David, I think every one of your analysts should have to be a broker for one day and see what it's like to walk in our shoes. They should only know what it feels like to come in each morning and have no idea if you're going to earn $1,000 or $1. All the analysts have their big fat contracts and their guarantees, so what do they care? Without the brokers, they'd be *nothing*. The analysts are costs. It's the brokers who generate the revenues. I'd like to see them… They have no idea…I could do better with *Value Line* …In fact, maybe that's what we should do, David, shut down the Research Department, give *Value Line* to each office and, with the money we'd save, raise the brokers' payouts by a couple of points…I think I'll recommend that to Paul Pitcher and Ed Koster the next time I see them …I think they're coming here to golf next month… they just don't realize, David…so what am I supposed to do…?"

* * *

As 3:00 neared and David prepared for his taxi ride

to *II* and back, Bill Griffeth began reporting a "Power Lunch" exclusive on CNBC. The story, he said, involved a hostile offer by Milbanks Media for the shares of Four Dimensions Media.

"As we reported to you several days ago, Milbanks Media, ticker MM on the Big Board, has offered one-third of a Milbanks share for each Four Dimensions share outstanding. Milbanks was trading around $52, I believe, at the time it made the offer, so the value of that offer to FDME was a little over $17 a share, at least initially. However, since the offer was made, and probably in response to what could be characterized as a lukewarm reaction at best from FDME's senior management and the fear that Milbanks might have to raise its bid, Milbanks has since traded down to $48, cutting the value of its current offer to about $16 per FDME share."

David listened but heard nothing new. "This is breaking news?" he asked of no one in particular.

"Well now this story is taking an interesting turn it seems, because just moments ago, Four Dimensions issued the press release I'm holding in my hands, and it says the following. First, Four Dimensions' Board of Directors has unanimously rejected the bid from Milbanks, calling it unsolicited, undesirable and substantially deficient. Second, it has filed suit against Milbanks to block that firm from proceeding with any offer that has not been approved by FDME's board. And third, and this is perhaps the most interesting part of the story, FDME has also filed suit against BC Securities and its analyst, Ron Vargo, charging that, and I quote, BCS and Vargo conspired with Milbanks to issue false and negative research reports on FDME in an effort to depress the price of FDME's shares and facilitate a hostile bid for FDME at a price that is disadvantageous to FDME shareholders, unquote.

"What FDME may be referring to," Griffeth explained, "is a report that BCS issued last month in which it initiated coverage of FDME with a Sell recommendation and a target price of $12. That report may well have contributed to a decline in the price of FDME's shares from $15 to just north of $12 immediately prior to Milbanks's launching of its $17–a-share bid for FDME. So, in this highly unusual step, FDME has filed suit against BC Securities and its analyst Ron Vargo, charging them with conspiring to deflate the price of FDME and thus make it vulnerable to Milbanks's hostile bid."

David pressed the Mute button and dialed Ron Vargo.

"Did you see it?" he asked.

"God, yes David, what should I do?"

"I've got to go get *II*. Call Patrick Erdenberger and ask him what he'd recommend."

"Will do, David."

"Oh… and Ron?"

"Yes?"

"Tell me you didn't do it."

"I didn't do it, David."

* * *

As David's car raced up Park Avenue South, Patrick Erdenberger sat locked away with Jerome Joh, reviewing new documents and scratching his head.

"We're not here," he told Jerome.

"We have to be. I've never seen it done any other way."

"I agree with you, but we're not here."

For 15 minutes, they read the same sheets over and over again, top to bottom, upside down, inside out. When they'd satisfied themselves that they couldn't find what they were looking for because it wasn't there, Patrick called Ken Lavery.

"Have you retained your outside counsel, Ken?"

"No," Ken answered, puzzled. "You said that you'd represent me. Why?"

"Well, you should get going."

"Why? What's wrong now?"

"Well, my friend, the two newest suits to arrive today look mighty familiar with one exception."

"And that is…"

"It seems that the *only* defendant named in these suits is Ken Lavery."

"Do they say how much?'

"You mean the damages they're seeking from you, personally?"

"Yes."

"Let's see… combined?… they want $5.5 million to compensate them and $100 million to punish you."

* * *

As usual, David arrived at *II* 15 minutes early. He was herded into one of the conference rooms where everyone chatted with Denise Murrell for a few minutes and watched CNBC. As usual, David was the only Director of Research in the room. He saw several Associate Directors whom he greeted and with whom he chatted, several administrative assistants and a bunch of messengers. Everyone just sat and waited. At exactly 4:15, the large manilla envelopes arrived, one for each firm. David grabbed his, signed for it, raced down the elevator and jumped back into his waiting car service.

Once the car headed for the FDR Drive, David finally braced himself for the envelope opening. All those months of long days and short nights, all his blood, sweat and tears, would now prove to have been well spent or not.

"Please, God," David whispered, "split the difference."

As he opened the envelope and took out the copy of the October issue and the letter that detailed how each BCS analyst had placed, he pictured the number 19 in his head.

"Nineteen All Stars, top-10 status and a $6 million payday. Please God, please, it isn't that much to ask."

Finally David opened the magazine to the page with the table called "The Leaders" on it. This was the table that showed how each firm had ranked over all, the number of first-teamers it had, the number of second-teamers, the number of third-teamers, and the number of Runner-Ups. The rank for each firm was based on the sum of those four numbers.

David knew that, if BCS had finished tenth, he'd find it just below the middle of the table because only 15 firms had any All Stars at all, so he started looking for BCS about a third of the way down the list, knowing that the sooner he saw it, the better he'd have done.

The first names David recognized were Goldman Sachs and Bear Stearns. "Shit!" No BCS.

He looked farther down the list. Deutsche Bank, UBS and J.P. Morgan. "Dammit! Where *am* I?"

Suddenly he saw it. BC Securities. "Thank God!" Just below him were Prudential, Bank of America and

Bernstein. "Good!" he said out loud, "I've leapt over them!"

But when David looked to the left of each firm's name, at the rankings, he realized that he and Prudential had *tied* for eleventh place, with BCS being listed first strictly for alphabetical reasons. Bank of America was thirteenth, Bernstein fourteenth.

The cab lurched as it changed lanes on the FDR Drive. David tried to concentrate, to understand exactly what had happened. Again he focused on the BCS line in the table. Number of All Stars: 14, up from 5 the year before. Rank: tied for eleventh, up from fourteenth last year. Number of first-teamers: 0. Number of second-teamers: 0. Number of third-teamers: 2. Number of Runner-Ups: 12.

David took a spreadsheet that he'd prepared and started plugging in the numbers. First he looked at last year's BCS All Stars. Of the five, Nancy Natolio had moved up to number three but was credited to Deutsche Bank because she'd left just before the job-hoppers' deadline had expired. Keith Jackman and Robin Lomax had fallen off. Only Tim Omori and Will Rivas had remained Runner-Ups.

Next, David looked at the 10 All Stars he'd hired and kept. Of the 10, seven had ranked. The eleventh hire, Liz Tytus had also moved up to number three from Runner-Up but, because she was unemployed when the deadline expired, she was listed as "Affiliation Unknown" and David had gotten no credit for her. Of his other new hires, Tom Batchelder had fallen off in packaging, where only three analysts were ranked and no Runner-Ups were named; Christopher Chadwick had fallen off in cosmetics and household products; and Katherine Lillard had fallen off in leisure. Six of the "repeaters" had maintained their status as Runner-Ups, while Daniel Roe had moved up to third.

Finally, David looked at the newly crowned All Stars who had been on board last year. Four had made Runner-Up for the first time: Matt Burlingame in managed care, Mark Noel in server and enterprise hardware, Laura Payden in specialty chemicals and James Hovanian in semi capital equipment. One had debuted at number three: Linda Logan. "God!" David thought, "I'll never hear the end of it."

As disappointed as David felt, he knew that he'd done what he could in such a short period of time. He'd kept those he could keep, he'd hired every ranked analyst he could hire, and he'd helped those who had missed out last year to maximize their chances this go-around. I'll put the best spin on it that I can, he promised himself, and I'll have made $4 million, which ain't $6 million but ain't $2.5 million either.

* * *

David stopped in his office for a second on his way to meet with his analysts and called Dieter with the news. Almost three times as many All Stars as a year earlier, and within two votes of number ten, up from number fourteen.

"Go tell your analysts, David," Dieter said. "I'll stop by and congratulate everyone after your meeting."

Up on the 74th floor, the whole Research Department, it seemed, had jammed into three small conference rooms that had been opened into one large one. David saw more seniors than usual, a ton of associates, a smattering of institutional salespeople, and Carl Robern sitting up front, to David's left as he faced the audience. He could feel hundreds of eyes on him, trying to glean from his walk, his mannerisms or his complexion whether he was happy or sad, satisfied or not. At first David played with them, giving no hint as to the outcome. Then he told them.

"We did very well," he said. "We placed 14 analysts on the All Star Team this year, up from five last year, and we moved from number fourteen to number eleven. We were within two votes of cracking the top 10. We had 12 Runner-Ups and two third-teamers."

The crowd burst into applause and hooting. Many of the analysts assumed that David was disappointed but they couldn't see it because David was acting so well. Everyone was dying to learn exactly who had ranked where.

"Let me get the bad news out of the way first."

Suddenly the room seemed edgy. If David was going to call out names, this was the moment when you sure as Hell didn't want to hear yours.

"Five analysts who made the team last year didn't this year: Keith Jackman, Robin Lomax, Tom Batchelder, Christopher Chadwick and Katherine Lillard. In many of these cases, the problem simply was that *II* ranked fewer analysts in these categories than they'd done in prior years so none of you should feel badly about this. We'll get you back on next year, I promise."

The sighs of relief elsewhere in the room were palpable. "Everyone else who was a Runner-Up last year was a Runner-Up this year, with one exception, Daniel Roe who moved up to number three. So that's Tim Omori and Will Rivas, Van Trudell and Marsha Yamamoto, Vivian Zimm and Anne Reiss, Grace Flagler and Tim Parish. Congratulations to all of you, and bravo to you, Daniel!" The room again erupted in applause.

As David paused to let the clapping die down, one of the side doors opened and two uniformed policemen stepped quietly into the room. One of them, Officer Gula, panned the crowd looking for a head of salt-and-pepper hair, probably up front. In a matter of seconds he found it. Leaving his partner by the door, Gula walked slowly towards the front of the room where David was standing, crossed over, said "Excuse me" softly to David who froze at what he thought he might be seeing, bent down and whispered something in Carl Robern's ear and then walked with Carl at his heels back to the side of the room. Gula's partner, who was fingering a pair of handcuffs in his right pocket, pushed the side door open with his left hand and let Gula and Robern out first before following them into the hall and closing the door behind him.

"Carl Robern," Gula said, "you're under arrest for the attempted rape of Heather Weeks. You have the right to remain silent. Anything you say can and will be used against you in a court of law. You have the right to speak to an attorney..."

As Gula read Miranda, his partner opened the handcuffs and closed one around each of Carl's wrists. When they were done, they all rode down to the lobby, walked out the front door and drove in Gula's squad car to the 1st Precinct station house near the Holland Tunnel. Carl, while defiant in demeanor, looked at no one and said nothing.

Back inside the conference room, over the mounting buzz of disbelief and speculation by the analysts about what they'd just witnessed, David congratulated Mark Noel, Matt Burlingame, Laura Payden and James

Hovanian on debuting as Runner-Ups, and Linda Logan on finishing number three in strategy. Linda, of course, wasn't in the room. She couldn't be bothered with nonsense like this.

"So, let me just tell you how proud I am of all of you, not just you All Stars but all of you future All Stars too, and let's never forget all the hard work that our associate analysts, research assistants and secretaries put in every day to help their seniors make this team." Again there was lots of clapping.

"You did extraordinarily well. I'm very happy with how we fared, and I'm sure our new parent will be too, so come see me at 5:30, grab some shrimp and a glass of champagne, and celebrate the new BCS Research Department. Thank you, everybody, and congratulations."

* * *

Everyone filed out of the conference room and walked slowly, buzzing all the way, to the elevator banks, while Nick Denisovich waited patiently on the British Airways line at JFK for his boarding pass to Geneva.

All he carried with him were a suitcase full of clothes, a passport, a second airline ticket covering passage from Geneva to Moscow, and six unanswered messages from James Klenger at the NASD.

Hope I don't need it, he thought, referring to the Moscow ticket.

But Nick knew that, if he ever felt the NASD or the New York Stock Exchange or the SEC breathing down his neck, he'd do what he had to do. Like Anna and Piotr, he too would disappear within the Wild Wild West of his mother land, where no one would know him or bother him or turn him in.

In Russia, $16.7 million would last a lifetime, or more.

Nick grabbed a copy of *The Economist*, made his way uneventfully through the metal detector, stopped for his last Nathan's hot dog and then vanished from sight, for good.

* * *

David returned to his office with Lisa Palladino to find the door closed, which surprised him. He knocked, heard some shuffling inside and waited to see who opened the door. It didn't take long.

"Dieter! I wasn't expecting you until later."

"Hello, David," he said, sounding a little strained. "How did your meeting go?"

It was then that David noticed two other figures in the room. One was Ed Koster and the other Vilhelm Drews.

"Wow!" David said with a grin. "I didn't realize we were going to get the royal treatment this evening."

Ed and Vilhelm rose and extended their hands. "Hello, David," Ed said, half-smiling. "Hello, David," Vilhelm said, nodding slightly and smiling insincerely.

"Did you hear how we did?" David asked.

"Yes, David, we did," Ed answered, "and in truth, that's why we're here."

David suddenly felt edgy.

"Please, David, sit," Vilhelm said, pointing to the empty chair. "You see, David, we know how hard you worked this year, and we appreciate all the progress you made in building up our new U.S. Research Department. We're very happy to now have 14 All Stars but, frankly, we'd expected more from you and we're not sure why we didn't get it.

"I think we agreed when you first were offered this job that it would take 40 All Stars, give or take, to become top-5 in *II*, which meant that you'd have to add almost 20 a year for two years to achieve our goal. You told us you'd need to spend $300 million a year to make that happen, and we didn't blink. You said you'd need to use headhunters extensively and, again, we didn't blink.

"Whatever you asked for along the way, staffing, office space, computers, keeping the cafeteria away from your analysts, whatever you wanted we gave you. Yet, here we are, with a net addition of nine All Stars in your first year, not the 20 that you'd promised."

David started to protest over the use of the word "promised" but quickly decided against it. He looked at Ed Koster for help but got none.

"So, David, what I've decided to do, is to ask Dieter to move to New York and to assume day-to-day responsibility for the U.S. research effort."

"What will happen to Dieter's global responsibilities?" David asked.

"He will maintain them, but instead of heading global while managing Europe day to day, he'll head global while managing the U.S. effort day to day."

"I have strong people throughout Germany and in London who'll assume day-to-day duties for Europe," Dieter explained.

"So you're firing me."

"We're relieving you of your responsibilities with respect to U.S. Equity Research. Perhaps there's another position in the firm that would be better for you."

David sighed and shook his head slowly. "You're on board with this, Ed?"

"I am," Koster said. He clearly knew who had acquired whom.

"And my contract…?"

"… will be honored," Vilhelm said. "You've earned $4 million for this year, and we'll pay you $4 million for next year."

"I probably would have qualified for more next year."

"We're going to pay you $4 million to go away quietly, David, instead of $5 million to do an entire year's work for us. You'll be free to seek employment elsewhere, and we'll part on good terms. Who knows? Maybe you'll get someone else to hire you for $4 million and thus make $8 million next year instead!"

Suddenly there was a sharp knock on David's door. David looked at Vilhelm. "Please, please," he said, "answer it."

David opened the door and found Mark Noel standing in the hallway.

"Mark?"

"David, I'm so sorry to do this to you right now. I know you want to celebrate and everything, and by the way, I really appreciate the kind words you said about me upstairs, but I have a job offer that self-destructs at the close of business tomorrow and I really need to talk to you about it today."

"A job offer? From whom?"

"Deutsche Bank."

"Don't they have George Elling?"

"Yes, but George is getting a *huge* promotion into some new management position."

"You're under contract."

"I know, but they told me they'll provide me with

whatever legal help I need if you come after me and try to enforce it."

David looked long at Mark with great affection. "I'm going to miss you," he said.

"I know, David, I feel exactly the same way."

"Come," David said, waving Mark into his office and draping an arm around his shoulders.

Inside, Vilhelm, Ed and Dieter looked up, perplexed.

"Mark," David said, "I think you know Vilhelm Drews, the CEO of BC Holdings." Mark extended his hand and shook Vilhelm's.

"And Ed Koster I know you know." Mark shook Ed's hand as well.

"And Dieter? Do you know Dieter?"

"We met once when you were doling out the new contracts," Mark said. Dieter, who was clearly drawing a blank, shook hands with Mark uneasily. All five men were standing a little too close together in an office that was, at the moment, a little too small.

"Mark, Dieter is going to be your boss now. He's assuming responsibility for our department. I'll be moving on, I don't know where, but close by, I'm sure."

"Dieter," David added, "Mark has something important he needs to discuss with you. Something about Deutsche Bank, I think."

And then, having made his introductions, David hugged Mark, winked at Vilhelm, let himself out, and closed the door, quietly but firmly, behind him.

ABOUT THE AUTHOR

MICHAEL CULP, CFA began investing at age 12 and later turned his love of the stock market into a 27-year Wall Street career. Following eight years researching health care companies, retailers, banks, and fast-food chains, and becoming a Chartered Financial Analyst, Mr. Culp was hired as a Senior Restaurant Industry Analyst by Prudential Securities in 1982 and was voted #1 in his field in *Institutional Investor's* All-America Research Poll—the same poll that features so prominently in *Conflicted*—in 1983 through 1986.

In March 1986, at the age of 33, Mr. Culp was named Director of Research of Prudential Securities, and 11 years later he was recruited by PaineWebber Inc. to serve in the same capacity at that firm.

Mr. Culp, who retired from Wall Street in November 2000 following PaineWebber's acquisition by UBS Warburg, resides in Southampton, New York, with his wife, Deborah Bronston, who was also a #1-ranked analyst and later Associate Director of Research at a leading securities firm before retiring in early 2003.